CALIFIA'S CRUSADE

Justin Hébert

This novel is the original work of its author and no part of its text was created using generative AI technology. The cover art was created by Mirela Barbu and not by generative AI technology.

To Gwen and Allie

My favorite warriors

Forward

Writing this novel began with trying to answer a simple question: Where does the name California come from? I vaguely remember from my primary school years that a textbook claimed that Califia was a Spanish goddess and that the name California came from that. When this question popped into my head as an adult, however, this answer suddenly didn't make any sense. The Spanish who colonized what is today Mexico and California were essentially Catholic supremacist reactionaries who had no tolerance to offer the native people, much less a pagan goddess from their own culture. After some digging, I discovered "The Adventures of Esplandian," the novel written circa 1500 CE which created, from whole cloth, the idea that there was a large island off the west coast of North America. When Cortez sent his scouts to investigate western Mexico after subjugating the Tripartite Alliance which we often refer to as the Aztecs, they returned with an exciting report: there was an island off the western coast. Today, we know that they had sited the Baja Peninsula, but maps of North America continued to be drawn with all of California rendered as an island well into the 1700s.

This novel was not an easy one to write. In keeping with the original novel's premise I kept the story's setting in 1500 CE, but soon discovered that I knew relatively little about Europe in 1500 CE. Being an American, my education for that time period broadly covered the British colonization of the Americas and concurrent events in Europe were relatively neglected. For a history nerd like me, it is always exciting to discover more history to learn.

I read all about King Louis XII of France and his adventures in northern Italy, the annulment of his first marriage, and the birthright of Constantinople which his predecessor purchased from the last living heir to the Byzantine Empire's throne. I read about Grand Prince Ivan III of Moscow and how he consolidated power in Russia, tangled with the Golden Horde, and suffered a succession crisis. It was relatively easy to find good English sources about the European rulers. The rulers of Asia Minor, Egypt, and Persia proved somewhat more difficult to pin down.

The documentation left behind by the Ottoman Empire (which was actually called the Osman Empire) was generally reliable enough to fill in any gaps. I read of Sultan Bayezid II and his consolidation of power after a civil war which pitted him against his brother, the crusade which was nearly called against his empire in the late 1400s, and his eventual usurpation through a coup of one of his sons. The Mamluks in 1500 were difficult to research in a way that made for compelling stories, thus I created the fictional general Al-Khulani and described his soldiers very broadly. Then there was the problem of the Timurids.

You cannot imagine how enraged I became upon learning that the Timurids did not refer to themselves as Timurids but instead used the objectively more awesome-sounding name "Gurkani." In the podcast I host (A History of Japan), I strive to use native names for cities, people, and places rather than their English bastardizations. I don't always succeed. But it seemed a crime to name one of the largest land empires in world history after its founder (Timur the Great) and then call it a day. It is exactly the type of laziness which I cannot tolerate.

As to whether the rulers of these mighty factions (on either side) could have actually put aside their egos and worked together to defeat a common enemy, the answer is almost certainly no. The Gurkani and the Osmans were notorious rivals, especially considering that the Gurkani Empire's founder, Timur, was the only person to ever capture an Osman sultan in battle. The Mamluks also clashed often with the Osmans and their own internal political instability would likely have prevented their involvement in the jihad which I have concocted.

On the side of the European alliance, things were little better. Both Louis XII of France and Ivan III of Moscow had semi-legitimate claim to the throne of Constantinople, which both used as propaganda in their homelands and never, as far as I was able to discover, made any practical plans for enforcing those claims upon the city. The involvement of the Genoese and the Venetians would have likewise been extremely difficult to coordinate.

Why would I create these historically unlikely alliances? 1) Because I write *fiction* and 2) because it's more likely than the original story, in which a band of Spanish crusaders seized Constantinople. If there had been a crusade against the Osman Empire in 1500, the French would have undoubtedly led it as they did nearly every other crusade. The Spanish, who were still largely consumed with driving Muslim influence from the

Iberian Peninsula, would almost certainly have had no involvement. While putting aside their rivalries would have been difficult for the Osman Empire, Mamluk Sultanate, and Gurkani Empire, I tend to think that it would not have been *entirely* impossible. Eventually, however, such arguments tend to boil down to: *What I have written, I have written.*

So what have I created? Hopefully something interesting. I linked the black Amazons of California with the mythical Amazons of ancient Greece, recasting the Trojan War along with the myth of Atlantis. In the early drafts of this novel, characters were far too prone to resolving their differences in a constructive, restorative manner, and the manuscript greatly improved when I simply let them fight. The Californians come from a nation which would have been perceived as something of a Utopia during its day and age, but I have done my best to preserve their humanity, warts and all.

I enjoyed writing this book; I hope you enjoy reading it.

Part I: The Visitor

1

On the isle of California in the year of our Lord 1500, a woman in a hut stared at two helmets and pretended she had a choice. Polished to a mirror shine, the left helmet glinted vividly in the morning sunlight that streamed through the open window. The swirling designs and intricate patterns of its visor and crown were perfectly accented by great golden wings that adorned either side. A purple plume sprouted from the top which would spill down the back of its wearer.

The other helmet was also composed of golden griffinsteel, though finished with a burnished, rustic look. It was adorned by no scrollwork nor intricate etchings of any kind, and was little better than a bucket beaten roughly into the large egg-shape of a head. It was practical, useful, and almost aggressively ugly.

Every young girl on California knew the story of the great exodus. Queen Amaltheia sacrificed herself for the freedom of the Amazons, who were saved from their sinking island home by griffins sent from the Triumvir Goddesses. Amaltheia's lover, Helena, led them across a vast ocean and a vast continent until finally they came to

California, an uninhabited island chain which served as their home for thousands of years.

The queen-elect prepared to commemorate that exodus with a procession of her own. But first, she had to put on her helmet. The woman who surveyed the helmets dearly wanted to don the shining helm and its matching set of decorative armor. Hera herself would envy its queenly majesty, and Aphrodite could not ask for a more beautiful raiment. But it was not Hera or Aphrodite whom her people needed today. They clamored for Athena, the goddess of warfare, craft, and wisdom. The goddess of *practicality*.

The hide flap door suddenly flipped open and Arianna poked her head in, smiling brightly. She glided past the door with casual grace, her many brightly-colored bracelets clacking as she approached the queen. She wore an elegant deerskin dress with white lace fringe tickling her slender thighs. Her cheeks dimpled as she smiled at the queen, a small scar at the left corner of her mouth flexing like a muscle. The queen loved that scar, and loved the lips which now kissed her own.

"This will be a coronation day to remember," Arianna said, pulling away from the queen and sighing.

"The campaign was memorable *enough*," the queen replied ruefully, glaring at the plain burnished helmet. "It should be Malachea who has to wear this dreadful armor."

"You'll look marvelous in it," the young woman said, giving the queen's shoulders a squeeze. "Our ferocious champion, the bold Hypa- oh!"

The queen turned, raising an eyebrow at her lover's sudden halt.

"I should call you by your title now, shouldn't I?" Arianna said.

The queen smiled, a little sad that she might not hear anyone call her by her chosen name for many years. Her mother would have called it a necessary sacrifice.

"Let me hear it first from you, my love," she said, smiling playfully at Arianna.

"Califia."

Califia turned and embraced her companion. They shared a long, indulgent kiss.

"If we don't leave soon, we'll be scandalously late," Arianna said, breaking away from the queen's lips and turning to leave.

"We wouldn't want any more *scandal*," Califia said, pulling on a padded cotton undershirt as she prepared to don the plain burnished thorax. She turned to see Arianna clenching her eyes in embarrassment.

"I didn't mean—"

"I know." Califia smiled as kindly as she could muster. She wasn't angry with her lover for invoking the controversy that haunted her election. Arianna left the hut after a small, awkward smile.

Califia tightened the straps of the thorax and opened the drawer where she stored jewelry and gifts. A bearskin-and-turkey-feather headdress lay flat inside, a gift from the Ohlone with whom she had arranged trade during a time of famine many years ago. Next to it sat a few small carved bears and some abalone jewelry— gifts from her daughter Chloe. The queen smiled at the thought of seeing her eight-year-old daughter at the coronation.

Califia had expected to be *less* exhausted once her whirlwind election campaign ended. The sitting queen had arranged everything and even led the delegation herself. They had started in the south, among those who hardly knew her. They proceeded to hold three-day elections in those regions approving her as the new Califia. The old woman's presence added considerable weight to her candidacy.

It was all perfectly legal-- nothing that hadn't been done before. Her critics, however, crowed that these tactics pre-emptively squeezed out any would-be competitors. A few even wrote formal complaints, but thus far it was only words.

"I was *joking* about being late," Arianna chimed, standing near the hide-flap door with her hands on her hips. "You do remember that your coronation is today, right?"

As she stepped out of the hut and into a harsh mid-morning light, Califia shifted her thorax with one hand while she adjusted her left breast with the other. She hated this armor for both its discomfort and its warlike appearance. She resented its necessity but knew in her heart that Basilea was right: little gestures could carry a lot of weight.

A cheer erupted and as her eyes adjusted she realized that her home was practically besieged by well-wishers and supporters. They chanted her title - her name - over and over as they pumped their fists in the air and clapped their hands.

Califia! Califia! Califia! Califia!

She smiled, her cheeks warming as she pushed a few stray braids behind her shoulder. Arianna grinned proudly and clapped, cheering loudest of all. She stopped clapping suddenly, her eyebrows lifting as she turned around and squatted before something which the queen couldn't see. Suddenly the air filled with the whooshing sound of flapping wings as ravens flew from the small wooden cage which Arianna had opened.

Ravens, Califia thought. *How fitting that she would choose the avatar of Artemis, the goddess of sound judgment, to bless this journey.*

The crowd parted as the queen stepped forward, forming a perfect promenade route for her march through the village. Behind the cheering crowd she spotted the roofs of other huts, as well as the longhouse and the three steeples of the temple to the Triumvirs. Laboneia had been a good home to her these last four years and, while she still sorely missed Ippaea, which lay on California's east coast, the people here had made her feel truly blessed to be apart of their community.

Califia clasped congratulatory hands with village leaders, religious elders, and even Tessa, the smith built like a bison who had forged Califia's armor. After surveying the queen's armor, she nodded with approval.

The sight of the chariots made the queen gasp. Their cabs were adorned on either side with griffins crafted beautifully from gold wire, standing proud with their wings flared up. The beasts' heads and wings framed her torso and head perfectly, which Califia realized made it appear as though she were riding the creatures into glorious combat.

The people of Laboneia waved and cheered as the chariot embarked, the two llamas first pulling slowly and then easing into a casual trot. The llamas were wearing their own set of wings as well. Her cheeks were sore from the last two months of forced smiling at campaign events, but today nothing could keep her from grinning like a child with a secret.

The Coronation March was a tradition stretching back into time immemorial, far beyond the current Third Republic and even beyond the distant Age of Tyrants. It was a symbol which endured every new regime, every mass reorganization and small-scale reshuffle. Whenever a new queen was elected, the Coronation March paid tribute to the great migration that brought the foremothers to this land.

Califia was thankful that the elaborate marches of the distant past were now considered antiquated and a direct route was favored both for the sake of the participants and national administration.

After long hours following the winding road which led southwest through several villages, the capital came into view around midday. The great city was easy to spot from a distance; it rose into the air like a mountain, but its terraces became clear as the traveler drew closer. Those bold enough to take their mothering journey to the realm of the Mexhica testified that those people built similar structures out of stone— places of worship and ceremony. A growing faction of Amazon historians believed that the capital had been originally built with a similar sacredness in mind long ago.

The people of Californopolis threw their hands rapturously into the air and cheered as she passed. Some had donned special costumes for the occasion; four large women wore massive crowns of red-dyed griffin feathers while three others wore heavy skirts woven with intricate patterns of multi-colored beads. Most of the celebrants had stripped to the waist and Califia envied them. Her breasts were beginning to ache beneath the heavy thorax.

"I've never been to the capital before," remarked the chariot driver, whom the queen realized looked quite young. Her bare arms were tattooed with many dot patterns which appeared like jeweled bands around her bicep and forearm, with a chain of dots connecting them running along her elbow. Below her lip, slender colored rainbow lines traveled down her chin and disappeared beneath her chestplate. She grinned earnestly, like a child who has learned a new game and Califia guessed that she was no older than nineteen.

"Is it everything you hoped it would be?" The queen replied, holding her palms out to receive a blessing being offered by a nearby devotee who was extending her arms as she recited a blessing.

"I did not know so many people could live in one place."

Califia felt briefly as though she were seeing the city for the first time. It *was* amazing that so many people could live and work side by side, shrugging at their differences and holding fast to that which they held in common. *If only the rest of the nation were the same.*

Califia's thoughts turned to her most vocal critic— the Strategos of the Gorgon soldiers. Malachea had been idly chattering for years about campaigning to become the next queen, and rumors swirled that Califia's campaign infuriated the strategos. The woman's infernal daughter, Dionysia, had even begun championing her mother's cause.

The second ramp led to a terrace dotted with a series of interconnected houses which were built by the Califia before her mother. Originally an experiment in communal living space, they were popular in the capital but had not sparked a trend in the rest of their island, save for the deserts in the south where such housing served to bond militia trainees together and help with their cohesion as fighting cohorts. A happy grin spread across her face as she remembered her own time in the barracks — the nights spent endlessly talking as well as the more passionate nights spent *not* talking.

After passing through several more levels devoted to housing, agoras, food storage, and farming, they arrived at last at the topmost terrace where a massive, tall longhouse sat amid an array of purple, red, yellow, and blue flowers. The palace was a magnificent building; red timbers held up the main structure while austere blanched oak pillars supported the awning of the portico. The roof was composed of dark, tightly-packed dried maize husks and the window shutters adorned with mosaics featuring mighty Californian warriors and their griffins.

The day was growing hot, and the soon-to-be-retired queen and her honor guard stood sheltered in the portico's shade. Flanking them were delegates of various tribes from across the eastern gulf. The Ohlone delegate gave a courteous nod, her abalone necklace shimmering. She was flanked by four men with bare chests painted with cougar paws and sunbursts along with three bare-breasted women wearing deerskin skirts and feathered hats that looked like hedgehogs. To their right stood their southern neighbors the Tepota'al, led by three matriarchs with headdresses of large turkey feathers and wearing long brightly-dyed robes woven from river reeds and deerskin along with a group of five men covered in swirling dotted black tattoos.

By the time they reached the palace her procession had grown to nearly three hundred women. The bright colors of their costumes along with the various shades of brown and black skin was a pleasing sight in Califia's eyes. Their joy was intoxicating; she smiled in spite of the armor and the unpleasantness that had surrounded the days leading up to this moment. *Malachea will come,* she thought to herself. *She will accept your installation and that will be the end of it.*

Arianna helped Califia step down from the chariot platform and whispered as she passed close, "The Kashaya are here!"

Califia looked upon them; their heads were covered by furred hats with a plume of feathers bursting from the crown, their torsos were covered only by intricate tattoos, and they wore short cotton loincloths decorated with colorful beads in a complicated concentric rhombus pattern. Their leader observed Califia with sharp, watchful eyes from beneath the curly mane of the bison helm. The Kashaya rarely concerned themselves with California. Basilea must have gone out of her way to arrange their presence and thus fortify Califia's image as a respectable queen.

Califia ran her fingers along the golden wire attached to the hull of her vehicle, marveling at the intricate craftsmanship on display. The swirling patterns tapered and then seemed to explode in a whirlpool of silver and gold.

"This must have taken months," she said to Arianna. "How did you keep this secret from me?"

Arianna embraced her but Califia barely felt the squeeze beneath her heavy armor.

"It wasn't difficult; you've been busy."

Califia felt as though a shard of glass sank into her heart. Her muscles stiffened defensively.

"You knew I wanted this," she whispered, irritated that her lover would choose *this* moment to start a fight.

Arianna released her and sighed, looking wounded.

"That's not what I meant," she said, hoisting herself onto one of the passing chariots. Califia wanted to call after her, but Basilea was looking at her expectantly which meant that it was time for the ceremony to begin.

"Greetings, our queen! May your reign bring prosperity and happiness to our land and the lands beyond!"

The retiring queen gracefully stepped forward, spreading her arms and smiling amiably. Califia hugged her friend warmly and although she had exchanged many embraces before this day, the woman felt strangely small and frail in her arms now. It was as though her body knew that she would be Califia no longer; from that day forward she would be called *Basilea*, a title which meant *honored matron* in the old tongue. She had served Califia's mother during her time as queen in years past, protecting the island as polemarkos during the Cochimi War. Those days were defined by famine, plague and conflict; the women from that age had a hardness about them, a solid edge that only the harshest conditions forge.

"She's not here yet, but she'll come," Basilea whispered into Califia's ear. "Don't worry."

The queen released Basilea and proceeded to greet the esteemed visitors, who each offered a blessing. Music rang out from within the palace, filling the air with hopeful melodies and playful tunes. The two guards who stood on either side of the building's large double doors pulled at the gigantic handles and they swung them open with the ease of a child pushing a ball downhill. It was a trick of engineering, a series of pulleys and networked gears, but even the queen couldn't help but look on with wonder.

The vast open space within the palace was filled with hip-high tables covered with broad platters of various foods. In the center, a flat circular dais had been erected for the ceremony, and above their heads stood a long, winding balcony supported by oaken columns covered in relief carvings of Californian folk tales. The walls were covered with bright bead and shell mosaics, and every niche featured several sculpted heads of the Califias who had come before. Basilea's likeness, its clay still shiny and unpainted, was kissed by the sunlight streaming in from opened roof panels.

Kyria, a sandy brown woman in colorful flowing robes patterned after the flowers of spring greeted Califia at the doorway, bowing gracefully and with far more theater than necessary. Her green eyes sparkled beneath her hairdo, an intricate inter-woven tower atop her head. Once more Califia wondered where Kyria's mother had found the man with whom she had produced such a beautiful and elegant creature.

"My queen, just as the chefs have created many wonders for your palate, I have prepared a feast for your ears and eyes." She smoothly took several shuffling steps to the side and held out her willowy arm toward the harpists and percussionists on the dais, who continued playing their lively, festive tune as Califia strode into the grand hall.

Basilea leaned close as she walked beside Califia.

"Kyria is a bit… enthusiastic, but I think you'll come to appreciate her passion for all things musical and theatrical."

Califia smiled at the fact that Basilea, so erudite and austere, had nonetheless given bombastic Kyria charge of royal entertainment.

"I like her enthusiasm," the queen replied, smiling toward the court entertainer. "She and I worked together some years ago arranging entertainment for harvesters."

"Ah, yes." Basilea closed her eyes for a moment and massaged her temple with her fingers. "I had forgotten that you know each other. That will help; I have yet to find a person who can resist her passion for the performing arts."

"Even Malachea?"

The corners of Basilea's lips curled up in a mischievous half-smile.

"Actually, the two of them became quite… *entangled*

after the festival of Persephone last spring."

Califia felt her cheeks become warm at the thought. A hard-ass bitch like Malachea falling into the arms of a gentle, artsy woman like Kyria? It seemed impossible; if anyone but Basilea had just told her she would have accused them of lying. Even as queen, the old woman always seemed terribly well-informed about such affairs.

Arianna appeared suddenly at Califia's side, sliding a spiced abalone into her mouth and pausing a few moments to admire the iridescent inner shell. "By Athena's bones, have you ever seen a party so lovely?"

"Blasphemy doesn't become you, dear," Basilea said, plucking buttered slices of potato from a nearby platter and daintily placing them in her mouth.

"It's only blasphemy if your heart is motivated by ill intent toward the gods," Ariana sang, smirking with the confidence of someone who joined a theology omadha two months before and was therefore now an expert on all things divine. Basilea's brows furrowed and Califia felt her own eyes glaze over at the prospect of a debate. She deftly backed out of the conversation before opening arguments.

She drifted between tables for a spell sampling various styles of steamed and flash-boiled shrimp, bundles of sweet and spicy peppers, and a pot of soup composed of turkey, maize, and diced potatoes. As she prepared to give the Ohlone a special greeting, suddenly she heard a familiar cry.

"Mommy! Mommy!"

She turned to see her daughter Chloe running toward her in tears. She rested one knee on the ground and Chloe nearly knocked her down with a ferocious embrace.

"Please don't do it, mommy," her daughter whimpered

between sobs. "Please don't be the queen."

Califia picked up her daughter and walked to a remote spot far beneath the balcony where they could speak uninterrupted.

"Why are you afraid?"

"They call you a tyrant, mommy. Krysta and Tayelli said you're a tyrant and promised that their mommies would stop you."

Califia's breath stopped for a moment. She closed her eyes and silently cursed the bitter adults who had been muttering within earshot of their own daughters. Chloe threw her arms around Califia's neck and squeezed tightly.

"I would be so sad if you died, mommy."

"I'm not going to die, my love." She backed out of the girl's embrace, squeezing her shoulders. "The strategoses will protect me. And I don't think anyone would dare to challenge Chloe the bold."

She tapped Chloe's nose and the child smiled at her mom's bravado, loosing a tiny giggle as Califia playfully put her fist over her heart and bowed solemnly. She gave the girl a sudden tickle and the giggles suddenly multiplied into a great cloud of laughter.

"Did you tell the caretakers about this?"

Chloe nodded.

"They made them apologize."

Califia squared her daughter's shoulders and looked her in the eye.

"There is always a space between what people say and what they will *actually* do. A griffin is not troubled by the threats of a turkey."

The girl giggled again, wiping her tears and drying her hand upon the bright purple dress she wore for the occasion. She reached out and tapped Califia's burnished armor.

"You look funny, mommy."

Califia smiled and her heart warmed.

"Oh really?"

"Like a big fat beetle!" Chloe giggled.

"How dare you speak this way to the queen?" She bellowed in a mocking tone. "You must suffer for this insult!"

Califia hoisted her into the air with one hand while the other deftly attacked each of her tickle spots. They walked back to the assembly hand in hand until Chloe spotted some children playing on the other side of the palace and sprinted to join them. It pained her heart to see her daughter leave so quickly but she was glad that she could help the girl overcome her fears.

Now if only Malachea would show up and help me overcome my own fears.

Califia easily rejoined the festivities and was in the middle of a discussion when the air was suddenly pierced with the clanging of palace alarm bells. Through one of the many open windows the queen spotted a large cloud of dust just past the city gates. Her heart thumped in her ears as everyone in the room gathered by the windows and stared, some curious and others panic-stricken, at the distant mystery.

Califia absently wondered if the anxiety that now coursed through her veins was comparable to what the Cochimi felt when the fury of the Californian Amazons bore down upon them during the reign of her mother. Basilea had punished the mainlanders for trespassing on sacred Californian ground but her later reign as queen had been peaceful. It was known, however, that some among the approaching Gorgons desired to reignite that conflict and win the glory which they had been previously denied by being born too late.

"Our noble strategos of the Gorgons blesses our gathering with her presence," Basilea announced, loud enough to be clearly heard over the ringing bells. As the gathered crowd politely chuckled, Califia saw the old woman whisper into the ear of a nearby page who sprinted toward the stairs and then ascended by leaping them two at a time. After a few more peals, the bells ceased their ringing.

"Always so dramatic," Strategos Aleksandra said, shaking her head and grinning with admiration. "Kass would be proud."

Califia smiled and nodded politely, though she had quite forgotten she had been speaking with the strategos of the central regions Ipíos and Jorgya. The queen hoped this woman was right, that this late arrival with a large retinue of Gorgon soldiers was nothing more than a tantrum.

"Excuse me, please," Califia said and Aleksandra nodded amiably and took a sip from her brown ceramic cup. Most of the attendees were already meandering back to the tables and she caught a few snippets of idle conversation on her short journey. A few were discussing whether Isikyai was superior to the way of Omu and whether the two could even be compared, while others marveled at some item of food and speculated about its ingredients. No one seemed concerned. *Good.*

"Don't fall for it," Basilea said as Califia came within earshot. "If she launched a coup, she would only make herself the tyrant."

"I'm not sure *she* will see it that way." Califia took a deep breath and felt the ground beneath her solidify.

"I have known Malachea since she was a baby; she values her *honor* above everything - even victory itself."

Basilea's voice held steady, which gave Califia some comfort. "Killing you would be *cheating*."

Malachea was easy to spot. She stood nearly a head taller than Califia and her muscles bulged beneath her armor with the definition and bulk of one who imposed diligent discipline over her body. She possessed an easy, natural confidence - a swagger, a proud posture - that others had imitated but only the strategos of the Gorgons had managed to truly capture.

Califia donned her most welcoming grin as her stomach tied itself into a hard knot. As the column of armored soldiers came to a stop before her, she spread her arms as she greeted them.

"Welcome to the celebration, my friends."

Malachea removed her helmet and nestled it in the crook of her elbow, displaying her beard tattoo, which was patterned like a thorny bramble. She bowed her head and smiled with a confidence that the queen did not like at all.

"I apologize for our tardiness… *Califia*. We arrived late because we were acquiring a coronation gift."

"We are happy to receive you, Strategos," Califia said diplomatically, "and all we ask is that you refrain from bringing any implements of war into the royal palace."

"We happily submit ourselves to tradition, my queen," Malachea glanced quickly at Basilea as if the title was meant for her. "We shall leave our axes, shields, spears, swords, staves, bows, and daggers by the fountain."

"*And* your armor," Basilea said, sounding almost offended that she even needed to say so. Califia held her breath; several members of Malachea's cohort looked indignant at the idea of removing their armor. Basilea continued, "How else will you dance?"

Some light laughter, as well as a series of hand-signaled

commands from Malachea herself, convinced Califia that the danger hand passed. *For now.* The gorgons removed their helmets, revealing their beard tattoos which marked them as elite warriors. Some were intricate, others followed geometric patterns, and some were just a mass of black ink.

The warriors revealed flowing wine red sleeveless gowns as they removed their armor. They had come prepared. The queen envied them, thinking of how such dresses would beautifully frame the tattoos that graced her arms and breasts. The image of Athena that graced her left bicep would look especially grand.

Cheers erupted from a few corners of the great hall as Malachea entered, throwing her massive arms wide as she received the greetings. How the queen envied the strategos and her very comfortable-looking gown. Her skin felt suddenly hot, though she couldn't be sure whether it was from genuine discomfort or from envy.

"Forget about her," Basilea reassured her. "Let's go talk with the Ohlone and the Kashaya while we have a chance."

The queen was once more thankful that Basilea was there to guide her. The Ohlone delegation, three women and a man wearing turkey feather crowns and intricately beaded loincloths, smiled as the two women approached. They chatted about the events in their homeland, how a flock of sparrows flitted through their camp during a coming-of-age ceremony— an omen of a prosperous year.

The Kashaya were similarly happy to talk about their many herds of bison that grazed throughout their lands and the mighty hunts which their chiefs organized to feed the people. California had its own bison herds, though they hunted them from the backs of griffins when they had need of their meat and hides.

As the party continued, the queen and Basilea gradually drifted apart. Califia spoke with one of the musicians who played a flute which she bragged about carving from a fallen sequoia. After a few boring discussions with some arkozhas and a strategos, the queen tried to enjoy a few restorative moments of peace.

"Quite the spectacle," Malachea remarked, appearing suddenly at Califia's side.

"It is no crime to celebrate an achievement," Califia retorted, rolling her eyes as Malachea grabbed some more food.

"An unannounced lightning campaign with no challenger," Malachea examined a cluster of spiced shrimp. "Some would say that such an achievement does not warrant a party this extravagant."

Malachea popped the shrimp cluster into her mouth and turned to take her leave. She nearly collided with Kyria, who had been approaching the queen. The two paused awkwardly and their expressions soured. Kyria fixed the Gorgon strategos with a glare that Califia believed would have frozen an erupting volcano and Malachea pursed her lips in turn and gave a heavy sigh. Malachea moved on and Kyria affixed a smile.

"My queen, the Ohlone would like to favor your reign with a dance."

"Yes, I..." Califia tried to clear her mind. The thought of the rude, brash Malachea resting in the arms of gentle and bubbly Kyria was too vast an equation for her to even conceive, much less hope to solve.

"Are you feeling okay?"

Califia nodded.

"I am only too happy to receive their blessing."

Once she had quieted the musicians and cleared the

dais of furniture, the dance began. The largest of them, a man whose height and bulk would rival a bear, began a low and intense chant as the dancers hit drums in time as they stepped across their elevated dance space. Some held feathered fans and tasseled scepters, waving them in patterns that expanded and contracted as the steady rhythm grew louder or softer. Califia noticed three or four couples taking the dance as an opportunity to slip away for more intimate relations in one of the many furnished rooms attached to the great hall. She smiled as she imagined taking Ariana's hand and leading her into one of the abandoned rooms, their bodies pulsing to the rhythm of the Ohlone chant.

The Tepota'al, not satisfied being outshone by their northern neighbors, insisted on performing a dance afterward. She naturally assented. The people of the coastal mountains celebrated a much more vigorous dance complete with battle whoops and acrobatic flips. The Kashaya performed next, blessing the gathering with a stomping, galloping dance meant to invoke the spirit of the bison. The Californians in the assembly clapped and talked to one another excitedly until Kyria at last commanded their silence, leading Califia onto the dais gently but firmly by the elbow.

"It is time for the coronation!" The mistress of entertainment announced, turning once more to the queen and smiling supportively. Basilea ascended the three steps to the top of the dais with the graceful ease of one well-practiced in poise and regal command. The gray hair braided and gathered on top of her head looked like a snowy crown.

"Eight years ago, I stood on this platform and swore an oath to protect this nation and its people at any cost, even with my own life," Basilea spoke with conviction and her voice resonated through the palace. "Before you stands she who will continue in my stead. Today she swears the same oath and submits her life to its demands."

From her belt, Basilea removed a dagger with a black sheath. Its hilt was likewise black, but shiny from centuries of handling. Basilea held it aloft for everyone to lay eyes upon; the room filled with a revered silence as each woman reflected upon the blade's meaning and history. Califia thought of Amaltheia who conjured it, sitting miserably in a prison cell on the island their people once ruled until tricked into defeat by their crafty enemies. In a desperate act of self control and determination, she had plunged that dagger into her own heart so that her people, Califia's people, might be saved from subjugation and slavery.

Basilea held the dagger's sheath with both hands and angled the hilt toward Califia. This part of the ritual she knew well and had practiced; she grabbed the proffered hilt and unveiled the gleaming blade, pointing its tip toward the heavens for a few moments as it shimmered. She placed her left hand upon its broad pommel and rotated the weapon until its point hovered over her own heart.

"Will you serve the Amazons, placing their desires, their needs, their futures above your own, even at the cost of your own life?"

Califia held the blade steady and took a calming breath before responding.

"I will."

"Kneel before your people."

Califia knelt, still holding the dagger toward her heart. Basilea turned to the assembly.

"Will you, the people of California, accept and

encourage your queen as she contributes her talent, energy, and indeed her very life on your behalf?"

"We will." The crowd replied, the resonance of the palace transforming their spoken assent into an enthusiastic roar.

Basilea stretched her hands toward the sky and enthusiastically spoke the words that her own predecessor, the mother of the new Califia, had spoken on her behalf twelve years before.

"Rejoice, my people! A new queen has come to serve us, to invigorate us where we have grown stagnant, to enrich us where we have grown poor, to enlighten us where our minds have grown dark!" She turned toward Califia, whose knee was beginning to throb. "Arise, O queen, and put away the weapon that guaranteed our freedom so many years ago!"

Califia rose to her feet and took the sheath from Basilea, sliding the dagger smoothly back inside. She tied the weapon into her belt and gazed regally upon her people who looked back with a mixture of reverence, respect, and open skepticism.

"My queen," Kyria interjected, beaming with joy and anticipation, "I humbly request the honor of being the first to present you with a coronation gift."

"Will you require use of this platform?" Califia asked.

"You know me too well," Kyria blushed a little and gestured for the actors whom Califia had noticed were standing near the far walls in outlandishly plumed costumes.

One of the actors was queen of the turkeys and the other was queen of the hawks. The narrator explained that there was a great war between them and the performers began slashing at each other, the hawks wielding polearms adorned with curved talon-like blades and the turkeys armed with great feathered shields. They fought constantly until the land was too ravaged for either party to find food. At last they learned that they must cease fighting one another and work together in order to survive.

Califia was enjoying the story until it transformed into a ham-handed attempt at a metaphor of reconciliation. *Damn you, Kyria.* She glanced at Malachea, who was rolling her eyes. The turkey and hawk embraced to tepid applause.

Afterward, several *Omadhas* presented gifts - the harvesters brought a gold sickle representing their hope of abundant yields during Califia's reign, the fishers of Amaltheia brought an intricately molded goblet with a salmon stem and rapid ocean currents surrounding the central cup, and the hatchery sent a circlet composed of griffin feathers and light, silvery eggshell steel.

After each gift, she glanced at Malachea to see if the Gorgons were ready to present whatever they had brought for her. They had been so vocal about opposing her queenship that she wasn't expecting anything, but Malachea had made it clear that something would be given. Califia shivered to think what it might be.

The Kashaya presented a wooden dagger carved from oak. As the queen held the curved dagger aloft for everyone to see, she saw that Malachea was whispering commands to her daughter, Dionysia. *Whatever it is, it will be here soon.*

Malachea stepped forward. Califia felt as though the tension in the room threatened to crush them all. She pushed visions of a bloody coup out of her mind.

"There are some who have scurrilously whispered that our new Califia is unsuited to the work of protecting our land, of protecting us."

You were behind those whispers, Califia thought, hoping her seething anger was not visible in her expression.

"Our gift is an opportunity to prove those doubters wrong and demonstrate your unwavering commitment to our safety and security."

She held up her hand and two of her Gorgons appeared at the large open doors at the entrance. As they stepped inside, Califia saw that they were flanking a third figure — someone dressed in a strange dark red robe which matched no style Califia had never seen. Both arms and legs were shackled and their head was covered by a dark woven sack.

"We apprehended an intruder this morning wandering the southern shores of Droserós, perhaps an enemy scout sent to spy our land for invasion. Because the griffins were locked away, he was spared the horrific death which their beaks and talons bring."

She pulled the bag off of his head and a brown-skinned man blinked and looked about, his mouth agape. He had bushy eyebrows and neatly-trimmed beard, and he spoke a few words in a strange language wholly unfamiliar to Califia's ears.

"Our gift to you, great queen," Malachea received a wide-bladed axe from one of the guards flanking the prisoner and immediately proffered it to Califia, "is the honor of performing this man's execution."

2

The stranger gazed at the weapon with wide eyes and quivering lips. Basilea gaped and Arianna stared at the man with curiosity. The hall was transformed into a sea of wide eyes and open mouths.

Kyria loosed a shrill, horrified gasp, which initiated a flurry of copycats and shattered the long silence. Califia glanced at the mainlanders, who looked on in horror and grief.

"I thank you, strategos, for this opportunity," the queen began, holding up her palm. "But I must refuse."

Whispers echoed through the hall and Malachea wore an uncertain expression. Briefly the queen wondered whether the Gorgon strategos had fully expected to force her into committing a summary execution.

"Should one of *us* execute the prisoner, then?" asked Dionysia, Malachea's eldest daughter.

"This is an unusual circumstance," Califia began, stalling for time. She glanced around the room hoping to think of something quick. A few of the arkozhas muttered to one another, their eyes stuck to the newcomer's frightened face. "I must confer with the civic council."

The room erupted once more in whispers and perplexed expressions as those gathered now strained to get a good look at the stranger's face. The Ohlone, Tepota'al and Kashaya peered at him and whispered to one another, but none of them seemed to recognized the bearded man.

Basilea gestured toward a room at to the far eastern end of the hall. The arkozhas followed and Califia closed the door behind her. The moment the door slid shut, Basilea jammed a finger in Malachea's face.

"This is beyond outrageous even for you!"

"I only have our people's best interests in mind," she replied defensively.

"You should have executed this man yourself; it is your duty."

Malachea's jaw clenched, and for a moment Califia worried that the two ladies would come to blows.

"I wanted to give our new queen the chance to demonstrate that her armor is not just for show!"

"If anyone doubts our queen's abilities," said strategos Traesta, gesturing toward Califia with a muscular arm, "it is probably because you have been allowing your soldiers to wag their tongues at anyone foolish enough to listen!"

"It is not forbidden to speak one's mind," Malachea said coolly, glancing at the queen as she might notice a gnat or other small annoyance.

"Violence against one's fellow Amazons *is* forbidden," said Arkozha Filai, maneuvering herself so that she stood between the strategos and the queen. "I still have yet to receive any reply regarding the two drunken gorgons who injured four people in Troyaste last month."

"What *brought* my warriors to that backwater outpost?" Malachea spat. "Next time deal with the Jaguar yourselves."

"Enough!" Califia stepped forward, gently moving Filai aside as the woman's dark face began to flush with rage. "Using violence to *solve* problems only multiplies them."

"Your mother was not afraid to use violence to solve *her* problems," Malachea replied.

"And she was wrong to do so," Califia said. "The war with the Cochimi was an avoidable tragedy which she regretted until her dying day."

The room suddenly seemed to fill with a stifling silence.

"We do not have many laws, my queen," Malachea growled, stepping forward so that she was just in front of Califia, "but the law is quite clear regarding trespassers."

"What weapons did he carry?" Asked Olympia, the strategos of the valley militia. She was at least a head shorter than Califia and her sandy brown skin looked soft to the touch. Yet there was a firmness, a resoluteness to her that the queen could not quite define or explain. She locked eyes with Malachea and raised her eyebrows as if she expected a quicker answer.

"He was… unarmed," the gorgon strategos glowered at the short, stocky woman who dared to challenge her.

"What was the manner of his watercraft?" Olympia asked, taking a defiant step toward Malachea.

"We found none," Malachea turned once more to Califia, "but it may have drifted away."

"There is much, it seems, that we do not know about this visitor," Califia said, pacing a little with what meager space she could claim in the crowded room. "No weapon, no boat… he does not sound like a trespasser. More like a refugee."

"We do not have many laws, Strategos," Basilea said,

clearly savoring this moment, "but the law is quite clear regarding refugees."

The islands did not often receive those lost at sea or fleeing their homeland but when the odd lost soul managed to avoid being devoured by griffins, the Californians prided themselves on giving that person the help they needed— even if that person was a *man*.

"We should ask the mainlanders for help," Strategos Traesta suggested.

"Basilea, would you…?" Califia had barely begun to ask when the former queen had already slid open the door and approached the various delegations of the Ohlone, Tepota'al, Kashaya, and all the others. She turned to Malachea.

"Take the visitor to a vacant house as close to the palace as possible. Keep him under guard but give him food and water. At this moment he is our guest and you will ensure that those under your command treat him as such."

Malachea clenched her jaw and glowered. She stormed out of the doorway, shoving the door loudly into its full open position on her way out. Her hands flashed quickly with urgent signals to the gorgons guarding the bound man. They hoisted him to his feet and hustled him quickly out of the palace. Malachea stopped briefly at one of the food tables as she stomped toward the exit, stuffing her mouth with shrimp and abalone before disappearing into the light of the outdoors.

Califia marched into the hall, gesturing for Kyria to start the music once more. As the music played, the whispers faded and those gathered continued celebrating as they danced, kissed, and grabbed the odd handful of food. The queen sighed, feeling already quite exhausted from her first day.

"You handled that well," Olympia said, appearing at Califia's elbow.

"Many thanks to you, strategos," the queen said, acknowledging the woman's contribution with a solemn nod.

"What will you do if the mainlanders cannot help us identify this man and his people?"

Califia's breath stopped for a moment as she realized she did not have a plan beyond *stop Malachea from making my first act as queen a bloody execution.* As if sensing her panic, the strategos put a hand on her shoulder and gave it a few good-natured pats.

"Always be thinking of what may come next," Olympia said, grinning in a way that made the queen feel warm inside. "I can promise you Malachea is already considering her next move. She's a pain in the ass, but she's brave and tough and her soldiers love her more than their own mothers. Don't underestimate her."

"I will be careful," Califia replied, adding when Olympia raised a skeptical eyebrow, "and I will think of what may come next."

The strategos of the valley militia nodded and grinned and promptly sought out a rather tall woman and began dancing with her. Arianna, who had been wistfully swaying to the music like a willow in a breeze, drifted over to Califia with a goofy grin on her face.

Wine sloshed in the glass tumbler she held precariously with her fingertips. Her delighted expression faded suddenly into deep concern. "Are you going to kill that poor man?"

"Not if I can help it, love." Califia smiled and took the glass just as her lover was about to drop it, playfully draining it and placing it carefully on a table behind her. "You should take a break from the wine."

"I will… as soon as you come dance with me!" She took Califia's hand and began dragging her toward a cluster of dancers who were swaying to the melodic rhythm of the harps and flutes. Califia released her hand as she spotted Basilea coming toward them.

"Soon, my love," the queen said. Arianna looked at her own empty hand with disappointment.

"Give me some good news," she said to Basilea as the woman finally wove through the dense crowd.

Basilea's face was distressed and apologetic.

"None of them recognize the man's clothing or his words. I walked them outside and bade the man speak but none of the mainlanders comprehended a single word."

"What is your impression of him?"

Basilea twisted her lips as she considered this, but Califia knew better than to rush the old woman.

"He's terrified, but I don't think he came here with hostile intent. He gazes in awe at every rock along the path, every face that crosses his eyeline, as though he's experiencing something novel, something beyond his imagination."

Califia took a moment to think. The man certainly wasn't Cochimi, and the other mainlanders had no reason to deny knowledge of him. The queen suddenly realized there was a piece of this puzzle that didn't fit. "Where did Malachea say they found the visitor?"

"The shores of…" Basilea thought for several moments, "…Droserós!"

The women grinned at one another.

"I have to speak with Malachea," Califia said, looking toward the doorway as she prepared to go.

Framed in the light of the open doorway was Dionysia, Malachea's daughter, who marched toward the queen with a sour look on her face.

"The strategos wants you," she said indifferently.

"What a lovely coincidence," Califia said, smiling warmly in spite of the rude young woman before her.

Malachea stood just to the side of the palace entrance, leaning casually against the outer wall with her arms crossed.

"I am not your enemy. I brought this man to you to solidify your coronation, not sabotage it."

"By making me into an executioner?" Califia said, baffled at the boldness of this woman's deception.

"A *protector*!" Malachea said, looking exasperated. "This was a simple test — I didn't expect you to fail it!"

"Speaking of failing tests, I wonder if the strategos of the Gorgons shouldn't have more knowledge of geography!" Califia felt triumphant speaking these thoughts aloud, a sensation which was only intensified by Malachea's confused expression. "How often do trespassers show up in Droserós?"

"What does that have to do with…" Malachea trailed off, her indignant tone quickly fading into one of sinking realization. "He's still a trespasser."

"Our bravest sisters have flown over the western ocean," Califia made a small step forward, forcing Malachea to give a tiny bit of ground, "and found nothing but saltwater. If you discovered him on our western coast then he must be from lands beyond those waters, which means he is almost certainly lost and, therefore, a refugee."

The strategos pursed her lips and exhaled sharply from her flared nostrils.

"It won't matter," she growled, at which Califia scoffed as she continued. "All anyone will talk about is how your first act as queen was to refuse to protect your people from a threat. I hope you're prepared to deal with the consequences."

"I will not murder an unarmed person who is simply lost! Such an act would invite the wrath of the triumvirs!"

Malachea scoffed, shaking her head as she shoved her helmet over her many snaky locks. "It is the wrath of the people you should fear. *They* are your god now, my queen!"

Before Califia could answer back, the Gorgon strategos turned her back and jogged away. The queen seethed with frustration. The infernal woman must have known that Califia, whose gentle nature was well-known, would never summarily behead someone— even a *man*! Califia had fallen into the ambitious soldier's trap but she couldn't think of any way she could have avoided it.

****

After donning a stout purple cotton dress, the queen strode to the hut where the visitor was being kept, which was easily found thanks to the armed guards flanking the doorway. She could see at a glance that they were Gorgons; one had an elaborate interlocking tattoo that circled her mouth while the other's cheeks and chin were covered by a trail of dots that circled her eyes and blended into her serpentine locks. Each wore a weathered breastplate of Griffinsteel, which shimmered in spite of many scuffs, and casually held a sagaris - the traditional single-edged battle axe of the Amazons.

"I'm going to speak with the prisoner," Califia told them, hoping they understood that she didn't need their permission.

"Good luck," said one, hastily adding, "my queen."

She pushed the thatched reeds hanging in the doorway

aside and stepped into the balmy hut. The prisoner lay on the ground, his bound hands cradling his head as he snored. She puzzled over his strange brown robes and turban; his beard was beginning to fray around the edges but its tapered shape suggested grooming. His skin was several shades lighter than that of most Amazons, close to the color of a beech tree's interior. She nudged his shoulder gently and he yawned as he sat up.

As he fixed his eyes upon her, he hurled his head and hands onto the ground before him as though bending in worship, jabbering away in his language which sounded to Califia's ears like the swishing of tidal currents against rocks. She sighed and pushed him upright so that he was sitting on his heels. His eyes were filled with abject terror and she gave her friendliest smile, hoping to calm him. In the dirt between them she drew an arrow pointing to him, shrugging when he looked from the symbol and then back to her.

Who are you?

His eyes shot back and forth as though he was puzzling over an answer. He drew a crude stick figure of a woman with exaggerated breasts and some kind of giant spiked hat that reminded her of a wooden palisade. He gestured to the figure and then pointed at Califia. She put her hand on her chest.

"Me?"

He nodded vigorously and before she could decide between being flattered or offended, he quickly sketched another stick man wearing a turban next to her and gestured to himself. Califia nodded. He then traced a rectangle in his hands, something he seemed to be offering her. He gestured to the object in his hand and drew little arrows in the dirt pointing to Califia's figure. He looked up with wide, hopeful eyes.

She tapped the rectangle and offered a confused gesture. He nodded and wiped away his illustration, beginning a new drawing composed of an elaborate set of vertical lines. He made jagged little connecting lines between them and Califia believed he was drawing walls. He drew little people standing atop the walls and then, with sudden quick strokes, he drew curving lines reaching up to the sky. Flames.

The prisoner smashed the city with his fists and looked up with a friendly smile. She returned a polite grin, then swiftly left the hut.

****

"It sounds like a declaration of war!" Exclaimed Malachea after Califia finished describing her interview with the prisoner. Basilea paced and tapped her finger against her chin. The war council had been assembled, consisting of the queen, Basilea, and the other six strategoses who stood around the room as well. It was midmorning and the cool of the early day still lingered in the small eastern room of the palace.

"He seems in no way hostile," Califia replied, puzzling over the matter like a Bison chewing its cud. "He smiled throughout our... *conversation*. He seemed more frightened than anything else."

"Perhaps it was merely a threat?" Basilea postulated, still pacing without making eye contact. "'Free me or my people will burn your cities?'"

Califia twisted her lips as she puzzled over it. In the image he was presenting her with... what? A threatening letter? A gift? Some trade goods? She turned to Malachea.

"Have your scouts discovered anything that might help

us?"

The strategos shook her head.

"News of the stranger has already spread to the Elysium Valley," Aleksandra said. "I have heard that many Omadhas have begun drafting statements of protest and are making preparations to take further action if necessary."

Califia's heart plummet into her gut like a stone falling into the ocean. Letters of protest, direct action, and political involvement were a way of life on California but she hoped she would have more time to solve this mystery before the chanting, demonstrating, and work stoppages began.

"We need to move quickly," Califia took a moment to think. She turned to Basilea. "I need you to travel to Elysiopolis and address the harvesters directly. They respect you."

"Not enough to accept the presence of a strange man on our island!"

"I'm not asking you to win their hearts, just try to slow them down. Tell them about him - what he looks like, what his language sounds like. Make him a curiosity rather than a threat!"

"I will do what I can." Basilea embraced Califia and then left the room. The queen turned to her strategoses.

"Think carefully whatever you are about to ask of us, Califia," Malachea warned as Califia opened her mouth. "The only thing our people hate more than a weak leader is a tyrant."

She felt the back of her neck burn with fury. Malachea was out of line, but the anxiety she saw on the faces of the other strategoses gave her pause. There were a thousand wrong responses to this situation and few which would be sufficient to quell the people's reactionary rage.

Califia chose her words carefully but spoke them firmly. "All I ask of you and the soldiers you command is that you protect the visitor."

"Trespasser," said Linnea, who led the militia of the southernmost desert regions. "The people refer to him as the trespasser."

Her expression was hard and impassive; her skin was like a craggy cliff face which, in spite of its cracks, has grown stronger from constant wind. She wasn't glaring or hostile, but there was no doubt in Califia's mind that she was sending a message. *We work for the people, not for you.*

"The people are free to decide for themselves what to call the man," Califia said, shrugging as though the matter was of little consequence to her. "Trespasser, however, implies malicious intent and all the evidence so far indicates that the man arrived here by accident."

Linnea squinted as she considered this, then gave a small nod. This, Califia knew, was as close to an affirmation as she was likely to get.

The queen attended to her other duties, sending various coronation gifts to other leaders who could find better use for them, being careful not to send a gift to the person or omadha from whom it had originated. The first messenger bearing a letter of protest arrived that evening, just as Califia was eating the last of her seared salmon, a belated coronation gift from a nearby resident named Feydra. The letter was from the Californopolis Weaver's Omadha, and while it was politely worded, its demands were clear: the undersigned were prepared to deny the palace any new rugs, tapestries, and blankets until the trespasser was gone from the island.

There's that word again. The queen rolled the document

up and tossed it into a basket reserved for petitions near the dais. Her bones ached as she shuffled toward her chambers and she twisted about, hoping to stretch the cramps and soothe her weary body. When she arrived at last at her chamber, she slid the door open and gasped to see someone sitting on the bed.

"Sorry!" Arianna blurted, following up with an awkward giggle. "I only just arrived. I thought you would be here by now, and I… well… I didn't mean to startle you."

"It's alright," Califia said, laughing at herself for being so jumpy. "I was hoping to see you today, but there was no time."

"I thought you might be busy," Arianna smiled and tucked one of her stray braids behind her ear. "The temple of Athena requested some murals, so I spent most of my day there, getting a feel for the space."

"I see," the queen replied, even though she definitely did not. While she enjoyed the art which Arianna created, she did not understand the woman's relationship with it. Nevertheless, she tried. "And did the space have a good… *feel?*"

"It did, though more than a few visiting *Isikyai* clearly did not appreciate my presence."

"That's not surprising," Califia chuckled. The Isikyai believed in waiting in silence to hear the gods speak and the movement tended to attract those who were easily annoyed by the normal behavior of others.

"Come sit with me," Arianna invited, patting the empty half of the bed. Califia smiled and took off her outer tunic, laying it upon the nearby desk and sitting on the bed in her shift.

The troubles of the world melted away with every caress, every deep, long kiss. Afterward they snuffed the candles and lay together under the covers, each enjoying the others' warmth.

"Everyone's talking about him." Arianna sighed, staring toward the ceiling with her hands behind her head.

"He'll be the primary source of conversation here for many months," Califia took a deep breath and let it out slowly.

"Has anyone tried to communicate with him since this morning?"

"Since he threatened to invade and raze the capital?" Califia grinned and shook her head. "Not really, no."

"We don't know what he meant," Arianna said. "Basilea has a talent for languages - maybe she could find a way to—"

"She's in Elysiopolis," Califia groaned, wishing there was some way for the woman to be in both places at the same time. "I need to be careful not to rely upon her too much."

"Just seems a pity," Arianna closed her eyes and her words sounded slow and tired. "Who knows what he could teach us about the world?"

The next morning, Califia cursed as she stepped in a pile of scrolls waiting for her outside the door. She scooped the pile into her arms and carried it to the table outside, plopping them onto the bench beside her and unrolling one at random. The Brewers Omadha of the Capital refused to provide drinks for the palace until the trespasser was removed. She scanned the others, quickly glancing through roughly half of them before coming to the inevitable conclusion that each of these messages was a demand for the trespasser's head.

Visitor, she reminded herself. *He's a visitor.*

She shuffled through the messages and found the one

she was thinking of, confirming that it was from Xirozesto. *How in Hera's name could the far south of the island have received word of the visitor?* She shuffled through a few more, finding one from Sillavuna in the far north and several more from Urafidyo, which was the southernmost region. After some searching she finally found one which was neither complaint nor petition: a message from Pholess informing her that the dignitaries from the mainland peoples had all disembarked and the Griffins were therefore released.

She looked into the sky and saw several soaring overhead, the watchful guardians and swift messengers of the Amazons. More petitions and protests were sure to arrive in greater volume. As Califia pondered how to address this pending influx, Arianna emerged from the large open doors at the palace's front carrying in both her arms a fresh pile of scrolls.

"You're certainly popular this morning!" Arianna said as she arranged her haul as neatly as possible on the only bit of table not yet covered.

"Quite the opposite," Califia replied, rolling her eyes at a crude poem scrawled in the margin of a letter of protest from the Carpenter's Omadha of Droseros. "Could I ask a favor?"

Arianna raised an eyebrow, then looked down and adopted a determined yet overly serious expression. "Alright, I will do it. I will kill the visitor for you."

Califia and Arianna shared a burst of laughter and for a moment the queen's heart felt light.

"Can you find the page responsible for bringing these messages to me and redirect her to this table?"

"Of course, love," said Arianna, grabbing a tumbling scroll as she rose from her seat. She peeked at its contents and smirked. "Wouldn't want to miss out on anything quite as important as this."

She handed the scroll to Califia before sprinting off to find whomever was on messenger duty that morning. The queen unrolled it and saw it was from the capital's poetry Omadha, threatening to withhold their verses from Califia's ears until the trespasser was properly dealt with.

I'll try to survive without your tired couplets. The queen felt a twinge of guilt at the thought. The greatest poets hailed from Urafidyo or Xirozesto, places where life and death existed in a delicate balance. The capital was remarkable for many things, but poetry was not among them.

Arianna soon returned holding a basket with yet more scrolls in one hand and chomping an apple with the other. Following her was a harried-looking young girl who held two baskets at least as full as Arianna's. She set them down by Califia's feet and left the queen's presence faster than a person fleeing a sudden encounter with a skunk.

One of the new scrolls caught Califia's eye. While most of the others were sealed with a bit of wax, this one was held closed by a bright blue ribbon and as the queen took it up, she also noticed that the edge on one side had been charred slightly as if someone held it for a few moments near an open flame. The blue ribbon indicated that it was from Basilea, and the charred side was a secret signal they had worked out during the campaign months. This missive contained a coded message.

The message was straight-forward and to the point, which was Basilea's usual style. While the Harvesters Omadha of the Elysium valley in Jorgya were not pleased at the news of a man on the island allowed to live, they were not bothered enough by this development to consider work stoppage or other direct action. Yet.

At the bottom of the page was the key to the hidden message - Basilea had chosen to end the letter with the closing "Your Humble Friend" but her first attempt at the phrase had been marred by a spelling error and she had crossed through it with a single line before writing it again. Califia began searching for the crossed out glyph and after following the pattern established for the code, had written the secret message on the bottom of a parchment where she had found space, adding punctuation where it seemed to fit.

This will not hold for long. Rumors claim you intend to use the man for pleasure. I believe Linnea is responsible.

Califia felt her blood suddenly boiling in spite of the coolness of the morning. To accuse her of such perversion - using a man for pleasure! - was a trick worthy of Malachea, but she never suspected Linnea capable of such disgusting skulduggery. While the return of the griffins may have helped speed the news of the visitor along, no doubt Linnea was the bigger reason why so many villages and settlements throughout the desert south were so quickly aware of what had transpired at the coronation.

"You look ready to pluck feathers from a sleeping griffin," Arianna remarked, smirking at the queen as she seethed.

"If that would put this matter to rest, I would gladly attempt it," Califia said through her teeth. She quickly tore off the bit of parchment where she had transcribed the hidden message. She rose and strode into the hall carrying the original missive and the transcription. A small fire had been lit at the great hearth and she eagerly pitched both documents into the flames.

"If only there was some way to make them understand," Arianna said sadly as the flames engulfed the scrolls. "They are reacting to rumor instead of facts."

"Perhaps there is a way," Califia said, wishing she had thought of this earlier. "The griffins' return means that the people can more easily send their complaints, but it also means I can more easily tell them the truth of this matter."

She spent most of the morning drafting a proclamation which she was certain would set the matter straight. It would be sent to the major cities and settlements throughout the nation, each of which managed their own communication circuit for ensuring that the words of the queen were heard by everyone in the smaller villages and outposts. She assigned the pages to organize the incoming scrolls in the meantime, a task for which she did not envy them. *They volunteered for these posts because they think they want to be the Califia someday. Let them see what they can expect on very bad days.*

The message she composed was simple and to the point: the man whom the Gorgons had brought to the coronation was *rescued*, not captured. He possessed no vessel and no weapons, and was no threat to the Amazons otherwise. For the moment, he was being treated as a refugee, a child of merciful Persephone who watched over all those who had been driven from the comfort and familiarity of their homes.

The last part was a bit more flowery and overly pious than she generally liked, but the outrageously scandalous nature of the accusations required the strongest defense she could muster. She nearly called the visitor a child of Aphrodite at first, but changed it to Persephone both because the goddess of the afterlife was more directly connected to refugees and because she realized with a blush that evoking the goddess of love would only add tinder to the rumors that she wanted to use the man to satisfy some perversion. She wrinkled her nose at the thought; she had done her duty and conceived Chloe in the usual way, by seducing an isolated man from the mainland, and while the experience had not been entirely unpleasant, it was in no way comparable to the passionate nights she spent with her fellow women.

She gave the missive to a page, who told her that they could transcribe twenty-three copies by the evening. Around midday someone, she did not see who, brought her a plate full of stewed bison wrapped in a firm but soft corn wrap. It was the perfect thing to eat while she read every new screed, marveling a few times at some truly original arguments created to malign her character. She had nearly cleared her plate when she heard the rapidly-approaching flap of griffin wings and looked up in time to see the creature land and its rider hop from the saddle and remove her wind visor as she ran quickly toward the queen. It was Traesta, the strategos of *Okeanostendron*, the northern regions.

"Califia, you need to read this," she said, tossing a scroll onto the table where the queen had just managed to clear a space.

The queen grunted at the invasion of that one clear space but smiled amiably at the strategos, who was already removing her riding furs in the midday heat. Califia unrolled the parchment and felt an icy stab within her heart as she read and re-read the message. It was short, and its script was unnervingly smooth and unflinching.

Killing a tyrant is the highest honor.

"I found that by my tent less than two hours ago," Traesta explained, thanking a nearby page for bringing her a cup of water. "I can only assume that the others will soon receive similar missives."

If they haven't already, the queen thought. She shuddered at what might come next; she knew enough of the history of California to understand that tyranny took two or three generations to be destroyed. The liberators often became worse than the oppressors they rose against.

She did not want to do what she believed needed to be done. There was no comparison, philosophical or otherwise, between the loss of a single life and the loss of thousands. She took a moment to silently curse Malachea once more for bringing this situation into existence. She opened her eyes as Traesta finished draining her cup.

"How long should it take for the others to be gathered at the capital - the strategoses and the arkozhas?" The queen asked, gesturing to the page who had come to collect Traesta's empty cup.

"Not more than a day, I should think," Traesta said, handing off her cup and thanking the girl.

"Bring me parchment and a stylus," Califia said to the page. The girl sprinted quickly away, fumbling the cup but luckily catching it before it struck the ground.

"What are you going to do?" Traesta asked, crossing her arms over her chest.

"I'm putting an end to this before things get any further out of control."

****

Califia woke the next morning to a wave of guilt over what she was about to do. When the foremothers traveled across a vast ocean, they came upon a continent which they now referred to as the mainland. It was a broad and fertile land and some of the Amazons proposed claiming this land for their own and conquering the people who lived there. Queen Helena convinced them to continue seeking until they found an uninhabited place to live instead. She is credited with the axiom *Do not visit upon others the evils which have been visited upon you.*

Eventually they found California. Helena's argument became a guiding principle for all future generations of Amazons, surviving even the darkness of the Age of Tyrants. Helena's principle was rolling through Califia's mind as she dressed herself, ate a meager breakfast, and prepared to receive the island's leaders. The strategoses and arkozhas, having received their invitations, gradually arrived at the capital within the day just as Traesta had predicted. They assembled in the main hall that afternoon, waiting on her pronouncement.

"Before I proceed," Califia began, "are there any reports of ship sightings, either within range of the coast or beyond it?"

She looked to the arkozhas of Filion and Droseros, but they shook their heads. She turned toward Malachea, whose scouts had been combing the distant seas in search of such vessels, but the strategos of the Gorgons gave only a subtle shake of the head before offering an indifferent shrug.

"If we had two more days, we could find them," Basilea said, the confidence in her voice almost making a believer of Califia herself.

"If Amaltheia and Helena had not fallen in love, we would live on Atlantis," Califia said, smiling sadly at her adviser who nodded and sighed. The queen felt a sudden impulse to make a grand speech, but this was not a time for speeches; this was a time for action. "It seems there is only one true path forward."

She stepped through the assembled council and signaled for the great palace doors to open. The pages turned the cranks that controlled the monstrous doors which now parted for the queen. Outside, an agitated crowd was already shouting and chanting in a great cacophony. The queen held up her hands and the noise subsided enough for her to be heard.

"Are you yet unmoved by the poor visitor's plight?" She asked, hoping that at least some would answer in the affirmative. Instead the air erupted once more with rage and bloodthirst and fear and hatred.

Her heart sank at the discord between herself and her people, but as their queen it was her duty to keep them safe. They would never feel safe with a man allowed to stay on their island.

"Bring him," she said to a nearby Gorgon who, thankfully, did not glance at Malachea before obeying the queen's order. The guard disappeared through the crowd and soon returned, escorting the man with his hands bound in front of him. He gaped at the crowd with wide, terrified eyes, and smiled when he saw Califia. His grin faded when he perceived her mournful expression.

"Silence!" The queen shouted, her voice booming over the crowd's rage. A quiet suddenly filled the air and Califia wasted no time in filling it. "This man was unarmed and without watercraft when he was found; he has threatened no one and I believe he means us no harm. Yet his continued presence here violates the law, and thus I must see justice done."

From somewhere in the back of the crowd, something flew toward the visitor and landed in the dirt just in front of him. The shouts and anger rose quickly again, and the queen knew that the battle was lost. Malachea handed her a sword and the Gorgon attendant shoved the visitor to his knees.

Taking one last look into the crowd, Califia spotted

Arianna, her eyes downcast and her shoulders slumped. Califia took up her position behind the man, grabbing his left shoulder with one hand and resting the point of the borrowed sword just behind his right collarbone. Malachea stepped forward and held up her hand. The crowd fell silent.

Califia adjusted her grip on the hilt, ensuring that this matter would finally be put to rest in the space of one single, quick thrust. She locked eyes with the crowd one last time, looking from person to person as she prepared for the moment of action. She sucked in a quick breath and felt her muscles tense.

"Hold!" Came a loud shout from the sky. Both the queen and those assembled looked toward the south to see two fast-approaching griffins and their riders. The queen feared that they would crash due to the speed of their approach, but the great beasts flapped their wings forward, slowing just enough to safely drop to the ground.

The riders jumped from their mounts, hastily placed hoods over the creatures' heads, and sprinted toward the queen. They were close enough now that Califia and the others could see their tell-tale Gorgon markings, beard tattoos and long locks of snaky hair.

"Strategos," the two gave Malachea an exhausted salute by tapping their fists to their hearts. Malachea ran to them and the three were just far enough away that Califia could not interpret their mutterings. The Gorgon strategos' face looked stunned. She strode briskly back to Califia.

"My queen," Malachea said, loud enough so that all besides the queen could hear her as well, "these two have located his friends."

A murmur rippled through the crowd, as if they

weren't certain how they ought to react. Califia took the blade from his collarbone and handed it back to Malachea, who quickly sheathed it without meeting the queen's eyes. The visitor himself suddenly jumped up and turned to Califia, his eyes wide as two full moons.

"Friends!" He shouted, matching the Amazonian pronunciation almost perfectly. "Friends! I are friends! We am are friends! Friends!"

He adopted the happiest grin Califia had ever seen in her life and the queen realized that she was also smiling.

3

In the sky above Califia, three griffins spun and whirled around one another like fallen oak leaves caught in an updraft. The queen gripped the hilt of the triumvir dagger, which she had unsheathed on the advice of Basilea. Baring the blade made for a stronger link between herself and the beasts now at her command. Many philosophers and scholars had puzzled over the weapon, which was the length of her forearm, but none could state with *certainty* precisely how it worked. The red gem which was affixed to the cross-section where the blade merged with the hilt glowed when the user successfully communed with the catbirds, but no one knew exactly why. It fell into the category of things not yet understood by humans: *magic*.

"Focus on what you want the creatures to do next," Basilea had instructed her two days earlier when the queen had come so close to executing the visitor. "Be patient with them - they are not machines. They have minds of their own."

The harmonic bliss Califia felt at every swoop, every turn, every spin was nearly euphoric. When thoughts of

Malachea or the visitor periodically drifted into her consciousness, the griffins began to disperse. She turned her attention back to them, commanding them to fly parallel with one another. They took up their positions one above the other and matched each other's movements as naturally as the shimmerfish schools which swam in synchronized clouds to guard themselves from predators in the bay.

Califia felt her stomach rumble so she reached into the pouch at her hip and shoved a handful of roasted pine nuts in her mouth. She savored the light crunch as she tried ordering the creatures to fly tandem, then switch places, then circle one another, all of which they did without hesitation. A few moments after she had swallowed the nuts, she felt suddenly very empty again and reached in for another handful.

"Looks like it's going well today," Basilea said, coming from out of the palace main hall. "Anything you have noticed?"

"They're very sensitive," Califia said, grabbing yet another handful of nuts and sighing as she realized the meager half-dozen nuts she had grabbed were the last in the pouch. "If I am fearful, they move faster but less carefully. If I am calm, their movements are slow and intentional."

Basilea gave the queen a knowing smirk. "The way you're putting away that snack, they're probably hungry."

"Oh, gods!" Califia said, cupping her hand over her mouth. "I was wondering why I started snacking so soon after lunch!"

"If you release them, they'll go to the keepers and eat their fill," Basilea said. The queen did so, sheathing the dagger. "It can be a tricky thing, discerning your own needs from theirs when you are linked through the dagger. It is good that you've developed such an acute sensitivity so soon!"

The last two days had been a whirlwind and it was nice to take a moment to acclimate herself to her regular duties as queen. First came the debate over whether to allow the visitor to write his people a letter with a map indicating their location. It was fairly easy to quell the civic council in this regard, for most had considered the timing of the entire affair to be a fortuitous sign from the gods that this man was important.

Once the scouts informed the queen that the ships were still a fortnight away after they had dropped the invitation on the deck of the largest boat, Malachea made a compelling argument for building rudimentary fortifications along the western coast in places where the armada was likely to make contact. Califia had nearly objected out of habit, but the wisdom in such a maneuver was obvious.

"He says they come in peace," she gestured to the visitor, who smiled stupidly as he listened for more familiar words, "but who knows what greed might grip their hearts when they see our fertile, undefended coast?"

The only times in California's history when it had grappled with an outside invader, the initial attempts at incursion had always come from the east and so those were the only parts of the country which had any defensive structures erected. The visitor coming from the west had changed everyone's perspective entirely and Califia had already begun making plans for more permanent battlements to be constructed there when the present crisis had passed.

"I've been thinking about the strategoses," Basilea said, her gaze following the griffins as they passed just out of sight. "How many informed you that they received messages encouraging them to kill you?"

"Traesta told me," Califia replied, glad that the griffins were gone so that they would not feel her sadness. "But no others."

"She wasn't the only one who received such a letter; count on it."

"Perhaps the others felt embarrassed by such a request, or burned the message in outrage?"

"One may have, but not more than two. The strategoses must be made to respect you. Unfortunately you lost a lot of credit in their eyes by sparing Yakov."

Califia was about to ask who Yakov was and then remembered that Basilea had managed to extract the man's name in the conversation she attempted shortly after the near execution.

"Surely now they see the wisdom in granting his life," Califia said, scoffing with exasperation when Basilea replied with a blank look. "If his companions had found us on their own and we had executed him, they would be justified in avenging his death with war."

Basilea tapped a finger against her lips.

"I respect the logic of that possibility," she replied, "but you are assuming the strategoses have deduced this on their own. Truth be told, even *I* didn't think that far ahead!"

Califia nodded as she saw the wisdom in Basilea's words. No matter what happened next, whether invasion or alliance or nothing at all, she needed the strategoses to know that she was not making decisions with her heart, but with the sort of steely-eyed pragmatism which they themselves aspired to.

"It's time you made a new friend," Basilea said, gesturing to the Triumvir Dagger. Califia handed it over and the old woman closed her eyes as the red gem glowed. A griffin whom the queen had noticed was circling in the distance changed course and was coming their way.

"This is Ektra," Basilea said. "She's the Royal Griffin."

Califia felt a growing sense of dread as the creature approached. She had never enjoyed the experience of flying and generally flew as little as possible. When she was sixteen, during her second year in the militia barracks, she trained in the basics of controlling a griffin, learned how to cinch herself properly into the saddle and give commands with halter and reigns. Only during the final fortnight of this particular training session were the students allowed to actually mount a real griffin and apply what they had learned, and Califia retired from the militia immediately after her first training flight.

She had ridden a few times since then, whenever it was necessary to deliver an urgent message or when her presence was needed somewhere quickly. As the Royal Griffin landed before them, Califia could not help but admire the beast.

Ektra was a massive catbird, standing as tall on her four legs as a human did on two. Her plumage was lofty and full, and her head quickly changed direction as if she were always observing her surroundings. She had arrived when the griffins had been released, and Basilea eagerly chatted with the creature as she attached the saddle.

"She's tough, but obedient," Basilea said, lovingly stroking Ektra's neck. "Don't jerk her around too much and she'll serve you well enough. She's a hunter, though, so don't be afraid to use the dagger to more directly control her if she spots a turkey, a beaver, or other such creature she might want to prey upon."

"She looks big enough to carry a bison," Califia remarked, gingerly extending her hand toward the beast's shoulder.

"Not too softly," Basilea said, fluffing up the creature's neck plumage as if giving an example. "Pet her like you mean it."

Califia pressed her hand harder into Ektra's feathers and felt her relax slightly. She moved her hand across the upper part of the creature's back, then repeated the stroke. With every repetition she felt it relax more and more, until it felt like stroking her pet marmot from her childhood.

"She's ready, and you haven't a moment to lose," Basilea said, giving Ektra one last scratch behind her ears. The beast leaned into her hand and Basilea grinned with happy familiarity. "Remember: you're there to help morale and give the militia the chance to meet their queen, but primarily you are there to help. Don't let them bait you, and don't let them discourage you from assisting in their efforts."

"I leave the capital in your hands, Basilea," Califia said, looping her right foot into the stirrup and swinging her left leg over Ektra, who now lay on the ground patiently waiting to take to the skies again. Califia attached all the safety straps and made sure to pull them tight and double check the bindings. "Send word to me if there are any further developments. I'm sure when I return you and Yakov will be good friends."

"Friends with a man?" Basilea chuckled. "I wouldn't know where to begin!"

With a flick of the reigns, Ektra flapped twice and then suddenly they were airborne. Califia's knuckles went white gripping the saddlehorn and her entire body tensed with anxiety as they lifted further and further up. Ektra cried out as she ascended, which nearly made the queen soil her riding breeches from fright. She sighed as she realized the creature was probably just reacting to her own stress and she closed her eyes and took a few calming breaths, imagining that she were sitting in the temple of the triumvirs in Droseros, sitting among the Isikyaist masters with whom she sat in blissful silence, waiting upon the gods to speak.

Her stomach lurched as Ektra leveled off. The queen opened her eyes, squinting against the wind. As if reading her thoughts, the beast gradually dipped just a little so that the air did not blow against them quite so furiously. Taking stock of their position and that of the midmorning sun, she gently pulled the griffin's head to the left and Ektra responded by steadily moving in that direction. They would go north first, she and Basilea had decided, among the regions of Okeanostendron - the sea of trees. The place was rightly named, from where Califia was sitting, as below them the massive green giants stretched for vast distances, covering the massive mountains upon which they sat.

The first stop was the region of Amaltheia, named for the last queen of Atlantis. It lay at the very northwest corner of the main island and included the large island of Vrachodis just off the coast which was where Califia was traveling. It was a rather barren place, hardly even inhabited except by ascetics, hermits, and those expelled from their home communities, but Traesta had insisted that it be protected.

Traesta was an old friend of Califia, and at first she questioned Basilea's wisdom in putting her first on this junket, but the former queen wisely answered that the best way to ensure a successful end was to arrange for a successful beginning. Working alongside an old friend would build the queen's confidence and she might even get Traesta to give her some helpful advice with the others.

The island of Vrachodis was much as she remembered it from her time serving as a temple caretaker. The temple of silence was still a squat circular structure with a large chimney in the center for releasing the rich smoke of the heather that grew on the island, used in various rituals by the Isikyai of the rocky land. Around the temple there sprawled a village of sorts, if an assortment of tiny huts could be called a village. There was just enough space on the outskirts of the town for her to land.

Once Ektra's claws touched the soil, it took every ounce of the queen's self control not to rip away the straps that composed her safety harness as quickly as possible and leap onto solid ground. She loosened everything in as dignified a manner as she could muster, forcing herself to go slow and steady as she realized she had already drawn an audience.

"To what do I owe this honor?" Traesta said, once Califia had been led to where the strategos now directed the construction of protective battlements.

"I came to help."

The strategos set her to work helping to build a proper palisade by digging the narrow trench required and then dropping in the long sharpened stakes which composed the threatening wall of spikes. The militia who worked alongside her were young women from fourteen to twenty-five, all thrilling hairstyles and unconventional tattoos and an excitement about life that the queen found quite infectious. They chatted with one another as they worked, speculating whether they would have to fight the invaders and what manner of weapons these new people might use and whether any of them might be attractive.

"Basilea doesn't seem to think there are any women

among them," Califia interjected.

"That's a shame," said the one who appeared to be the youngest. Her eyebrows were decorated with tattooed dots that hovered above them, each one a different hue. She sighed wistfully, leaned on her shovel and adopted a faraway look in her eyes. "So much for love."

The rest of their group burst with laughter and the queen laughed as well. She noticed at that moment Traesta looking over at their group from a portion of the palisade that had not only been completed, but had a high walkway attached and secured. The strategos smiled when she noticed Califia's gaze, but the queen noticed the expression she had previously worn for just a moment before breaking into a grin. She looked worried.

"You lot could use a break!" Traesta shouted to Califia's group. "Go get some water and stretch if you like, have some food if you're hungry."

"We're only too happy to oblige," said the girl with the eyebrow rainbow dots.

When they had gone beyond earshot, Traesta produced a scroll from a pouch she wore at her side.

"Do you know anything about *this*?"

Califia unrolled it and quickly scanned its contents, which were brief. It announced an emergency meeting of the war council, which would take place at the capital at noon the next day. The queen felt as though the message had knocked the wind out of her, then saw the official mark at the bottom which made her blood boil. It was signed by Malachea.

"Damn that woman," Califia said, rolling the message back into shape and handing it to Traesta. "Wait — did any message arrive for me?"

"None that I am aware of," Traesta said, her voice wavering a little at the implication. "You don't think she would—"

"It's irrelevant," the queen shook her head. "I know it's happening, so I'll be there. Whatever she plans to discuss, she won't be able to circumvent me, if that was her goal."

"Of course," the strategos offered a wooden smile but the queen could still sense worry behind her eyes. "As you say."

"Is there something more I should know about?"

"I cannot tell you what I have not been told," Traesta began, rolling her eyes at her own pathetic attempt at deflection. "The truth is, Basilea was trying to tell me something about Malachea at your coronation. She was interrupted and assured me that we would talk more later, but then everything happened with the visitor."

Califia paused.

"There have been several moments in which she has made strange comments about the Gorgon leader to me as well, but told me she was still investigating the matter and that she would bring it to my attention when the need arose."

"What in Athena's name could it be?"

There was just enough time for Califia to fly back to the capital, cursing Malachea the entire time. More infuriating than the woman's infernal politicking was the fact that she had interrupted what surely would have been a productive junket and, more importantly, she forced Califia to ride a griffin twice in the same day. The former was an annoyance; the latter was unforgivable.

She slept fitfully, overcome by a wicked combination of indescribably painful muscle soreness and nightmares of falling from a griffin. She sipped a nice hot willow tea prepared by the kitchen staff in the morning and ate a plate that was mostly meat - bison sausage, turkey fillets, and salted salmon patties - which the page informed her would help with the muscle soreness. Apparently the complaints she had made to Arianna the night before had not remained private.

Noon seemed to arrive sooner than usual. Califia was exhausted and in the sourest of moods when the strategoses began arriving, those from the farthest reaches landing first and those closest to the capital last.

"Now that the war council is duly assembled," Malachea began, taking the lead since she had been the initiator of this meeting, "I can share with you the unsettling details of our newfound *friends*."

"How close are they?" Traesta asked, getting her words in just before Malachea continued.

"Our estimates have not changed: they should arrive in approximately thirteen days." Malachea nodded as the others muttered to one another over whether they were doing all they could to prepare. Then she held up a hand and continued, "They bring strange weapons which we have had the opportunity to observe. A gull flew close to their ships and one of them pointed a strange sort of pipe at the animal. There was a great boom, followed by a cloud of smoke around the weapon, and the bird was killed."

A few of the strategoses gasped at the bird's death, and Califia did likewise.

"What killed the bird?" Linnea asked, her tone mostly cold but carrying a slight tremor of dread.

"We aren't certain," Malachea said, holding up a hand to hush the inevitable muttering. "It could be some kind of crossbow that makes a loud noise, or perhaps the sound killed the bird through some kind of magic which we do not possess. But that isn't the worst part. There are seven ships in this armada, and each of them has several large metal tubes which we believe work in a similar fashion to the smaller tubes carried by the sailors."

"We should double-reinforce our fortifications," said Aleksandra. "I will bring extra workers if it will help."

"Very generous of you," Malachea said, unable to completely conceal a dismissive tone in her voice, "but there was nothing left of the sea bird except a cloud of feathers. If these larger tubes are capable of greater destruction, as we suspect, I don't know how we would stand a chance against them."

"Every weapon has a weakness," Linnea said, thumping her staff on the wood floor. "And they would shit their pants at the sight of our griffins."

"These weapons might be capable of killing our protectors," Malachea said, shaking her head at the prospect. "I'm not saying that *any* attempt to fight them would be doomed, but we need to ready ourselves in case the visitor's friends decide they are interested in more than collecting their lost companion."

A dead silence filled the room. Califia pictured men who looked like Yakov pointing their strange pipes at Basilea, at Arianna, and then a boom, a puff of smoke, and a pile of hair and clothes where her friends once stood.

"We are already fortifying the island to discourage hostility," Traesta said, crossing her arms. "What more can be done?"

Malachea frowned. Califia was certain that she was going to dislike whatever the Gorgon strategos was about to suggest.

"We deploy the militia - the *entire* militia - and appoint a polemarkos to lead them in case this visit turns violent."

Califia closed her eyes for a moment as the purpose of this assembly now became clear. *Malachea is using this as an opportunity.*

"I nominate the queen," Aleksandra said, without hesitation and with an almost defiant air. Califia was touched; she had always maintained a fairly amiable relationship with the strategos of Ipios and Jorgya, but it wasn't until this moment that she believed the reserved woman *actually liked her.*

"I confirm the nomination," Traesta said, standing next to Aleksandra.

Malachea looked toward Califia with something approaching pity. "If circumstances were otherwise, I would happily agree. But there is a question of experience."

Califia glared at Malachea, who pursed her lips and cast her eyes downward. *A disgusting show of humility.*

"Thus far she is the only candidate," Traesta said.

"I nominate Malachea," Linnea said. When a few other strategoses shot quick glares, she added, "With her years of service, she deserves our consideration, that's all."

"I'll confirm the nomination," chimed Danaea, who served in the desert regions north of Linnea.

"Before we continue," Basilea said, hushing the group as they began to whisper, "I must ask both Califia and Malachea to leave the room so we can deliberate. Unless there are other nominations?"

Califia's blood froze in her veins and she must have appeared alarmed because Basilea gave her an especially reassuring look. After a few moments of uncomfortable silence, Basilea's motion was carried. The queen and her foe left the chamber and the deliberations began. The rest of the war council would not leave until they had reached a unanimous decision. Califia's heart burned with rage at Malachea for this entire debacle and she decided to let her know it.

"You had your opportunity to campaign against me and you decided you would rather hunt jaguars and greatbears and whatever else you Gorgons do in your spare time," the queen seethed. "Are you really so incapable of respecting the people's will?"

"By the time I discovered you and your *auntie* had initiated an election, nearly half the nation's votes had already been counted."

"You could have contested," Califia hissed, struggling to keep her voice from becoming a shout. "Nothing was done that couldn't have been undone."

Malachea squared her shoulders and locked eyes with the queen.

"Which of us worked harder to get where we are?" She said, in a tone that was so even and measured that it made Califia's rage burn all the hotter.

"You think I'm just some former princess who followed in her mom's footsteps," Califia felt her voice rising but could not prevent it, "but I mean to actually improve things all over the islands for everyone."

"If this grand plan of yours fails and there's a famine or a drought or a plague or a fucking invasion, what then? Have you even conceived the possibility that you might fail, and all of us will pay the consequences? Gods, how did your mother allow you to grow up thinking you were the center of the universe?"

"Don't talk about my mother."

"You're the one who brought her up," Malachea said dismissively. "And you and I both know that convincing the arkozhas to organize a contested vote is more difficult than wrestling a greatbear."

"I think you were just too afraid of losing."

Malachea's nostrils flared, her brows furrowed, and each of her hands was now balled into a white-knuckled fist. The loud creak of the chamber door as it was slid open across the hall brought their confrontation to an abrupt close and the Gorgon shook out her hands as the remainder of the war council emerged. Califia breathed out a lungful of air she hadn't realized she'd been holding onto.

"The council has spoken," Basilea said as the other strategoses gathered close. "The title of polemarkos shall be granted to Malachea, strategos of the Gorgons, by unanimous decree."

Califia's heart sank into her stomach at the word unanimous. She knew that this was a consensus decision, but hearing it out loud stung more ferociously than an infuriated hornet.

"There is, however, a special exception," Basilea continued. Califia felt a small lift as she saw her rival's cocky grin suddenly melt away. "Malachea will be entitled as polemarkos and will command the troops who fight on foot. In the interest of the long-term health of our griffins, however, the council was concerned that putting them through a bonding process with another handler when they have only just begun the process with the queen would create too much mental strain on the simple creatures. Thus Califia will still have command over the griffins as needs be."

"What about cavalry?" Malachea growled, clearly upset by this unorthodox declaration.

"As the need arises, the polemarkos and the queen will decide on cavalry deployment together and as amiably as possible."

Malachea frowned and turned her head to the queen. She flexed her hands into fists for a brief moment, then turned once more to Basilea.

"I humbly accept the council's decision and hope only that I may honor the office which now honors me."

Basilea nodded and offered congratulations. The strategoses followed suit and when they had finished, an awkward silence settled onto the hall as they waited for Califia to do the same.

"May your leadership secure the safety of our people," Califia said, doing her best to keep her bitterness from leaking into her voice.

"This council is dismissed," Malachea said, smiling at each member in turn. "You may return to your homes for now and await further instructions. Stay vigilant!"

With that, the war council disbursed and when Califia was alone with her adviser, she kicked a nearby pillar.

"You were right," Califia began. "I should have been focusing on improving my relationships with the strategoses."

Basilea grabbed her by the shoulders and stared piercingly at her.

"It is not your fault. It's mine."

The conviction in the old woman's voice made the queen realize she was not just taking the blame as a matter of course. Something was *wrong*.

"What do you mean?" Califia said.

"Malachea has a dark secret and I was too much of a coward to investigate it."

Califia looked at the large open door of the main hall, then to the smaller door of the chamber where the war council had just convened.

"Perhaps we ought to discuss this in a more private setting," Califia said, "and you can tell me whatever you planned to tell Traesta at the coronation."

4

It had been fourteen days since Malachea was elected polemarkos, fourteen days since Basilea had informed the queen of her suspicions. Great hulking ships lumbered southward as they approached the town of Paraleya on the center of California's western coast. Califia had wondered whether the polemarkos had exaggerated the capabilities of their new acquaintances but now that she saw the ships for herself, the queen believed that Malachea had undersold the imminent danger. Not only were the top decks littered with ominous bronze tubes, but the hulls of the ships also had tubes sticking out from hatches. The largest of these ships, which now lowered a smaller vessel into the water, had four rows of the devices jutting from the ship's hull like metal penises.

"Yakov confirmed what the scouts feared," Basilea mentioned to the queen, muttering in her ear as men from the ship's deck descended into the boat using a rope ladder. "Those devices, cannons he called them, throw great heavy spheres of metal which can wreak destruction even against solid stone walls."

"They probably weren't very impressed by our wooden

palisades, then," Califia said. She saw a bearded figure from the ship descend into the small craft who wore some kind of silvery hat, a bright blue coat, red sash, and shock-white breeches with a silver stripe across the outside of both legs.

"Our demonstrations should be sufficient," Basilea said, turning around and nodding. Califia followed her gaze to see Malachea standing about twenty paces behind them with nearly the entirety of the Gorgon order standing at her back.

"*Should* is not good enough. I need to be *certain*." Califia brushed a stray braid behind her ear.

"Of course, my queen," Basilea said. "I hope you are not still dwelling on Malachea's promotion."

"Haven't given it another thought. I pray to Nika for her success."

Basilea gave her a wry grin.

"Even if you'd managed to visit the other strategoses, I doubt the vote would have come out differently."

"Malachea defeated me in a lightning campaign of her own," Califia said.

"Our people dislike giving one person too much power. Even your mother needed a brave warrior to serve as polemarkos while she reigned as queen."

"My mother did not suspect you of killing your own sister."

As soon as the words left her mouth, Califia regretted them. Basilea's eyes went wide and she gazed all around them, looking for any sign that the queen's foolish words had been overheard. Califia felt her own eyes wandering as well, but most of those nearby were eagerly discussing the newcomers as they pointed at their ship and commented on their manner of dress.

"Every time I think you are beginning to sound like a

queen, you do something so foolish..." Basilea trailed off and Califia had the impression that the old woman would rather not finish that sentence.

"Apologies. But this will not be the last time we discuss this."

"Obviously."

Califia's inner voice scolded her for this slip; she had no excuse. She had been carrying around a dark and perilous secret which, if not kept hidden until accusations could be properly investigated, could tear the nation apart. Califia remembered the incident well — Kassandra, the strategos of the Gorgons and several of her closest lieutenants had fallen victims to a sudden rockslide in the desert highlands of Helena, far to the south. Shocking and tragic, certainly, but still an incident that most people will shrug at and tell themselves *these things happen.*

As the small craft approached the shore, two sailors jumped into the shallows and dragged the boat onto the beach, then held out their hands to the finely-dressed man so that he could step onto the shore without wetting his boots. Califia wondered who this man was that these others honored him so. He seemed older, and for a moment she convinced herself that it was possible these outsiders shared the same reverence for elders as the Californians. However, he conducted himself with such an air of absolute confidence that the queen realized the truth: the outside world was much the same as when the Amazons fled their home, preferring coercion to cooperation, tyranny to liberty. She sighed as she watched the arrogant man march up the beach with a stern look on his face as his subordinates hung their heads and followed apace.

As he drew closer, she saw that his beard was

well-trimmed and his mustache waxed into fetching curls on both sides. He bowed his head when he came within a few paces and rattled a few words in the language which he and Yakov shared. Yakov related it to Basilea, who then translated for the queen.

"He offers you the blessing of his god," Basilea began, smiling politely as she continued. "His name is Admiral Kemal Reis. He thanks you for rescuing his servant and keeping him safe."

"Translate precisely, as if you were the original speaker," Califia advised. "We would like to invite you and your men to a special dinner celebration to celebrate Yakov's safe return and to better acquaint ourselves with your nation."

Basilea spoke to Yakov, who spoke to the man in the silver turban. Now that he was near she could see that it was indeed a turban with a red gem and feather adorning its front. He smiled and nodded, offering his hand to the queen.

"I think you are meant to place your hand in his," Basilea whispered.

Califia placed her palm against that of Admiral Kemal's, and he promptly raised it to his lips and gave her knuckles a kiss. It took every ounce of her self control not to gasp or giggle at the tickle from his whiskers.

The longhouse of Paraleya was much smaller than that of Californopolis, as the town normally supported far fewer people. What it lacked in engineering marvels like the pulleys of the capital hall's doors it more than made up in flexibility. The local climate was usually very mild, but occasional heat waves were not uncommon, so the permanent fixtures of the hall itself were really just the four corner posts and the roof. The walls themselves were removable and folded up in a rather attractive fashion which allowed them to be stacked and utilized as the bases of short tables for events such as this one. Everything had already been prepared - platters of seared salmon and spicy shrimp, fried saltbush and fresh piyida leaves, skewers fully laden with Bison steak and charred onion bulbs and peppers - and Admiral Kemal and his subordinates sniffed the air with delighted anticipation as they arrived at the open hall.

"After you, of course," Califia said, holding her smile through the translation process. The sailors immediately started grabbing handfuls of the various foods and the Admiral contented himself with organizing a wide assortment on his trencher and taking small bites of things. Around each of the tables was an assortment of cushions, which the visitors sat upon as they enjoyed their food.

Califia made a go ahead motion to Kyria across the hall, and she smiled and nodded. The woman looked to her left for a moment and pursed her lips as though displeased. The queen followed her gaze and saw that Malachea had just entered that side of the hall wearing heavy armor along with the traditional polemarkos helm, which was shaped like a griffin's skull. Basilea's assertions about the polemarkos, which the queen had been trying very hard to keep captive in the back of her mind, now came to the forefront. She tried to focus instead upon the newcomers and their reaction to this hospitality.

Yakov sat next to Admiral Kemal and the two chatted busily as they stuffed their faces with food. Basilea sat nearby and appeared very focused on her skewer of Bison steak and onions. The queen believed they were most likely discussing Yakov's time so far among the Californians, how his life was initially spared and then how he was almost killed by the queen a second time when word came of the ships. She hoped very much that the Admiral would not take offense or think that there was anything to be avenged about Yakov's situation; she and the others reasoned that they would probably suffer a similar fate if it had been they who were shipwrecked among Yakov's people. Whether or not this was actually the case remained to be seen.

"Can't hide from me," Arianna said, wrapping her arms around Califia's shoulders and kissing her on the cheek.

"Not here," the queen said, pushing her away instinctively. The Admiral looked toward her at that very moment and raised a glass of manzanita wine, as if in tribute. He smiled amiably and she gave him a small and humble bow of her head.

"Sorry," Arianna replied, and from her breath the queen deduced that she had been drinking a fair bit of the manzanita wine herself. "I didn't mean to embarrass you."

"It's not that, it's just—" Califia held out a hand to stop her, but Arianna was already away. The queen sighed, once more feeling the disparity of their ages. Seven years did not seem like much when they first coupled but at times like this it may as well have been seventy. The young woman seemed determined to take everything personally. Califia had a sudden urge to imbibe some manzanita wine herself. She took a cup from a nearby serving table and strolled to where Admiral Kemal sat with Basilea and Yakov.

The Admiral's face seemed granite hard, even when he smiled. His brown skin had a reddish quality which the queen assumed was either from the biting winds of the open sea or from too many hours spent in the sun. He raised his cup once more when the queen sat upon her cushions, and she did the same. They drank in unison.

"The Admiral was just telling me," Basilea said, "how grateful he was to have recovered Yakov alive. Apparently their mission was in jeopardy without his presence."

"I am only too happy to see him returned safely," Califia said, speaking directly to Admiral Kemal and pausing occasionally to allow for translation. "Our gods look kindly upon refugees, as we were once refugees ourselves."

"And yet," Admiral Kemal said, "he tells me that you nearly killed him. Strange hospitality, I would say."

Califia paused and considered her next words. The Admiral was right, and she was embarrassed that she had allowed herself to be so easily swayed by the shouts of angry mobs. But this was not a time to express anything except a united front.

"It is our law," Califia explained, "that any man who sets foot on this land uninvited should be killed."

Admiral Kemal continued eating as the translation was relayed, pausing when it had finished and raising an eyebrow at the queen, then Basilea, then Yakov. He spoke a few words in rapid succession to Yakov, who replied just as quickly. Then finally the words were passed to Basilea, who relayed them to the queen.

"He has never encountered a people who do not have men among them. He wonders if Yakov is making sport of him. From his tone, I would say he is offended at the prospect."

"Look around, Admiral," Califia said, sweeping her hand around the room. "You will find only women here besides yourselves, and our people have lived in this way for centuries."

"But if there are no men, then who fights on your behalf?" Admiral Kemal asked. Though she did not yet speak his language, the queen could hear exasperated confusion in his words. "Who plows the fields and hunts the animals which we now feast upon?"

"We do," Califia said plainly.

The Admiral's eyes went a little wide and he gazed around the room at the many women gathered among them. After a few minutes of pondering the admiral popped up his index finger as if he had just solved a sphinx's riddle. He muttered at length to Yakov without pausing to allow him to translate, and Yakov seemed to be offering answers but it was clear from both men's glances and even Admiral Kemal's occasional finger jabs that the two were discussing their hosts. At length, Yakov finally spoke.

"The admiral apologizes for his ignorance and hopes that you will not take offense to his inquiries," Yakov said, his tone very friendly and diplomatic. "He has a particular question which I fear may be a little sensitive, and he asks purely from curiosity."

A long pause passed between them until Califia realized the man was actually seeking permission to ask a question. She chuckled a little at the awkwardness.

"Ask whatever you wish," the queen said, doing her best to smile magnanimously.

"Admiral Kemal wants to know who protects your land, who defends you when your barbarian neighbors take up arms against you?"

Califia felt her body stiffen at the tone of the question, particularly the barbarian neighbors phrasing. The occasional diplomatic incident between themselves and the Ohlone, the Tepota'al, or even the Kashaya was inevitable, but it never went beyond a few empty threats at worst and more often was resolved peacefully. Even hostile groups like the Cochimi were never thought of as anything but a fellow tribe equal in both dignity and station. Barbarian wasn't a word the Californians used for any other people; it was a word their long-ago enemies used to describe the foremothers.

"You told him about the griffins, I assume?" Califia asked, after taking a moment to collect herself.

"He doesn't believe in them and no doubt thinks I am mocking him with tall tales."

"Very well," Califia smiled at the Admiral, who returned a polite grin. "Tell him that we have strength of arms enough to discourage any would-be invaders among our militia, all of whom are women of course."

The Admiral waited patiently as Yakov explained, holding a bit of saltbush-wrapped shrimp he had been preparing to devour. He tilted his head as the translation finished, and pursed his lips in an expression which the queen believed was amused skepticism. She also thought she spotted just a hint of something else behind his brown eyes, perhaps the greedy idea which she had hoped to snuff.

"Polemarkos!" Califia called to Malachea, who was standing around with some other Gorgons chatting and laughing. She looked to the queen with a knowing smile. "I believe you have prepared a demonstration?"

Malachea tapped the shoulder of one of the nearby Gorgons. The fighters, already arrayed in their thoraxes, skirts, and greaves, slid on their helmets and fastened the chinstraps, then picked up two wooden sagarises nearby. The axes themselves were single-bladed and about as long as an arm from shoulder to fingertip. The polemarkos did a few spinning moves with her sagaris, transferring it effortlessly from one hand to the next as it whirled like a cyclone. Her partner did the same, even tossing her weapon into the air and catching its hilt perfectly as it spun toward the ground. Both prepared a ready stance and began to circle each other, sidestepping smoothly like prowling jaguars.

The Admiral gazed upon them with what looked to Califia like something between awe and disbelief, as if he once more was encountering something he had never conceived could possibly exist. The queen enjoyed this expression, and assured herself that their plan to sufficiently intimidate these potential invaders was blossoming nicely.

Malachea and her partner traded a set of basic strikes and blocks first, warming up in the same fashion as any militia trainee. Then each struck twice and was blocked twice. Next, they traded a more intricate series of strikes and blocks, still keeping to the basic training forms but executing all of them flawlessly.

"Shields!" Malachea called, and a round shield was tossed to each combatant. She struck for her partner's head and the axe-head glanced off the shield. Her partner swung for her midsection but she likewise blocked with a shield. Then suddenly Malachea stepped in close, shoving her shield into her opponent's shoulder and isolating the woman's right arm. The polemarkos swung for the head and her opponent lifted her shield to deflect. Malachea's sagaris smacked hard against the shield but she quickly hooked it behind her opponent's shield and yanked it away. Her partner tried to bring the aegis back up, but the polemarkos' wooden axehead came to a stop just before it struck her opponent's neck.

The admiral winced and sucked his teeth at this maneuver, as if picturing what would happen next in an actual battle. Califia felt more confident each moment that everything was at last working exactly as she intended. The fighters continued for some time, modeling many different fighting techniques. Admiral Kemal and Yakov became avid observers, commenting to one another and even mimicking some of the motions with their own hands.

"Thank you, Polemarkos," Califia said after quite a long time had passed. "Your technique is without reproach and you honor us with your service."

"My queen," Malachea said, putting her fist over her heart and giving a respectful nod. "We would like to invite our guests to join us on the field just east of this hall for a more comprehensive demonstration of our martial prowess."

"I don't know that such a demonstration is really necessary," Califia began, wishing she could stop Yakov from translating almost as much as she wished she had not reacted so swiftly. *They are sufficiently impressed; any further display might be interpreted as hostility.*

"Our good queen wouldn't want the labor of her soldiers to go to waste," Malachea declared, inspiring a few supporting claps from the gathered militia. "They prepared this entire battle demonstration themselves."

Califia bit her lip and glanced quickly at Basilea, who closed her eyes and shook her head. Her only chance at shutting this down had already passed. She sighed.

"Lead the way, Polemarkos."

The wide grassy meadow that lay inland from the hall appeared already prepared for this demonstration; archery targets loosely grouped on the far side of the field and various sets of bundled armor sat on the near side. The Gorgons and other militia quickly dressed for combat, save for Malachea and her partner who were already dressed. Soon the warriors were fully arrayed on the grassy field, their griffinsteel helms and breastplates glinting in the afternoon light.

Califia thrummed her fingers against her legs as she waited for the admiral and his men to join her and the others. They were filling their arms with food and Yakov said they would be along. She didn't doubt that they were spending a few moments to themselves, discussing the Californians away from Basilea's listening ears.

"Are you sure it is wise to show them a complete battle demonstration?" Basilea asked.

"Not my idea," Califia said nervously. "I thought she would arrange some light sparring, not a full battle."

"Don't let that stop you from taking credit," the former queen said, a hint of admiration in her voice. "The idea is right, it's just that it should be you on the field instead of her."

"You don't think this will provoke our honored guests?"

"They seem eager for a show, actually," Basilea looked back toward the hall and Califia followed her gaze. Admiral Kemal and his officers were pointing and gesturing with a look of awe upon their faces.

Califia crossed her arms against her chest. When she was a child, she would sometimes feel disappointed when her teachers would choose other students when asking for answers. She had worked very hard to overcome that feeling of disappointment, and she resented it creeping back into her life now that she was fully grown and also the duly elected queen. She pondered her reaction for a moment; was it possible that Califia herself was so blinded by her rivalry with Malachea that she was unable to recognize when the infernal woman managed to conceive a good idea?

"Truly your army must be the envy of your neighbors,

great queen," the admiral said, stuffing a spicy shrimp into his mouth as he surveyed the assembled force with a hawkish gaze as Yakov translated. "Your soldiers look fierce and prepared."

"Indeed, admiral, these young women are eager to demonstrate their skills."

"Spears front!" Malachea shouted and her soldiers came together in a snap, pressing their polearms forward and forming a wall with their shields. At the back of the phalanx, archers nocked their bows and crouched just as they would in an actual battle. In their center was Malachea, marked by a large flag bearing the image of Medusa herself in all her twisting snake-haired glory.

"March One!"

Her platoon responded with a loud ha! that made a few of the sailors flinch. Califia could not help but smile proudly. The phalanx marched forward at a steady pace, preserving the integrity of their shield wall as well as the uniform presentation of their spear-points. There were no gaps in the front of this cohort, no dips in their interlocking shields.

When they neared the end of the field, they quickly raised their spears and the formation adopted a loose grouping that allowed the spear-women to race through the avenues made by the archers to get to the other side of them in a flash. The spears pressed together and the archers turned around and likewise grouped closer, ducking slightly so that they would not make easy targets for ranged enemies.

"Good discipline," Admiral Kemal muttered. Basilea whispered the translation quickly before Yakov caught on but Califia saw that both he and his overlord were possessed by the spectacle before them. Malachea gestured to the pages waiting on the flanks of the field

and they hustled to the center carrying round targets
which they quickly propped up before sprinting back to
the edge of the meadow.

Still at the very edge of the field, at least a hundred
paces from the target, Malachea hollered for her archers
to take aim. They stretched their bowstrings, which
groaned slightly, and held steady with anticipation.

"Loose!" The polemarkos called, and the arrows
clouded the sky for a moment before raining down on
the five targets at midfield. Not every fletch struck its
mark, Califia knew from her own training that this was an
impossible expectation, but each target had at least five
arrows stuck in its middle and those that missed sprung
from the ground close by like deadly flowers. The
admiral raised his eyebrows and pursed his lips. Califia
dared to believe he looked impressed.

"Hydra!" Malachea shouted. Immediately the platoon
divided into 5 smaller groups, each consisting of six
spears and three archers. They spread themselves over
the width of their battlefield, each group marching with
all six spears holding up their shields in front of the
archers. When they reached a point about fifty or sixty
paces from the arrow-covered targets, the soldiers put
their spears on the ground and arranged themselves so
that the six shields were stacked in pairs, two in front of
each archer. When the shooters each yelled, the top
shield of their pair lifted and they immediately loosed,
their missiles striking one of the targets every time. As
soon as the arrow flew, the shields closed again,
protecting them from return fire from their imaginary
enemies.

Califia nodded in approval as she observed that the
arrows they were using in the Hydra formation had their
shafts painted red, whereas the previous arrows from the

mass volley were green. *It is wise of Malachea to demonstrate that the accuracy of our archers does not depend on any one formation.*

"Spears front!" Malachea shouted once more, initiating what looked at first like a mad rush from her platoon to come together but then suddenly they all stopped and were in their previous configuration - spears at the fore, archers to the rear.

"March five!"

As soon as the words left the polemarkos's mouth, the phalanx charged at nearly a full sprint toward the maimed targets, striking through them with their spears and shredding the bundled reeds into mulch. The admiral smiled and clapped his hands, whispering something to one of his men who hustled back toward the hall, then continued toward the beach. Basilea shook her head; she hadn't been able to hear what he had said.

"Wonderful," he smiled at Califia, then gestured toward the Gorgons. "Your enemies surely lose many nights' sleep at the thought of crossing swords with you."

Before Califia could think of a reply, an eerie bellow erupted suddenly from the woods. At first she thought it was a sentry's horn but the tone tapered roughly and in the same manner as an animal.

"What could that be?" Basilea sad, turning her gaze toward the forest along with everyone else at the demonstration.

Once more, loud and low, like the sound of angry thunder, the bellow echoed through the meadow and the assembled warriors gripped their weapons in anticipation. Suddenly, crashing through the trees came a massive bison bull, thrashing its head and ripping through a stray archery target as though it was a pile of cut grass.

Califia's heart jumped into her throat as the beast

charged straight for the Gorgons, who quickly raised
their spears and shields in response. There was no time
to form a proper wall of spears and the bison easily
pushed past their pikes. The nearest warriors rolled out
of its way and the archers fled. The animal stopped and
looked around, as if challenging them to a fight.

The sailors and the admiral were chattering excitedly
among themselves as Malachea shouted orders and her
platoon split into three separate phalanxes, each with
their spears concentrated on the center of the mass of
shields. The archers dodged the creature's charges with
expert precision, rolling just into its blind spot while
narrowly avoiding the deadly hooves.

The three phalanxes closed in around the beast, the
thirty spearwomen moving in unison whenever it
flinched. Califia's heart leapt with terror every time the
beast moved. Basilea grabbed her hand.

Suddenly arrows whistled past the hoplites' heads and
stuck into the beast's thick hide. It bellowed and began
whipping its head toward one of the bundle of spears. As
it knocked them away, the two other platoons charged
into it, goring the animal in its stomach and ribs. It
whipped its head around and broke several of the spears,
their tips still stuck in its gut as it thrashed and roared.

Califia's breath caught in her lungs, certain that at least
one of these brave Gorgons was marked for
Persephone's gates when suddenly a warrior leapt onto
the monster's back. The beast bucked and snorted, trying
desperately to throw her from his hump. The Gorgon
held onto the woolly hair on its back with her left hand
and drew a long dagger from her belt with her right. She
probed at the animal's ribs until she found purchase, then
shoved the blade fully into its upper chest.

Blood poured from the arrow wounds near its back

legs and the creature made a sound which, in spite of its loud volume, was unmistakably a whimper. It collapsed in a heap as the Gorgon who had just jammed a knife into its heart jumped and tumbled away.

The air was thick with silence as if everyone was waiting for the monster to rise again. Everyone loosed a sigh in relief as the animal finally breathed its last. Then the air was split by raucous applause. Basilea tapped her on the shoulder and the queen followed her gaze to see that it was Malachea who had so valiantly slain the beast with her own blade.

"If you thought she was insufferable before," Basilea said, rolling her eyes. The polemarkos, her armor still splashed with blood, jogged to them and removed her helm when she came close. She breathed heavily, trying to catch her breath.

"How was that for a demonstration?" Malachea said, grinning playfully.

"You were nearly killed!" Califia said, feeling a touch of awe at Malachea's martial skills.

"Coming close to death makes one appreciate life," she said, shrugging as though the entire thing was a small matter.

"It is unusual for bison to stray this far south before the summer," Basilea observed, her tone nearly straying into an accusation. Malachea winked and the queen felt rage once more rising within her chest.

"Did you…" Califia could barely make the words come together. "Did you arrange for this Bison to attack us?"

Malachea looked at her as though she had just asked whether her beard was real. Then she clenched her jaw.

"It's one thing to look impressive when you are pretending to fight. I wanted them to see how we react to the unexpected." The polemarkos sniffed and put her hands on her hips as her breathing slowed.

"You are as reckless as you are stubborn," Basilea scolded. "Someone could have gotten hurt!"

"Better a few twisted ankles and bruised shoulders than getting our throats cut while we sleep!" Malachea said, stepping into Basilea's space. "You were a warrior, once. Tell me I'm wrong."

"If you had bothered to ask," Califia said, "we could have discussed this little maneuver."

"I don't *need* your permission to command the army," Malachea said, thumping her chestplate. "*I* am the polemarkos."

Basilea cleared her throat and gestured to their guests, who were staring wide-eyed at the dead bison. Califia's heart sank into her gut; she did not doubt that the men were probably making urgent plans to depart as soon as possible. And yet... they appeared to be engaged in a very involved discussion or even debate. The admiral was speaking in a strong, confident cadence and the officer he addressed seemed to be objecting. Admiral Kemal's eyes suddenly glanced toward the Californians and he thrust a finger in the man's face and said a few quick words very aggressively and the man fell silent and shrugged.

"My apologies, admiral," Califia began, but the man held up a hand and shook his head immediately after the translation. Admiral Kemal gave his men a resigned look and muttered a few words as he gestured toward the sky. He turned to Califia with an apologetic expression began speaking with a stately, diplomatic air as Yakov conveyed his words.

"It is I who must apologize, fair queen, for I must now confess to you a most dreadful insult for which I can only beg your mercy."

Califia started to protest, but both the admiral and Yakov continued and so she relented.

"I have traveled far with this fleet, in search of worthy allies to aid my country in its struggle against a wicked army of blasphemers who have formed against us."

This was somewhat broken up by Yakov and Basilea trying to find the appropriate words in Californian for wicked and blasphemers, which had not come up in Yakov's conversational learning.

"My nation is strong, but our enemies seized our capital in a surprise assault nearly a year ago. I had heard of some islands to the north of the East Indies which were said to possess warriors of great determination and martial skill. I see now that it pleased God instead to send us to you, and to plead with you now to help us retake that which has been stolen from us."

Califia looked to Basilea, whose face was just as stunned as she felt her own must appear. The queen closed her eyes and recalled her first attempt at communicating with Yakov, how he had drawn the boats and the city in flames. At the time they worried that it was a threat. It seemed obvious now that he was trying to convey his mission.

"While we are only too glad to have your nation's friendship," Califia began, suddenly very eager to see the backs of these men, "we are not seeking to involve ourselves in whatever wars are being fought in lands far away."

She added the last bit hoping that it sounded polite, but worried she may have nonetheless offended the admiral. He waved his hand as if brushing away such concerns and redoubled his efforts, looking her in the eye as Yakov translated.

"Wars are far away until they are not. The people with whom we are at war have invaded our lands many times without provocation. They deal in lies and blasphemies and cannot be trusted to keep their words any more than a mule can be trusted not to pull against its reins."

Califia was tempted to ask what a mule was, but thought better of it. Admiral Kemal continued.

"You are obviously a wise and benevolent ruler - surely *you* see the wisdom in striking a troublesome foe before he has the chance to strike you first? These people are not like us and do not know how to content themselves with what God has given them, so they take from those they believe are too weak to resist them."

"But surely you see the wisdom," Califia began, finding at last a pause long enough for her to speak, "in not looking for trouble where you don't need to? I have no doubt these enemies of yours are terrible and wicked, but they have done nothing to us."

"In time, they will," Admiral Kemal gestured toward the ocean. "Already their boats circle the world in search of whatever they can steal. Their names are known well in my homeland, but they grow more and more famous in the lands to your west."

"Tell us their names, then," Califia said, determined to end this conversation very soon, "that we might know them if they come here and know not to trust them."

The admiral sighed, no doubt sensing that he had failed.

"They call themselves by many names," he said, slumping his proud shoulders a little. "The Franks, the Muscovites, the Greeks—"

As Yakov translated this last name, Califia gasped. Malachea, Basilea, and every other Californian near enough to hear likewise made a horrified sound. The first two names were without meaning to the Amazons. The last, however, was a word that came from their own language, a name that sent shivers down the spines of even the least superstitious among them.

"Why did you choose that word?" Califia demanded of Yakov. Flabbergasted, the man sputtered a little before giving his answer.

"The language you speak is similar to the tongue of the Greeks," he explained. "I recognized the word *friend* that day you nearly executed me, and I've worked out much of the rest of it by recalling what I remember of that language."

"Could it be?" Basilea wondered aloud. "Those who drove the foremothers from their ancestral home, could they really still exist after all these years?"

"I see no reason why not," Malachea said. A strange glint shined in her eyes, one which inspired an uncomfortable feeling in Califia. "*We* still exist."

"Greeks or no," the queen said, turning back to Admiral Kemal, "we simply cannot—"

"Apologies, my queen," Malachea interrupted, "but it's only appropriate that we bring this matter before the war council."

"The war—" Basilea interrupted herself, scoffing at the notion. "We are not at war."

"As polemarkos it is my right to call such an assembly," Malachea looked at the admiral and Yakov, who waited eagerly for an answer. "You will have your answer tomorrow gentlemen, we thank you for honoring us with your nation's friendship."

As Admiral Kemal and his staff walked toward the small boat on the beach to retire to their ships, Califia rounded on Malachea.

"I am the queen," Califia stepped so far into

Malachea's space that their noses were only two finger-widths apart. "I say we will not go to war against the Greeks or anyone else."

Malachea sighed, and stepped back from the queen. For a moment Califia dared to hope that she was about to back down. Then the two women locked eyes and Malachea spoke.

"I am the polemarkos. I don't need your permission."

5

The villains in the story of the great exodus were the Greek tyrants. The Amazons of Atlantis provided shelter for Greek women who fled the cruelties of slavery, marriage, and servitude. When Helena, the queen of Sparta, sought the protection of the Amazons, the tyrants put aside their disputes with one another and invaded Atlantis.

A brutal siege ensued for ten months or ten years depending on the account. The walls of Illayos, the capital, held strong against assaults and many noble warriors perished in personal duels as the siege dragged on. When their strength was finally exhausted, the Greeks announced that they were leaving. As a token of their apology, they left behind a gift: a large wooden statue of a griffin.

At night, those hiding within the bowels of the statue sabotaged the city gates, allowing the allied Greek army to take the city by treachery. The King of Sparta locked queen Amaltheia in a closet and raped Helena, who had become the queen's lover.

In that small closet, with her lover shrieking on the

other side of the door, Amaltheia prayed to Athena, Hera, and Aphrodite. She asked for the safety of her people to be secured, even at the cost of her own life. The Triumvir goddesses honored the queen's prayer. A dagger materialized in front of where she knelt. Understanding this blessing as an invitation, she picked it up, held its point over her left breast, then plunged it deep within her own heart.

Amaltheia's sacrifice was not in vain. The Amazons were saved and the Greeks perished beneath the waves. The phrase "a Greek oath" was a longstanding pejorative among the Amazons when accusing someone of lying. The idea that the offspring of these monsters were still thriving and that they, like these newcomers, might some day sail across the Great Western Sea to once more imprison, enslave, and subjugate the Amazons was unacceptable.

It was little wonder that the ensuing War Council meeting was probably the shortest in Californian history. Califia was unsurprised that Linnea and Danaea had so vocally supported punishing the Greeks for their ancient crime, but she was shocked that Olympia, Zephyra, and even Traesta had likewise adopted very aggressive stances.

Califia was a little perplexed at Malachea's seeming cooperative attitude in calling a War Council when she had the authority to declare war, and the whole affair felt to her like a waste of time until it occurred to her that the polemarkos wasn't actually interested in the strategoses' input so much as their personal investment. If the war went poorly, no one would be able to set all of the blame upon Malachea's broad shoulders; they had voted for this war, and thus all had a stake in prosecuting it to the fullest extent.

The queen entered the hall, its walls now put back in place to allow some shelter from the cool night. She found a cot and plopped down, staring blankly at the ceiling and trying to relax the muscles in her back which had been clenched tight since the meeting's end.

"It went that poorly, eh?" Basilea said. The former queen stood over the cot, her face twisted with sympathetic concern.

"I had no idea," Califia said, "that our strategoses were so eager for war."

"It can't have been a total surprise," Basilea chuckled wryly. "When the only tool you have is a spear, every problem looks like an enemy."

Califia smiled at the jest, then winced as a cramp slithered its way north between her shoulder blades and then settled on the left side of her neck. She rubbed at the spot and closed her eyes.

"I have to confess that I am a little excited to face the Greeks in battle," Califia said, as the cramp in her neck began to calm.

"What is good for tomorrow is not always good for next month," Basilea said, sighing. "My entire time as queen was dedicated to reducing the militia's influence in political affairs. This war only further entrenches them."

"If only I could have prevented Malachea from becoming polemarkos."

Basilea sat up and rotated so that she was sitting sideways on the cot.

"Regrets get us nowhere. We need to find a way to center *you* in this war. Swing the pendulum back to civilian leadership."

"How?"

"When I have an answer, I'll let you know," Basilea yawned, then stretched out once more on the cot.

"According to Yakov and the Admiral, the journey to fight the Greeks will be extremely long. I am sure we will think of something on the way."

After a fitful night's sleep, Califia woke up angry. She stepped out of the hall and immediately cursed the sun, which seemed far too bright. She then heard a proclamation being announced throughout the town — the polemarkos was calling for the militia to be assembled and volunteers were needed to help load supplies and provisions upon their new allies' ships. The queen spotted two young women laughing as they walked, arm-in-arm, toward the town's agora where tasks would be assigned and the process of loading the ships properly organized.

The agora was already filling up with volunteers who lined up to be given assignments by the day's supervisors. Califia quickly noticed a commonality among those assigning tasks: each bore the tattooed beard of a Gorgon. She got her task from the supervisor, who said that Califia could be useful as a stevedore, hauling the boxes of dried maize, muscat raisins, and salted meats from the far end of the agora down to the shore where they would be loaded onto small craft and taken on board the hulking ships.

She busied herself hauling heavy foodstuffs to and from the shore and as her muscles burned like dried twigs in a wildfire, she felt the anger and frustration she had been accumulating since becoming queen likewise begin to burn away. While she was not a devotee of Isikyai, some of their practices had proven useful. She had found that focusing on one's immediate task had a cleansing effect, what the practitioners referred to as a clarifying objective.

More than a few times in the course of loading the

boats, she thought she spotted her lover among the other stevedores, or the crate-makers, or musicians playing a rhythmic tune. Each time it was a different young woman whose hair, eyes, or mannerisms were merely reminiscent of Arianna. Califia chuckled to herself when she thought she spotted her among those constructing a larger dock so that the ships could be loaded directly. Arianna was a wonder with clay, wood, and even marble, but was absolute rubbish when it came to practical craft like construction.

Her thoughts were interrupted by the sound of someone calling her name. It was a man's voice, which is why it took her a few moments to realize they were indeed calling for her and not shouting some profane word in the Osman tongue.

She looked toward the sound and spotted Yakov, standing beneath a shady cypress. Next to him was Admiral Kemal, sitting on a padded stool and snacking on dried fruit while he observed the Californians in action. Behind them, standing just beyond the great tree's penumbra, a young man was waving a large palm leaf so that it provided both the admiral and the young emissary with cool, moving air. Admiral Kemal gestured with his hand for Califia to approach.

"Hot today, yes?" Yakov translated for the admiral as Califia came near.

"Early spring days here are very hot."

She worried that Yakov might not know the word *spring* but apparently he was familiar.

"Have a drink." The admiral gestured mid-translation and one of the boys standing nearby handed her a goblet and filled it with a rich red liquid. It's fruity scent filled her nostrils as she raised it to drink. It was thicker than she expected but very sweet and refreshing. She thought at first it was wine, but it did not have the sharp bite of fermentation.

"Many thanks, admiral."

"I see that you and the other leaders are working hard alongside your subjects. Is this a usual custom among your people?"

"A usual custom?" Califia turned the words over in her mind, trying to make sense of them. She looked the admiral over; he was dressed in his finest clothes and lounging while his sailors back on the ship did the hard work of hauling the supply crates filling the cargo hold. "We always work together."

"This would be very unusual in any other place," he said, taking a sip of his drink. "Most remarkable."

Something about the admiral's tone of voice made the queen uneasy. She fiddled with her drink, watching the thick nectar ooze back and forth in the goblet, leaving a light fruity coating on either side.

"I thank you for the refreshment but I really should get back to helping."

"I brought another stool, if you would like to rest with us."

The queen became suddenly aware of an ache in her back, sensing a pain just below her shoulder blades which cried out for relief. As if he spotted the hesitation in her eyes, he continued.

"We will bring some food, perhaps some grapes if you prefer. You could sit in the shade with us. Yakov could rub your feet. It is too hot for a queen to be doing this kind of work."

Yakov blushed at the suggestion that he rub Califia's feet. The queen considered the offer for far longer than she knew she should, imagining how good it would feel to sit in the cool of the tree and be fanned and drink fruity beverages and have her feet rubbed.

"It's not too hot for me," she said politely, quickly handing her goblet to a page and walking back toward the crates while Yakov was still translating. As she picked up yet another impossibly heavy bag of dried maize, she heard the echo of the admiral's laughter in her ears and it burned her skin far more ferociously than the sun. What burned even more, however, was the shame she felt at how eager she had become to shrug off her duties and sit in luxury while her people toiled.

At midday a group of older women brought food and Califia joined the nearest line. A gray-haired woman with a faded Gorgon beard handed her a massive maize wrap filled with bison steak, roast potatoes, round lettuce, and avocado slices. She tore through it much faster than she had intended and as she popped the last bit into her mouth, it seemed to her as if she had taken the first bite only a few moments before.

She spotted a few Gorgons sitting on some crates nearer the shore, and among them was none other than Malachea herself. Califia wondered why she hadn't spotted the polemarkos before now, but it was clear that the woman had not just arrived. Her taut, muscular skin glistened with sweat and while she was not devouring her meal as quickly as the queen herself, she had more than half-finished her wrap, which she was gesturing with between bites.

"Hotter than Zeus's armpits today," Califia said as she approached the polemarkos and her entourage.

The polemarkos took a bite from her wrap. "It gets much hotter in Thermydia."

The other gorgons nodded as they chewed.

"I wonder what Kassandra would think of this," Califia pretended to gaze into the distance as she watched

Malachea out of the corner of her eye.

"She would have already built the dock herself!" Exclaimed one of the Gorgons. She smiled and nudged the polemarkos and Califia thought she spotted a strange expression come over Malachea's face.

"Kassandra always was eager for a fight," the polemarkos said, staring intently at Califia. "Even *she* never dreamed of fighting the Greeks. She would mock our softness by continuing her tasks while the rest of us sat and ate."

"It's tragic that she cannot be with us," Califia said, turning now to her foe and watching her much more closely.

Malachea was about to take another bite of her wrap when she paused. Her eyes darted to the queen and she adopted an expression that most would take for indignation. There was a hint of suspicion in her gaze, however, which the queen noticed.

"Disasters befall the good and the wicked alike," Malachea replied. "We must do what we can with whatever time we have."

"Well said, Polemarkos!" chimed the same Gorgon from before. She was as large as most Gorgons but her hair had been cropped short and she appeared to be still growing out the snaky locks so beloved by their group.

"It's scripture, Deanna," Malachea scoffed, staring hard at the last third of her wrap. "The words are attributed to Hera speaking through the Oracle Zemonastrya."

"I *know*!" Deanna said, a little too defensively. "It was still well said."

"I have had sufficient rest," Malachea said, setting the remaining third of her wrap on a nearby crate. "The sun will not wait for our permission to set, nor the stars our consent before they shine upon us."

The few other Gorgons who still had remainders set them down and followed their leader to the dock where they began hauling piles of lumber to be added to the structure. Califia pondered the polemarkos' reaction. She had not expected a confession, but Malachea did seem shaken. The speed with which she changed the subject away from her sister was odd. And while Malachea was not known for her religious devotion, she had quoted scripture. Still, it was a well-known verse often employed by devotees seeking to comfort the bereaved. Califia was not yet convinced of the woman's guilt. She was also not quite convinced of her innocence.

Music lifted into the air as everyone returned to their labors and Califia was suddenly struck with an idea. There was a patch of flat grass along the route which the stevedores hauled provisions where the musicians were plucking their lyres, tweeting their flutes, and striking their xylophones. Conducting the group was precisely the person whom the queen was searching for.

Kyria made her wait until the song was finished before she set one of the musicians in charge of conducting in her place and joined the queen.

"My mother's favorite song was Blue Herons by the Sea," the queen explained over the din of the performers. "Would you mind playing it sometime before the sun sets today?"

"Only too glad to, my queen," Kyria said, smiling politely and already turning toward the band.

"It seems like a good day to remember those who came before," Califia quickly continued, hoping she didn't sound like someone who is trying to get information. "Do you happen to know if Kassandra had a favorite tune?"

Kyria stiffened at the mention of the name, then she sighed and shook her arms as if trying to rid them of flies.

"You probably don't know this," Kyria began, "but the polemarkos and I were lovers a few years back, for a while."

"I didn't know," Califia replied, feeling an intense wave of guilt at the lie.

"We were very private about it. Unfortunately, I wanted something more than secret liaisons and sweaty dalliances in dark corners and unlit hallways. Oh, the things I had to endure from that woman!"

"I understand," the queen said, trying to find the right words for the question she wanted to ask. "Still, she might like to be reminded of her sister as she toils in the hot sun."

Kyria fiddled with her fingernails.

"I'm not sure she would want to be reminded of Kassandra. On the few occasions when we did sleep in the same bed, she always woke me up in the night by talking in her sleep. Talking to her sister."

Califia raised an eyebrow, forcing herself to pause before asking so as not to appear too eager.

"What kind of things did she say?"

"I'm sorry, Kassandra," Kyria performed the words, adding dramatic flourish to them. "Over and over, apologizing until I would wake her. I tell you, that woman pushed me to the limits of my endurance even in her sleep!"

Califia nodded and made many sounds of agreement as Kyria prattled on. She didn't hear a single word, however, but only pondered what Malachea could have done to feel the need to be so apologetic to her dead sister. She never bothered apologizing to anyone, as far as the queen knew.

"I must return to my duties," Califia said as soon as Kyria needed to take a breath. "Thank you for all you do."

"You're quite welcome, my queen. You know I—"

Califia had already started walking away and barely heard whatever Kyria said next. She had a sinking feeling in her gut that she knew couldn't be satisfied with a hundred bison maize wraps.

That night, Califia wished very much that Basilea was with her instead of being back in Californopolis preparing those who had been chosen to steward the nation in the queen's absence. The Arkozhas had worked out some kind of power sharing arrangement between their various provinces and Basilea was determined to hone the finer details before she returned to Paraleya to embark alongside the militia toward glory and destiny.

The builders had made tremendous progress and the dock was about three quarters to being finished. Malachea believed it would be finished by the middle of the next day, and called for a celebration of their first night preparing for the coming war. The village of Paraleya provided more food, manzanita wine, maize whiskey, and all manner of celebratory consumables.

Califia was far too preoccupied to think about enjoying herself. The savory, spicy smell of the bison and abalone fresh from the grill held no interest for her, neither did the wine, whiskey, or dances. Her mind bounced between the situation with Malachea and her own situation with Arianna. The words she had spoken to the young woman in anger now rang in her ears and, determined to find her absent lover, she began asking around.

"Saw her this morning," Deanna the Gorgon said,

taking a big drink of manzanita wine, "but that was the last time. Are you sure you don't want a drink?"

Malachea began walking towards them at that moment, fresh from dancing in the agora and Califia deftly made her escape when Deanna glanced in the polemarkos' direction. The last thing she needed was a drunk conversation with Malachea. While the woman might very well confess with her usual judgment softened by the influence of strong drinks, any such confession would likely be stricken as untrustworthy by an actual tribunal. The queen also didn't want to risk becoming an object of the woman's wrath when her judgment had been thus impaired.

The only thing more exhausting than the day's events was the thought of joining the festivities in the agora, so the queen chose the only sensible option currently available and decided it was time to sleep. She entered the hall and was pleased to see, as her eyes adjusted to the dim lighting, that it was full of empty cots. She had the room to herself, which was an abundant blessing because she was of the opinion that reigning queens should not weep in despair in front of their people. She found the cot that she was fairly certain she had slept in the night before and laid upon it.

"I wasn't sure if you'd come," said a voice, and the queen felt her entire body tense firm as a statue for a moment before realizing it was Arianna. The young woman was lying on a cot only a few paces away from her own, wrapped in blankets which cloaked her presence. Califia let the air out of her lungs and turned to look her lover in the eye.

"I see no reason to celebrate," Califia said, feeling a wave of relief as she spoke one of her inmost hidden thoughts aloud. "The task at hand is not yet finished and we haven't even fought in a single battle yet, let alone gained a victory."

"People like to celebrate the *possibility* of things," Arianna said, turning over so that she faced the queen. "They also like to celebrate beginnings."

"I'll be only too happy to celebrate the *end* of this war," Califia said, feeling another wave of relief. Arianna sighed.

"You're doing it again."

"What?"

"Taking burdens which are not yours to carry," the young woman reached out her hand and the queen took it in hers. "You do not control when any of this begins or ends."

"That doesn't mean I'm not responsible," Califia said, regretting instantly how defensive she sounded.

Arianna sighed again. She squeezed Califia's fingers, then brought her free hand up and caressed the far side of the queen's face, turning her chin toward herself at the last moment so that they sat nose to nose.

"Let me help you relax."

Heat rushed into her body as Arianna kissed her softly, but passionately. Califia felt weak but emboldened and brought arms around her lover, pressing their bodies together. She pushed firmly against Arianna, who understood and lay back on the cot as the queen climbed atop her and set about kissing her neck.

Arianna unfastened her top from around the back of her neck and pulled it down, exposing her breasts to the cool night air. Califia kissed the space between her lover's collarbones as she pondered which side to bless first.

"My queen…" Arianna moaned softly, untying the back of Califia's tunic with one hand while the other cradled Califia's head. "My mighty warrior queen…"

Califia paused mid-kiss, then decided to ignore the comment as she continued downward, her lips traveling down her lover's breastbone. She cupped Arianna's left breast in her hand and felt her heart thump hard and fast with excitement.

"Conquer me, my warrior queen..." Arianna continued, gasping with pleasure. "Let me feel the wrath of the Amazons."

The heat which the queen had felt at first suddenly cooled.

"I don't like that," she said between kisses, hoping her lover would go back to wordlessly moaning.

"Oh!" Arianna said, her voice filled with hurt. "Sorry."

I must have sounded much harsher than I meant to.

Califia kissed her way toward her lover's waiting nipple, admittedly rushing her usual process a little. Arianna responded by grunting and nudging the queen to get off of her.

Califia took her hand from Arianna's breast and her lips from the woman's chest. She stood and felt the back of her tunic sag now that it had been untied. Arianna propped her elbows behind her.

"What's wrong?" The queen asked, feeling a little hurt at the interruption.

"Maybe you should ask Kyria," Arianna spat, pulling her tunic back up and tying it once more behind her neck.

"What?"

"Did you think I didn't notice the two of you today?" She said, her voice filled with hurt. "How happy you looked, whispering to one another and blushing!"

"There is nothing between me and Kyria," Califia said, feeling the heat of blush rushing into her cheeks. "We were chatting and she shared something private with me."

Califia clenched her eyes shut as she realized how bad that sounded.

"I'm sure she did," Arianna said, standing and fixing her rumpled clothes as she turned away from the queen. "Perhaps you offered to make her *sing*."

"That's not true," Califia said, placing her hand gently on her lover's shoulder. "I would never betray you."

Arianna stood silently for a moment and the queen knew better than to press for an answer. This was not the first time she had erupted in a jealous rage and Califia had learned that patience was the best way to soldier through them.

"I'm sorry you don't like me calling you a warrior queen," Arianna said, turning to Califia. A tear trickled down her cheek. "When I saw you with her today I worried that you were growing bored of me. Kyria's so beautiful and you've known her for many years…"

"She's a friend," Califia insisted, embracing her lover. "Nothing more. And I don't want to be anyone's *warrior queen*."

She felt Arianna stiffen suddenly in her arms. The woman gently but firmly pushed away from her.

"Then why are you going to war?"

The question hit Califia like a charging bison. She sputtered a little, but Arianna continued.

"When you told me you were running for queen," the young woman said, "you said you wanted to promote creative expression and art, that you wanted to reduce the power of the militia, which you believed was growing too strong."

"All of that is still true—"

"Listen!" Arianna's eyes welled with tears and Califia clamped her lips together. "I know you; I know you still want those things. I don't think you will accomplish *any* of them if you go to war."

The queen was tempted to interject, to protest that Arianna didn't understand. Her lover was obviously building to something, and Califia felt the same dread she experienced every time a lover told her that it was time to end things.

"I have no choice," the queen said, feeling tears beginning to form at the edges of her eyes.

Arianna nodded and Califia feared that at any moment she would leave the building and their partnership would be at an end.

"There is more to war than fighting," Arianna said, sounding suddenly upbeat. "At least as important, possibly more important, is the story of the war itself. Your mother's war against the Cochimi was costly. Some say that we nearly lost our soul as the fighting dragged on."

After a period of silence that lasted long enough for Califia to be certain that Arianna wouldn't mind if she spoke, the queen replied.

"What are you suggesting?"

"You need people who will help you tell the story of this war," Arianna squeezed Califia's fingers, holding them tight in the same manner as when she was nervous. "If you're going to that cursed place to fight those wretched tyrants who drove out our blessed foremothers, then I'm coming too."

"Arianna—"

"I am proficient with bow and arrow, and one of the captains of the Droseros division has been trying to recruit me into their company."

An unspoken question hung in the air. *Do you want me to come?* Califia sensed it just as she felt the first drops of rain late on a spring day or the brush of the wind against her skin. Instinctively, she wanted her lover as far from danger as possible. The thought of breaking poor Arianna's heart by telling her to remain behind, however, was just too difficult to bear.

"It will be my great honor to fight alongside you and bring glory to our people together," Califia said, hoping she sounded more sincere than she felt.

Arianna hugged Califia, who fought the urge to wriggle free and tell her the truth. They each lay on their own cot, side by side, holding hands and occasionally giving the other a loving squeeze. When Califia realized that Arianna had fallen asleep at last, she let go of her lover's hand and sighed in relief. Though she had let the matter pass between them in the name of making peace, she wanted nothing more than to wake Arianna and tell her she must stay. Califia had run on a platform of reinvigorating art and culture among her people, of ushering in a new age of peace defined by innovative creativity. Instead, she was leading her people into a war far from their home against an enemy who had probably forgotten about them.

Califia stared at the beams and thatch which composed the hall's roof. She fell asleep while trying very hard to convince herself that she was not making a terrible mistake.

Part II: The Fires of Battle

6

Shortly after her mother died, Califia felt as though her life was empty and her pursuits meaningless. She withdrew from public life and sought the will of the triumvirs on the remote northern island of Vrachodis among the Isikyai practitioners there. After a month of sitting in silence before Aphrodite, she surmised that the goddess was advising her to have a child. This was eight years before her election as queen.

The act of impregnation was simple enough, but safely finding a willing partner was tricky and sometimes fraught with danger. The usual manner was to travel to the mainland via griffin and find a man to provide seed. Their nearest neighbors - the Ohlone, the Tepota'al, the Kashaya and others - saw such ventures as a blessing upon their people. They welcomed Amazon visitors and allowed them to choose any willing volunteer. Consuming the roots from the Bruchna shrub ensured that any child produced was likely to be born female, though the occasional infant boy was gifted to the friendly mainland neighbors to raise as their own.

Califia had traveled far to the north and eventually

found a man from among a tribe she did not know. The end result was young Chloe, the daughter whom she now left behind. The journey which she was about to undertake would mark the second time in her entire life that she had left her island home.

She chose, along with the rest of the war council, to take up residence on the Göke, the Admiral's flagship. A four-masted vessel with a black hull and spacious deck, the ship also carried a complement of long red oars which the admiral explained were useful for maneuvering in battle and moving the ship when the wind died. The old sailor seemed to think of this ship with the same affection which Califia thought of her daughter.

When their homeland finally disappeared on the far horizon, the queen's heart sank into her gut as she looked in the direction the boats were traveling only to see… nothing. No outlying barrier islands or small fishing canoes, no seagulls patrolling their home waters. Everywhere she looked was just more ocean.

"How long did the admiral say this trip will take?" Ariana asked as they sat together in their sleeping quarters that first night.

"Many months. I was quite certain he was exaggerating." Califia grabbed the sides of the bedpost as the ship lurched.

"I smudged three perfectly good charcoal sketches today, thanks to this bloody ship's lurching," her lover complained sadly. "It will be some time before I can make anything worth sharing under these conditions."

"Yakov claims that we will soon be jogging across the deck and not think twice about the ship's incessant bobbing about."

"Big talk for a man who fell off one of these boats," Ariana laid back across the mattress and Califia laid across her. The artist stroked the queen's hair. "What do you think they'll look like?"

"The Greeks? From the stories, I expect they have protruding fangs and breathe fire."

Califia's head bounced as Ariana chuckled.

"Perhaps they have bat wings and fart as loud as thunderclaps?"

"Obviously their farts are like thunder."

They shared a good laugh and for a moment everything felt normal. If she closed her eyes, Califia could convince herself they were back in her hut on dry land, the motion of the boat only a faint dream. Then the ship lurched again and the illusion was shattered.

A scowling Basilea had informed her in the morning that the others were complaining that the queen was slumbering on a soft bed while they were made to attempt sleep in moth-eaten slings. The admiral laughed incredulously when she informed him of her intention to vacate the guest quarters and sleep among her people.

Dozens of days were spent floating along, eating food that grew more and more stale with each passing day, and shitting over the rails of a moving boat. Yakov was right; after half a fortnight, Califia barely noticed the bobbing and lurching.

There was no shortage of sights to see along the initial stretch of their voyage. They sailed close enough to a vast continent to their north to see its many ships and sprawling coastal cities. Other vessels had a variety of design variations— some broad boats utilized flat segmented sails while others made use of billowing sheets and narrow hulls. Arianna and other artists sketched furiously, some adding their own design flourishes to the eclectic vessels.

Every fourteen days, Admiral Kemal would order the

ships anchored in place and every man would go below decks immediately. Then, the Californians opened the kennels to allow the griffins to stretch their wings.

The queen used that time to practice commanding the beasts. Basilea told her that the griffins were learning to listen to their new queen. She started with five, the most she was able to command at one time, but after one month at sea she had expanded her cohort to ten griffins. She could manage them flying in synchronous patterns, taking turns doing flips or rolls or other tricks, splitting them into two groups and giving them different commands simultaneously. It was exhilarating, feeling so completely connected to the beasts as they soared, dove, and twirled in the sky above. If she closed her eyes, she swore she felt as if she was flying herself.

After a long month and a half had passed, they finally came within sight of land. Califia's heart melted as she saw that it was a chain of islands and not the large, contiguous land mass which Admiral Kemal had described. They roughly followed a coastline far to their right for another half a month and then they were gliding once more through open ocean without a speck of land in sight.

During this long journey, Califia began regularly chatting with the Osman Admiral, who regaled her with many amusing stories of his time as a sailor. One night, as he imbibed a strong drink called *raki*, she dared to ask why he had been sent on this mission.

"I lost a battle," he said, taking a quick swig from a small flask. "The Venetians were charging this ship and I panicked. I signaled the other ships to come defend us and then the enemy ships surrounded us and crippled the Sultan's fleet. If it had not been for my many years of service beforehand, I would have been *executed*."

Califia shuddered at the thought. To the Amazons, executing trespassers was the will of their gods — the griffins generally did the work for them. An Amazon *might* be executed if their actions were directly treasonous, but even then, leniency was favored. The thought of executing one of her own people as routine punishment was shockingly scandalous.

She dared not ask the Admiral any further detail of the incident at the time but Yakov was happy to fill in the details later. The defeat of the Osman fleet had allowed the Venetians — whoever they were — to take control of the waters south of Constantinopolis and later seize the straits that surrounded the city. The Greeks and their allies who later allegedly conquered the city were brought by these Venetians as well as another people called *Genoans*. The queen's head could only take so much, however, so between these strange backward history lessons and learning the Osman tongue along with the language they called Greek, she had little desire to investigate further.

After two and a half months at sea, at last a broad stretch of land lay before them and the queen immediately assumed that they had arrived. When the admiral informed her that the land she sighted was actually the coast of a different land called Africa, her heart felt as though it was sinking into the ocean.

As they followed this coastline south and then several more months due north, the queen made a habit of waving at the natives who came to the shore to gawk at the passers by. They possessed the same dark skin tone as her own people, even darker than their mainlander neighbors. She idly pondered whether these people were distant cousins from an ancient branch of the Amazon family tree.

The Californians passed their time in the usual way; playing games, competing at various tasks around the ships, and finding dark corners for quick sex. Califia herself had snuck Ariana into such a hidden place a few times, and likewise had received the occasional sensuous surprise from her lover in return.

Everything settled into a stable equilibrium. Then one dark night while in the midst of a deep sleep, Califia was called back into the waking world by shouting and shrieking coming from the deck above her.

She rolled out of her hammock and listened. When she heard the squawking of griffins and the shouts rise to a fever pitch, she ran full-force up the stairs to the upper deck and nearly fell on her face as she stumbled through the open doorway.

Two sailors lay unmoving on the deck as blood pooled beneath them while ten other sailors gathered spears, curved swords, and the strange pipe weapons which she had learned were called *arquebuses*. They shouted and waved their weapons at the sky. Califia followed their gaze and saw the silhouettes of two griffins soaring against the blanket of stars.

"What happened?" The queen asked.

"Your *monsters* killed two of my men!" Admiral Kemal shouted as he pulled the crank on a large crossbow.

"Those cages are not easily breached by *griffins*," Califia said, her heart burning with anger as she realized that the dead sailors were the most likely culprits. Curious and stupid; a dangerous combination.

"I want them shot out of the sky, lieutenant!" The admiral shouted as he mounted an iron bolt onto his crossbow.

"Shoot at those creatures and you sentence yourself to death," Malachea declared, marching out from below decks with a sagaris in her hand. "They are not to be harmed."

"They are just *animals*!" Admiral Kemal shouted, stepping into Malachea's space with a boldness which Califia thought inadvisable. "You have many more!"

"We will not fight for your Sultan if you harm the griffins," Califia declared, inspiring several gasps from the Amazons who were starting to fill the deck. "We will *fly* back home if we must."

She sincerely hoped that Admiral Kemal backed down because she had no practical idea how they would find their way home from wherever they were at the moment.

"Are two dangerous animals really worth undoing everything we have accomplished?" The admiral shouted, his face beginning to turn bright red.

"They are sacred to us," Califia declared. "They are not to be harmed. Your men shouldn't have been anywhere near their kennels, much less unlatched them!"

Admiral Kemal bit his lip as if considering his options. Then he took the metal bolt out of his crossbow and turned to the others on deck.

"Lower your weapons," he said. Califia had learned enough of the Osman language to understand at least that much. He shot her a smoldering glare. "I will take the men below; get those beasts back where they belong."

Califia took hold of the triumvir dagger, feeling the internal glow of connection to the two beasts flying overhead. *Return,* she thought. She closed her eyes and listened. She felt the cold air rushing against her skin. From the two beasts, however, she sensed only resistance, refusal. *Return,* she thought again, hoping the creatures could sense the insistence she was trying to convey.

Home. The word crept into her mind but she realized that the thought was not her own. Her eyes welled with tears and she felt a wave of sadness crash over her.

"Should I mount upon Elena and fetch them for you, my queen?"

Califia glared at Malachea. The infernal woman's face appeared sincere enough, but her gorgon entourage smirked at the queen's apparent difficulty. Her daughter, Dionysia, was wearing a particularly belittling sneer.

"They miss home," Califia replied, focusing on the creatures overhead and pleading with them once more to come back to the ship. "They are sad."

"Their sadness is a luxury," the polemarkos said. "We should have left them at home."

"*Quiet*, Malachea," Califia said, her irritation threatening to transform into rage. "I need to concentrate."

Return.

One of the griffins drifted down toward the deck, but then relented and flapped back up into the sky. Califia closed her eyes and focused her thoughts on what she wanted, picturing both of the creatures landing softly on the deck.

Return.

The queen focused her thoughts on the sights, sounds and smells of home. She imagined tossing one of the griffins a raw, fresh cut of bison. She pictured the massive trees of the griffins' roosting grounds, recalled the strong scents of pine and clover.

Return.

The queen opened her eyes, gazing at the creatures and hoping they would listen. Slowly, one of the griffins descended in a spiraling flight path. The other followed. Everyone on deck watched with wide eyes and Califia suddenly realized she was holding her breath. She exhaled slowly as the first beast laid its paws and talons upon the deck and folded its wings against its back. The other followed suit and the two stood upon the planks and looked around at the women who now surrounded them.

The queen sent feelings of gratitude through the triumvir dagger, then approached the prodigal catbirds. She stroked their necks as she cooed sweet talk, telling them they had done well and that she was proud of them. Two of the women on deck who had worked periodically as wranglers groomed the griffins a little before coaxing them below, where they placed them securely into the kennels from which they had escaped.

The Admiral spoke some words over his two lost men, who were wrapped in cloth and had large iron weights fastened around their feet. When he finished, he nodded to the attendants and they gradually tilted up the boards which the bodies lay upon until both slid down and splashed into the water below.

She had been worried that Admiral Kemal might ignore them for the rest of the voyage but after the funeral service he invited Califia and Malachea — and *only* the two of them — into his cabin. The room where the Admiral slept had many rectangular storage spaces built into his walls which contained a variety of books, tools, beverages, and scrolls. In the middle of the room was a table upon which a great paper map had been mounted.

"Here is where we are," he announced, jabbing a middle finger against the map. "In two days, we will reach the Cape of Storms and then we can start traveling north."

"How far north?" Malachea asked, looking with

wonder upon the map.

"Here is our destination," he said, tracing his finger around the western part of Africa and then around its large northern edge. Califia thought this path would never end until at last his finger rested upon a point on the southeastern edge of the continent which lay north of Africa.

"Can the world really be so large?" Malachea said, tracing her own finger along the path which the admiral had just charted.

Admiral Kemal turned around and rifled through his storage spaces, moving aside strange brass instruments and thick bound books. He grunted with affirmation and returned with a scroll.

"Consider this a gift," he said, handing it to Malachea who held it, still rolled, up against a light streaming in through a nearby window. She gasped.

"It's a copy of the map laid out before you," Admiral Kemal said, smiling. His grin turned a little sour as he continued. "After interrogating my men, it is clear that those who were killed by your... *beasts* were trying to entertain themselves at the creatures' expense. Those responsible, those who *survived*, will receive their due punishment soon, but I wanted to put this matter behind us in the spirit of good relations. Are you satisfied?"

Malachea grinned as she tried to compare the two maps without unrolling the gift she had just received. Her face was almost childlike as she found corresponding shapes and continents.

"We are satisfied, admiral," Califia said. "And we are grateful for your continued hospitality."

The *due punishment* which Admiral Kemal referred to was meted out the next day. The Amazons watched, first from curiosity and then from horror, as three men were brought onto the deck, stripped to the waist, then bound to the ship's rail. The charges against them were read aloud by Yakov, and sentence pronounced: ten lashes each. The whip made bloody lines across each of their backs, one at a time. Califia rushed to the stern and vomited from the sight. She was accompanied by many of her fellow Amazons.

Africa appeared massive on the map which Malachea gladly showed off at every opportunity. It felt much larger as time continued to pass. Days turned into fortnights, which turned into months. Three months passed since they rounded The Cape of Storms and endured the rain and wind for which that area was apparently famous. They celebrated the festival of Persephone by singing songs to their departed loved ones, and the festival of Hera by painting themselves with phalluses and dancing topless upon the deck. The sailors especially enjoyed the festival of Hera until they learned that the phalluses were meant to represent the penis and testicles of Zeus, which Hera was credited with removing during the revolution.

One day, whilst looking through a magnifying scope which she had fashioned after those used by the sailors, Arianna cried out.

"There is land on our left side!" She shouted, clapping her hands.

The admiral explained that they were passing through an area called Gibraltar and that the journey should be much smoother from here. The Osmans controlled the northern coast of Africa, and Califia once more felt her head spin as she tried to comprehend just how big that broad land could possibly be.

Another fortnight passed and they flew their griffins for the last time the day before they made landfall. The admiral referred to the place they docked as Thrace.

"We cannot land nearer to Constantinopolis because that area is controlled by our enemies," the admiral explained.

"The Greeks?" Malachea asked.

"Venetians," Califia said, as though she knew all about them.

Admiral Kemal handed his spotting scope to Califia who looked through the lens and saw what appeared to be a gaggle of large ships, many larger than the boats that carried the Californian army.

"They must be a mighty people," Malachea said, looking through the scope as Califia handed it over.

"They should not be taken lightly; a lesson I learned at great cost," Admiral Kemal spat. "However, they are nothing more than lovers of money. The Muscovites pay a great sum to use their navy. If the coins stopped flowing, they would happily leave their employers to rot in the city."

Califia felt a familiar ache in her mind that always came up whenever Yakov or the Admiral mentioned money. She had examined many of the small metal disks which their Osman allies assured them were quite valuable but she never understood what gave them their value. *You cannot eat metal disks.*

The plan was to march from the port city of Gelibolu to what the sailors described as the most magnificent city in the world. The Californian army donned its armor and put the cages of griffins atop carts that required six-horse teams to pull. They gathered outside the city and Malachea stood atop a makeshift platform composed of pallets and crates.

"I, the polemarkos of all California, request the favor of the triumvirate goddesses. Great Athena, give us your wisdom!"

"Give us your wisdom!" They all responded, Califia included. Basilea stood at a distance to her, something which the queen knew would need to end soon. She and her chief advisor had not dared speak any further about their suspicions of Malachea for fear of being overheard, but now that they were departing the ships that would probably come to an end.

"Great Hera, give us your honor!"

"Give us your honor!"

"And great Aphrodite, give us your love!"

"Give us your love!"

Malachea pointed with her spear into the massed army, scanning and searching until the point hovered toward Califia.

"My queen, won't you join me?"

She felt her blood run hot at the request, but was determined not to let her nerves become her master. She silently walked through the crowd until she arrived at the stage. A few nearby Gorgons helped her scale the rickety thing safely and she muttered her gratitude.

"With the blessings of the gods," Malachea began, "we shall soon have revenge on those who drove our foremothers from their home many thousands of years ago!"

Califia nearly jumped as the polemarkos grabbed her hand and thrust both their arms into the air together. The Californians cheered.

****

"I know I'm still learning your language," Califia said to Yakov on the fifth day of their walking journey to the besieged city, "but Constantinopolis does not sound like an Osman name."

"You don't think so?" Yakov answered coyly as he shifted the heavy duffel he carried to his other shoulder.

"It sounds like a name that originated from our language."

"You're not far from the truth. It is a Greek name with a Roman inspiration."

She puzzled at this as they straggled along, a great herd of clanking soldiers shuffling further along an endless road. A band of Osman soldiers from Gelibolu were leading the great column. She had heard Yakov refer to them as Yenisherries and he seemed most pleased to have them nearby. Califia believed she and Yakov were somewhere near the middle of the Californian army who composed the column's rear.

"Tell me more."

"As I understand it, a thousand years ago the city was founded by a great emperor who wanted to give his nation a fresh start. Constantine was his name."

"He was an Osman emperor?" Califia felt very confused by this, since Yakov and the other Osmans always referred to their leader as the Sultan.

"Roman, actually."

"What is a Roman?"

"A mighty people whose empire was crushed under the weight of their greed. They were great builders and engineers. Many cities in Osman lands still receive fresh water from aqueducts built by Roman hands centuries ago."

Califia wondered whether there were any such aqueducts near Constantinopolis, but did not want to interrupt Yakov's stories.

"Like many Romans, Constantine was a Christian, but we must not judge him for that," Yakov insisted. Califia nodded as though she agreed but was a little confused that Yakov would think she would judge him thus. "He treated *my* people little better than the Spanish."

Yakov had spoken of his people before and how the Osman Sultan had rescued them from the Spanish who were bent on exterminating them like pests. She attempted to get him back on track.

"How did the city come to be in Osman hands?"

"It was… a gift," Yakov waved his hands as if shooing the question away. "A gift from God."

"Like California?"

"Sorry?"

"How our people had to abandon Atlantis and that the goddesses led us to a new home."

"Ah, yes," Yakov answered. He paused and seemed like he was about to say more on the matter, then just smiled. Califia wondered whether the admiral's answer would be much different, or indeed if the Sultan's response would be quite this diplomatic.

"*There* you are!" Basilea appeared suddenly about a stone's throw ahead of Califia, hers the only face in a sea of griffinsteel helms. She pressed through the column, an easy feat because the former queen was quickly recognized by the other soldiers who gladly provided a path.

"Yakov was just telling me—"

"You are needed," Basilea said, giving Yakov a friendly nod. She gestured for Califia to follow her toward the front of the column, which suddenly came to a halt without warning. Thus they had to abandon their initial route through the crush of soldiers and instead walk along the edges of the road, which was hemmed on both sides by steep shoulders which they periodically had to climb to get around wider portions of the column.

"What is it?" Califia asked when they were well out of Yakov's earshot.

"Our allies have stopped, and Malachea needs your guidance," Basilea explained.

Califia paused.

"She didn't send for me, did she?"

"I never said she *wanted* your guidance," the former queen turned and smirked and they continued their hike. Califia shook her head and laughed. When finally they came to the head of the Californian army, Malachea and the other two strategoses, Traesta and Olympia, were up on a ridge away from the army. The murmur of the idle warriors meant that whatever the polemarkos was discussing with the other two leaders was completely inaudible until Califia and Basilea came close, straining up the steep ravine and arriving almost out of breath.

"You've seen what their weapons can do," Olympia was saying, gesturing toward the front of the Osman column, which was obscured by a bend in the road and dense forest. "Do you really want to see griffinsteel tested against arquebus bullets?"

"What does that mean?" Califia demanded, finding her breath. "Who is going to shoot at us?"

"Our allies might," Traesta said, "if they mistake our scouts for an ambush."

A rapid series of pops like dozens of cracking tree limbs erupted from somewhere up ahead. Every Californian head that wasn't already gazing toward the head of the column now snapped in that direction.

"Arquebuses," Malachea said, thrusting a finger in the direction of the sound. "We cannot wait any longer."

"What do you propose?" Califia said.

Malachea shot her an annoyed glare.

"As I have already informed the strategoses," she

gestured to the three women, "I think we should send a small but well-armed strike force to skulk through these woods and see if our allies require our assistance."

Califia nodded, trying not to blush with embarrassment. She wanted to be angry with Malachea for making her feel like she was getting in the way, but she could see that it was the truth. Basilea gave her a reassuring look, but that only made her feel worse.

The polemarkos gave orders to the strategoses, who ran down the ridge to relay them. With great haste, about fifty Amazons helped one another up the steep ravine until they stood atop it with Malachea, Califia, and Basilea.

"Keep together," Malachea called to the troops who were now assembled alongside them. "Unsling your shields from your backs so that our allies might recognize us. The way that the sailors gaped at griffinsteel makes me believe its likeness is unique among the peoples of these lands. Hopefully they'll see that it's us. Stay safe and support the lieutenants."

Califia counted five lieutenants among the fifty warriors, each with griffin wings forged onto the sides of their helms. One of them looked very much like a younger version of the polemarkos and Califia quickly realized it was the woman's daughter - Dionysia. In addition to her mother's fashion sense, it was said that she had also inherited her hot temper. Malachea donned the polemarkos helm - a magnificently beautiful head covering which was shaped like a griffin's skull. Malachea pulled the visor closed, effectively shutting the helm's beak and leaving her only a narrow slit for her to look out from.

The lieutenant nearest Califia signaled for her to follow, while pointing to nine other warriors in turn including Basilea. The five groups, each composed of about ten Amazons, rushed through the forest one cohort at a time, orbiting their lieutenants and heeding their commands.

Another rapid set of cracks split the air and Califia thought she saw movement beyond the trees up ahead. Grayish, silvery smoke likewise filled the air ahead, and the queen realized very suddenly that the sounds were coming from a broad clearing ahead of them.

"Keep low!" Malachea shouted, an order which was quickly obeyed as every warrior, including Califia and Basilea, hunched as they continued their rushed pace to join in whatever troubles their allies were facing.

At last they came to the tree line and witnessed the source of the loud cracking booms that had brought them here. In the vast meadow were several armed bands of warriors in dress which looked very strange to Califia's eyes. Some wore plates of metal but many were covered only by rags and cloth caps. The few who were mounted did not charge against the assembled Osman column, but were fleeing quickly in the opposite direction.

"It's an ambush!" Malachea said. "Form lines and prepare to charge!"

Califia and Basilea stood side by side, axes and shields in hand. They exchanged a nervous glance as their fellow warriors lined up next to them and prepared to shock their enemies into flight. Califia let out a lung-full of air, having only just realized she'd been holding her breath.

Malachea raised her axe, no doubt preparing to give the order to charge, when Califia noticed something peculiar about this enemy. The three bands each had perhaps sixty soldiers, but two of these groups were already fleeing in terror while a lone third was still advancing at a halting, uncertain pace. Right at the

moment the polemarkos was about to lower her spear to
signal the advance, another series of booming cracks
erupted from the Osman line, specifically from the
Yenisherries. Smoke rose from their arquebuses and
more than half of the remaining enemy force fell to the
ground. The surviving half turned and fled, screaming
and crying with sounds that reminded Califia of panicked
animals more than humans.

"Hold," Malachea said, lowering the butt of her spear
so that it rested upon the ground.

"We can still catch a few," said one of the lieutenants,
stepping just out of the trees.

"I said hold!" The polemarkos barked, shooting an icy
glare at the offending officer, who stepped back into the
cool shade of the dense trees. Califia felt a little guilt
because of her amusement at the exchange, for it was
Dionysia, Malachea's own daughter, who had
contradicted the polemarkos' orders.

Mounted soldiers from the Osman line now leapt onto
the meadow and chased those who fled, chopping and
hacking at them with curved sabres which Califia
remembered were called scimitars. There was one who
tumbled just as a horseman slashed for his head,
narrowly dodging the blade as he fell to the ground. The
commonly-dressed man laid upon the grass as if
pretending to be dead.

As the horseman who had chased him ran after more
tempting prey, the man slowly rose from the ground and
looked in several directions around himself, assessing his
surroundings. *Don't do it, find another way*, Califia thought
as she realized what the man was planning. He gazed for
a few moments toward where the Californians were still
hidden, looking at the trees the way that a starving
person would look at a plate of roast turkey. He looked

toward the nearest groups of horsemen, who by now were very far away from him, and bolted for the trees.

"With your permission, Polemarkos," Dionysia said, picking up her shield from where she had rested it against a nearby tree.

"Go," Malachea said. "Avenge our foremothers."

Califia felt a bolt of pity as Dionysia charged from the tree line, axe and shield at the ready, bearing down on the fleeing man. His eyes went wide and he stumbled backward and cried out in terror, crawling away for a moment in sheer panic. He reached into his tattered boot and produced a dagger whose blade was no longer than the width of Califia's hand. Dionysia knocked her shield with her sagaris a few times and laughed as the man aimed his tiny blade at her, holding his arm way out in front of his body as beads of sweat dripped from his face.

Dionysia crouched and cocked her weapon arm back. Her opponent lunged, jabbing wildly but she easily deflected the small blade with her shield and then shoved him back. She brought the pointed tip of her battle axe directly in front of his chest, then suddenly aimed its point toward his feet. She jabbed at one, then the other, forcing the man to hop back and forth as he dodged the blows.

"See how he dances!" Dionysia shouted, laughing uproariously at her joke. Some of the other Amazons laughed along, but Califia did not think the jest was particularly clever or funny.

Where is the honor in toying with one's enemy?

Dionysia continued her ghoulish, catlike play when the man suddenly lifted his foot before she struck at it and stomped firmly upon the axehead. Dionysia dropped her weapon and her opponent charged towards her with the speed of a bison bull with an angry hornet stinging its rump. He smashed into her shield and forced her to tumble onto her back.

Dionysia wrestled side-to-side with her assailant, who jabbed at her helmet with his blade. A fellow Gorgon who stood next to Malachea stepped out of the tree cover and took a few steps toward them.

"No," Malachea said, holding out her spear in front of the Gorgon. "She can handle this herself."

Califia felt a wave of illness suddenly wash over her as she pictured her own daughter Chloe wrestling with this man in Dionysia's place. That Malachea would allow her own daughter to be hurt or even killed to fulfill some abstract notion of honor in battle only served to bolster Califia's suspicions about the fate of her older sister.

The man had been clever in nullifying Dionysia's weapon but it was clear from his wild slashing and stabbing that he was relying on luck to win this fight. It was likewise clear when Dionysia at last properly leveraged her shield to roll her assailant onto his back that his luck was swiftly coming to an end.

She pulled a dagger from her belt as she straddled her opponent, whose legs thrashed and kicked like a trapped animal. Shoving her shield onto his weapon arm, she raised her blade and shoved it straight into the man's throat. Califia watched in horror as his legs stopped their thrashing and then went limp.

Dionysia stood up slowly, leaving her dagger planted in the dead man's neck as she picked up her shield. Then she pulled her weapon from her victim's body and raised its bloody blade above her as the Amazons cheered and applauded the spectacle. Califia worried for a moment that she and Basilea were the only warriors among their cohort to refrain from such base encouragement, but the queen noticed from the corner of her eye that Malachea likewise withheld applause. The polemarkos held up her spear and waved it forward, signaling their entire party to follow her into the meadow.

"That was sloppy," Malachea said to her daughter.

"I was never in danger," Dionysia said, cleaning the blood from her dagger with a cloth she produced from inside of her thorax.

"He came too close, nonetheless."

"I had it under control."

"Never hold back when you are fighting for your life," Malachea said, taking the stranger's dagger from where it lay near his motionless hand. She tossed it to Dionysia, who nearly dropped her shield while catching it. "Next time, spare us the theatrics and spare *him* the indignity of being made into an object of entertainment."

Dionysia threw the dagger so that it stuck in the ground near Califia's feet.

"Worthless spoil," she spat, pausing a moment to stare upon the wide open eyes of the man she killed before following her mother to chat with Admiral Kemal, who had ridden his horse near to them.

Califia looked at Dionysia's opponent (she thought of him as her victim). He wore several layers of clothing, but it was moth-eaten and threadbare. The small cap on his head had fallen off, and while it looked much sturdier than his rough tunic and faded trousers, she didn't imagine that it would provide any protection in battle, much less keep his head warm on even a mild autumn day.

She plucked the small knife from where Dionysia had discarded it, and saw that it was not really a weapon at all, but a flimsy, impossibly thin slice of metal bolted roughly to an unfinished wooden handle which was pitted and blackened by rot.

Is this what we left familiar shores and warm fires and loving family to do? Murder people whose condition is more wretched than even our most severe ascetics?

She wrapped the small knife in a cloth and tucked it safely into her chest plate. She heard Admiral Kemal and Malachea share a laugh nearby and wondered whether this entire venture was a terrible mistake.

7

"A pity you arrived so late," Admiral Kemal said to Califia as she approached. "It is good that one of you got a taste of battle, at least."

"A snack," Dionysia said, grinning like a wolf. "When is the great feast?"

"Patience, lieutenant," Malachea said tersely. "How much longer until we arrive at Constantinopolis?"

"We'll be there before sundown," the Admiral replied, absently rubbing the waxen curls of his mustache with a thumb and forefinger. He looked at the queen. "Califia, won't you join me in the vanguard for the remainder of our journey?"

Califia tensed as the eyes of every Amazon suddenly fell upon her. She decided it would be better not to offend their host.

"It would be my honor, admiral."

Malachea pursed her lips at this response and Dionysia appeared almost wounded that the admiral had not asked her instead. Basilea's was the only face whose expression resembled approval but the queen even spotted the tiniest smidge of doubt in her ancient eyes.

"We go to rejoin our people," Malachea said, speaking in a commanding tone as if she intended only to relay an order to her own warriors and cared not even the weight of an autumn leaf whether the queen rejoined them.

Califia walked alongside the Admiral and the great beast which he rode. While she had recovered from her shock at discovering that horses were not just a mythical fancy of the foremothers, she still was not comfortable being quite so close to one. They seemed to possess a gentle nature, but so did the griffins. Knowing what the latter was capable of, she shuddered to imagine the great rippling muscles of these monsters employed for violence.

"I apologize for this delay," Admiral Kemal said as they rejoined the column and the other cavalry came galloping back from their chase. "These roads are not as safe as they once were."

"Are these men Greeks?" Califia said.

"Not at all," the Admiral scoffed as though this was a silly question. "They come from a land rather far to the north. They are Majyars and Wallachians, I believe."

"Majyars. Wallachians." Califia wondered how many of these groups she would need to keep track of. "Why did they come here, so far from their home?"

"Why did *you*?" Admiral Kemal said, looking down at Califia with a raised eyebrow. He chuckled gently, amused by his own retort. "One of the infidel monarchs convinced them to join in their great crusade. For many years, my people lived on the other side of that sea," he pointed south toward the narrow straits in the distance, where Califia saw many large ships on patrol. "When the Sultan's father conquered Constantinopolis and subdued the many Greek towns in this area, others began to fear that they might be next."

"Were their fears reasonable?" Califia asked, growing more and more uneasy with this conversation. Admiral Kemal raised his eyebrow at her once more but looked not at all amused this time.

"It has been nearly fifty years since Constantine's city fell to our cannons," he said, looking ahead and pointing to a large plateau looming far in the distance. "Sultan Mehmet, peace be upon him, is remembered as a righteous king, a fair ruler, and a mighty warrior. The current sultan is eager to be likewise remembered in such a favorable light."

"What will happen to the Sultan if he fails to retake the city?" Califia asked. A nearby Yenisherry turned his head slightly and seemed to glower at her for a moment.

"It is unwise to discuss such things in a way that might be overheard," the admiral said, speaking in Californian tongue. "The Sultan is greatly indebted to the red-hatted soldiers, and likewise they become angry when they hear anyone speaking against him."

Califia understood that red-hatted soldiers meant the Yenisherries, who wore tall red caps topped with a wide red cloth that hung behind their heads. She wondered what would have happened if the same man who glanced back at her had understood what the admiral had just said. *These must be their equivalent of Gorgons.*

"As long as we are speaking freely," Califia said, deciding to ask a potentially risky question, "what is your opinion of the Sultan?"

Admiral Kemal gave her a long, measuring look, once more fiddling with the waxed curl of his mustache.

"The man is a paranoid old fool who is either unable or unwilling to discern who are his real enemies and friends. Some day, I expect, he'll find a dagger planted in his back and will have no one to blame for the betrayal but himself."

Califia blinked a few times in surprise and shock to hear the admiral speak thusly. He and Yakov had done nothing but praise the Sultan on the entire journey here. The Admiral must have been keeping such thoughts to himself until this very moment.

"When we meet the Sultan tonight," he continued, still speaking Californian, "I would be very grateful if you didn't mention a word of what I've just told you. I meant no mischief by it - you should know who you are fighting alongside. You're owed at least that much."

"I see no reason to bring it up," Califia said, feeling the pull of her curiosity grow too strong for her better sense. "What might happen to you if these thoughts became known to the Sultan himself?"

"A lot of things, I expect," Admiral Kemal scoffed at the thought. "I would be beaten senseless, have my bones yanked out of their joints and then broken, and eventually, when the torturers grow weary of my screams, I would be strangled."

"Gods," Califia's stomach turned. "I will not mention these things to the Sultan, of course."

Admiral Kemal sighed, then gazed toward the channel clogged with enemy ships for such a long time that Califia nearly gave up any hope of receiving an answer.

"I have been at sea for nearly two years," he said softly, speaking Osman language once more. "I love the life of a sailor - the swaying of the waves, the gulls calling softly in the morning air, the excitement that lays around every undiscovered corner. I once hoped that completing this mission would convince the sultan to reinstate me as head of his navy, but God knows that man makes a religion out of being stubborn."

The queen was once more struck by the difference

between her own people and the Osmans. If California had a navy, the leader would be selected by the people on the ships, not appointed by the queen. She again shook her head at the backwardness of their newfound allies.

Califia and the Admiral walked, side by side, on foot and on horse, for many hours after that until they came close enough to the distant plateau ahead for the queen to realize it was not a plateau at all, but a massive walled city. Her heart felt overwhelmed as it often did when she gazed upon a beautiful valley, or the vastness of the western sea. She did not need to ask the name of this place. Here at last was Constantinopolis.

Arrayed around the city like worshipers around an idol was an ocean of brightly-colored tents and innumerable soldiers armed with great halberds, long pikes, and arquebuses. As they drew nearer to the massive army, Califia began to notice differences between various sections. In the central group, which was the largest, she spotted the tell-tale red caps of Yenisherries alongside heavy infantry wearing pointed helms and segmented plate mail, curved heavy blades hanging from their belts and long pikes in their hands. While the tents were brightly-colored, they were mostly plain solids unadorned with decoration or pattern. She surmised that this large central group was the Osmans themselves.

On their right was a camp filled with plainly-colored tents with little outward decorations. Around them swarmed men whose skin, in general, was noticeably lighter than either Amazon or Osman. They mostly wore turbans and well-used plate armor over loose-fitting but protective chain male. Their trousers were wide near the hips and knees but were tapered and tucked into tall boots at their calves. They carried all sorts of weapons among them - bows, sabres, arquebuses, crossbows, and long daggers - and some wore small round shields on their backs which were about half the size of the shields employed by the Amazons.

To the left of the great Osman host was a group that appeared to have nearly as many horses as they had armed soldiers. Their tents were plainly colored but featured bright decorative patterns around their fringe and on certain panels. Their helms were round but had flaps on either side that framed their wide faces and went all the way past the neck. The armor they wore looked like rectangular scales from this distance, and most had thin mustaches and walked with a wide gait that struck Califia as boastful.

The walls had massive gates and at the foot of one, the queen was fairly certain she saw two people fighting. The rest of the army didn't seem concerned, however, so she decided to ask about it later.

The Yenisherries who had accompanied them from Gelibolu abruptly broke off but Admiral Kemal and his sailors continued on their original path. The Amazon army fell in with the queen and the Admiral as they continued.

Admiral Kemal led them toward a massive brown tent with colorful banners flying from its central post. It stood about as tall as the great hall at Califomopolis and appeared to be almost perfectly cylindrical, though when they drew nearer she noticed a slight taper from its broad base. Two large and cross-looking men with bushy mustaches armed with halberds and outfitted in heavy plate guarded the entrance to the tent. Admiral Kemal dismounted his horse and approached the guards with a friendly but commanding air.

"I, Kemal Reis, have returned," the admiral said. "Please announce me to his majesty."

One of the guards went swiftly into the tent while the other stayed at his post glaring at the would-be entrants. After a few moments of dutiful staring, he furrowed his brow and his eyes began wandering over the many faces in the crowd before him. His expression transformed from cross to perplexed and he looked at the admiral as though wondering whether the man had lost his mind.

"The Sultan will see you now," said the other guard as he emerged from the tent. "Your... friends may send in three of their leaders. No weapons."

Admiral Kemal smiled broadly at Califia and sauntered into the tent. Malachea, and Olympia (whom the polemarkos had pointed to imperiously) relinquished their arms with the nearest Amazon. Califia turned to Basilea and handed over her sword, axe, shield, the triumvir dagger, and the small knife she had filched from the unfortunate man whom Dionysia had killed for sport. Basilea raised an eyebrow at this item, and Califia shrugged.

"Athena's wisdom go with you," Basilea said, squeezing Califia's shoulder as she pocketed the knife.

The queen nodded and followed the two other women inside, ducking beneath the flap just before the guards let it fall. Within the tent sat a bearded man wearing an enormous turban with a sparkling red jewel resting where it covered his forehead from which sprang three massive soft, bright blue feathers. His robes were made from fine red cloth and covered with swirling patterns of shimmering gold. Several cushions jutted out from beneath his royal posterior, and he reminded Califia of a flower.

On his right and left stood two frowning older men with tightly-groomed mustaches and beards dressed in fine clothes of their own. Flanking each man were four guards wearing scale mail shirts, plate mail over their hips and thighs, knee-high plated boots, and the red caps which Califia knew marked them as Yenisherries.

"So," the Sultan said, looking from Admiral Kemal to each of the three Amazons in turn before returning his gaze to the admiral. "You've returned."

"Your majesty, I have the honor to present the Amazons of California, who have brought five hundred troops to aid in the jihad. This is one of their generals, Olympia," Admiral Kemal gestured for her to step forward, which she did. "Their mighty battle leader, Malachea," He paused for the polemarkos to step forward. "And their queen, Califia."

Califia stepped forward and gave the Sultan a polite bow. He picked up a steaming cup from a small table near his elbow and sipped the concoction within. After smacking his lips a few times, he looked up at Admiral Kemal with an expression that was equal parts annoyed and enraged.

"Sultan Bayezid," Califia began, "we are honored to join you in fighting against our mutual enem—"

"You have not lost your talent for disappointing me, Admiral," the Sultan said, never bothering to cast a second glance at the Amazons. He brought the cup close to his lips, pausing to inhale its vapors. "In the two years you have been at sea, these women were really the best you could find?"

"If I may be so bold, your majesty," Admiral Kemal said, a confident smile spreading over his lips, "you wouldn't assume a tiger is harmless simply because you'd never seen it kill."

"*These* are not tigers," the Sultan chortled, sipping his drink and placing it back upon the small table by his side. He gave Admiral Kemal an icy glare for several moments until sighing and shaking his head. "You have technically upheld your end of our bargain, Admiral. You may go. As for the rest of you, I'll send word if I have need of you. Good day."

Admiral Kemal bowed and walked backward several paces before turning and pushing open the tent flap. He held it open and waited for Califia and the others. The queen was stunned and it took her a few moments to realize that they had been dismissed. She mimicked the admiral's mannerisms, bowing and walking backward, then strode quickly out of the tent in dismay.

Basilea was waiting for her, still holding onto her weapons. Those who had watched over the possessions of the other two were waiting as well, but the rest of the Amazons had disappeared.

"Sorry," Basilea said, handing her the small knife she had swiped from the dead Majyar. "I thought you might be attending the Sultan for much longer, so I had the rest of our group begin setting up camp."

"Very sensible," Califia muttered, trying to make sense of the icy reception. "Malachea, do you have any idea what just happened?"

"What were you expecting?" the polemarkos retorted, taking up her axe and shield. "The Sultan does not know us and has no reason to expect we know the axe's head from its shaft."

"I feel like a fool, traveling nearly half a year just to be greeted like that," Califia said, strapping her shield to her back.

"If we want the Sultan's respect, we need to earn it," Malachea said, shrugging as if the whole affair hadn't affected her at all. Califia looked around for Admiral Kemal, intending to ask his opinion, but he had already mounted his horse which was now galloping fast toward the edges of the siege lines, as if he wasn't about to risk his opportunity for escape.

"Do you know where our people have made camp?" Califia asked Basilea.

"An empty space near the rear of the Osman camp, follow me," she answered, nodding to Malachea and Olympia and their companions to follow as well.

The camp site was a stretch of flat ground around which tents were already being erected while Amazons arranged stone circles in the middle area for cook fires. A gaggle of warriors were gathered near one of the circles, where Califia spotted Dionysia holding court. She passed nearby, intending to claim a spot past the group for her own campsite when she overheard the conversation.

"…he carried a huge sword so I needed to work him with my shield first, get him tired out." Dionysia was saying, her voice puffed up with prideful boasting. "He slashed at my face but I deflected. He tried to grab my axe, so I dropped it and quickly drew my dagger…"

The queen knew she should just walk past and prepare her camp site and find Arianna and celebrate their arrival and think nothing of this ridiculous scene but she stopped in her tracks, feeling quite unable to do any of those things.

"Where is his sword now, Dionysia?" Califia asked, moving in between the audience until she was standing very close.

"Moldering in the ground alongside the man's corpse, I suspect," she said, her voice full of bravado.

"You should have kept it as a token of remembrance," the queen said, her tone only slightly admonishing.

"I'll have more to choose from before long," Dionysia shrugged, as if her own heroism was a foregone conclusion.

"You're in luck," Califia said, reaching into her satchel and producing the crude, half-rotten knife whose nubby point had been rounded and whose blade was thin from too much sharpening. "I kept it for you, in case you later regretted leaving the fearsome weapon behind."

The queen held the dagger at eye level, allowing everyone to get a solid look at the pathetic weapon which the lieutenant had described as a sword. Several of Dionysia's entourage let loose tittering giggles which soon turned into a tidal wave of laughter. Dionysia snatched the knife from Califia's hand with a glare. The queen pressed onward to find a place to pitch her tent. The spot she had been eying was now taken, but she was so pleased with herself that she didn't care. Thankfully Arianna had already found a decent spot and reserved the neighboring plot for Califia.

Two days later, they had yet to hear from Sultan Bayezid.

"What do you think?" Arianna said, lifting a filthy cloth from the small clay sculpture. "I call it The Battle of Gelibolu."

The sculpture portrayed three Amazon hoplites crouching in battle stance with their spears forward and their shields together while two Yenisherries stood behind them with arquebuses aimed at their mutual enemy. Califia ran her eyes over the small statue, admiring the folds in the loose clothing the Yenisherries wore over their armor, as well as the rippling arm muscles of the Californian warriors.

"We were closer to Silivri, I think," the queen said, peering closely at the face of one of the Yenisherries and seeing that Arianna had included a little bushy mustache. "And our escort did most of the fighting."

"This is more about the feel of the battle," she

explained. "It's not meant to be understood literally."

Califia gave Arianna the approving smile the young woman was obviously looking for. The sculpture, a model for a larger piece which Arianna was planning to create, was competently assembled and indeed the feel of it was correct. Still, the queen felt bothered by it and could not say why.

The griffins sat in their kennels playing with the various toys which the wranglers had brought for them, but whenever Califia communed with them, she could sense their anxiety at being in a foreign land, the uneasiness of their confinement. It had been nearly a fortnight since they were last allowed out of their kennels, and while they had adjusted to a routine of occasional freedom on the journey across the ocean, the queen believed they were expecting that schedule to be upheld now that they were on land.

Annoyed by Arianna's sculpture and unsettled by the griffins, Califia decided to track down Yakov and demand some answers. Now that he had returned to his home, he seemed to be acting as a sort of royal messenger, roaming the camp to deliver the Sultan's blessings and appreciation to the various groups gathered for the sake of his cause. Every time Califia managed to catch his eye line, he swiftly looked away as if the mere sight of her was indecent to him. Instead of trying to predict his movements, she stood before the sultan's great tent for the better part of an hour, enduring the guards' leering and whispered comments until finally he arrived.

"Oh!" He yelped as he came near the tent entrance and spotted Califia. "H-has the Sultan summoned you?"

"No, and I would like to know why," Califia spoke in the Amazon tongue so that the Guards would not understand. "I want answers, Yakov."

"Heh-heh," Yakov chuckled nervously, looking at the guards with a pleading expression but turning back to Califia when they ignored him. "It's nearly midday; you must be getting hungry. I will come to your camp in an hour and bring such a feast—"

"I do not require food," Califia produced a wrap from her satchel and took a bite.

"I have business with the Sultan at the moment—"

"I will wait," Califia said. "Don't be too long."

Yakov looked once more at the guards, who still appeared indifferent to his presence. One of them sniffed a little and the other fiddled absently with his mustache.

"As you wish, your highness," he said, bowing and entering the tent. He emerged much more quickly than Califia expected and she stuffed the remaining half of a maize wrap back into her satchel and walked beside him.

"We have traveled farther from our home than any of our people before us save the foremothers themselves," Califia began, reciting the lines with even greater passion than she had rehearsed them. "Why does the Sultan ignore us?"

"Before I give you an answer," Yakov said, "I would like some assurance of safety."

"Assurance of..." Califia rolled her eyes. "You must think we are savages."

"It's not that!" Yakov protested, stepping in a pile of horse manure and cursing. "If I told the Sultan what I am about to tell you, he would take my head without a second thought."

She rolled her eyes but understood.

"I hereby swear upon the three goddesses who care for the heavens and the earth that I will not kill you for anything you say," Califia said, giving Yakov a pat on the back which she hoped he would find reassuring. He nodded as though satisfied with her oath.

"I have spent many an hour singing the praises of your army to the Sultan," Yakov said, his voice quavering with a weariness she had never heard from him before. "I told him of the demonstration, and how Malachea killed that terrible monster. He does not listen, and often interrupts me when I try to assure him of your worthiness."

Califia felt like a child with a puzzle box, poking and pulling at various places along its surface trying to find a panel which would help her open it. None of it made sense.

"Even if the quality of our warriors was poor," Califia said, "why does he not give us a scouting assignment or some other menial task? I wasn't expecting we would be placed in the vanguard, but I also didn't think we would be ignored."

"It is because you are women," Yakov said, sighing. "The Sultan is embarrassed to have you fighting in his army. Among Osman women, such activity is strictly forbidden."

Califia stopped in her tracks. She suddenly realized that the only women she had seen in the camps of their allies were cooks and launderers. All of their soldiers were men. The Californians must seem equally odd to have an army composed only of women.

"Why would Admiral Kemal bring us here?" Califia asked, suddenly enraged at the absent man whom she had thought of as her friend. "He must have known the Sultan would find us unacceptable."

Yakov sighed as if weary but also seemed somewhat relieved. "The Sultan wanted to banish Admiral Kemal after his failure against the Venetians. He relented, for the Admiral has many powerful friends, but gave him the quest to deliver another army to help retake the capital as a kind of soft exile."

An impossible quest. Califia sighed, thinking of the impossible quests given to Amazon heroes of legend.

"But instead, the Admiral found us," Califia shook her head at how stupid it all was, how she and the Amazons were just pawns in some kind of game played between the admiral and his sovereign.

"Convincing your people to come fight fulfilled the conditions of his return," Yakov explained. "The fact that you are all women, something he knew the Sultan would think unacceptable... that was his way of sticking a finger in the sovereign's eye."

Califia did not know how to respond to any of this. It pained her to think that they had come all this way just to be used and then neglected entirely.

"What do you think we should do?" Califia asked, hoping that her trust in Yakov was not misplaced.

"If I were you, Califia," Yakov said, continuing his pace as the queen followed, "I would go home. This is not your fight, and the Sultan does not want you here."

"I thank you for your honesty," Califia said, "and I hope that you understand we consider you a friend."

"You honor me, truly," Yakov halted and bowed. "Now, if you will excuse me, I need to convince some Yenisherries to travel to Rodoschuk to retrieve the cannons awaiting us there."

"*Convince* them?" Califia felt great confusion at this. "I thought the Sultan's word was law."

"The Yenisherries are not like other soldiers in his majesty's army," Yakov explained. "He relies on their support, so sometimes they flaunt his commands to remind him that they control his fate."

"They really are Gorgons," Califia scoffed and shook

her head. "Why does the Sultan insist on pressing them?"

"He wants the cannon to arrive safely and as they are his fiercest warriors, he believes it is their duty. They see it as servant's work, which they are of course too proud to perform."

Servant's work. The phrase was considered a compliment in California and an insult here. It baffled her to think of a people who considered serving an ignoble pursuit. It also gave her an idea.

"What if the Yenisherries were not needed for this mission?" Califia asked.

"I don't understand," Yakov said.

Califia looked at the tent and then told Yakov what she intended. He announced her to the Sultan himself and within a few moments the matter was settled. The Amazons had a mission and Califia had a chance to undermine the polemarkos.

****

When the queen had brought the idea to the war council that night, they immediately loved it and praised the queen for thinking of it. Malachea tried to object to some of the finer points, but ultimately the plan to travel to Rodoschuk and retrieve the canons was ratified with a unanimous vote. Even the polemarkos grudgingly assented. The next morning, the camp came alive with preparation.

Yakov arrived midmorning, explaining that he was ordered to accompany them and supervise the transport of the cannons. Four divisions, each a hundred strong, were chosen for the task while the remaining hundred agreed to stay and hold prayer vigils for the safety of their compatriots.

The journey to Rodoschuk was both arduous and dull; the three-day journey was filled with marching and eating, and nights reserved for pitching tents along the roadside and sleeping until the sun rose. Yakov tried to pass the time by chatting but after having just spent several months with the man on a sea voyage, there was little about the man that remained a mystery. His people were called *Sephardim*, which he said was a type of Jew, as though that clarified the issue. They lived in Spain but the Christian king persecuted them and Admiral Kemal had rescued them from certain doom, bringing them to the Osmans to serve at the sultan's pleasure. It was easy to understand his loyalty to the sovereign, whom he endlessly praised at the slightest hint of provocation.

When they arrived at Rodoschuk the city gates were shut to travelers due to increasing sightings of Majyar and Wallachian raiders. Yakov, terrified at the mention of these enemies, insisted they not spend the night in the city but take the cannons to the Sultan as quickly as possible. The wagons pulling the great heavy weapons, however, slowed the whole army's pace to a crawl.

Several times on the journey back to the siege camp, between debates with Basilea and others over the nature of the triune goddesses and the limits of human perception, the queen thought she saw movement from the corner of her eye. Every time she turned her head to spot whatever was wandering in the thick forest that crowded the road, she saw only trees.

On their fifth day since leaving the city, Califia realized they were crossing the same meadow clearing where the Majyar had attempted to ambush the Yenisherries. She could see why it was chosen; the grasses and weeds there grew as high as her hip.

She froze, her eyes locked onto a particular stretch of

field where she was certain she had just seen a dark patch of light brown that did not match the black soil of this area. The wind blew and she caught another glimpse, this time even spotting a bit of cross-hatched texture. She scanned the field, her mind spinning with terror, and nearly screamed as she saw hidden among the ocean of waving grass the sharp gray of heavy mail and the chestnut brown of war bows.

"Halt!" She yelled, her throat squeezing tight with panic and urgency.

Malachea, marching a short distance ahead, turned to see what was happening as the massive column came to a stop. She strode quickly to Califia, frowning with disapproval.

"What is the meaning of this?" She hissed, following the queen's haunted gaze and looking at the meadow with a confused expression. Before Califia could answer, the polemarkos' eyebrows twitched and her breath caught in her throat with a gasp. She drew her sagaris and held it in the air, then angled it toward the meadow. "Battle line left!"

The Amazons quickly shoved their baggage onto the right side of the road and sprinted to take their place in the phalanx. The archers went to the back, the hoplites to the fore and arranged themselves in four ranks. As they were still getting properly arranged, a man covered from head to toe in thick iron plate mail stood in the meadow and shouted something Califia did not understand. The meadow then seemed to come alive as hundreds of men stood and started charging toward the still-forming Californian line.

The front two ranks thrust their longaxes forward and prepared for impact as the third and fourth ranks were still shoving themselves into place. The enemy seemed to be charging wildly, almost individually, at first, but they quickly coalesced just before throwing themselves against the Californian line. Califia's arm jerked backward with the impact as a man's shoulder was impaled upon the point of her weapon but when she glanced to her left she saw that the central hoplites were being pushed back by heavy-plated enemies whose armor deflected their stabbing strikes. Most of the front rank dropped their halberds as a result and drew their battle axes, jabbing and hacking at their foes from behind their shields. The line held firm.

Califia's muscles tensed with anticipation as she heard the familiar stretch of bowstrings. The other Amazons were shouting at their foe, hurling insults and roaring with wild, animalistic noises. Califia likewise shouted and jabbed her longaxe repeatedly at the men before her.

A horn blasted a flat-sounding note that resounded through the clearing. From behind the trees at the far side of the meadow charged at least a hundred armored men with horses outfitted with armored plates. They formed up in two tight clusters and rode together toward the wings of the Amazon army.

A small cloud of arrows flew overhead and showered on the enemy. The armored warriors held up their shields but even the fletches which struck home bounced off the plate armor.

A crude knife struck at the edge of Califia's shield, its wielder pulling against her hoplon with its chipped, jagged blade. She saw similar sights along her line and realized the men fighting on the wing she currently defended had bypassed the longaxes of the front rank. She dropped her own halberd and drew her sagaris.

Her assailant pulled once more on the top of her shield and during one particularly laborious effort she jabbed her axe beneath the shield and felt the tip sink into something dense. The knife clattered against the inside of her aegis as it fell from her enemy's grasp and she believed the thump she heard shortly after was the man falling to the ground. He was swiftly replaced by someone with a sword that battered against her shield and periodically tried to jab around it.

As another volley of missiles loosed, the enemy who punished Califia's shield stumbled back, then fell to the ground with a fletch jutting up from his heart. The hoplite line stumbled forward a little as their resistant pushing overcame the rapidly falling front ranks of their foes.

Califia dared to lower her shield a little and peer over the top of it. Screams of pain and terror erupted before the queen as the Californian arrows thunked into flesh and tore through them like paper. Fountains of blood flowed from many unlucky victims as their eyes went glassy and their limbs slack. The vanguard who had pressed against them so viciously was mostly dead, and those behind began running for their lives, disrupting the charging cavalry on the left flank, causing a few warhorses to fall and the cohesion among enemy horsemen collapse as they spread out to avoid the fleeing men.

Energy surged through the queen's body as she watched the enemy rout, but the euphoria which now coursed through her veins turned suddenly cold as she looked toward the center and saw that the main body of their enemy was still pressing hard against Malachea's division. The heavy cavalry which had charged the right flank had connected with brutal efficiency, the riders slashing their swords onto the helms of the Amazon infantry there. The archers at the back were loosing at-will, but their missiles bounced off the enemy armor like twigs.

"Form up on my lead!" shouted a nearby lieutenant. She charged into the meadow, stopping about a spear's throw from where the central enemy division was pressing into the Californian middle, which was beginning to bend like a bow pulled taut. Califia and those in her company formed a front line, followed by an eager second rank which set their halberds upon the vanguard's shoulders. The lieutenant watched eagerly as the third and fourth rank took up their positions, and for a moment Califia thought the woman, whose face was obscured beneath the protective helm, looked like Malachea. Then she realized that she had been following Dionysia, who now nodded as if satisfied that her phalanx was ready.

"Charge!" Dionysia shouted, tapping her shield with her sagaris and then running as hard as she could toward the enemies who were pressing against Malachea's cohort. Califia followed and the mass of them crashed into the enemy like a wave against loose rocks.

The front rank jabbed and hacked. Califia tried to aim her blows toward the enemy's legs, which appeared to be protected only by cloth trousers. She avoided the plates which covered their torsos, and their heads which were almost completely covered by helms that resembled steel baskets.

Another phalanx of Amazons was pouring toward the beleaguered enemy from the opposite flank. They charged at a run, but kept their close formation and struck the enemy heavy cavalry on the army's right with a terrible crash. Men tumbled from their mounts, horses screamed in terror, and the battle cries of the Amazons seemed so loud and boisterous that Califia wondered whether Athena herself was secretly fighting among them in disguise.

The enemy heavy cavalry who remained turned and fled back to the trees at the far end of the meadow, followed by the screaming mass of the armored foot soldiers who clanked along behind them.

"Do not pursue!" Malachea shouted, repeating the command a few times as various soldiers wandered a few steps toward the forest where their enemy had fled.

The queen surveyed the battlefield; those enemies who remained were either dead or wounded. Many of the enemy dead looked no different from those poor souls who had been killed by the Yenisherries so many days before, wearing little or no armor. Many of the wounded wore heavy plate, some wearing steel trousers as well.

"Hashem be praised!" Yakov said, approaching the queen from behind. "The Sultan will hear of your heroism this day!"

"It didn't feel heroic," Califia said, her eyes lingering for a moment on a man dressed in ragged clothes whose throat gushed a fountain of blood.

"Speak for yourself," Dionysia said, kicking a man who was clutching at a bleeding arm.

"Enough!" Malachea shouted, approaching them as the other soldiers began checking on the survivors.

"He's an enemy," Dionysia protested, looking incredulously at her mother.

"Put him with the others," Malachea said, gesturing to a group of about a dozen enemy soldiers who were being bound together with a length of rope.

"What will become of them?" Califia asked, keeping a close eye on Dionysia as she escorted the bleeding man to the gaggle of prisoners.

"That will be for the Sultan to decide," the polemarkos

took a long swig of her water bag, filling her mouth until her cheeks puffed out. She swallowed gradually savoring it like fine manzanita wine.

It took another two days to return to the siege camp, two long days of jumping at larks, boars, and anything else that moved in the periphery. It was midday when they finally arrived, and to Califia's surprise, they were greeted with applause.

8

As the Osmans built fortifications and battlements for their newly-acquired cannons, the Californians constructed twenty-three pyres and abstained from food for the rest of the afternoon and evening. Califia crafted a clay remembrance totem alongside Arianna, who seemed deeply troubled.

"You didn't tell me Philomena died," she said as she worked a lump of clay with a slender shaping tool.

"I did not know her," Califia said, immediately regretting the defensiveness in her own voice.

Arianna pressed the tool firmly into her clay, making a texture of deep ravines in its surface.

"There's no reason for you to know her," she said, smoothing over part of her sculpture with gentle presses of her thumb. "She was not a strategos, or an admiral, or a sultan."

"That is not fair," Califia said, cursing as she accidentally tore off a portion of her clay totem. It was meant to be a whale, as she remembered that Touraena and Esme were lovers who enjoyed watching the whales play around the ships during the voyage. The whale in her hand was now missing its tail.

"Be gentle," Arianna admonished, dipping her fingers in a shallow bowl of water on the table before her. She added a drop to Califia's clay and the queen smushed the busted tail back onto its body, smoothing over the jagged scar that resulted from the unintended amputation. "I have heard rumors that we might be leaving soon."

"Depends upon tomorrow," Califia said, absently smoothing and shaping the whale back into submission. "A short war."

"Not short enough," she replied, a tear rolling down her cheek and dripping onto her lap.

Califia walked away, still shaping her totem and trying not to rip any more of its limbs off. Arianna had always been her escape from politics, the one person in her life without a thousand opinions whom she could cry to and bitch to and feel better with afterward. Perhaps they might return to that dynamic, but the artist was too close to all of this now.

That night the Californians wept for their lost sisters, placed their totems upon their corpses, and lit the pyres as they prayed to the triumvirs and the other goddesses. Within the flames, the remembrance totems hardened. Apart from the ash, the tiny statues were the only physical remains left behind by the departed.

In the morning, Califia woke in an empty tent. She dressed herself, donning her griffinsteel armor, then went to the funeral grounds. Malachea had arrived before her and greeted her with a solemn nod. The queen fished among the ashes for her totem. She gripped it tightly in her fist as she gazed at the twenty-three piles of ashes which lay behind their campground. Twenty tree of her sisters whose lives were now gone, scattered like the pine tree's pollen on a windy day.

"Your highness!" Yakov's voice called. He sprinted towards where she had been standing with the war council in the middle of the *agora*, as the empty space in between their tents had come to be called. "I have come to extend to you a most excellent honor! His majesty the Sultan would like to invite you to join him at his pavilion to witness our armies crush the enemy."

Califia remembered the many times Admiral Kemal had offered special treatment or accommodations because of her position as the leader. She knew better than to invite resentment from the other Amazons.

"My place is with my people," Califia said, shrugging as though there was nothing to be done.

"If I may, my queen," Malachea chimed, "it has already been decided that we will deploy far back from the vanguard due to our diminished numbers. One less will not make a difference."

The queen shot a glare at Malachea, who shrugged.

"It is not right for a queen to set herself above those she serves," Califia said.

"The army is under *my* command," Malachea reminded her. "Plus, we wouldn't want to violate local customs. Given the circumstances, isn't diplomacy one of your most important duties?"

Califia glanced at Yakov, who was staring at her with wide, hopeful eyes. Malachea was correct, and Califia hated her for it. *I won't be needed on the field and, given their attitudes toward women, the Sultan is probably breaking some tradition by inviting me in the first place.*

"Tell his majesty that I am happy to accept his invitation," the queen said.

Yakov looked overjoyed and ran quickly out of their camp, no doubt to inform his sovereign of the good news as he sipped coffee and barked orders. She glared at

Malachea, who was already walking away.

The Sultan's pavilion was much easier to find than she expected— it lay on top of a tall hill and was shaded by a brightly colored canvas umbrella. She took one last look around the camp and was satisfied that the officers were already rousting late sleepers and helping them prepare.

The hill was tall but not steep, so climbing to the pavilion in full armor was no difficult task. Beneath the shade of the great umbrella sat the Sultan, sipping a steaming cup as a turbaned man in large-fitting robes was chatting with him. Sitting near them was a man with skin as bright as the midday sun, popping dates into his mouth from a nearby bowl. Around the three men were servants or slaves, Califia did not know if there was a difference, who fanned their masters with broad fans that resembled flattened brooms as well as men holding intricately designed silver platters covered in food. Yakov was sitting just behind them and had just stuffed some manner of roll into his mouth, which he hastily chewed as he stood and sprinted to the queen.

"Your great and sovereign majesties," Yakov said as he stood in front of Califia and turned toward the Sultan, "I have the honor of presenting the queen of California."

Califia bowed in the manner of the Osmans and the three men sitting on the cushions nodded in a manner which the queen chose to interpret as respectful. The Sultan gestured to an empty spot among the cushions next to him, and she marched over and sat among them.

"Your highness," Yakov said, addressing Califia, "I have the honor to present to you Sultan Husayn of the Gurkani," The man in the baggy robes nodded solemnly, "and General Al-Khulani of Egypt," the light-skinned man now bowed his head and smiled in a way that seemed strange to the queen. She nodded back and watched as the preparations for the assault began below.

"Your land must be made of gold," Sultan Husayn said, grabbing a handful of salted nuts, "considering how you use it for armor."

"It's griffinsteel," Califia explained, taking off her helm and handing it to Sultan Husayn to inspect. "It is made by mingling iron and pulverized griffin bones."

"It's light," the Gurkani leader said, rapping the cheek plates a few times with his knuckles. "Sturdy, too!"

He handed it to Sultan Bayezid, who pulled at it as though he believed he might bend it with his hands. He pursed his lips and turned it over in his hands a few times, then handed it to the third man, the one with bright skin, a small red turban, and a thin mustache. General Al-Khulani tested the helm from inside the dome which covered Califia's head, pulling and banging various regions until finally giving an impressed nod and handing it back to the queen.

"Let us hope we have no need of your protection up here," said the General, smiling as he popped a grape into his mouth.

"I daresay," Sultan Bayezid scoffed, "if the battle goes so poorly that we end up trapped on this hillock with only Queen Califia to protect us, we would have a decent chance at escape."

"No need to fear, fair lady," Sultan Husayn said, gesturing to the massive army assembled before the city. "Even if God is not with us today, your protection will not be necessary."

Califia felt a little astonished at this welcome, which was positively scalding compared to the coolness of her initial reception. The blast of a horn split the air and the armies below raised a great battle cry in response. More horns joined in the blast, from all over the army, raising a din so loud that Califia was tempted to shield her ears from the racket. The drone of the horns, however, was soon dwarfed by thunderous booms that shook the very ground.

The queen gasped loud enough for the others to hear and they shared a chuckle over her surprise. Great clouds of dust erupted from the city walls, and she could see cracks in some places. Just in front of one of the outer walls, she saw a mound of black dirt which had not existed a moment ago. Cheering rose from the army, and Califia realized the terrible noise had been the reports of cannons, which she could see now were being hastily reloaded by their crews below.

"My father took this city," Sultan Bayezid remarked, "by smashing down their walls with cannons. Soon the infidels will feel the bite of our blades and regret the day they left the comforts of their soft beds."

"Your father did not smash *these* walls," General Al-Khulani remarked, throwing an unsuitable grape on the ground. "He targeted the Blachernae walls, to the north. Much less fortified."

"You have already made your opinion on this matter known, General," the Osman Sultan said, waving the comment away with his hand. "It is too risky to concentrate our forces to the north as long as the Genoese control the seas. Cannon fire from those ships would threaten this entire endeavor."

"Besides," the Gurkani Sultan said, "we already have a plan for taking the Theodosian walls, so why waste time chasing an ideal situation which we have no means of creating?"

"I only mean," General Al-Khulani said, examining a date, "that it is a pity we do not have a brilliant naval commander at our disposal. Such a man would be an invaluable resource, if only such a man existed."

"I agree," Sultan Bayezid said, crushing some leftover pistachio shells in his clenched fist. "It is a pity that there is no such man upon whom we could rely."

Califia realized they were discussing Admiral Kemal. The Sultan was too proud to ask him to help with the naval side of the siege, so he sent him away on a hopeless quest instead. Even now, when his allies subtly tried to encourage him to reach out to the admiral, he refused. She wondered if they had discussed herself and her people in such similar, obscured conversation. She decided such things were best left unpondered.

The cannons continued firing through most of the morning and while many places along the walls now had dents or cracks, not a single spot along the barriers had been breached in any meaningful sense. Just before midday, the horns blew once more and a cheer rose from the army, but Califia could not see why. Then she saw the great formations of troops cluster tightly together to allow great ramps to be wheeled through, wide enough to accommodate four people with their shoulders touching. The soldiers then manned stations alongside the ramps where thick lumbers jutted out from the body for them to push against.

The queen was greatly surprised at the speed of these ramps, for it seemed to take only the span of perhaps twelve heartbeats before the ramps had reached the outer walls, which were unmanned. The whole time they pushed the ramps into position and then lined up behind their entrances to prepare a great charge, arrows and rocks rained down on them from the inner walls, which were considerably taller than the outer walls which were now being breached.

Along with the armored men who defended the tops

of those walls, Califia suddenly spotted several metallic cylinders being put into position peeking between the jutting patterns of the parapets. *Cannons,* she realized. *Our enemies have cannons too.*

And as this thought ran through her head, the enemy guns began to fire.

The queen saw now that there were four ramps, targeting four different areas of the walls. The first connected with the outer wall it was aiming for and the men shoving it did something to the wheels which Califia assumed stabilized the structure so that it did not roll away. The cannons poking from the inner walls still had not fired. *What are they waiting for?*

"Behold," Sultan Bayezid said, raising a jeweled goblet filled with something with a fruity smell, "our forces will now crash over their walls like ocean waves."

The queen wondered how the Osman, Gurkani, and Mamluk soldiers who had just crested the outer wall would manage the steep drop which she knew awaited them on its other side. As if answering her question, she saw that the outermost soldiers on the ramps carried long, sturdy constructions of planks which she now realized resembled a staircase. They shuffled the stair forward and the men closest to the inside of the outer walls fixed them in place and led the way into the space between the inner and outer walls.

As the queen wondered about how they planned to overcome the considerably taller inner walls, men with great crossbows loosed a strange and loud payload straight into the air. Whatever they had let loose had two claws upon its head which dragged long chains behind it. As the first mechanism grabbed hold of the parapets and men began to climb, she saw that these missiles were actually chain ladders.

"Our reserves move forward at last," the Gurkani sultan said, watching the troops down below with two telescopes which had been fused together so that he could look through them with his eyes. "No doubt they are cursing their luck that they will get last choice of the city's spoils."

Califia searched the assembled masses below until her eyes fixed on the group of soldiers whose armor blazoned like burnished yellow suns in the brightness of midday. She saw the tall feathers of the lieutenants, the bright blue helms of the strategoses, and the griffin skull helm of Malachea, the polemarkos who was prepared to lead them to glory.

The now familiar boom of cannons interrupted her admiration of the Californian army. Puffs of smoke drifted from parts of the inner walls and she realized the cannon fire had come from the city itself. The front ranks of the reserve troops, which were now approaching the city to bolster the assault, caught the brunt of the cannons' wrath as great plumes of dirt were raised in the middles of their formations and men screamed in pain and fear.

"Are we in danger?" Califia asked, suddenly filled with cold terror as she imagined a cannonball smashing into their little pavilion.

"The guns can't reach us up here, your highness," General Al-Khulani said, sniffing as if he was witnessing something mildly boring.

"Why do we not pull our troops back?" Califia flinched as a cannonball exploded into the middle of an Osman formation.

"They are brave enough not to run," Sultan Bayezid said, "and the cannons will stop once our men take the walls."

"*If* they take the walls," Sultan Husayn said, handing his strange double-telescope to Bayezid. Califia did not need far-seeing lenses to understand the Gurkani leader's meaning. The defenders on the inner walls were suddenly out in force, pouring pots of steaming viscous liquid on those who tried to scale the walls, and hammering them with large boulders and rocks as well.

The enemy cannons, meanwhile, kept up their fire and more of the reserve troops were killed or wounded. Califia looked toward her people, and breathed a brief sigh of relief that they were still out of range just as she was. The units ahead of them, however, were just struck by a flying ball in their front ranks, so in a few moments the Amazons would also endure this horror themselves.

Califia looked about the battlefield, hoping to see something that might turn the tide, and when she peered northward, she spotted several sails in the distance nearing the far shore. Sultan Bayezid was handing the scope back to Sultan Husayn and Califia snatched it in mid handover. She aimed it toward the ships.

"Your highness?" Sultan Bayezid said, sounding surprised.

"They're landing troops," Califia said, watching in horror as the ships lowered ramps and armored men poured onto the northern coast. She handed the scope to Sultan Bayezid, who stared through the device and laughed.

"We'll be inside their city in a moment," he said, arrogance dripping from his voice like water falls from a duck. He handed the device back to Sultan Husayn and turned to one of the nearby runners. "You there! Tell the cannon to turn toward the north and prepare to fire on these interlopers!"

The runner sprinted away very quickly and Califia

gasped as a cannonball fired from the walls struck very near the Californian divisions. She looked toward the inner walls, hoping that the Sultan was correct about the troops breaching them very soon. Instead, she witnessed the troops at the foot of those walls in complete disarray. They had crowded too densely into the space between the inner and outer walls and the Christians were exacting a massive penalty for this mistake. The boulders, boiling liquids, and arrows which they hurled down upon the Osman Alliance's heads did double their usual mischief.

A torch dropped from the defenders on one segment of the walls and when it struck the ground, the black liquid that was laid there ignited in a terrible blaze and forced a panic among the alliance soldiers. Men screamed and pushed against their advancing fellows as they tried to escape a painful and horrific death.

The other leaders started barking orders at the runners, screaming for the troops to be withdrawn so that they could defend against the newcomers charging from the northern shore. Califia stood and donned her helm, pulling the chin cinch tight.

"Send your forces north as quickly as possible," she said, preparing to join her people and prevent them from walking into a tragedy.

"Where are you going?" General Al-Khulani asked.

"I will lead our people to defend the northern flank," she said. "Pray to your god that we will not defend it in vain!"

The queen nearly stumbled twice because of how swiftly she bolted down the hill, but she kept her feet. She was fairly certain she heard Sultan Bayezid shouting for her to stop, but ignored the man. *I am not your subject.* She ran through the spaces between the armed divisions, following the shimmering gold which flashed in the spaces between Osman troops. The cannons on the city wall fired another volley, but the sound of their impact sounded far from where she sprinted, and the spray of dirt and bodies far to her left told her that the defenders were still targeting the foremost reserve troops.

"Polemarkos!" The queen shouted, waving her hands as she approached the Amazon army.

"Califia?" said Malachea, giving her lieutenants the hand signal to halt, which they passed along to the rest of the troops. "You should not be here."

"We are in danger," Califia panted. Malachea shouted for the other strategoses to join them, which they did quickly. By now the nearest body of troops was about a javelin's throw ahead of them, still marching toward the wall. The queen explained the situation to the hastily assembled war council.

"You should return to the Sultan," Malachea said to Califia, in between barking orders for their assembly to prepare a northward excursion.

"We will need every warrior we can muster," Basilea chimed, inspiring a look of exasperation from the polemarkos. She seemed to be preparing herself to argue the matter, but then shook her head.

"Fine," Malachea said. "You don't have time to fetch a halberd, so your sagaris will have to suffice. We go to defend the north flank!"

Califia fell in with those troops in the rear who also didn't carry spears or longaxes, mostly archers but a few lighter-armored axewomen who served as shock troops in the battle, smashing into the enemy flanks swiftly and brutally to cause panic. The queen herself had received only rudimentary training in this manner of fighting, but there was no time to argue qualifications at the moment.

They traveled north, jogging along an arcing path behind their allies whose various divisions were mostly still charging for the walls. Califia risked a glance at the Osman and allied troops at the foot of the inner walls to see that two of the segments were abandoned and soldiers from one of the two remaining segments were actively fleeing back over the ramp, obstructing the reserve troops who were attempting to rush into danger. She turned her eyes forward; it would not do to allow distraction at such a crucial moment.

Someone up at the front of their formation shouted something, then several others shouted the same words, but the queen still could not understand them. At last some of the closer lieutenants barked *Enemies ahead!* and Califia shivered as though someone was pouring slushed snow down the middle of her spine. She glanced at their flanks but so far no allies were coming to their aid. *We are on our own.*

The Amazons slowed their pace to a quick walk, then a stroll, then a halt. The clang of shields being overlapped stung the air and from her position near the back, Califia could just see that the spears near the front were lowering in preparation for engaging the enemy. Between the axewomen and the hoplites stood a fair number of archers, at least 100 by the queen's counting, and they spread themselves out and nocked arrows in preparation for the polemarkos' orders. The queen spotted Basilea among the archers and she was trying to find Arianna as well when the orders were relayed through the lieutenants.

"Archers, prepare!" they commanded. The archers raised their bows and drew the bowstrings back to their cheeks, their missiles ready to launch. Califia could not see the enemy warriors yet, but she could hear them and, much to her alarm, she could feel them. The ground rumbled as their foe charged toward them. Malachea shouted something from the front which the queen could not understand.

The collective thrum of bowstrings was like the beat of a thousand drums. Califia heard the tinkling bounces of the arrows as they struck against hard metal. The back rank of the phalanx, their shields aimed toward the heavens, reverberated slightly with the impact of the enemy charge. The clanging, bashing sound of armed combat filled the air and Califia hoped that their forces were prevailing. She looked behind them and to their flanks, but still they were alone, about two bowshots from the main army withdrawing at last from their failed attempt to take the city walls.

"Follow us," the woman next to her said, giving her a friendly rap on the shoulder. Califia joined the axewomen as they marched toward their army's right flank, glancing behind her to see that the axewomen on the other side were likewise going to the left. The archers loosed another volley.

"Stick close to me, my queen," the same woman said to her. Even with her helm obscuring her face, Califia noticed the telltale tattooed beard of a Gorgon, this one styled as a tangle of octopus tentacles. As she glanced to the other axewomen, she saw that they likewise bore the signs of Gorgon membership.

They jogged clear of the phalanx, then wheeled around in a great sweeping arc toward the center. Califia now at last received her first glimpse of their enemies; foot troops covered head to toe in heavy plate mail wielding long isosceles blades and oblong shields. Some carried brutal-looking maces and others wielded broad-headed axes and round shields.

"Charge!" a nearby lieutenant shouted, and Califia sprinted with the rest of their group toward the left flank of their foe. Being that she was still in the back of the formation, her role was to push and shout encouragement to her fellows, which she did gladly. However, now that she was at a vantage where she could survey the enemy soldiers more thoroughly, she felt her heart jump into her throat at how many there were.

A sword jabbed into their formation, missing the two ranks of soldiers ahead of her and jabbing the top of her thorax near the collarbone. She shoved her shield beneath it and pushed it upward. The queen heard the sound of steel squelching into flesh, saw a spray of blood and smelled the odor of defecation. From somewhere within the enemy ranks, the sound of an arquebus firing split the air, but Califia believed it was only a single gun which made the report.

One of the soldiers to her front cried out and suddenly lurched forward, a mailed fist clutching her rope-like hair. The queen pressed forward and sheathed her blade, grabbing at the plate that covered the woman's back and stopping her assailant from capturing her. The Amazon shrieked as two sides fought for her, grabbing and pulling. The women to Califia's right and left grabbed the poor warrior, who flailed and jabbed at her attacker.

The poor woman's shrieks set Califia's blood to a rolling boil. *I have already buried twenty-three of my sisters. I will not bury this one as well.* A narrow gap opened before her and she quickly raised her sagaris and swung it down onto the arm of the man who was pulling Califia's neighbor into the enemy ranks. The blow dented his armor and he let go of her hair as he cried out, but the arms of his compatriots suddenly took up his task and clutched at the unfortunate Amazon, dragging her away from the grasps of her own fellow warriors.

Califia dropped her shield and raised her battle axe, gripping the handle with both hands. The helmet of a nearby enemy warrior had fallen off and she hacked the smiling blade into the man's skull. His blood sprayed into his neighbors' eyes as he slumped to the ground. She held her weapon firm and yanked it from his head.

The enemy ranks had loosened a little to allow the Amazon captive to be pulled into them. The queen held her sagaris in her right hand and with her left she drew a dirk as long as about two hand-lengths. She kicked, stabbed, and chopped her way into the enemy's midst, keeping her captured sister within her view. She thought she spotted her fellow warriors on her flanks a few times, but she focused on the captive to the exclusion of all else. The poor woman was being shuffled along by two lightly-armored men.

The man on her left wore a leather jerkin and the tip of Califia's axe pierced it like soft cheese. The Amazon prisoner balled her left hand into a fist and mercilessly punched the man on her right until he fell to the ground and crawled away. She turned and ran past the queen. The enemy's front ranks thinned and they seemed to be falling back. The queen felt a surge of joy at an impending victory until an impossibly tall man with shoulders broader than a bison stepped forward and roared.

Califia did not know that humans could grow so tall—he was at least a head taller than Traesta who was the tallest among them. He roared at the Amazons and bashed his massive sword against the oblong shield he carried, clanking toward them in a suit of plate mail and a helm that covered his entire face. The enemy troops pulled back but held their formation and kept weapons ready.

Califia looked at her own soldiers — many were wounded, about a dozen lay so still that she was certain they were dead, and those still on their feet looked almost too exhausted to stand. If this champion managed to rally his fellow warriors into redoubling their effort, the Amazons would be overrun.

Califia picked up a shield and hunched slightly, letting the aegis cover more of her body. She recalled her training, in spite of her years. Keep the *hoplon* between yourself and the enemy, stay light on your feet, and be careful where you step. She leapt aside as the man suddenly raised his massive sword overhead and brought it down where she had been standing only moments ago. The tip of the blade sunk into the black earth but not very far. He swept it toward her and she caught the strike with her shield. The blow pushed her slightly to the left, but she held her ground and did not stumble.

He raised the sword again, preparing for an overhead blow. She jabbed the point of her sagaris into his right armpit but it struck chainmail that undergirded his plate. She brought her shield up just as her assailant's weapon came crashing down. The enemy's blade slid off the shield to her right, twisting him around and giving her an opportunity to fall back. The man righted himself, then turned and said something in his language to his fellows. A few titters welled up from his compatriots but his own laughter boomed like a cannon, as if the queen was a source of limitless amusement.

He raised his arms and turned briefly toward his people, which evoked cheers from them. As he turned back toward Califia, his arms still up and out as if he were inviting an embrace, she noticed that his armor rode up when he raised his arm, enough that she saw a hint of flesh just below the hem of his mail shirt which fit a little too short for such a tall subject. She shouted a battle cry, daring the man to charge once again. He obliged, running full tilt toward the queen.

She ducked and rolled away from him at the last possible moment, rising quickly enough to smack his armored backside with the flat of her axe. This drew laughter from the Amazons and even some surprised chuckles from the man's compatriots and he turned toward her in a rage, smacking his shield and roaring like a cornered puma. He raised his sword once more and she charged him with the point of her sagaris aimed for his exposed midsection. He brought down his weapon upon her shield and a little of it struck her helm and knocked her back.

Scrambling, panicking, she crawled backwards and rushed to regain her feet. *Where is my sagaris?* The large man sank to one knee, the hilt of an Amazon battle axe jutting out from his midsection, a waterfall of blood staining its leather wrapping. Her head swam for a moment but she gathered herself and approached the champion as he dropped his weapon and shield.

He was muttering something to himself in a half-whisper and although Califia could not comprehend the words, she understood that it was a prayer. He fell on his left side and rolled onto his back. The hilt of Califia's sagaris angled toward the sky and blood no longer flowed from the wound. She gripped the bloodied haft of her weapon and yanked it from his gut, and it was only then that she saw the enemy army staring with wide, awestruck eyes at the sight before them. She lifted the axe in the air, showing them their champion's blood.

Without warning, a cloud of arrows suddenly fell upon the enemy warriors who now fled in full panic. The earth rumbled like a Bison stampede. The queen turned to the direction where the arrows had been launched, and saw many armored men riding on horseback with bowstrings pulled to their cheeks. They loosed again and more of the fleeing enemy fell, then the cavalry drew curved blades and hacked at the stragglers. The ships on the far shore had already begun pulling away. While the walled city was still in enemy hands, the main body of the army was safe from potential ambush.

"Califia!" Basilea's voice cried. The queen ran toward where she heard it, finally spotting the old woman after she shouted a few more times. She was kneeling on the ground, cradling a young Amazon archer who had been wounded in the shoulder by something that left black scarring around the edges of her armor. As the queen came closer, she gasped as she recognized the face of Arianna.

9

The *medikos* tent was a sprawling structure, stitched together from many smaller tents and resting upon poles hewn from the local forest. It was located far from the agora so that the wounded could recover in peace and quiet. The interior was essentially a long hallway filled with cots, with the occasional stool set aside for visitors. Califia sat upon one of those stools as Arianna woke from her long slumber at last.

"By Hera's eyebrows," Arianna said, "you look anxious enough to chew the tail off a bison."

"My love," Califia said, enveloping Arianna's right hand in both of her own. "I've been so worried."

"Just a scratch," Arianna said, grinning mischievously and squeezing the queen's hands in return. "The doctors say I should be able to return to the battlefield tonight."

A nearby physician looked up, eyes wide, from where she had been examining a woman with a heavily bandaged leg.

"We most certainly did *not!*" The woman exclaimed. She looked only a little younger than Basilea, but possessed a sturdier frame and a much less polite countenance. "You'll need at least a fortnight's rest, wicked girl!"

"You see the rudeness I've had to endure?" Arianna gestured to the doctor and gave an impish grin. "The medicine is worse than the injury."

The physician rolled her eyes and walked further down the corridor until she came to a woman with a bandage around her right arm. Califia turned back to her lover.

"You shouldn't antagonize them," she said, shaking her head.

"They've been wonderful, to tell the truth," Arianna smiled sleepily, which led Califia to believe she had taken medicine recently. She closed her eyes for a moment and the queen thought she might perhaps drift off to sleep, but then her eyelids fluttered upward and she tilted her head. "Am I really the sole source of all this anxiety?"

Califia sighed.

"Everyone is anxious today. The battle went to shit and no one knows what's coming next. The sultan probably sent Yakov to search for me."

"You don't have to stay," Arianna said, squeezing the queen's hand. "I understand you are very busy."

Califia squeezed her hand in return.

"I always have time for you. How are you feeling, really?"

"My shoulder aches but the doctors said the bullet just grazed it. For a while I really thought I was bound for Persephone's court."

Califia stifled a sniffle but could not stop her eyes from welling with tears. A single one escaped down her right cheek and she tried to smile through it.

"By Athena's hands, I'm glad you are alright."

"I don't feel the same, though."

"What?"

"I feel... different somehow. I've been trying to think of a way to describe it, but words fail me. If, for example, the doctor came and told me I would be dead by the end of this day, I don't think I would be terribly upset."

"Don't talk like that," Califia said, feeling the tears beginning to stream onto both cheeks. "You're going to get better. You'll be painting and sculpting and driving Basilea crazy with your blasphemies again very soon."

"It's not that I *want* to die," Arianna objected, looking upon Califia with a wounded expression. "It's just... if I were going to — *if!* — then... I don't know, it would just be something that is going to happen. Like next year's harvest or the snow melting in spring."

Califia's tears fell upon Arianna's bedsheets.

"Get some rest, my love," the queen said, wiping the excess tears from her cheeks.

"Probably a good idea," Arianna agreed, squeezing Califia's hand one last time before letting go and rolling onto her right shoulder.

Califia stood and started toward the exit, when she felt a hand on her shoulder. She turned to see Arianna's physician looking concerned.

"Are you alright, my queen?" the doctor asked.

"Arianna was just... saying some troubling things about death. Is she really going to be okay?"

"Physically, she will recover without too much lasting damage," the doctor turned her gaze toward where the artist snoozed. "The minds of the wounded sometimes venture to very dark places. Coming near to a violent death has something of a haunting effect."

"I see," the queen sniffed and blinked her stinging eyes. "Thank you for your care, doctor."

"Be sure you get some rest yourself," the doctor said, striding toward another of her patients without wasting another glance at the queen.

As Califia left the medicos tent, she suddenly felt an eerie presence watching her. From the corner of her eye, leaning against a nearby tree, she spotted a figure and nearly jumped out of her skin before realizing who it was.

"Califia!" Basilea hissed, wincing as the queen gave a start.

"What are you doing sneaking through the trees?" Califia said when she caught her breath.

"Surely a hero of the Amazons is not frightened of an old woman like me?" She said, laughing as she clapped a hand on the queen's shoulder.

"A hero of the…" Califia felt suspicious of her chief advisor. "What are you up to?"

"Solving a problem," Basilea looked around, checking for eavesdroppers as usual. "We need to capitalize on your recent success."

Califia wracked her brain for a moment to decipher what the old woman could possibly mean. She glared when she understood.

"You mean killing the warrior yesterday?"

"*And* saving the life of your sword-sister! That woman has been especially talkative this morning — she's practically campaigning on your behalf!"

"What is the point of this, Basilea?" Califia felt the beginnings of a headache as the sides of her head began to throb. "Yesterday was a disaster and my *victory* was mostly luck!"

"You mustn't say things like that!" Basilea interjected. "Your actions were heroic, end of story. It wasn't luck: it was *providence*."

"Was it providence that we cremated nine more of our sisters last night? By the triumvirs, so far all we have to show for ourselves is casualties!"

"Now you're just being cynical," Basilea said, smiling in a way that made Califia even more unsettled. "The sultan of the Gurkani has sent over a fine collection of illustrated books, the Osman sultan gave us five massive urns of *raki*, and the Egyptians gave us a small chest filled with coins!"

"How many do we need to buy back the lives of our lost sisters?"

"You're not seeing the big picture," Basilea paused to give a frustrated grunt. "Our allies think more highly of us than ever and it is all thanks to you! They honor us because of you and everyone in camp knows it!"

"The woman I love is laying in *there*," Califia pointed to the medicos tent. "She's wounded and she's sad and she's not acting like herself. Forgive me if all of this positioning and politicking seems a little *fucking pointless*."

"It has been many months since we discussed it," Basilea said, almost growling, "but we cannot allow the army to remain fully under the command of a *sorocide*."

Califia gasped at the word, which was one of the few real taboos of the Amazons. Murdering a fellow Amazon was already considered a high offense against the community and the gods; murdering one's own blood-sister was practically *unspeakable*.

"I will confess I have not thought about Malachea's alleged crime as much as I should have," Califia said. "We have only hearsay."

"Regardless," Basilea continued, "you have a duty to protect your people — *especially* from a power-hungry strategos. We must enhance your reputation in order to diminish *hers*."

"I do not wish to use the queenship as a cudgel against my personal enemies," Califia said. The idea of drawing all this attention to herself, of potentially creating a cult of personality, repulsed her more than Arianna's strange words.

"Consider this a *sacrifice* you must make for the sake of your people," Basilea said, looking somewhat sympathetic to Califia's plight.

"Fine," Califia sighed and crossed her arms.

"I knew you would see reason," Basilea grinned and took Califia by the shoulders. "Come with me. I have prepared a little surprise."

Califia followed the old woman through the woods toward the agora. She saw that many Amazons were already gathered there, most chatting with a few others or rushing about performing various camp-related errands. As they reached that flat space in the center of the Amazon camp, the queen felt herself suddenly hoisted into the air and nearly cried out as she was set upon the shoulders of two massive gorgons who enthusiastically marched around the agora's perimeter. Those present soon transformed into an audience and they cheered and clapped for their queen. Her gorgon escorts signaled for the cheers to grow louder. Amazons who had been on the periphery or even gathered outside the agora now wandered in and joined in the adulation.

What on earth is Basilea trying to do? Her handlers marched around the agora and various Californians touched her legs and the hem of her skirt. From one end of the agora, she heard some chanting her title over and over while on the other end, they were chanting something else.

Hero.

She spotted the polemarkos standing just beyond the rough boundaries of the agora, staring at Califia and shaking her head in disgust. Califia tapped the shoulder she sat upon, trying to signal them to let her down, but they did not notice. Eventually, they set her feet on the ground of their own accord and the queen rushed away, waving and smiling as cries of *Champion!* and *Hero!* and *Goddess!* floated in the air all around her. Yakov arrived as the chants were dying down, flanked by four Osman guards.

"The sultan would be honored if you would join him and other distinguished guests for a gathering," the emissary said, smiling at Califia as though he was proud of her. She glanced at the spot where she had seen Malachea before, but the polemarkos was gone. Whether she was about to ask the troublesome woman to join her or gloat that the sultan had chosen the queen over the commander-in-chief, Califia could not say. She nodded to Yakov and followed him out of the camp. Basilea came as well, and the sultan's representative noticed her but did nothing to dissuade her attendance.

"I bid you welcome, fair queen," said Sultan Bayezid, bowing to Califia as she appeared before his tent. The top of the structure had been opened completely, the large flaps reshaped and restaked so that the tent was now an open-air pavilion. Many other important-looking men in fine coats and fancy headwear were milling about, drinking from decorative goblets or earthen cups and chatting with one another while servants rushed to refill their libations at the slightest gesture.

"You honor me, great Sultan," Califia said, bowing along with Basilea. "Are you celebrating something?"

The sultan's eyes hardened and he clenched his jaw, but it only lasted a moment before he donned an amiable countenance once more.

"Yesterday was nearly a complete disaster," he said, blowing on his steaming cup. "We are celebrating the quick actions your people took in protecting us from humiliation and defeat."

"We are also celebrating your great victory over the Christian giant," said a man who approached them from a food table nearby. He was slender but not especially tall, though Califia had to admit that his face, even with its slim mustache and tiny chin beard, was handsome, as far as men's faces went. The intricate, geometric style on the hems of his fine gold-flecked red robe reminded her of Sultan Husayn and she assumed that he was also Gurkani.

"Queen Califia," Sultan Bayezid said, accidentally making a name of her titles, "may I present Alishir Nava'i, who serves at the pleasure of Sultan Husayn."

The newcomer bowed and Califia mirrored his gesture, secretly very pleased with herself that she had deduced correctly. He smiled warmly and took a sip from a silver goblet embossed with designs and accented around its dome with bright red gems.

"I understand we have your people to thank for chasing away the invaders yesterday?" She said to Alishir as Sultan Bayezid turned to chat with the leader of the Mamluks. Someone had informed her that the horse archers who arrived after she slew the giant were Gurkani.

"It is *you* who should be thanked, your highness," he said, in smooth, flowing Greek, "for your valiant efforts against our mutual foe. While it was my own army that gave chase, our foes were already routing by the time we arrived. I bore witness to this myself."

"You were *with* them?" Califia said, very impressed with his bravery. "Then I thank you for your aid, nonetheless."

He smiled and took another sip.

"Our labors were made easy by your hard work. If not

for your quick thinking and valiant fighting, many more of my warriors would be trying to restore their honor today."

Something about his phrasing made Califia curious.

"How do your people restore their honor?"

Alishir blinked as though perplexed at being asked such a simple question. Then he smiled warmly.

"Yakov has told me much of your people," he said, somewhat cryptically. "Meeting you in person, however, is quite different. For a failed warrior to restore his honor he must challenge an enemy to single combat."

Califia recalled the accounts of the siege of Illayos when great Amazon heroes would respond to such challenges from Greek warriors. The royal griffin Ektra was named after one such hero.

"I understand," the queen said. "For us, restoration is a much different process, but our foremothers understood the way of your warriors in this regard."

Alishir nodded politely at this, then took a hasty sip of his beverage. He looked at the queen, then quickly around the area as if preparing to share a secret. She braced herself for what she suspected would be some kind of grave news.

"If my question inspires offense, please forgive me," he said, speaking in hushed tones. "Is it true that you have banned men from your society?"

Califia smiled and breathed a small sigh of relief that he was only curious about something trivial.

"That is true," Califia said. "It must seem strange to you."

"I would make myself a liar if I said it did not," Alishir allowed, shaking his head at the oddity. "Still, I see the merit in keeping men out. As soon as one shows up, your people go off to war!"

Califia laughed at this jest a little more loudly than she meant to. She had not yet encountered such wit among any of their new allies.

"I often pray for peace," Alishir continued, "yet it seems that God keeps it just beyond my grasp. Though war is an unfortunate necessity, I do hate to see good people caught up in it because they did not understand what was happening."

Califia raised an eyebrow, wondering if perhaps his command of Greek was not as high as she originally believed.

"My own people are acquainted with war," she said, trying to find a way to agree with him, "but not to the same degree, I think, as the Osmans, Gurkani, and Egyptians."

"You should count that as a blessing," Alishir said darkly. "When my sultan claimed his birthright, his first task was to pacify those who rejected him. You would think our people would grow weary of war, but instead it has become routine for us."

Califia shuddered a little at the idea of war becoming intrinsic. It did not seem very long ago that she feared civil war might erupt during her own coronation.

"When I was elected as queen, there were many who objected," Califia said. "None took up arms against me, however. Such things have happened in times past, but it seems strange for us to imagine it now."

"Your people are truly blessed," Alishir sipped from his goblet.

"Yakov told me that your people were once enemies with the Osmans," Califia said.

"Not very long ago, if you must know the truth. The Mamluks— whom you call Egyptians— have likewise pursued disputes with their northern neighbors in times past. If not for this *jihad*, our three peoples would probably even now be plotting to destroy one another."

Alishir put his goblet on a nearby servant's tray. He locked eyes with her with an intensity that made her worry, for a moment, that he was going to try and kiss her.

"When you first arrived, Sultan Bayezid thought you were a nuisance," he said. "Now that you have proven your worth in battle, he may expect more of you."

"We did not come here to admire the view," Califia replied. "We are eager to do our part and bring this conflict to an end."

Alishir tilted his head in a way that the queen understood as skepticism.

"Be careful about what you offer to powerful men like the Osman sultan. He has a short memory for success and a long memory for failure."

Califia thought of Admiral Kemal and his longstanding conflict with Sultan Bayezid. She nodded, believing that she understood him at last. He seemed well-intentioned enough, so she resisted the tendency to feel insulted. *They think we are like children.*

She spoke with many others at this little gathering — some high-ranking Osman lords called *pashas* as well as one of General Al-Khulani's marshals — and availed herself of the food and drink. Basilea kept her distance, which seemed wise given that Califia still felt vaguely irritated at her for planning the ridiculous celebration at the agora without her knowledge. As night began to fall, she spoke with the Osman sultan once more.

"I hope we can count on your people's help in constructing new ramps and other siege engines," he said, grabbing some dates from a nearby tray. "Yakov said that you all have a knack for engineering."

Califia was taken aback by this compliment and indeed the entire party was making her head spin. Just a few days before she had been the leader of an unwanted army, while today she was a mighty hero worthy of flattery and adulation.

"We are happy to help wherever we can," she replied, looking for Basilea only to realize she had lost track of the woman. "I don't have much of a head for machines and gears, but many among our number are extremely clever in that regard."

"Splendid, splendid," the sultan said, popping a few dates into his mouth and nodding.

The sultan smiled at her amiably but she felt a familiar twinge in the back of her mind — an instinctual certainty that she had just been *tricked*. Her stomach clenched into a hard fist as her mind caught up to her instincts. By agreeing to help with the construction of new siege equipment, she had just committed them to stay at least another month. *Possibly longer.*

She cursed herself for a fool. The war council had not even convened since yesterday's battle, so she had no idea what the strategoses were thinking, much less the *people*, who may very well resent their queen volunteering their labor.

"Your majesty," Califia said, just as the sultan seemed ready to turn aside and take his leave of her. "How long might it take to build these new engines?"

"Many hands will make the effort much shorter," the sultan replied. "I think two months is a likely timespan."

The queen took in a deep breath, closing her eyes for a moment and trying to imagine two long months of sitting in camp while her army grew ever more discontented. She had the upper hand against Malachea for now, but how long would that last?

She would be remembered as the Califia who sold them as slaves to Osman overlords and the brave polemarkos Malachea would challenge her immediately upon their return and wrench the queenship from her hand.

I will have accomplished none of the goals I had when I first thought of becoming queen.

The sultan had fully turned away by this point and Basilea returned to her side. The queen's mind raced as she tried to conceive some way she might shorten the commitment she had just agreed to, a quick-fix to undo the mistake she had just made. The polemarkos technically commanded the army. What could she do as a mere queen? With that thought, she realized she still had one advantage over Malachea. *It is time to use it.*

"Your majesty!" She shouted, a little too loudly as it made the Osman sovereign start. "What if this siege could be ended sooner?"

The sultan turned toward her, his face intrigued. *The polemarkos may command the army, but she is no queen.* Califia told him the idea she had cobbled together in the last few moments. She felt as if this entire journey might indeed be the work of providence after all.

****

Convincing the Sultan and his advisers had been easier than she expected, thanks in large part to Yakov's eyewitness testimony. The War Council was a little displeased that the queen had once more acted independently of their purview, but Basilea was quick to point out that the queen was well within her rights. They ratified the decision, though Malachea and Olympia abstained.

The next three days were a whirlwind of activity as the Amazons helped the rest of the camp take precautions for the day of the battle. They helped build extensive awnings to conceal the allied troops, and helped repair the salvageable ramps and construct new ladders with which the assault teams could seize the walls. If this plan worked, there would be no need to spend two months building a full contingent of ramps, ladders, and towers.

On the fifth day since the nearly-disastrous assault, Califia once more joined Sultan Bayezid, Sultan Husayn, and General Al-Khulani on the shaded pavilion overlooking the battlefield. Basilea stood by her side, dressed in gold griffinsteel armor. The troops below huddled beneath the awnings and only the siege ramps and ladders could be seen from the hillock. One band of armored soldiers stood in the open, their golden armor gleaming in the morning sun.

Malachea was easy to spot, her griffin skull helm distinct even from this distance. The other two strategoses, Traesta and Olympia, were likewise easily found because of the large plumes they wore in their helms to distinguish their office.

"Take a moment," Basilea told her, placing her hand gently against the crook of the queen's elbow. "Reach out to the creatures first without drawing the dagger."

"I've never done that before," Califia said, her hand drifting toward the magic weapon. "I didn't even know it could be done."

"The dagger assists in bonding the griffins to its bearer," Basilea explained, "but that bond exists apart from the implement itself."

"Are you still bonded to the creatures?"

"For the first few months of your ascension, I felt an occasional sensation, but the bond they had with me has since faded."

Califia closed her eyes, trying to reach out with her thoughts to the creatures in their kennels. She imagined a large crabapple tree with thousands of spring blossoms floating to the ground, dancing in the sunshine as they drifted around. Still the creatures did not respond.

"I have a long way to go," the queen said, sighing.

"As do we all," Basilea said in a far-away voice. She grinned at Califia and nodded toward the item hanging on her belt.

The queen drew the triumvir dagger. She reached out to them now through the dagger's connection, hoping to feel the usual eagerness and joy. Instead, she felt a prickling, stabbing sensation which reminded her of a numb limb when it recovers its circulation.

She gazed at the city walls, those monstrosities of stone, and then turned toward Basilea, who was holding the banner expectantly. She nodded to the former queen who stepped out from beneath the shelter, held the banner by its hilt so it was fully lofted in the air, and waved it back and forth with vigor.

She could feel their relief in finally being let loose upon the world and the elation that they were no longer prisoners. She was uncertain whether they felt the sensation of apology she was trying to send to them, so enraptured were they in their newfound freedom.

"Whenever you are ready, your highness," Sultan Bayezid said, sipping a cup of nectar.

The queen closed her eyes and reached out.

I am here.

A few griffins responded with simple acknowledgments. She paused, calmed herself once more and tried again.

I am here.

A much more robust set of responses flooded into her mind.

So are we.

What do you want?

I do not like my cage.

I want to fly!

Califia smiled. The creatures once given as a gift from the triumvirate for the protection of their people would now help avenge the foremothers.

To the walls, she commanded through her mind. *Kill all that you find there.*

The queen felt the griffins rouse themselves. The tension in her own muscles disappeared as they stretched their wings and backs. She had to open her eyes and steady herself as they swiftly took to the air, flapping their cramped wings with an eager ferocity.

"They are coming," Califia said, looking above to spot their flying mass but forgetting that they were covered by a large umbrella for both shade and the safety of the Sultans and General Al-Khulani. Soon after, she spotted massive wings just past the horizon of the enormous parasol, a narrow line of catbirds which quickly grew into a broad, dark column of feathers, talons, and beaks.

"God preserve us," Sultan Bayezid said, his mouth gaping afterward like a trout.

"How are they?" Basilea asked.

"Hungry," Califia said. "Eager and hungry."

"Strange," the former queen said, tilting her head. "They have been fed twice a day just as they would be at home."

"Hungry might not be the right word," Califia felt an

incredible surge of murderous glee as the creatures neared the inner wall. "It is not just a hunger for food, but a hunger to *kill*."

"Is something wrong?" Sultan Husayn asked, peering through his magnifying lenses and clearly trying to keep the tool from trembling in his hand. Califia realized that the Gurkani Sultan's suspicion had been piqued by the fact that she and Basilea had been speaking the Californian tongue.

"Apologies, your majesty," Califia said, speaking the Osman language once more. She took her hand from the hilt of the triumvir dagger, leaving the griffins to themselves for now so she could focus on her fellow national leaders. "The creatures are very eager to do violence."

"Good, good," he replied, his voice afflicted with just the slightest tremor. The queen's heart warmed with the vindication that this decision had been correct. Just seeing the griffins in flight was enough to make these great rulers of vast empires tremble in abject terror.

The griffins swooped upon the crusaders who manned the inner walls, plunging onto the leftmost section of the fortifications and spreading quickly toward the right.

In spite of the considerable distance, Califia and all those in the Sultan's pavilion could hear panicked shouts and shrieks from the crusaders on the wall. Alishir handed Califia a telescope and she felt ill at the sight of the ensuing carnage. A man desperately holding a snarling griffin at bay with a pike was attacked from behind. A cannoneer howled as one of the monsters tore his forearm from his elbow, snapping it like a twig. A warrior with a two-handed sword swiped at one of the creatures still airborne but it dodged and he fell from the wall into the trench below and crumpled in a sickening heap.

"Voracious brutes, aren't they?" Said General Al-Khulani. He winced as he peered through his scope, then grinned and lightly chuckled.

As the griffins abandoned the leftmost sections of the walls and swarmed upon the center, Califia peered hard through her scope to spot survivors and found none. A chill slithered down her spine as she surveyed the aftermath; the blood that slicked the walls could almost be mistaken for red paint if not for the severed limbs, abandoned weapons, and loose feathers.

Califia wrapped her fingers around the dagger's hilt and reached out to her creatures through the magic bond. The griffins were unanimous in their single-minded pursuit of carnage. They were not feeding— they were feasting. She brushed her hand against her chin, certain she felt some warm liquid dripping out and yet her hand remained dry. She winced as she felt her fingernails ripping away some plate armor before plunging into some poor warrior's guts.

"Remarkable," said Sultan Hussayn, wincing as he watched the battle unfold with his conjoined magnifying lenses. The queen nodded and tried to conceal the profound disturbance she felt as the beasts tore limbs and ripped throats.

"I would hate to be in the path of such a creature," Sultan Bayezid remarked, smiling with great amusement at his enemy's misfortune.

Califia nodded, trying to put such thoughts out of her head. Suddenly she pictured herself stabbing the sultans and the general, ripping their chests open, and devouring their organs as they screamed and flailed. She gasped and took her hand from the triumvir dagger.

"Are you alright?" Basilea asked, having noticed the

queen's distress.

"They are overwhelming me," Califia said. "Gods, but they are ferocious."

Basilea stiffened and the queen noticed. The old woman gave her a worried look.

"Some of the chronicles tell of an attempted invasion by mainlanders along our northern borders, possibly the Kashaya. It was written that when those enemies landed a large army on our land that the griffins behaved like sharks swarming a dead whale, ripping and tearing and gorging themselves beyond reason."

"How did they manage to regain control of the creatures?" Califia failed to keep the tremor out of her voice as her heart felt the icy grip of fear.

"They had to wait until the griffins had eaten their fill," Basilea said. "Only when every enemy was dead and they were sated did the creatures listen to the Califia of the time."

"Hera's eyes," Califia let out a lungful of air which she didn't realize she'd been holding. "Our allies will just have to wait a little longer."

She took a breath and tried to center her wildly flailing emotions. *Let them have their fun and then we can rein them in.*

"My queen!" Basilea cried suddenly. She looked to where the old woman pointed and gasped. From beneath one of the awnings below, a division of Osman soldiers suddenly emerged carrying ladders. The troops from under the neighboring awning likewise left the shelter of the canopies and raced toward the city as quickly as their legs could carry them.

From far to her left, the queen heard a noise that froze her heart. The groan of timbers, the squeak of wheels. Like a great distant wave lumbers toward shore, one of the siege ramps on the army's left wing begin to slowly roll toward the outer walls on that city's side. As Califia stared, disbelieving what she was seeing, the next closest ramp likewise began to slowly be shoved toward the undefended red walls of Constantinopolis.

"Get them back!" Califia pleaded with Sultan Bayezid. "They are charging too soon!"

The Sultan waved his hand and a message runner sprinted quickly over. He told him the message and the young boy mounted a swift horse and galloped quickly out of sight. She tried to draw the triumvir dagger but as her fingers made contact with the hilt, her mind flooded with horrific images of violence and bloodshed.

"Try reaching out to them without the dagger," Basilea said, gasping as the Osman ladders were propped up against the far left side of the walls.

Califia closed her eyes and tried to focus on the catbirds. At the edges of her consciousness, she felt their anger, their confusion, and their single-minded devotion to their mission. *Kill all men. Kill all men.*

The first of the Osmans was nearly at the top of the wall by now, and no matter how she attempted to plead with them, the griffins would not return.

"Your majesties!" Yakov called, pointing to the leftmost walls.

Sultan Husayn turned his dual scopes toward Yakov's finger. "Those greedy sons of dogs!"

Sultan Bayezid took his scope away from his eye and looked at Califia with a red face.

"Now would be a good time to send your animals back to their cages," he said, with a slight tremor in his voice.

"I am sorry, your majesty," Califia said, once more wincing as she tried to draw the dagger. "I don't think I can."

10

"Your Majesties," Califia said, turning to the Sultans and the General, "You must pull your troops back now!"

The allied commanders relayed orders through nearby runners who informed the signalmen who held large banners on the hill but by the time the banners began waving, four more siege ramps had begun their slow crawl across the battlefield.

She looked at the triumvir dagger and saw that the red gem which usually shined clear and strong was animated only by a weak light which periodically winked out entirely. Califia closed her eyes and gripped the weapon, feeling the connection open in her heart and mind. Their rage and bloodlust churned within her as they slashed their way through the last of the defenders on the wall. She closed her eyes.

Return.

The queen felt a small tickle of confirmation, and believed that some of the creatures had heard her. She opened her eyes to see the gem was shining a little bit brighter, but still shy of its usual brilliance. She pushed past the frustration she felt and focused her mind on them once more.

Return.

A slightly greater confirmation this time, as if more of the creatures were joining the responsive group. The gem grew brighter but still winked like a spent candle. She glanced below and saw that the leftmost group of soldiers were nearly at the outer wall and soon would begin piling over.

Return!

She could feel many responding and even flapping their way off of the wall and starting to fly back to the kennels. Far below, she heard the siege ramp slam into place against the outer wall and heard a great cheer from the men who began charging over it. The griffins who had started flying toward Califia looked toward the sound.

The queen gasped as one of the returning griffins looped about and dove straight toward the advancing Osmans who were raising ladders to climb the city's inner walls. She begged, pleaded through the triumvir dagger for the creatures to return swiftly but she could feel her desperation and fear weakening the bond and making it easier for the griffins to ignore her.

A diving griffin scooped up two of the allied soldiers, screaming and flailing, in its claws. It rose high above the inner walls before tossing both soldiers into the air and letting them fall to their deaths. Another thump sounded from the wall as the next ramp struck home and its soldiers charged over, apparently unable to see what was happening to their fellows in the section immediately to their left. They raised the ladders and scaled quickly, just as their neighbors were struck by two more griffins who tore into their ranks.

"Those monsters are killing my men!" Sultan Bayezid

shouted, his cheeks crimson. "Call them back, damn them!"

"Your men charged too early," Basilea shouted back. Califia tried once more to summon the creatures but it was like trying to convince a stone to transform into a potato. She wasn't certain whether they were ignoring her on purpose or if their frenzy had somehow made them unable to hear her call. Her heart leapt with hope as she saw the second group whose ramp had touched the outer walls successfully climb onto the taller inner wall, shouting their celebrations as they reached the walkway that ran along the wall.

She looked toward the rightward walls, where the defenders had made their last stand and the beasts had just silenced the final enemy. Sitting triumphant atop the rightmost walls, they snapped their heads toward the newly arrived soldiers on the wall behind them and alighted in a great cloud of blood and feathers and death.

The Sultans and the general were all speaking at once, demanding that she accomplish the very task which she was attempting. She closed her eyes and blocked them out, focusing on the griffins.

Get back here. Now!

A few of the catbirds' heads turned toward her, and she could feel some alarm through their connection which she initially believed was a good sign. But the heads turned back to the Osman, Gurkani, and Mamluk soldiers being massacred on the walls and they continued their work unabated.

You will return or I will punish you.

This got their attention, but only for a moment. Another company of soldiers was mounting one of the center sections of the inner wall and the flock turned once more toward the new arrivals as their former quarry fled back toward the safety of the hides.

From the allied lines, horns began blowing a variety of patterns and rhythms. Califia believed that the messengers carrying the Sultans' orders had finally passed the message along to those leading on the ground. Unfortunately, these patterns and cacophonous blasts created a chaotic symphony which only sowed confusion in the ranks of soldiers below. Some began abandoning the walls right as others were charging onto them, all the while the griffins grabbed, tore, and snapped at any living creature in sight.

"What is happening out there?" Shouted Malachea's voice from a little below them on the hill. She was marching up with Traesta, Olympia, and several captains in tow.

"They've gone mad," Califia said, fighting back tears. "We've tried to recall them but the stubborn beasts refuse to listen."

Malachea borrowed Basilea's scope and peered through it for a moment, waving it around as if scanning the griffin flock. She paused for a moment, squinted harder, then pointed a finger toward the direction of her scope.

"There is Elena, my mount," the polemarkos said, tracing her finger around as she followed the creature's dives and swoops. "She's larger than many of the others, they listen to her. Her wings have dark spots underneath and her talons are pitch black."

"What am I supposed to do?" Califia said, frustrated at Malachea's meddling.

"Think of her, focus on her," Basilea said. "Call her by name, look at her while you do. Tell her Malachea is here and waiting. You," she pointed at one of the captains, "have the polemarkos' saddle brought up as quickly as you can."

The captain sprinted down the hill as if her hair was on fire.

Califia centered herself, closed her eyes, pictured the large catbird with its dark spotted underwings, its black talons, and pictured Malachea riding upon it. She gripped the dagger's hilt.

Elena.

She felt something, not the usual surge of interest as she had experienced before, but more like a bolt of attention.

Elena, Malachea needs you.

A griffin somewhere along the wall shrieked loudly and in the same moment, Califia felt the sensation of assent. One of the larger griffins broke away from the group along the wall and soared toward the pavilion. Califia sent her thanks through the dagger. The captain had returned with two grooms who carried the polemarkos' saddle.

Elena landed on the hill near the pavilion and it was only then that Califia realized the Sultans, the general, and their entire staff had all abandoned the pavilion at the creature's approach. The grooms saddled it quickly and Malachea made some final adjustments to the fore-cinch that wrapped around the beast's chest.

As Malachea flew away, Califia used the same technique and summoned Ektra, her own mount. Basilea sent for the queen's saddle and the polemarkos arrived at the wall just as they were finishing tying the mountings onto the queen's griffin.

Malachea flew among the other griffins, shouting as her mount squawked and shrieked. The creatures ignored her, each focusing with rapt attention upon the prey before them. An Osman soldier tried to face one down with a pike and shield; the griffin he resisted snapped his spear in half and slashed his face with its razor-edged talons, shredding the man's helm and head. A Mamluk archer attempted to loose an arrow into one of the creatures; when the shot went wide, the griffin snapped his right arm off.

The queen had nearly finished strapping herself into the saddle when things somehow got worse; while Malachea was flying and shouting, some of the griffins that she flew near began swooping close to her. They repeated this a few times and then one of the creatures slashed at the polemarkos' shoulder. Another took a swipe at her feet. Then her head.

Califia tapped Ektra on her shoulder and the beast leaped into the air, flapping hard and rising fast. She flew toward Malachea, who was shouting and cursing and ducking as the griffins around her slashed and shrieked. *I'm coming, polemarkos.* As the queen neared the wall, three of the beasts who had been swarming the Osman attackers suddenly turned in the air and raced toward Malachea, their talons outstretched and gleaming.

The polemarkos braced herself, hunching over the saddle and holding fast as her mount rolled to protect her. Ektra tucked her wings and entered a shallow dive toward the embattled Malachea, arriving just as the beasts were nearly upon them. Califia waved the triumvir dagger, shooing the creatures away like bothersome flies. Now that she was in the air alongside them, she was almost overwhelmed by their rage, their eagerness to shed blood and tear flesh.

They responded, she realized. Being closer to the creatures must make the connection stronger. The distraction of so much fresh prey was overpowering her ability to command them, but now that she was in their midst, she couldn't be ignored. She held the dagger high, the red gem gleaming like the sunrise.

A new boldness surging through her bones, the queen flew toward the nearest griffin and focused on it, holding the dagger and trying her best to think of love, safety, and the kennel. The creature turned its head and looked her in the eye. It tilted its head as it as if it didn't recognize her. Her heart began to plummet, certain that the griffin would soon go back to its maiming, when it suddenly broke away from its fellows pillaging the wall and flew toward the waiting Californians. The queen watched as the beast neared the kennels and was promptly herded inside. The handlers closed the door and tossed in some salted meat. *One so far,* she thought, ducking as one of the beasts dove very close to Ektra's wings.

"Califia!" the polemarkos called, her mount hovering nearby. She pointed to the one that had just swooped close to the queen and then pulled at Elena's reins to chase the beast down. The queen followed closely, gripping the dagger's hilt and focusing. As if confirming that it heard her, the creature turned its head aside and shrieked. She could feel anger and irritation from the beast, who dove suddenly for the wall. Califia and Malachea dove after it, the queen doing her best to give the errant creature some sense of calm and security.

Just as it neared the soldiers on the wall, who wore the black scale mail that marked them as Gurkani, the beast banked sharply away at the last moment. Ektra strained through the sharp turn and the queen's knuckles went white from gripping the reins.

The griffin they were pursuing gave an enraged shriek, so angry that Califia could feel it through their shared connection, but nonetheless broke from its attack and flew toward the kennels.

Something whistled past the queen's head. She ducked and then turned her head carefully toward the direction they came from, spotting holes in the walls of the tall buildings behind the walls. As she looked, another bolt shot out but it went wide.

She guided Ektra back from the walls to take them out of range of the hateful missiles. While surveying the walls, however, her blood froze as she spotted a lone assault division of Osman troops who had taken the far right side of the walls, the last of their soldiers climbing the ladders and occupying the rightmost section. They celebrated their conquest with trilling shouts that would have otherwise sounded to Califia like a pleasant chorus of a flock of starlings.

The griffins coalesced high in the air as one single, relentless mass and then crashed like a waterfall upon the celebrating soldiers. Shrieks of pain and panic now echoed throughout the city and beyond. Califia and Malachea spurred their mounts to pursue, though the queen noticed that Ektra was already breathing heavily. Califia was exhausted. She tried to press through it. *I'll rest when the danger has passed.*

As if they knew what the two Californians were planning, two pairs of griffins broke from the walls and flew straight toward the queen and the polemarkos, screeching as they stretched out their razor talons. Ektra broke at the last moment, rapidly spinning in a roll while the queen clung tightly. Both of her assailants slashed at her griffin as they passed overhead, but neither landed a blow.

Califia turned around to pursue them, gripping the dagger in one hand and Ektra's reins with the other. *Perhaps I can convince both of them*, she thought, at once directing her attention toward the errant birds and straining to conceive images of trust, love, and returning to the kennel. One griffin acquiesced immediately, flying a little higher and then flapping straight toward the Californians. The other shrieked and flipped quickly around, charging once more.

Ektra dodged again, but Califia felt a disturbing twinge of extra confidence from the beast. It was expecting this dodge, and as Ektra rolled beneath her assailant, the other griffin shoved her toward the ground. For a moment, the queen was certain that she was falling, that at any moment her skull would smash to pieces against the ground like an overripe melon. Ektra quickly corrected and they were comfortably aloft once more, but Califia's entire body clenched up tight, her muscles becoming hard as bone.

She glanced toward Malachea to see that she was evading her attackers as she cursed and shouted. The queen looked toward the griffin they were chasing and from it she felt anger, resentment, and despair.

Offering the creature vague promises of comfort and rest wasn't working, so Califia decided to try a different tactic. She thought about Arianna, about the pain that she felt when her lover had said hurtful words, how much she missed lying beside her at night and feeling her close in the morning. The creature slowed for a moment, then turned its head toward the queen, a gleam of recognition in its eyes. The queen sensed feelings of sadness and regret.

The creature flew toward the waiting Amazons and their kennels. Califia wiped the tears from her eyes; she was now certain that this could be put right. There was still time for the walls to be conquered, taking the rest of the city would be up to their allies. They could end this war and return home as heroes. She would be known as the queen who avenged the foremothers. It was *destiny*.

From somewhere to her right, Califia heard Malachea scream and curse. She turned to see that the polemarkos was being attacked by two circling griffins working as a team, slashing at Elena's wings and grabbing at her back legs in turn. One lurched for the mount's head and the other slashed toward its right wing. Elena cleverly rolled to evade them. Malachea cried out in the middle of the maneuver, and Califia soon saw the reason; one of the attacking griffins had slashed through some of the polemarkos' safety straps. Elena lurched around as Malachea hung from her by one remaining strap and both mount and rider tumbled toward the unforgiving ground.

Califia urged Ektra into a dive, her stomach turning as Malachea and her mount circled one another, flailing as they fell. The queen realized that the polemarkos' mount was trying to angle itself underneath her in a way that would swing her back into the saddle. The ground seemed to rush toward them, the queen felt bile rising in her throat, then Elena curled under Malachea and swooped quickly upward. They were not saved yet; they were now in the space between the inner and outer walls and the momentum of the fall carried them forward. Just as Califia believed they were about to smash themselves against the shorter outer wall, Elena beat her wings fast and hard, lofting them just over the crest of the battlement.

Through the dagger, Califia could feel Elena's exhaustion. The beast was being crushed under the weight of overwork. Just after they passed the wall, they descended swiftly. *Too swiftly*. Elena's legs scrambled against the ground as she attempted to land, but they crumpled beneath her and Malachea bounced out of the saddle as they came to the ground.

Don't be dead don't be dead. Califia ushered Ektra safely to the ground near where the pair had crashed and unfastened her safety straps before her mount was fully on the ground. She leapt from the saddle and sprinted to where the polemarkos lay.

"Malachea!" she cried, her heart overwhelmed at the sight of the lean, muscled, seemingly invincible bitch of battle laying on the ground cradling her left arm and breathing heavily.

"Check... Elena..." she said, wincing as she choked the words out.

Califia leaned over and looked into the eyes of the downed griffin. The creature was breathing heavily, but it perked up its head at the sight of the queen. She patted its forehead, smoothing its soft feathers as tears rolled down her cheeks. She looked toward the cloud of griffins still flying, slashing, and biting at the allied forces.

All along the rightmost sections of the wall, men screamed and fought and bled and died as the griffins' merciless attack rained down upon them. Men fell to the ground below, shrieking and flailing as they scrambled to find purchase in the empty air. From where she stood on the ground, the spray of blood looked almost like morning mist at sunrise. A chorus of panicked shrieks filled Califia's ears and she shuddered.

"My queen, we are here."

Califia turned at the sound of Traesta's voice, startled to see the entire division of Amazons had joined her on the field. The noise of the dying soldiers above had masked their approach, and the queen nearly wept with relief. *Time for that later.*

"Take the polemarkos to the medicos tent," Califia said, "and see to Elena as well, make sure the wranglers check her very closely for injuries."

Traesta signaled to a few of the troops and they cut Malachea's remaining safety strap with a dagger and carried her from the field. A few more coaxed Elena to her feet and she limped away.

The queen looked at Traesta, then at the walls, then to the great flock of griffins making quick work of the assault crew, who were now fleeing down the ladders which they had worked so hard to erect. Along the outer walls the siege ramps and ladders had been abandoned in the mad rush to flee from the bloody death that had awaited those who took the walls.

"What would you have us do, my queen?" Olympia asked, gazing at the horror on the wall.

"We need to get them down, but I don't know how," Califia admitted.

"We saw two at least fly back to their kennels," Traesta said, putting her hand on the queen's shoulder. "How did you manage to convince them?"

"That takes too long," Califia said. When Traesta and Olympia met her gaze with expectant looks, she continued. "I had to focus on them individually, flying close with Ektra, who is now exhausted."

"I see Hypolita!" said one young woman, whom the queen guessed was no older than twenty. She smiled as she said this to her neighboring soldier, a fond smile of adoration. Califia remembered how thinking of Arianna had helped her break through to the second griffin she had convinced to return.

"Tell me about Hypolita," Califia commanded the woman, who looked at the queen with large, startled eyes. The queen subtly gripped the hilt of the triumvir dagger.

"I, uh…" she began, sputtering a little. "She has beautiful feathers— they are black with deep purple.

Sometimes when she needs a rest from patrolling I sit against her and read poetry."

Califia felt a wave of relief as she detected the faintest bit of recognition and even longing through the dagger's connection. She pictured the woman leaning against the dark bird, purple highlights and all, the both of them beneath an old cypress tree staring out from the coast. More emotions trickled from the catbird — happiness, contentment, peace. *It is working.*

"Can you recite any of the poems now?" The queen asked.

As the young woman recited line and verse, one of the beasts in the distance suddenly departed the wall, flying toward them and circling the Amazons, cooing happily. *Return.* The creature obeyed, flying toward the kennels as it transmitted feelings of joy and happiness through the triumvir dagger.

"Everyone who serves in cavalry, step forward!" Olympia called. About a hundred Amazons came in front of the formation, laying down their spears as they prepared to help call their friends home

"Who is next?" Califia asked, sighing heavily as she tried not to think about how much longer this was going to take. By now the last of the allied warriors had abandoned the walls, and the queen's sole concern was getting the creatures back where they belonged.

One by one, Califia and the riders coaxed each of the griffins to return to their cages without further incident. By the time the final creature returned, the sky was quickly turning dark. The Amazon army marched back to the siege camp as crusaders cautiously retook the inner walls, a few offering jeers and insults (the queen assumed, as she didn't understand any of their languages) as the women walked away exhausted.

As they approached the camp, the smells and wafts of smoke floating up from various quarters of the site told her that their allies were already busy with dinner and likely just as eager as the Amazons to forget this ill-fortuned day. She paused to take a last look at Constantinopolis. Sunset painted the distant western skies a bright orange which reflected on the surface of the great city walls. If she squinted, Califia could almost pretend the city which housed the foremothers' great enemy was being razed to the ground.

Part III: The Challenge

11

What now?

The question had been rolling through the back of Califia's mind since the last griffin was put back into its kennel. She remembered Olympia's advice on California so many months before— *Always be thinking of what may come next.* She had done her best to anticipate the situation and stay one step ahead of Malachea. Her best had failed.

The war council meeting extended late into the evening without Malachea. The injured polemarkos needed to recover from her wounds and Califia felt guilty that she had caused Malachea to be hurt in the first place.

While Califia expected heated exchanges and recriminations, instead it seemed that the strategoses were too exhausted to engage in such distractions. The question of what to do next loomed over them like an icy shadow. Olympia suggested making an official apology to their allies, whom they had undeniably failed. Although her original recommendation was that Califia *alone* apologize to the Osmans, Gurkani, and Mamluks, Traesta convinced her that the entire council needed to participate because it was important to present a united front. The queen was too exhausted to try to parse whether this was meant as a criticism of Califia's eagerness to utilize the griffins.

She fell asleep late and was awakened early, a terrible combination even under ideal circumstances. The council gathered shortly after first light and marched toward the Osman camp. They planned to start with the Osmans and then travel later to the Gurkani and the Mamluks but when they arrived at Sultan Bayezid's tent they found that a meeting was already taking place. The tent was still deployed as an open structure and Califia immediately spotted Alishir, Yakov, and General Al-Khulani standing and loudly deliberating among the many other attendants in bright robes which were intricately embroidered.

A hush fell on the assembly as the Amazons approached and they all turned toward the newcomers. Their expressions were mixed but most looked some variety of unhappy. Anger, fear, and disappointment were all clearly displayed as Califia and her strategoses marched toward them until their feet rested upon the carpet.

"We have come to offer apology," Califia said, setting her knees upon the rug. She placed her hands on the ground in front of her in the manner she had observed from the sultan's servants. There had been vigorous debate among the war council over whether she ought to bow, but they eventually came to a consensus that the blood of the Osman army demanded humility.

"Why does the queen bow," Sultan Bayezid said, standing from his cushion, "while her generals stand?"

Califia rose.

"It is our custom, great sultan, for the queen to take such matters upon herself," she said, being sure to use the flattering language that the war council had also agreed upon. "In this particular instance, I was directly at fault."

"On that we agree," said the sultan, pacing with his hands clasped behind his back. He stopped before Califia and looked her in the eye. "Do you have *any* idea how many of my soldiers your monsters killed yesterday?"

The queen had to reject the answer that came first to her mind. *They would all still be alive if they had not so greedily charged the walls before it was time.* Instead, she looked at the ground.

"How many?"

"Two hundred and thirty-eight!" he shouted, continuing his pacing. "And *those* were just mine. The Gurkani lost one hundred fifty-six while the Egyptians lost over two hundred and fifty!"

Califia winced every time he recited a number. If the Amazons suffered these losses, everyone in their army would be dead.

She looked to the other representatives of the allied factions. Alishir, the Gurkani poet who had tried to warn her about the sultan's machinations, appeared stone-faced and disappointed. General Al-Khulani looked as though he was prepared to draw his sword and decapitate her on the spot. The only friendly face was Yakov's, and even he appeared extremely solemn.

"My sultan is extremely upset by this turn of events," Alishir said. "He awoke with a terrible ailment of the stomach which keeps him in constant pain."

"Please pass along my apology," Califia nodded to him but he looked away.

"The creatures should be put to death!" Al-Khulani said, jabbing his finger at the queen. "It is bad enough they are combined from two *haram* beasts - having them on the battlefield risks the wrath of God!"

His words struck Califia as odd until she remembered what Yakov had told her about dietary customs.

"God will only be angry with us if we *eat* one of them," Alishir said, turning to the Mamluk general. "They do us no harm by their mere existence."

"Do not lecture me on the tenets of Islam, book-fucker!" the general shouted, placing a hand on the hilt of his sword. "I did not come here to debate the Koran!"

"You would need to actually *read* a book in order to debate it," Alishir replied, grinning at his own cleverness.

"Enough!" Sultan Bayezid said, turning on the two of them. They both stiffened visibly at his outburst. Califia thought she knew the reason; they were not subjects of the Osman sultan, therefore he had no right to give them orders. A tense moment followed but it quickly passed as both men rolled their eyes. The sultan turned his attention back onto Califia.

"Because of yesterday's disaster," he said, pacing once more, "I will be forced to call upon other subjects to reinforce this army, lest we all be run off the peninsula by Christian raiders!"

"I understand," Califia said. "We will continue to support this effort in any way we can. In California, we do not merely apologize, but also seek to repair whatever damage has been caused. Nothing can bring back the lost soldiers, but we will do our best to ensure they did not die in vain."

Alishir looked satisfied. General Al-Khulani still ground his teeth, but nodded grudgingly. Sultan Bayezid pursed his lips, still clearly unhappy. Just as she feared he was going to start another round of recriminations, he turned toward Yakov.

"Go tell the guards that I need an escort, then return. You are coming with me."

The man bowed, then sprinted away from the tent toward a group of heavily armored Osman soldiers who carried halberds. The sultan turned back to Califia.

"You will lead me to your camp," he said. "I want to see these creatures for myself."

"We are only too happy to welcome you," Califia replied, waiting until he turned away before giving the strategoses a worried glance. Olympia took a deep breath and let out an annoyed sigh. Traesta shrugged.

As they trekked through the Osman camp, Alishir caught up with Califia and walked beside her in silence for several steps. As the others in their group began conversing, the Gurkani nobleman cleared his throat.

"I apologize for my outburst earlier," he said, giving a slight bow of his head as they walked along. "I have never been fond of Al-Khulani, but it was improper to shame him like that."

"I appreciated the thought," Califia replied, glancing behind them to see the Mamluk general walking toward the rear with a scowl seemingly carved into his face.

"He wears a face of anger, hoping we won't notice his fear," Alishir kept his voice low in spite of the fact that the section of camp they walked through now was especially noisy. "Sultan Bayezid is also frightened, and my own sultan as well."

Califia almost stopped in her tracks but Alishir gently placed his hand on the corner of her elbow and urged her to keep moving. It occurred to her that he might be risking something by being this frank with her, and that she ought to do whatever she could to protect him.

"The griffins," Califia said. "You are all frightened of the griffins."

"Cannons and guns are horrific weapons," he said, shaking his head, "but the devastation wrought by your beasts felt like an act of God. It is one thing to hear a scary story of a deadly monster who can casually rip men to pieces; seeing it for ourselves has changed how we see your people, and you."

"I had the distinct impression," the queen said, "that the sultan did not think highly of us when we first arrived."

"When you saved the army after the failed assault, you earned his respect and gratitude. He… *we* thought of you as equals. Now, however, it has begun to creep into his mind, and into *ours*, that your people might be more powerful than we are."

Once more Califia felt her head swim at how utterly alien these people were compared to the Amazons. The last time they spoke, Alishir mentioned that the Osmans, Mamluks, and Gurkani had been longtime enemies before the crusaders seized Constantinopolis. They worked together at the moment, but she believed that this cooperation would come to an end soon after the capital had been retaken.

They came to the outskirts of the Amazon camp, walking along a path that led through a row of tents and into the agora. The sultan paused at the end of the large space and his entourage filed into it from behind him. The Osman sovereign gaped wide-eyed and slack-jawed at the mass of women engaged in trade, argument, and prayer.

"Is this some kind of eating space?" He demanded, looking on with confusion at what Califia perceived as the usual day's activities.

"It can be used thus, certainly," Califia said, confused by the sultan's reaction. "It's a public area where our people can conduct themselves in whatever they please."

One of the sultan's advisers cupped a hand over his mouth at the sight of two women who had been strolling hand-in-hand suddenly stop so that one could give the other a playful kiss.

"It is little wonder that God has abandoned our cause," General Al-Khulani said, shaking his head in disgust.

Alishir gave the Mamluk general a sharp look, but he ignored it. The Osman sultan turned toward the queen.

"Where do you keep the monsters who slaughtered my men yesterday?"

Califia led the way, walking by herself this time as Alishir fell into formation next to Sultan Bayezid. They strolled through the agora and past the medikos tent which the queen gazed upon until they came to the kennels. The creatures could be heard pacing in their cages and occasionally shrieking as their caretakers distributed their morning helping of raw meat.

The sultan asked questions about the creatures — how much they ate, how big they might grow, how many eggs the females usually laid — and Califia soon deferred him to one of the more knowledgeable caretakers who spoke the Osman language. Several Amazons apart from the caretakers themselves were gathered around the kennels, many of them sketching on paper or working with clay. Griffins were a common source of inspiration among her people, and Califia casually glanced at the works in progress.

One was drawing a griffin wearing its own set of plate armor, in a similar fashion to the armored horses ridden by the the allied heavy cavalry. Another was sculpting some kind of tapered cylinder which the queen could not discern, and she assumed it was part of an abstract piece.

Still a third artist was drawing a siege ramp with two curved hooks attached to the front, which extended into a sloped ladder which could be climbed. It seemed to be an improvement on the chain ladder crossbows which the Osmans had tried to use during the first assault.

Califia sighed. She was perusing artist sketches and works because she longed to visit Arianna, who should be leaving the care of the medikos very soon. She also dreaded searching for her at the tent because Malachea would be there.

The guilt which she had been trying to ignore still hung around her neck like an anchor. The sultan's words earlier that morning had only deepened her profound weight of responsibility.

She took her leave of Sultan Bayezid, who nodded and waved her away while listening to a caretaker describe the process of bathing griffins. As she jogged toward the medikos tent, she felt that her heart would burst if she happened to come upon the place right as Arianna was leaving. She pictured them running toward one another, embracing, and kissing passionately. Perhaps Malachea would be sleeping.

The tent was, happily, relatively empty of wounded Amazons but Califia immediately surmised that Arianna had already been released. Of the seven that remained, only one was wearing a sling on her massive right arm.

"The physician says I should be able to rejoin the rest of you tomorrow," the polemarkos said, standing and tapping her wounded arm. "Just a bruise, but she wants me to rest."

"I feared your injuries were much more severe," the queen said, averting her eyes from where a shock of purple shown through the thin fabric of Malachea's sling. "It is good to see you walking about."

"You won't be rid of me that easily, my queen," the polemarkos said, punctuating with a good-natured smile. Califia, nevertheless, blushed with shame.

"I am sorry everything went so wrong," the queen blurted, nearly unable to contain her tears. "I am sorry that you now suffer for it."

"Using the griffins was a mistake," Malachea said, putting a hand on the queen's shoulder, "but it was a bold mistake. If it had worked, everyone would now be praising your cleverness."

Califia looked sidelong at the polemarkos, waiting for the punch line to drop.

"*You* did not approve of using them for an attack," Califia said. "Yet now that it is a failure, you say it was a good idea?"

Malachea sighed.

"I was trying to pay you a compliment, but I see that is a fruitless endeavor. Have you spoken with our allies yet?"

Califia told her all about the apology and the allies' subsequent tour of the Amazon camp. Malachea sat down on her cot.

"While the griffins did not herald a successful attack," the polemarkos mused, "they may have served a greater purpose."

"What purpose can that be?" Califia felt completely lost.

"I have no problem working with these allies on this *specific* venture," Malachea said, "but there is something about their general demeanor toward us that I do not trust. If they had any thoughts of making war against our home, I hope that seeing the griffins in action have laid those thoughts to rest."

"That was *not* my intention," Califia said, feeling

suddenly *more* ashamed of the allied lives lost to the claws and beaks of the Amazons' protectors.

"We all get lucky sometimes," Malachea said, laying across the cot and adjusting her wounded arm for comfort.

Califia wished the polemarkos well, then promptly exited the tent. She had prepared herself for a great number of likely reactions from Malachea — angry resentment, sarcastic repartee, or glum indifference seemed the most likely. She never expected to receive the woman's warm approval. Somehow this was much worse.

She strode toward the griffin kennels, hoping to catch up with the allies and their entourage. Before she had taken three steps, she heard a loud voice calling for her from the other direction. Traesta stretched tall, waved her arms and called for the queen. They jogged toward one another and met in the grassy field.

"We didn't know where you had gone," she said as Califia arrived. "The sultan is addressing our people in the agora."

Traesta snatched her wrist and practically dragged her to the edge of the large open square, where a thick crowd had gathered around the sultan, who was speaking to them in Greek.

"...light of God may shine into the darkest corners of the earth!"

He had his hands raised and kept them frozen in the air for a moment as though waiting for some signal of approval from the crowd. He was greeted only by murmurs from the Amazon crowd, who seemed even more confused than Califia.

"*There* you are!" Basilea hissed, coming close so that she could speak in secret to the queen. "Did you know about this?"

"I was visiting the wounded," Califia said. "Has he broken some rule? Anyone may speak in the agora."

"The Mamluk and the Gurkani started arguing while we were at the kennels," Traesta explained, pausing to give Califia a disappointed glance. "General Al-Khulani demanded that we convert to Islam and take husbands. Alishir argued with him, but I could not grasp much of their conversation. The Osman sultan proposed a compromise: offering voluntary classes on Islam to any of our people who want to learn, which he has just done."

Califia paused to think this over. Was there anything nefarious about offering free education? The Amazons held no prohibitions on religion, and faith was largely considered one's own business. Nonetheless, the whole affair created an uneasy feeling in the pit of her stomach.

"Did he say anything... *odd* in his speech?" the queen asked.

"He said something about cultures learning from one another," Basilea said, tapping a finger on her chin as she looked to her left. "He said that in order to foster a spirit of cooperation and friendship, that we should actively seek ways we might benefit one another."

"When the Mamluk and the Gurkani were arguing," Traesta said, "I watched the sultan to see his reaction. He appeared to be incredibly anxious."

He fears his coalition is about to unravel, Califia realized. *Their armies are demoralized and they have nothing to show for it. How long before desertions begin en masse?*

"My love!" Came a voice from Califia's right. She turned to see Arianna, smiling and eagerly running toward her. "You must see what I just started making!"

"I was looking for you!" Califia said, embracing her

lover. "I will come as soon as I am able!"

"Go, by all means," Basilea said, smiling warmly at Arianna. "No use discussing these things without the entire council present. You look more anxious than a squirrel who wandered into a jaguar den. Go find some relaxation; this will keep until dinner!"

Califia walked arm-in-arm with her lover, who glanced at her from the corner of her eyes a few times.

"Tell me about what you are making," the queen said.

"If you're not interested, it's fine," Arianna said, glumly, looking at the ground as they strolled past the crowd.

"I wouldn't ask if I wasn't interested!" Califia said, a little too sharply. Arianna sighed.

"Sometimes I think you feign interest in my work out of some misplaced obligation," she said, disentangling her arm from Califia's. "It's fine if you don't care about art."

They walked a few steps in silence. Califia stopped and gripped Arianna by the shoulders, turning her toward herself and looking deeply into her eyes.

"If it's important to you, then it's important to me."

Arianna gazed back into her eyes uncertainly for a moment, then nodded and brought the queen into an embrace.

"I'm sorry. My shoulder still bothers me and it puts me into a dark mood. I don't mean to lash out."

"It's fine," Califia said, releasing her from the embrace and looping their arms back together. "Tell me about it while we walk."

"Kareana from the festivals omadha asked me to design the tunics for the upcoming Tikawich match," she said, blushing at the high honor which had been shown to her. "I think I am going to use an overlapping pattern with circles at the center, which will expand into—"

"Tikawich match?" Califia said, trying to recall what time of year this was in their home calendar. "For the Nika festival?"

"We celebrated that two months ago aboard the ships," Arianna said, laughing. "Your head really must be addled if you've forgotten about the Triumvir Games."

Arianna described her design in great detail, as well as the techniques she planned to employ in order to achieve the desired result. Califia nodded and made approving noises where it seemed appropriate, but she heard very little of her lover's description because suddenly every pressing problem seemed to crystallize into a simple, workable solution that would make everyone happy.

"Can you help me find Kareana?" Califia said, interrupting her lover mid-sentence.

Arianna looked as though Califia had just spoken to her in the Ohlone tongue.

"The member of the festival omadha who asked you to design the special tunics — can you help me find her?"

"I... yes, but why?"

"We're not going to settle for a mere game of Tikawich," Califia said, looking back toward the crowded agora. "We are going to make this the best Triumvir Games ever!"

12

Overstating the importance of the Triumvir Games was an impossible task. Athletes from across California competed in a variety of games and competitions, spectators ate delicious traditional food, and bright decorations lifted everyone's spirits just before the fall harvest. However, these events were generally open only to Amazons. After Califia argued passionately with the more conservative members of the army's festival omadha, they agreed to allow the participation of *men* in the games for the first time in history. Their allies would be allowed to compete.

The replies of those allies varied wildly. The Osman sultan's advisers had many questions about whether participating in the games themselves constituted an act of worship, an issue which the queen was happy to refute. The Gurkani sultan, who appeared somewhat pale and ill, asked about the events themselves and this led the queen to believe he was already thinking of soldiers who might make a good showing for his nation. The Mamluk general received her coolly, thanked her stiffly for the invitation, then vaguely indicated that he might send some officers to spectate and report back to him.

It wasn't until late that evening that Califia finally found time to look at Arianna's tunic design. It was even more beautiful than she had described it, with a center of swirling, overlapping circles of every color which merged with other shapes that fanned out in a layer of many-colored squares followed by a ring of rainbow hexagons. It was a geometric sunburst which would please the eyes of any aesthete. It was perfect, save for one small detail.

"It needs to cover the *entire* chest," Califia said, pointing to the void on the tunic's left where the left breast would naturally hang out.

"What? Why?" Arianna looked horrified at the suggestion. "Exposing the left breast is tradition!"

"It will offend our allies," the queen explained, "who will be our guests at these games."

"If they don't like it, their attendance is not required!"

Arianna's cheeks glowed bright crimson and Califia could not recall ever seeing her this angry.

"Over five hundred of their soldiers lie in the ground because of us," the queen said, trying to encourage rational thought in her lover. "This is a conciliatory gesture."

Arianna looked wounded in spite of Califia's measured, explanatory tone.

"These games are a celebration of our people," she said, her voice growing even louder. "To use them as a diplomatic ploy feels… *dirty!*"

"You don't understand," Califia placed a hand on Arianna's elbow but the young woman jerked her arm away.

"You are using these games as a way to cover your failure to take the walls!"

Arianna fumed as she picked up the tunic and threw it into the wall of the tent. Califia felt a hot fury rising within her.

"What do you suppose would happen to us," Califia said, "if our allies decide we are their enemies? They could crush us easily with their numbers alone!"

"I don't see why that—"

"You busy yourself with petty artwork and idle projects while the rest of us worry about keeping up good relations with the neighbors. I am sorry you won't get to see any extra breasts at the festival—"

Arianna snatched up the tunic and stormed from the tent. Califia, her hands shaking with rage, stormed after her.

"Being wounded in battle does not give you license to act like a *bitch*!"

Califia knew she would regret the words later, but in the moment they felt *good*. Arianna froze in mid-stride, then turned upon her with an expression that was equal parts furious and annoyed.

"Fuck you!" Arianna gestured with the tunic crumpled in her right fist. She half-turned away, then marched back to Califia and stared into her eyes. "The queen is supposed to sacrifice for the people, but you are asking *us* to sacrifice for the sake of your standing among your tyrant friends!"

Arianna stormed away, the offending tunic crumpled into a tiny ball beneath her white knuckles. Califia tried to think of something to shout after her, some lingering insult that would stick to her the way that her lover's words now pierced her own heart, but nothing came to mind. As the queen lay in bed that night, sleep came slowly as Arianna's words continued to wheedle their way into her soul. She was, thankfully, too exhausted for tears to come before dreams.

The next morning Califia dreaded telling Kareana that they needed a new designer for the competitors' festival tunics. When she arrived, the omadha was already very busy decorating the agora with colorful flags made from donated fabric and Kareana was humming happily as she anchored a ribbon to a nearby tree.

"There was a problem with the competitors' tunics," Califia began. Kareana looked at her with a confused smile and raised eyebrow.

"Are you worried they are too beautiful? Too celebratory?"

Califia must have looked confused because Kareana took her by the hand and led her to a nearby crafting area where Amazons were cutting and sewing fabric around a rug covered in materials on the ground. She reached down and pulled up an item of clothing that looked like Arianna's tunic design, save for the fact that the chest of its wearer would be completely covered.

"Your little marmot dropped this off early this morning," Kareana said, admiring the design. "Poor thing looked exhausted. What did you think the problem was?"

"I, um, thought that Arianna would not be able to finish the prototype in time for the others to duplicate it," Califia said, admiring how the design had likewise been re-centered on the sternum and radiated out like a geometric sunburst.

The queen couldn't be certain whether her lover had remade the tunic out of love or out of spite, but at the moment she didn't have time to ponder. She spent the next two days helping the festival omadha any way she could, including recruiting competitors, arranging trade with the other camps for the food and spices they would need for the traditional foods (or their nearest facsimile), and balancing the Tikawich teams so that none could claim the others had an unfair advantage.

Califia felt certain that they would never get everything ready in time. She was wrong; the banners that were erected the night before held firm throughout the windy night, the Tikawich field was suitably demarcated, and the javelin throw was moved, at the last moment, to a grassier field which was much less muddy. Everything that needed to be in place was in place, and the few things which weren't precisely to the queen's liking were so insignificant that she paid them no mind.

At home, the provinces sent their volunteer athletes to compete for local honor; here there would be three basic teams consisting of volunteers from the Gorgons, Traesta's division, and Olympia's division. Califia was still uncertain whether their allies would actually deign to compete against women, something that bothered her like a seed stuck between her teeth, but she had been assured by Yakov that many would at least attend as spectators.

A humble covered passage had been constructed between the various fields of play and the agora, through which each athlete was expected to enter. This was a rather spartan copy of the athletic field in California, a permanent fixture updated every season with wildflowers, colored parchment, and multi-colored maize kernels, but it didn't matter. Every Amazon face the queen passed on her way to the playing field was grinning brightly with excited anticipation.

Basilea's face, however, was filled with disapproval and no small amount of anxiety.

"Have you reconsidered?"

"I have. The answer is still no." The queen said as her

adviser fell in beside her. They continued toward the playing field.

"I've never known you to turn down an easy victory," Basilea continued, her tone adopting a familiar needling aspect which Califia loathed.

"And I've never known you to miscalculate," the queen replied, quickly adding, "but there's always a first time."

"Three years ago, you threw a javelin over half a stadia. I'm not saying you have to do the same, Nika knows you're out of practice, but you could still get pretty close and more importantly—"

"I have decided," Califia said, rolling her eyes. "I'll find some other way to outdo the polemarkos without rubbing her nose in shit."

Basilea pursed her lips but kept silent. Everyone knew what skill Malachea possessed with the javelin throw; for Califia to show off her own abilities when the polemarkos was injured and unable to display her own skills felt wrong.

"You may be certain," Basilea said warily, "that she would not hesitate to rub *your* nose in shit if the situation were reversed."

Califia looked askance at the former queen, wondering if someday she herself might become as cynical.

They arrived at the field, walking outside of the covered archway so that no one would think the queen intended to compete. The main field, where they would play Tikawich as well as many other team sports, was abuzz with women jogging up and down the field, tossing small hide-bound balls back and forth, and doing calisthenics to warm up their muscles. Each was wearing the special festival tunic designed by Arianna but wore the specific solid-colored headband of their team.

The heralds blew their horns, signaling the beginning of the competition. Califia was a little startled to see that the heralds themselves, who were normally devotees of Nika, were instead three Gorgons who had all shaved the sides of their heads to honor the goddess of victory.

Califia and Basilea quickly ran toward an area just off the edge of the field near its center and many Amazons gathered around them, chattering excitedly and giggling. It warmed the queen's heart to hear such happiness in the midst of this miserable siege.

The main field featured foot races of varying distances, all measured and remeasured beforehand to ensure conformity to the races at home. North of the field, just behind and to the left of where Califia and Basilea now stood, a ring had been demarcated for grappling as well as one for stick fighting and another for boxing. Those events would not begin until after lunch. Late-arriving Amazons streamed toward the field as the first Tikawich match began between Traesta's and Olympia's teams.

The players had all been drawn from the respective militia divisions they commanded. Traesta's women, wearing gold headbands, scored a goal very quickly, but then the game settled into a nearly even match, both sets of women racing across the field, passing the ball into each other's nets, getting smacked on their helms with a ball or, occasionally, another player's netstick. Olympia's team, who wore red headbands, managed to even the score just before the long break at the halfway point of the match, which they celebrated with jumping chest bumps and a few kisses.

As the players took their break, drinking water and eating handfuls of nuts and berries while the crowd eagerly chatted, there was an eruption of noise from the far end of the field. Califia gasped as she saw that Sultan

Bayezid and his entourage were arguing with some women on the periphery, the sultan's face growing redder by the moment. She sprinted to where they stood to intervene.

"Your majesty," she said, offering a polite bow. "Thank you for gracing our humble games."

"Humble, yes," the Sultan said, smiling politely but still appearing thoroughly unimpressed. "God smiles upon humility, my dear. May I introduce Balyemez Osman, the Agha of the Yenisherries."

Balyemez stepped forward, a short, stout man whose beard matched his frown. He had bushy eyebrows, dark skin, and wore a tall white hat with cloth streaming down the back which matched that of the Yenisherries in everything except the usual red color.

"Majesty," Balyemez said, nodding.

"An honor," Califia said, surmising that the title *Agha* must mean that this man was the Yenisherries' commander. It seemed strange that she had not met him before.

"Your highness," he said to Califia, "we wish to secure a space for his majesty to watch the games."

"Come with me," the queen replied, escorting them back to where she had been standing with Basilea. Sultan Bayezid followed along with his guards, pages, and commanders, who pressed through the crowd politely but firmly.

"How is this game played?" The sultan asked when the Tikawich match resumed.

Califia explained it to him, how the ball was passed between players and eventually one would attempt to hurl it into a net. He nodded as she explained about illegal maneuvers and special rules for when one player injured another.

"That one just cheated!" The Sultan exclaimed, pointing to where a woman was jogging off the field and handing her netstick and headband to a waiting teammate, who eagerly charged the field and took her place. "What is the punishment?"

"It's not cheating," Califia said, a little stunned at his assertion. "Any player can leave the field provided someone from their army division volunteers to take their place on the team."

"What?" The man's nostrils flared and his eyebrows raised as he squinted at the game. Califia suppressed a laugh as his expression suddenly seemed funny to her. "Those two are doing it now!"

Califia followed his point and nodded as she saw that a member of the other team, Olympia's division, was indeed handing her netstick and headband to a woman jogging onto the field.

"It seems most irregular," commented Balyemez, shaking his head in disapproval. "What is the point of such a game?"

"The mainlanders who taught it to our people many years ago," Califia explained, "said that it was training for war."

"It certainly doesn't teach endurance," the Sultan remarked.

The members of the Sultan's entourage who were within earshot all nodded their heads.

"Still, it *is* fun to watch," the queen said. The sultan shrugged and his entourage matched his indifferent expression.

"The uniforms are very beautiful," said Balyemez, the newcomer. "Did you bring them with you on the voyage?"

"We started making them two nights ago."

At this the sultan's jaw dropped.

"But there are so many!" He gaped as his eyes drifted around the Tikawich field and then also beheld how many spectators were thusly adorned. "Did you bring *two* armies - one of warriors and one of seamstresses?"

"Not at all," Califia found the question odd at first, but then remembered something the sultan's emissary had mentioned. "Yakov told me that your people commit their lives to producing leatherwork, or smithing metals, or growing food. It sounds... *strange* to our ears. We generally each cultivate several different skills and use them as they are needed."

"You do not have *tradespeople*?" The Sultan asked, turning to her and, for the moment, ignoring the match. "How do you ensure that enough food is grown for your people to eat? How can you be sure you will have enough weapons if invaders come? Do your people even produce enough goods to trade with your neighbors?"

"Lifelong commitment to a single skill is not *completely* alien to us," Califia explained, "but most of us explore many interests, hobbies, and productive labors."

The Sultan shook his head, as did every one of his followers who heard the queen. He spent the rest of the match in silence, no doubt wondering as Yakov had how a society could possibly function without the constant threat of violent coercion.

The match nearly ended in a tie, but some members of Olympia's team managed to score one final game-winning goal in the last moments of the second half. The field was cleared for some more races, and markers were laid out at equal intervals for the upcoming javelin throw.

"I wonder, fair queen," the Sultan said, sipping a cup of nectar that one of his attendants handed to him, "if you would be willing to have your ladies play against a team of my finest warriors?"

Califia glanced at Balyemez, who grinned and nodded at the suggestion as if it had been his own. His grin exuded the faintest hint of arrogance, of self-assured triumph.

"That sounds like fine afternoon entertainment, your majesty," Califia said, delighted at the thought of these men, so confident in their effortless superiority over women, learning a lesson in humility.

As more foot races began on the main field, the smaller sections around it began to host other events. Noticing the Sultan staring at the grappling ring, she invited him to join her closer to the action.

Two enormous women stepped into the ring covered only in loin wrappings and binding cloths compressing their breasts. One bore the beard tattoo of a Gorgon while the other had an arm covered in the intertwining branches of a tree, which Califia believed marked her as a resident of Silavunna, the wooded, mountainous land where griffins were raised. It was also home to trees which, if they were cut down, would be longer than the main field, longer even than the Sultan's great ships. This woman was built like such a tree— tall but solid and thick around her middle.

The Sultan gasped as the match commenced and both contestants hurled themselves into their opponent, slapping and grabbing and twisting and squeezing. It was over quickly, the tree-tattooed woman setting one foot just barely outside the circle in which they fought.

"The other way to win," Califia told the wide-eyed Sultan as he fanned himself, "is to cause both of your opponent's hands to touch the ground."

"A test of domination," the man said, nodding

approvingly at Balyemez, who seemed unimpressed. The Sultan turned back to Califia. "Sultan Husayn has arrived."

She turned her head toward where he pointed and saw that the Gurkani Sultan was indeed rapidly approaching along with a retinue of about thirty guards with twenty or so men in plain clothes whom she would have thought were slaves or pages except for the haughty manner of their proud strut. Alishir led them, smiling broadly as he surveyed the games around him.

"Some of my men request the honor of trying their skills against your finest wrestlers," Sultan Husayn said, gesturing to the unarmored men who walked alongside him.

"They are more than welcome," Califia said, gesturing toward the ring. Sultan Husayn barked a few words in the Gurkani tongue and a bulky fellow shrugged off his tunic and gave his bulky chest muscles a few slaps as he stepped into the ring.

The Amazon wrestlers whispered among themselves before deciding who would face him, choosing a woman somehow even taller and thicker than either of the two who had just competed. She and the Gurkani man faced off, readying themselves for the moment the officiant brought down her scepter.

They were upon one another in a flash, each trying to work their arms against their opponent's shoulders and elbows. At first the shoving seemed even, neither moving even a hair's breadth. Then each began weaving sideways before renewing their push, moving alongside their opponent to keep their balance and resist them in turn.

"He is trained in the Persian style," Sultan Husayn said, giving Califia a significant look as if he expected her to understand without any elaboration. She nodded as if she did, and hoped that would prove sufficient for the sultan.

The Amazon wrestler's footing shifted just slightly and her Gurkani opponent took full advantage, guiding her to the edge of the ring in a few short steps. Her heel pressed against the border, but she managed to stop short of toppling over. She stepped forward with that foot and planted it right behind the opposing foot of her competitor, who realized his predicament when it was too late. She shoved forward, the muscles in her arms and back bulging with the effort, and the man tried to take a big step back but his heel caught against the crook of her knee and he toppled to the ground, his right shoulder landing just outside the border of the ring.

The Amazon grappler offered to help him up but he swatted her hands away and rolled onto his knees, standing up and breathing heavily. Sultan Husayn shouted something in Gurkani and the entourage behind him laughed while the grappler glowered at the ground. He went back into the ring and stood ready, waiting for another opponent to face him.

Califia suddenly realized how dangerous this might become if the man felt he need to avenge some honor and, looking toward the main field where they were changing events once more, she concocted a plan.

"Perhaps your grapplers," Califia said to Sultan Husayn, "would be interested in teaching some of the Persian techniques to our wrestlers? We always value the chance to learn something new."

"I suppose we could do this for you," the Sultan said idly, yawning into his fan.

"Why don't the rest of us go and watch the javelin throw?" She turned to Sultan Bayezid as well, who looked at her blankly as though he hadn't been paying attention.

"That suits me," Sultan Husayn replied, and the Osman Sultan nodded as they all walked back to the main field, this time lining up behind the throwers as spectators were being ushered away from the sides of the field in case of stray missiles.

"You know," Califia told Sultan Husayn, glancing back toward the wrestling ring to see that the the Gurkani grapplers were indeed demonstrating techniques to the Californians and everyone seemed to be smiling and getting along, "I used to be quite the javelineer myself. I won the feathered crown for the event three years past, before I became the queen."

"Will you be throwing today?" Sultan Bayezid asked.

The tone of his question, as well as the expectant looks from both Sultans made Califia hesitate to respond. She felt certain that this was some kind of test, and while she would normally ignore such posturing, her position among these two leaders felt just tentative enough to make her care what they thought.

"It would not be appropriate," she said, fabricating the reason from whole cloth. The way the two men nodded at this answer told her that she had chosen the correct response.

The Sultans and their retinues were perfect spectators, clapping politely when athletes threw especially far, and even expressing sympathy when the occasional contestant had the weapon slip from her hands at the last moment or stumbled over the line and invalidated her throw.

The final contestant was announced, and Califia's heart froze as the name was shouted through a megaphone.

"Dionysia!"

Cheers erupted from the spectators and even from the

contestants playing smaller contests on the little fields and grappling ring. Far too many cheers for the queen's comfort. Califia felt a shiver as she remembered how Dionysia toyed with the poor Majyar man armed only with a small knife. The queen didn't even realize that the polemarkos' troublesome eldest daughter knew anything about javelin throwing.

Dionysia approached the starting point, looking downfield and taking a big breath in before squeezing it all out in a huff. She took a few bouncing steps forward, holding the throwing spear diagonally across her body, and then hurled it high into the air.

The queen thought at first that the unlucky woman had thrown the javelin at too high an arc, and that any errant wind might blow it short of its goal. It reached past the second-place weapon, and Califia prayed silently to Nika for a headwind. When it landed it was the clear winner, sinking into the ground beyond the former leading javelin by at least two spear lengths.

Dionysia jumped and shouted triumphantly and the crowd of spectators now roared their delight and congratulations. The woman composed herself quickly and waved, smiling with the pride of a woman who has just given birth. Some began to chant her name, and this continued as the spectators traveled back to the Tikawich field.

As the field was prepared for the final match, in which the allied soldiers would participate, Califia and the Sultans wandered back to the individual sports, where the wrestling matches were winding down and the single combat was just starting up. Two combatants entered the ring clad in padded safety armor and wielding a wooden sword with a small round shield also composed of wood. A hit anywhere on the pads or the helm scored a point, and two judges circle the fighters ready to raise one of their paddles to record a hit. Only if both judges raised the same paddle was a hit scored, five hits won the match.

"If any of your warriors wish to participate," Califia told the Sultans as a match between two Amazons began, "they will need to use our equipment, for safety."

"There is no such safety in a real fight," Balyemez said, giving the competition a disapproving look.

"This is not a real fight," Califia said. "It is a game."

"Don't look so dour, Balyemez," Sultan Bayezid said. "A wise man appreciates games for what they are, not what he thinks they ought to be."

A look passed over Balyemez's face that sent a chill through Califia's bones. *A wise man should not antagonize the man who decides whether he continues sitting upon the throne.* She recalled Yakov's words about the Yenisherries and their growing power and wondered if Bayezid himself realized just how much he still needed their support. Suddenly it occurred to her that this was probably the reason why their commander was now attending the sultan.

Several Osmans, Gurkani, and even a few Mamluks came over to try their hand against the Amazons in single combat. General Al-Khulani sent a messenger to deliver his regrets. Some situation in the Mamluk homelands required his immediate attention, so he wouldn't be able to attend. He did give his army permission to compete as they liked.

As Califia watched the various men being fitted into Amazon safety gear and facing off against either her people or one another, she admired their different techniques. The Osmans preferred to begin with heavy slashes followed by rapid glancing attacks at their flanks if their opponent held their ground. The Gurkani were nearly the opposite, beginning with uncommitted strikes before launching into heavy attacks. The Mamluks were nearly indiscernible in their tactics, some preferring mostly light jabs and quick strikes while others threw their bodies into the fight, and some changing almost at random.

"Careful of your legs, Murat!" Sultan Bayezid shouted. "This one likes to jab for the thighs!"

Murat yanked his foreleg backward just as his opponent swept for the knee, tapping her on the arm and scoring a point for his trouble. Sultan Bayezid applauded his efforts and continued shouting advice from the sidelines. The poor man nevertheless still lost his match and sulked out of the ring after the last blow struck right on his heart. The Sultan shrugged.

The next contestant to face an Amazon warrior was Gurkani, but his opponent was a Gorgon whose agility and canny instincts led to a 5-1 loss for the poor fellow. This time it was Sultan Husayn who shouted advice and encouragement in the Gurkani tongue, but to no avail.

The first victory for the allies came at the hands of a lithe Osman fighter who had mastered the art of dodging and counterattacking in the same motion. His match was somewhat close at 5-3 but it was a win nonetheless. Califia overheard Sultan Bayezid mutter to Balyemez that the contestant should find himself 300 *Akche* wealthier the following morning. From what she had learned of coins and money, this was a considerable sum and she was a little shocked that all that stood between the rough life of a common warrior hoping for loot and a wealthy fighter who lived in comfort was an arbitrary gift from his sovereign. *No, not arbitrary.* The man had earned it through victory in single combat.

As the afternoon wore on, several dozen more

matches unfolded and both Osman and Gurkani fighters won the occasional victory, each time leaving their rulers smiling magnanimously and whispering rewards to their advisers. The more impressive the victory, the higher the reward.

At last the final match of Tikawich was held, the Gorgons facing off against the Osman team. The Gurkani contestants had exhausted themselves entering the contests of grappling and single combat, and the Mamluks contented themselves with observing from the sidelines. The officiant blew her whistle and threw the ball in the air, which was immediately followed by a scuffle at midfield before the Gorgon team managed to whip the ball to one of their runners on the right flank. She sprinted ahead, keeping a sure hold on her netstick as it bobbed with the motion of her quick strides. Several Osmans tried to block her but they failed to set their feet in time and she charged straight through them, knocking them to the ground as she prepared her stick for a shot on the goal.

She kicked her front leg out as if preparing a very forceful shot, then curved her netstick at the last moment and passed the ball to another Amazon who had chosen a spot right in front of the net, whose guardian was now all the way to the right side as he anticipated the first woman to shoot. The ball flew blindingly fast but the second Gorgon caught it, gave a playful spin, and hurled it straight into the unguarded center of the goal. The officiant blew her whistle and the ladies celebrated, running toward the center of the field and lifting both the shooter and the one who had initially run the ball down the field on their shoulders.

"I don't expect our team to win this contest," Sultan Bayezid said frankly, sighing a little as if disappointed nonetheless. "Still, I think it is worth playing."

The rest of the game was much more even than either Califia or the Sultans were expecting. The score remained 1-0 for much of the time, neither side able to penetrate the opposition's defense. As the match neared its close, the Osman team suddenly found a second wind and charged headlong into the mass of defenders who were taken by surprise at the sudden burst of energy. Sultan Bayezid smiled as his men passed the ball between them and charged through the hastily assembled Amazon blockade to tie the score. The spectators clapped eagerly and the players quickly took their starting positions as the officiant readied herself to toss the ball into the air at center field. She glanced at the timekeepers, who closely watched the sands spilling through their time-glasses and gave the signal that play could continue.

The Osmans were not the only players capable of displaying a sudden burst of energy. The Amazons raced into action, catching the ball as it fell and tossing it to one another as they sprinted in looping circles as their opponents struggled to keep up. One woman caught the ball and began sprinting forward. The Osman defenders formed a wall to stop her, setting their feet and readying themselves to stand against her charge. Califia held her breath from the excitement. As she was nearly upon the enemy wall, the Gorgon with the ball leapt into the air and passed backward to where another Amazon waited just in front of the center line. The first woman crashed into the line of defenders, utterly toppling them.

The Amazon who caught the ball brought her netstick far back behind her, leapt into the air so that her body shifted sideways and she spun. She quickly planted her feet and brought the end of her netstick all the way to the ground. The ball launched quickly into a rising arc that soared across the field. Califia gasped at the sight; the woman had clearly practiced that move and was probably saving it for a moment precisely like this. The ball sailed high through the air, well above the heads of any defenders who could only watch helplessly. The keeper realized the ball was coming towards him, but too late to leap high enough to catch it. He jumped just after it struck the net, sailing just underneath the top bar of the goal.

The crowd erupted in thunderous applause and raucous shouting. The Amazon team ran toward mid-field and crushed into a huge mass, laughing and smiling and screaming with joy. Califia's heart swelled with pride as she cheered for her people. As the Osman team returned to midfield to reset for the beginning of the next round, a horn sounded from where the timekeepers sat, signaling the end of the game. At first their opponents did not understand so some of the Amazons broke away from their teammates and explained.

"That was delightful," Sultan Bayezid said, clapping his hands rapidly like an overexcited child. Balyemez also looked impressed and was commenting on the match to other members of the entourage.

This entire event had been one big success, and Califia felt as though things might once more return to an even footing in their relationship with these allies. Their soldiers enjoyed some recreation and could return to the battlefield with a song in their heart.

The swelling of pride in Califia's heart, both in her people and in her own cleverness at arranging these games, suddenly deflated as she saw that several members of the Osman team were shouting and pointing, slapping the back of one hand into the palm of the other. The Gorgon team seemed confused for the moment but some of the perplexed faces of her elite warriors were starting to transform into dangerous anger. The Osman spectators on the other side of the field were looking on as if preparing to join in the argument, something which Califia absolutely could not allow to happen.

She rushed onto the field to separate the two parties when suddenly she spotted Dionysia charging onto the field as well, javelin still in hand. Califia arrived just as several armored Osmans also stepped into the conflict, their hands hovering dangerously close to the hilts of their swords.

"My good sirs," Califia said to the Osman team, shouting louder than she needed to in order to draw their attention more fully. "You played honorably and made your sovereign proud. Whatever could be wrong?"

"*They* told us," the leading Osman player said, thrusting a finger at the Amazon players, "that taking a shot like that was against the rules!"

"I had not crossed the mid-field mark," said the Gorgon who had scored the winning shot. "You cannot shoot from behind the midfield line, but anywhere in-bounds on the opposing side is fair shooting territory."

"We were deceived!" The man shouted, thumping his chest. "You cheated!"

The Sultans and their retinues arrived, which initially relieved Califia because the nearby armed Osmans now moved their hands away from weapon hilts, apparently reluctant to draw a blade in the presence of their sovereign. This relief did not last long.

"It seems there was some miscommunication," Sultan Bayezid said, looking at the Amazon players with a disappointed gaze as if the whole affair was clearly their fault. "Perhaps my players should be allowed an opportunity to even the score?"

"The game is over," the Gorgon who had scored the winning goal said forcefully and far too directly for the Sultan's liking. "We won."

"This is a *fine* way to treat honored guests," Sultan Husayn added, looking shocked at the rudeness of the Gorgon's reply. "It is not the Osmans' fault you did not explain the rules properly."

"We explained them *several* times," the Gorgon continued, but Califia held up her hand and the woman rolled her eyes and turned away.

"Your majesties," Califia adopted the most reasonable tone she could muster, "I think it is important, in this moment, for us all to remember that this is just a game. I apologize for any confusion, but we-"

"Confusion?" The accusatory Osman player said, taking two steps toward the queen. "Confusion is all you have brought to this holy undertaking. Confusion and death!"

The man spat near Califia's feet, nearly striking her sandals. She looked to the Sultans, expecting that they would reprimand the offending soldier. They looked at her expectantly, as if she was still in the wrong.

"It pains me to say it, fair queen," Sultan Husayn began, stepping forward and clasping his hands, "but the man has a point. What have you and your army contributed to this effort besides confusion and chaos?"

"We saved your lives," Califia said, stunned at this turn of events. "We secured the transport of your cannons when your own soldiers were too *precious* for the task and then when your siege was failing, we held the line against the warriors who came from the boats. And it cost us many lives to do so."

"You were also defending yourselves," Sultan Bayezid said, stepping forward with the same air of superiority adopted by Sultan Husayn. "You can't expect us to commend you for saving your own lives, just because you *happened* to save ours as well."

Califia felt like a cornered marmot facing down two hungry jaguars. She looked to Yakov, but his eyes were downcast. She looked next to Alishir, but he only looked grim and resigned. She looked for Basilea, but she was nowhere to be found. Her eyes skimmed a hundred faces but none belonged to her chief adviser or to either of the strategoses or even Malachea. She felt a little surprised to be wishing that the troublesome polemarkos was by her side in this moment, but whatever trouble the woman gave her, she would certainly know how to get these two to back off.

What would Malachea do?

In that one single thought, she found her solution.

"I was going to make this announcement at the end of today's festivities," Califia said, doing her best to look as if she were disappointed in the two men for assuming otherwise, "but I suppose telling you now will make no difference. Apologies are just words; I mean to take action. One fortnight from today, I will present myself at the walls of Constantinopolis and challenge them to send out a champion for me to fight in single combat."

Sultan Bayezid's eyes went wider than she thought possible and Sultan Husayn's jaw dropped as well. Alishir's eyebrows shot up but he looked mostly impressed. Yakov looked worried, as usual. The two sovereigns considered the idea, no doubt working out the same equations which she had needed only a fraction of the time to solve.

"You understand the consequences if you lose this fight?" Sultan Bayezid said.

"It is the duty of Amazon queens to place themselves in danger for the sake of protecting their people," she said, speaking loudly so that those gathered would hear clearly. "If by undertaking this duel I can prove our contrition for recent events, then I will do so gladly."

The sultans both nodded and the nearby Amazons already began whispering over the matter. It was some hours later, when she was in her tent alone, exhausted yet still unable to fall asleep, that she realized Sultan Bayezid had probably planned the entire spectacle just to try and force her into committing once more to seeing the siege through until it was finished.

It doesn't matter, she thought, pulling her covers closer around her to keep away the chill in the night air. *Malachea herself could not have conceived a better solution.*

13

The War Council hastily assembled the morning after the triumvir games to give their own assessment of Califia's pledge.

"Even for *you*," Traesta said, pointing a finger at the queen, "this is too fucking reckless."

"What do you mean?" Califia asked, wounded by her friend's words.

"First you endanger the griffins," she said, each word cutting into the queen's heart, "and now you want to challenge a crusader to single combat, as if you're Achilla herself?"

"I think what the strategos is trying to say," Malachea said, stepping between the women and speaking in a much softer tone than Califia expected, "is that the council would have appreciated some consultation yesterday. The Sultans knew before *we* did - if we had not attended the crowning ceremony then this would be the first we had heard of this venture!"

"I don't believe she needed to consult us," Olympia said, raising an eyebrow as Traesta gave the ground a good kick. "The queen is not leading this army, so she does not owe it the same responsibilities as a polemarkos."

Califia was glad to have some support from Olympia for once, even if she felt as though the woman was opening old wounds, reminding her of how Malachea had outmaneuvered her.

"It still would have been nice to know ahead of time," Traesta said. "Whether the queen was *required* to tell us has nothing to do with whether she *should*."

Califia knew that Traesta was correct. She felt tempted to admit that she came up with the idea in the heat of the moment, but decided against it; their scolding would only get worse if they knew she had been improvising. Their criticism was already starting to feel a bit patronizing.

"When I decided to issue this challenge," Califia stepped around Basilea and toward Traesta, "my only thoughts were of Amaltheia and the example she set for all queens. I desired to fight on behalf of my people, to give them some measure of satisfaction from this entire adventure."

The council was silent for a moment and seemed stunned by this answer. Califia believed she saw in their eyes the same weariness that she felt in her soul, the same longing for this journey to be ended so that they might return to their familiar shores, mountains, and forests. Malachea pursed her lips and squinted slightly, looking somewhat suspicious.

"How far are you willing to follow Amaltheia's example?" she asked, stepping closer to the queen.

"As far as the triumvirs may lead me," Califia said cautiously, the familiar sensation that she had just stepped into a trap shivering up her spine.

"Even unto death?"

The hush that followed this question made the

previous tense silence seem raucous by comparison. The breeze became slight, which reduced the noise from rustling leaves overhead. It was as if the trees were also waiting patiently, silently for a response.

"If giving my life keeps our people secure, then I am willing to risk it."

As she spoke the words out loud, Califia realized that she truly was willing to lay her life down if it meant her people would be kept safe.

Malachea smiled in a way that almost appeared impressed. "I'm satisfied."

"It's your life," Traesta said, glumly. "I hope you know what you're doing."

"You have my vote," Olympia said, beaming broadly. "That is, if we are voting?"

"I don't see why not," Malachea said, calling the matter to a vote. The queen's decision to challenge a champion of Constantinopolis to a duel was ratified unanimously.

"Thank you for your confidence," Califia said as the three women lowered their hands. "I shall do my best to recover our honor."

Malachea dismissed the council and Califia walked out of the grove toward the agora. She had not seen Arianna since their fight over the tunics and she thought the agora was as good a place as any to try and locate the elusive young artist.

The space was filled, as usual, with various groups of artisans practicing their craft, women chatting or debating, and a few just idly laying about on the makeshift benches as the day went by. One of the artisan groups was sculpting, but Arianna was not among them. From the corner of her eye, the queen spotted a young woman sketching with a charcoal stick but as she drew closer she saw that it was not her lover.

Near the eastern side of the agora, Califia spotted pointed helms and scale armor behind a group of women locked in some heated debate. She moved to see the visitors from a better angle and saw the familiar scale armor and distinctive flaring faceguards of the Gurkani. Leading this procession of eight was Alishir and Yakov, whose presence gave Califia pause. *Why would the Osman sultan's emissary accompany a leader of the Gurkani?*

She strode toward them and arrived just as the debating women took notice and decided to take their conversation to the other end of the agora. Alishir smiled and bowed his head at her arrival, while Yakov bowed from the waist. The bodyguards who accompanied them gave her a disinterested glance and then looked about the camp with bored expressions.

"Peace be upon you, fair queen," Alishir said, offering a friendly grin.

"Your majesty," Yakov said, giving another deferent nod after he finished bowing.

"Gentlemen," Califia said, glancing at one of the bodyguards who idly spat on a nearby tree. "I am honored by your visit."

"I bring my sultan's regards," Alishir said. "He wishes you good fortune in your upcoming duel."

"As does my own sovereign," Yakov said. "Though he did not send me to tell you such, specifically."

"Why *did* he send you?" Califia asked.

"He wished for me to accompany the honorable Alishir," Yakov smiled at the Gurkani nobleman, who gave a tight-lipped smile in return. Califia must have appeared puzzled at this because Alishir explained.

"Sultan Bayezid prefers that my people go through *him* if we wish to speak with you," he explained. Califia detected straining in his voice, as though he was not entirely pleased with this arrangement. "You were brought here by his vassal, after all, so he has a more direct claim to alliance with you than we do."

She supposed that made sense, as far as any of these peoples' ways of doing things made any sense.

"Hail, Califia!" shouted an Amazon from the other end of the agora. "Amaltheia reborn!"

"You have won the admiration of your people," Alishir said. A few other women in the agora offered cheers of their own. "Perhaps we should take this conversation to a more suitable place?"

The queen took up stride between Alishir and Yakov and their escort shuffled behind them. Califia thought at first that they were walking toward the Osman camp and as she was deciding whether or not this should distress her, they turned aside and instead trekked up a small hill with a flat area on the top. It was the same hill where the sultans and General Al-Khulani sat during the assaults.

"I've always thought the city looks beautiful from here," Alishir said. The six guards who accompanied them sat or laid on the grass. "Once I came just before daybreak as the sun rose over the towering walls. A positively overwhelming sensation of joy and peace came over me."

He sighed, and Yakov nodded politely.

"I assume you brought me here because you have something to discuss?" Califia asked, eager to seek out her lover at the Amazon camp and leave these men on the hillock.

"I fear a great mistake has been made, and that I am partly to blame for it." Alishir's voice was terribly grave, and Califia dreaded whatever he was going to say next. An awkward silence passed and she realized he wanted her to say something.

"I doubt it is worse than what I tried to do with the griffins," she offered, hoping to elicit a smile and see a glimpse of his usual happiness.

"I don't know how to compare the two," he said, which only deepened the queen's trepidation. "While they are satisfied with your declaration yesterday, the sultans never wanted you to challenge a crusader to single combat."

"I assumed they wanted a gesture or deed, something to reinforce the apology with action," Califia said.

Alishir scoffed and shook his head.

"I sometimes forget how different your people are," he said. "They wanted *money*."

"They wanted…" she paused for a moment, struggling to recall the name for those little metal disks, "*coins*?"

Alishir chuckled and nodded. Yakov shrugged but then gave a small nod. Califia could not believe the matter could have been resolved so easily. They still had many coins leftover from the original gift which Admiral Kemal had given them when they first agreed to join this war.

"Ah, now you will see why I brought you up here," Alishir said, pointing to the city walls in the distance. Califia squinted to see that there were some armored soldiers standing near a large gate, which she remembered was named *The Golden Gate*. She thought she heard a distant din of horns and she gasped as she realized the gate itself was opening with a slow, steady rumble.

"Here, your majesty," Yakov said, handing Califia a collapsible brass spyglass.

She thanked him, then pulled it open and peered toward the soldiers standing before the gate. Most were dressed in the same scale-mail as the bodyguards who accompanied Alishir and Yakov, but one stood apart from the others. The armor he wore appeared golden and from the top of his helm there sprouted a bright red plume of feathers.

"That young man hails from one of our noble families," Alishir said. "During the previous assault attempt, he failed to protect the cohort under his command. They were all eaten by griffins while he escaped."

"I am glad he survived."

"*He* isn't."

Califia brought down the spyglass to give Alishir a quizzical look. Yakov pursed his lips and nodded.

"The men under his command were under his *protection*," Yakov explained. "Instead of protecting them, he saved his own life and thus has been accused of cowardice."

The queen felt a chill run up her spine and her shoulders clenched.

"He is fighting to regain his lost honor."

"Precisely," Alishir said, gesturing toward the wall with his index finger. "Here comes the Christian champion now!"

Califia looked through the spyglass to see a grim figure emerge through the city gate. He was covered in broad plate armor and wore a plumed helm through which only his eyes and nose could be seen. In his left hand he carried a round shield a little smaller than the hoplons used by the Amazons. In his right hand, he carried a straight-bladed longsword.

"Is the crusader also a man who is fighting to restore his honor?" Califia said, wishing she could hear what was being said by the two warriors she was watching.

"That is possible," Alishir replied, "but I think it is
more likely that he hopes to gain some kind of reward
from his liege."

The fight began as both warriors readied their
weapons. The young Gurkani wielded a colorful round
shield which was the same size as his opponent's and a
slender, curved sword. They traded a few preliminary
blows, sizing each other up as they struck, blocked,
retreated, or advanced. Califia thought she could almost
hear the shield thumps from their vantage point on the
hillock.

"How much money would the sultans have wanted for
the lives of their soldiers?" She asked, wincing as the
Gurkani warrior landed a blow against the side of the
crusader's helm. The Christian stumbled, but brought his
shield up before his opponent could follow through with
another attack.

"The money would not actually be for the sultans,"
Yakov explained, hissing through his teeth as the
crusader trapped the Gurkani warrior's sword between
his sword's guard and the rim of his shield. He wrenched
it away and the Gurkani stumbled backward reaching for
his belt. "The money would go to the families of the lost
soldiers."

The Gurkani warrior drew a flanged mace. It was
much shorter than his sword, but he handled it with
reassuring confidence.

"That makes sense," Califia said, thinking once again
that nothing about these people made any sense. The
families of fallen Amazons from the Cochimi war would
not need money because their needs would be provided
for regardless. She still did not see what, if any, benefits
were conferred by the incorporation of money.

"Watch the crusader closely," Alishir said. Califia

glanced at him and realized he was watching through his own scope. "His swings are too aggressive and young Salman is about to punish him for it."

The crusader was indeed swinging so hard that his sword clanked against the side of his armor on the follow-through. The Gurkani warrior, whose name was apparently Salman, was dodging but had his mace-arm cocked behind him, ready to strike when the opportunity arose.

The crusader had swung back-handed, but neglected to bring his shield in front to protect himself. Salman bashed him square on the forehead, which knocked the man back. As he stumbled, apparently dazed, the young Gurkani bashed his opponent's sword-hand and the long blade went flying to the side.

"In truth, I take little joy in viewing such displays," Alishir said, taking the spyglass from his eye, "but I hope you understand why I thought it important for you to see."

Califia took her own scope away from her eye, wishing she could say that she did understand. She looked to Alishir, then to Yakov, but could discern no clue from either's somber expression. Yakov, apparently noticing the queen's confused expression, explained.

"Fighting as part of a group is different than fighting alone," he said, gesturing to the duel in progress at the foot of the walls. She saw what he meant; the two began grappling after the crusader successfully pulled Salman's shield away from him. "You would be well advised to prepare yourself — to *train* yourself — for your impending encounter."

"I am no longer an amateur in battle," Califia objected. "Before your horsemen showed up to chase the crusaders away during that initial assault, I bested one of their giants in single combat!"

Alishir gave her a sidelong glance.

"It was not my intention to insult you, great queen. I only mean to offer guidance to aid your success. Many impetuous young warriors think that they cannot be beaten. Young Salman and his opponent no doubt both believe themselves invincible, but believing does not make it so."

Califia put the spyglass back to her eye and witnessed the final stages of the duel. Salman was shieldless but still held his flanged mace. His opponent now wielded an axe, but still held a shield in his left hand. Salman raised his weapon as if he intended to smash the weapon down on his enemy's head. He never got the opportunity. With a surprising quickness, the crusader leapt forward and jammed the narrow edge of his triangular shield against Salman's throat. The Gurkani warrior slammed his mace against the shield but his enemy had already ducked underneath it. His axe connected at Salman's knee, at the armor's joint. Even through her scope, Califia could see blood spurt and flow from the wound.

The Gurkani warrior fell, his screams distant but audible from the top of the hillock. He grabbed at his ruined knee, dropping his shield and rolling away from his enemy. She expected the crusader to immediately leap upon him and end his life, but instead he strode slowly toward his downed opponent, axe and shield at his side as though he expected no further threat from the man.

"Fortune was not with poor Salman today," Alishir said, his voice suddenly grim and hard-edged.

"Why does the crusader hesitate?" Califia asked.

"He is asking Salman if he yields," Alishir sounded as though he were talking to a child. "If the young man agrees, he will be held prisoner until ransom is paid."

"*Ransom?*"

"Money which his family is expected to pay for his release," Yakov explained.

Once more, it all centers around money.

Califia stared through her spyglass, transfixed at the scene unfolding before her. Salman rose, favoring his wounded knee and holding his mace out before him as if trying to keep the crusader at bay. His opponent raised his arms for battle, then swatted the mace aside with his shield and sank his axe directly into the Gurkani's neck. The young man fell to his knees, dropping his mace as blood poured from his wound. Califia winced as the crusader removed his weapon, then swiped his axe fully upon Salman's neck. She tore her eyes from the scope as his head rolled off his shoulders.

"Salman's family is very wealthy," Alishir said, mournfully. "They could have easily paid his ransom."

"Then why did he choose to die?" Califia felt horrified, both at the scene she had just witnessed and the mystery of why this man had chosen to end his life rather than face imprisonment.

"This was not about money; it was about *honor*," Alishir said. "The only way young Salman could restore *his* was to either defeat this opponent or die in the attempt."

"That's reprehensible," Califia said, her heart smoldering with anger at such an unjust system. "To us, honor is something that can be restored through service to the community, *never* through bloodshed."

"To us," Alishir said, sadly, "bloodshed sometimes *is* service to the community. Without brave warriors like young Salman, our empire would long ago have been subjugated by our neighbors."

"More importantly," Yakov said, "you need to

understand exactly what it is that you have volunteered for. You need to start training immediately with those who know how to fight individual duels or else you may share poor young Salman's fate."

Against her better judgment, she looked through the scope to see that Salman's body was being carried back by the Gurkani guards and the crusader was walking back into the city through the gate. One of Salman's escort carried the unfortunate young man's head and another held the empty helm.

"If I may be so bold as to advise you, your majesty," Alishir said, collapsing his own scope and sliding it into a pocket of his long coat, "I think you should spar with as many different warriors as you can from both your own people and your allies' until the day of the challenge."

"My sultan sent me, in part, to tell you that he is willing to provide sparring partners for this purpose," Yakov said, smiling amiably. "He earnestly prays for your success."

"I am surprised," Califia said, glancing at the Golden Gate as the doors finally eased shut. "I assumed both kings were still cross with me because of the incident with the griffins."

"They respect that you are trying to rectify your mistake," Alishir said. "Any victory against the crusaders is something we can all celebrate. I have selected a few of our finest fighters to aid you in this endeavor. They will begin arriving at your camp tomorrow, so please make sure someone knows where to send them."

"Understood," she said.

"Consider carefully who you choose among your people to train you," Alishir said. "You are not only honoring that person; you are placing your life in their hands."

As the three of them walked back to the Amazon camp, their Gurkani escorts trailing idly behind them, Califia thought about what she had seen. For the Amazons, single combat was a sport, a *game*. Warfare was something that was understood primarily as a collective affair. While it was true that great heroes like Achilla and Jactra were renowned for their prowess in single combat, it was their ability to inspire their fellow Amazons that made them legendary. If anything, their engagement in one-on-one fighting was almost considered a *sacrifice* which they made on behalf of the warriors who depended on them, not a means to gain fame and wealth.

It is a sacrifice which I am willing to make as well.

As they neared the short hide tents of the Amazons, she began to feel as though a weight was pressing upon her shoulders. She already had to find a trainer and begin daily sparring sessions, now she realized she also needed to set her affairs in order in case she lost this upcoming battle.

Alishir and Yakov took their leave of the queen and she walked toward the agora. A few Amazons took notice and gave her warm smiles. One even shouted *Hail Califia!* which caused many others to look toward her and do likewise. She smiled and waved graciously at them and was about to leave the square entirely when suddenly she saw a familiar face.

She ran toward Arianna, who was standing at the far end of the agora carrying a bundle of parchments in one hand and several charcoal sticks in the other. The queen wanted to embrace her lover and assumed Arianna wanted the same thing, but she made no effort to set the parchment and charcoal sticks down, so the queen instead stood awkwardly in front of her.

"I take it your shoulder is improved?" Califia said.

"It is still somewhat stiff," Arianna said, coldly.

"Walk with me," the queen said, smiling and leading her lover away from the noisy public square and into the woods nearby. "I did not see you at the games."

"I watched some Tikawich, but it only made me homesick," she said.

"We have been away far too long," Califia said, wondering what was bothering the normally cheerful young woman.

Arianna looked the queen in the eye. "I was hoping that we might consider returning home soon."

Califia turned toward her, utterly shocked.

"The Greeks still hold the walls," she said. "We sent some of them to the afterlife, but the foremothers have not, in the minds of our army, been properly avenged."

"Do me the honor of dropping the rhetoric," Arianna said, letting go of the queen's hand. "The foremothers are gone, as are those who enslaved and oppressed them. We, however, are still alive and I think we should try and stay that way."

Califia winced. "You have been only too happy to create monuments and plan murals for the glorious battles we have fought so far. What changed?"

Arianna grabbed the right side of her own tunic and peeled it carefully down her shoulder, revealing the bandage that still covered her bullet wound.

"As I lay in the medikos tent, do you know what I realized? I don't want to die for this."

"It's too late for second-guesses," Califia said, trying to pretend that the sight of the bandaged wound did not bother her. "We crossed the ocean, spilled blood, and you want us to give up this cause because you sustained an *injury*?"

Arianna rolled her eyes at the queen's words and she

carefully pulled her tunic back where it belonged.

"Staying here will only inflict greater injury," she said, plopping her art supplies on a nearby stump. "You promised me that this was more than just some empty quest for glory, then you decide to fight a duel?"

Califia winced. She had hoped her lover would be impressed at the actions of her *warrior queen.*

"The duty of the queen," Califia said, "is to sacrifice whatever is needed to protect her people, including herself."

"This is not sacrifice," Arianna said, jabbing a finger in Califia's face. "This is glory-seeking. This is fame-worship!"

"I won't have my motives questioned," Califia retorted, slapping away her lover's hand from out of her face. "I know why I am doing this and if you don't believe me then *fuck off!*"

Arianna stepped back, her eyes wide. She rubbed her hand where Califia had slapped it.

"Sorry to trouble you, oh mighty queen," she shook her head as she gave a mocking bow. "Don't worry, I won't question your asinine decisions any more."

"If you're not going to help me," Califia said, nearly shaking with rage, "then stay out of my way. I can't afford self-doubt. What you are doing is worse than *useless!*"

As soon as the words escaped her lips, the queen felt a stab of regret. Calling someone useless is an insult in nearly every culture, but among the Amazons it was practically a slur. Arianna turned and stormed away, striding deeper into the woods until she disappeared from the queen's sight.

Califia sighed. This exchange was nothing like what she had been picturing. She thought Arianna would be proud of her, would offer to commemorate the occasion with a statue or painting. It seemed like all they ever did was fight, and it made Califia feel utterly drained. *I can't afford fatigue right now.*

Bells began ringing at the agora and Califia realized that dinner would soon be served. She walked back toward the square, glancing behind herself periodically to see if perhaps Arianna was already seeking her out for a mutual apology. By the time she arrived at the agora, the food line had dwindled to only a few surly Amazons waiting for bowls of dark, rich stew.

Cradling the hot bowl and wooden spoon in her hands, she spotted an old stump on the edge of the agora which would serve well enough for a place to sit and eat. Before she had even finished chewing her first bite, a bulky woman approached carrying a steaming bowl. She stood there a moment before the queen realized she wanted her attention. Califia looked up and beheld a wide woman of average height with thick snaky hair and a familiar-looking tattooed beard. She twisted her lips in a way that made the queen believe she was nervous.

"Yes?"

"May I sit here?" She gestured to an unoccupied stump next to where Califia sat.

"Consider yourself invited," Califia said, gesturing to the seat and cramming the final bit of cold flatbread into her mouth. The woman sat and the queen was about to get up and leave.

"I guess you don't remember me," she said a little sadly, poking at the hot meat and maize in her bowl.

"Are you one of the captains?"

"Nothing so impressive as that."

The woman put a stray braid back in its place so that it did not wander into her food. Her beard tattoo was composed of interlocking octopus tentacles, but still the queen could not think of the woman's name.

"I must apologize," Califia said, after a long enough silence made it clear the woman was waiting for her to speak. "A queen should be more familiar with her people."

"I am not offended," she said, smiling shyly. "I only came here to thank you for what you did for me. You saved my life."

Califia felt hot with embarrassment. *Whom have I saved?* Then she remembered the melee during the first attempted assault, how the enemy warriors tried to pull one of the Gorgons into their ranks to kill or take prisoner and how Califia had stopped them and then slew the crusader champion. That woman had an octopus tentacle beard tattoo.

"Oh!" The queen said, trying to recall her name. It was right on the edge of her memory and she tried to fight for it and said the first name which materialized. "Daniera?"

"Deanna, my queen," she put a fist over her heart and bowed her head in a little salute.

"Of course," Califia said, pretending she remembered more clearly than she really did. "You guided me through that battle, as I recall. I doubt I would have known what to do otherwise."

"You did fine, better than I did," Deanna said. "I must confess that I am rather excited to see you slay another one of their big fighters."

Califia felt cheered by this woman and her faith in the queen's natural fighting ability. Her presence was a welcome relief after the bitterness of her exchange with Arianna, and suddenly she remembered the moment during the single combat game the day before when someone with thick, rope-like hair just like Deanna's had stared at the queen from behind the helm which concealed her face.

"Do you practice single combat, Deanna?"

Deanna flushed a little at this question and she shoved a spoonful of steaming food into her mouth, wincing slightly as it must have still been to hot to comfortably eat. Through her wincing, she nodded and smiled as she chewed.

"How did you perform yesterday?"

"I did not win," she said, looking slightly disappointed, "but I came within three contestants of the crown."

Califia could hardly believe her luck. She looked upon the Gorgon's face and estimated that she was probably between twenty-two and twenty-five. She was young, strong, eager to prove herself worthy of advancement within the Gorgon order, and she practiced single combat. *Surely Athena's hand is at work here.*

She took a deep breath and asked.

14

The sand-filled ball once more knocked the wind from Califia's lungs as it thumped into her chest. She wrapped her arms quickly around the projectile and nearly dropped it on her foot as her biceps burned. She paused to catch her breath then heaved the orb back to Deanna. The queen hoped that this time the ball would at least force the woman to take a step back to keep her balance. She was deeply disappointed when her opponent grabbed the object out of the air and still betrayed no sign of even being a little bit tired.

"That was better," Deanna said, sounding not at all convinced of her own words. "Let's drill for a bit."

Califia fought the urge to sigh with relief. In the two days she had been training so far, she had grown to hate that little heavy hide-covered ball more than anything or anyone she had encountered before. She selected one of the staves from the rack nearby as Deanna grabbed another. The muscles in the queen's back strained with an embarrassing soreness and she took deep breaths while trying to ignore the white-hot pain coursing through her forearms and shoulders.

Both women took up their ready stances, left feet leading as they aimed the tips of their polearms at one another's throats. Deanna pulled her weapon back in an obvious preparation for an attack and Califia readied herself to deflect the thrust. She swatted the tip of the quarter staff away. In a fluid motion that she had practiced many times, she thrust her own staff towards Deanna. Instead of striking her opponent in the chest as she had intended, however, she ended up shoving the tip of her weapon directly into the gap between the woman's arm and torso. Deanna looked down at the weapon's tip, a non-threatening length of wood wrapped in burlap and the queen thought she saw the woman give a little disapproving shake of her head. Califia was certain that in the shadows of Deanna's helm, the woman's eyes were rolling.

"You must complete the counter," she said patiently, tapping her leather padded breastplate with a warrior's pride. "I am in no danger."

We'll see about that. As they moved through the drill, she steadied herself and when the moment came, she put as much energy into her jab as she could muster.

"That was better," Deanna replied, appearing in every way unbothered. "Again."

The rest of the morning proceeded much the same, Califia performing drill after drill with spear, sword, sagaris, and every combination of arms Deanna could conceive. Some of the movements and techniques were familiar from her time serving with the coastal militia but as they grew more complex, she slightly regretted leaving after only one year.

The first visitors arrived at midday, Osman warriors escorted by Yakov. They brought a variety of wooden weapons in the shapes and varieties which she was likely to encounter from a crusader. Most were straight blades, but a few shorter sticks sufficed as practice maces and a few curved sabers were included because, according to Yakov, it wasn't unusual for the enemy to use weapons they had won in combat.

Califia practiced first against longswords, using the beard of her wooden sagaris to hook the blades and the rims of shields. The Osman soldiers demonstrated several counter-maneuvers and helped her find ways to mitigate them in an actual fight. She found them very helpful, and Deanna observed them closely and incorporated their techniques for later sparring practice.

They were sparring, Deanna swinging a long two-handed sword toward the queen's shield when their practice was interrupted by Yakov clearing his throat. The queen and her opponent released one another from their holds, brushed the dust from their greaves, and looked expectantly toward the emissary and his companion - a handsome and swarthy young man dressed in a shiny, well-polished set of chainmail characteristic of the Osmans, smiling politely.

"If it pleases you, fair queen," Yakov began, his annunciation lilting the same way it had in the Sultan's presence, "this is Prince Kasshim of Dulkadir."

Califia nodded and arced her torso into a polite bow, doing her best not to wince as her tortured muscles stretched and strained. Deanna did likewise, watching Califia and mimicking her motions uncertainly. *You're in my world now, Gorgon.*

"Thank you, Yakov," Califia said. "If you have other duties to attend, I don't want to keep you."

"Begging your pardon, your illustrious highness," Prince Kasshim said, his Greek practically flowering with politeness, "but I prefer that Yakov stay so that our honor might be preserved against gossips who might slander us with accusations of sinfulness."

Deanna turned to Califia with a face so twisted in confusion that the queen almost burst with laughter.

"He doesn't want anyone to credibly accuse him of having sex with me," she muttered to her trainer in Amazonian. She nodded her head as if she understood, then looked suddenly angry.

"As if he deserves such an honor," she said, suddenly blushing as she turned and pretended to organize the wooden weapons she had previously stacked haphazardly against a nearby oak.

"Yakov tells me you wanted to know more of how our enemy fights, yes?" Prince Kasshim spoke in a silky baritone and swaggered with an easy confidence. He held out his hand and Yakov gave him a wooden longsword. He spun it behind himself with a flick of his wrist, then brought it forward, aiming the pointy end toward her as he brought up his small convex triangular shield in a ready position. "Whenever you are ready."

Califia raised her sagaris and shield.

"Is sparring really the best way to begin?" Deanna asked, looking a bit concerned as the queen and the prince circled one another.

"Before a sculptor can shape his masterpiece," the prince said, smiling impishly, "he must familiarize himself with the clay."

He winked at the queen as he delivered the final part of his metaphor, though she wasn't sure why. With a sudden, swift motion, he swatted at her axe with his shield and charged forward, raising his wooden longsword as he closed the gap. The queen raised her shield while sweeping the underside of her sagaris behind his knee at the precise moment he struck. She shoved her shield into his chest with her full weight. He stumbled as she pulled the axe back, sweeping his leg and causing him to fall backwards, nearly dropping his practice sword as his back struck the earth.

Califia pinned his sword arm to the ground with her shield, dropped her sagaris, then drew a wooden dirk from her waist and held it near his throat. He swallowed as he realized what had happened, his throat nearly brushing against the wooden dagger as he gulped.

Something strange happened to his expression within the space of a few moments. At first he looked angry, almost enraged as his cheeks flushed and his brow furrowed. Then he closed his eyes, sighed, and then smiled amiably.

"Very good," he managed, his steady voice concealing the burst of emotions he had just experienced. "You kept a cool head in the midst of the fight, that's important."

Califia looked at Deanna, who was visibly trying not to laugh. The queen looked back toward Kasshim, worried she might start laughing herself and either embarrass or offend the young man.

"Shall we go again?" she asked, affixing the dirk back into her belt and lifting the shield so that the prince could wriggle out from under her clutches. They continued sparring for the better part of an hour, and the prince managed to impress Califia with a few new techniques and maneuvers.

"Women usually treat weapons as if they are dancing partners, but you do not," he commented during one of their breaks. "I can see why some men fear you."

"Do *you* fear me?" She asked, catching her breath enough to take another drink of water.

He grinned warmly.

"If I were afraid of you, it would be foolish to train

you to become more deadly, wouldn't it?"

"I suppose so," she quipped, noticing that he didn't actually answer the question.

"A whole nation of only women," he remarked, pouring some water on his face which trickled down his well-manicured chin beard. "Do your neighbors follow this custom as well?"

"Not exactly," Califia suddenly felt a pang in her heart at the thought of their neighbors. She pictured the Chumash wearing elaborate feathered headdresses, the Ohlone with their rainbow shell headbands, and the Kashaya with their bison horn necklaces. Her eyes suddenly burned as her heart ached to see them again. "Our neighbors aren't as… radical as we are, but their women are often leaders, ambassadors. I think women have much more status in their society than yours do."

Prince Kasshim looked wounded.

"You would not speak thus if you met our women. They are fierce as lions and graceful as deer."

"I have yet to meet any on the battlefield or among the Sultan's advisers. Those in the camp tend laundry or offer sex for coins."

His smile faded into a grave frown, the corners of his mouth growing taught as he lowered his gaze.

"I suppose that's true. Still, you cannot expect to understand us based solely on our organization on the battlefield," he took a swig of water from his gourd. "You should know, also, that he is not my Sultan."

"You are not an Osman?"

"I am Turk, but my people are not *Osmans*," his voice swelled with pride. "We do not bow and scrape before the great tyrant. We are a free people with our own leaders."

"Then why have you answered his call for Jihad?"

"Nearly all of our neighboring *Beyliks* have fallen to Osman domination. When the Sultan called for Jihad, I led our warriors here because we were promised fifty years of peace between us and the Osmans in return."

"So you are fighting on behalf of a king you do not trust in exchange for a promise with a time limit?" Califia's head spun at how ludicrous the entire arrangement seemed to her.

"I am doing what I must to ensure that my people can live in peace," he picked up his wooden sword and idly slashed it to the side a few times. "I am sure *you* understand the weight of duty."

"As queen, I certainly understand it," she agreed. "It's just… you described your people as free yet in order to preserve that freedom, you must come and serve a man you've described as a tyrant."

"Freedom is just a poet's word," he said grimly. "It sounds lovely but all of us are born into obligation one way or another."

"Speaking of obligation," Califia picked up her armaments and walked back into the sparring area.

They continued drilling and sparring until dusk began to blanket the sky. The prince made ready to leave for the night. She thanked him for his time and expected that Yakov would leave as well. The prince gave Yakov a significant look before tapping the left side of his nose twice. Then he left. Califia was curious about the strange gesture but waited until Prince Kasshim had strolled out of earshot.

"What was that?" She asked as the last bit of the prince's cloak flapped and then disappeared behind a tree in the distance.

"A great honor, your majesty," he said, practically giddy. "The prince would like to convey his deepest affection for you and wants to know if you will accept his suit."

"His *suit...*" She forgot the meaning of the Greek word for a moment but quickly remembered it had something to do with love. "Prince Kasshim is... in love with me?"

"His passion cannot be contained!" Yakov turned to Deanna, who looked as though she couldn't decide between confusion and fear. "Surely you must have seen it as well, his little smiling glances, the way he put his hand against your hip during the cutting drill... I do apologize if he was too forward, but clearly your beauty has enchanted him to the point of—"

"Stop, please," Califia's head spun with every word out of Yakov's mouth and she needed a moment to compose herself. "Just stop talking for a moment."

Had he really been trying to signal a romantic interest? How could she have missed it? She pictured the moments Yakov described but nothing seemed out of the ordinary. Then she decided to reimagine those moments but replaced the prince with an attractive woman and immediately felt her cheeks flush.

"He has entrusted me with a gift," Yakov continued after a moment, "should you accept his suit and agree to be courted by him."

"What is it?" Deanna asked before Califia could stop her.

Yakov took a long, slender box from his robe and the Gorgon stared at it as though expecting it to come to life and bite her.

"That won't be necessary," Califia said. "I won't be accepting his suit. Thank him for me, Yakov, and please convey my deepest respects and well-wishes for him and his people."

The emissary looked shocked and hurt, as though she were rejecting him. He put the gift back in his robe, looking like someone had just struck him. Like a boiling kettle suddenly overflows with scalding water, Califia suddenly felt cynical suspicion rising in her chest.

"Yakov," she said, hoping he might be a little more frank in his stunned state, "why would he want to marry me?"

"Well, he..." Yakov paused for a moment to wipe the sweat from his his forehead with his sleeve. "Prince Kasshim wants insurance that the Sultan will keep his word to respect Dulkadir's independence."

"So this would be a political arrangement?"

"Something like that, I think," Yakov cleared his throat and tried to recover his composure. "He would make a fine husband. I have only met one of his wives, but she was very amenable and—"

"*One* of his wives?" Califia felt suddenly scandalized. "How many wives does the man have?"

"Well... two, I think..."

"So, not only would I be marrying a man," she wrinkled her nose at this, "but I would be his *third* wife?"

"You mustn't take offense," Yakov continued nervously. "Your people would become wealthy if you accepted his suit! Dulkadir trades with some of the most skilled nations on earth! You could get spices from Aleppo, silk from the great Khans, steel from Damascus. In time, who knows but that Prince Kasshim's people and yours could forge your own empire!"

"I did not come here to forge an empire," Califia said, walking away from the drill ground with her Gorgon compatriot in tow. "Bring me sparring partners, not suitors."

Yakov did so over the next several days, escorting

Gurkani, Osman, and even a few Mamluk warriors, none of whom offered a proposal. Califia learned much from these volunteers and Deanna incorporated their fighting styles into their regular training routine. The queen hoped that Alishir might accompany the Gurkani fighters but Yakov said that he and Sultan Husayn had been buried in some kind of intense discussion for days.

On the fifth morning of her training, a company of men on horseback approached the clearing where Califia was slashing her wooden sword at the guts of a straw dummy. Most of the newcomers were Osman guards, dressed in their customary chain-and-plate armor with pointed helms but the man in the center was dressed in a fine coat and jeweled turban. At first she suspected that he was another potential suitor but something about his neat, pointed beard and his finely-waxed mustache seemed distantly familiar.

"When we last spoke," the man said, "I assumed we would never see one another again. How happy I am to be proven wrong!"

In addition to his fashion sense, his deep, warm voice and infectious smile gave him away.

"Admiral Kemal," Califia said, throwing down her weapons and removing her helm as she approached. "I didn't recognize you without a spyglass in your hand and the ocean splashing at your knees. Life on land doesn't suit you."

"Living on land might not be a problem for me much longer," he said, sounding a little sad, but quickly shaking his head at whatever thought lay behind his cryptic words. "They tell me you are going to challenge a Christian to single combat? How very chivalrous!"

"Just trying to make up for past mistakes."

Califia kicked at the dirt.

"None of these men speak your tongue," the Admiral suddenly switched to Amazon language, "so I may tell you that I don't think you are to blame for the disasters which have fallen upon this army. Our Sultan is a petulant child who delights in sentencing others to fates which he himself deserves."

Some of the guards raised their eyebrows, no doubt some understanding the word *Sultan*. If Admiral Kemal was concerned about this, he did not show it.

"I thought you had retired." Califia switched back to the Osman tongue. "What brings you to this place?"

"I was summoned by our wise and merciful leader," Admiral Kemal sounded piously sincere. Califia assumed this was for the sake of the guards. "It seems I am must be sentenced to whatever fate he thinks I deserve."

Califia's breath caught in her throat. She recalled all of the things which Yakov had told her about Admiral Kemal and the Sultan, how the man had barely kept his neck from the noose when the Venetians crushed his fleet and took Constantinopolis. The sultan sent him on an impossible mission as a sort of unofficial exile, believing the troublesome man would never return. Then he returned with an army of women. Now these women were blamed for nearly making shipwreck of the entire siege.

He is being executed because of us. Because of me.

"I will speak to the sultan on your behalf," Califia offered but the admiral waved away the gesture before she had finished speaking.

"I have entrusted my life to God," Admiral Kemal said, looking to the heavens as if expecting the deity to appear. He smiled at the queen. "Besides, I would not want the Sultan's wrath to fall upon *both* of us."

Before Califia could make a further offer to advocate

for the poor man, he pulled the reins of his horse and turned his mount away. The Osman guards fell in around him and continued their escort as the lot of them walked their horses toward the large brown tent wherein Admiral Kemal would meet his fate.

The queen's arms burned as she drilled and sparred through the morning but she was beginning to grow accustomed to the sensation, even welcome it. There was something very satisfying about hitting things. She could almost understand why some chose to remain enrolled in the militia long-term. As midday arrived, a young page with braids bound tightly to her skull brought them hot wraps stuffed with rice, maize, and spiced meat.

As she finished her meal, Deanna looked at the queen as if she was about to say something but her eyes wandered past Califia and fixed on something behind her. The queen turned to see Malachea approaching.

"Forgive the intrusion," the polemarkos said, sauntering forward as the women stood. "Though I have heard countless reports of your prowess and ferocity, I came to see your progress for myself."

"You want a demonstration?" Deanna asked, appearing flatfooted and stunned.

Malachea nodded. Califia and Deanna donned their sparring pads, picked up the wooden weapons and gave the polemarkos a demonstration, smacking shields, parrying thrusts, and periodically changing weapons. The polemarkos observed them quietly, occasionally rubbing her left elbow as though the pain from the injury she sustained some days before was lingering.

"You're coming along," Malachea said, after the demonstration had gone on so long that they were both worn out. "You're definitely faster; I see real improvement. Deanna, a word?"

After a brief glance at the queen, Deanna trudged over to Malachea and Califia stripped off her sparring pads, which were now hot and soaked with sweat, and put some distance between herself and the two gorgons. She tried to catch her breath, periodically glancing toward Deanna and seeing her expression grow darker. The queen saw the large woman nod a few times, but Malachea's voice was too low for her to catch even a single word.

The polemarkos strode away without so much as glancing at the queen. Deanna sighed and gestured toward the pile of discarded sparring pads on the ground.

"Suit back up," she said, sternly, picking up a wooden longsword. "We're not finished."

"Alright," Califia said, strapping the pads back onto her torso, legs, and arms. "Is something wrong?"

"Yes," Deanna said, a hard edge creeping into her voice. "You are fighting a duel in ten days and you are nowhere close to being ready."

"What did Malachea say to you?"

The large gorgon opened her mouth and for a moment appeared contrite and apologetic. Then her brow furrowed and her lips pursed as if she were frustrated.

"It doesn't matter. Pick up your axe and shield!"

They sparred through the afternoon, then went back to simple dummy-hitting drills as the sun began to sink low in the western sky. Califia walked back to the agora that evening, grabbing a bowl of meaty stew on her way. Her muscles were so sore, even eating hurt.

She did not bother asking Deanna what Malachea said. It seemed to Califia that the polemarkos simply was not satisfied unless she was making the queen suffer.

Every day started with the heavy toss bag followed by hours of nonstop sparring, dummy striking, and firm instruction. Deanna's previous friendly demeanor had been put to death by whatever Malachea said. It was almost as though Deanna had been replaced by that infernal woman.

By the thirteenth day of training, Califia finally felt that she was able to really keep up with her instructor. The moments when Deanna's weapons managed to connect grew more and more rare as the queen became faster, more agile, and reacted with greater precision.

Califia had been hoping that Arianna might show up and she searched for the young woman every time a group of Amazons came to observe the training. She was certain that if she could just get a few moments alone with her, that she could apologize and they would make up. After nearly a fortnight, however, her lover still had not sought her out, nor had Califia found time to perform a search of her own.

At mid-morning on that thirteenth day, Malachea once more arrived at the sparring circle as Deanna and Califia were working through a few tactics for countering an overhead slash from a longsword. This time she was dressed in sparring pads herself, and carrying a wooden sagaris and shield.

"I have come to check the queen's progress," Malachea said, tapping her shield a few times with the side of her wooden axe.

Deanna nodded and stepped aside without a word. Califia had not expected her to object but the woman didn't even wish her good luck. Whatever Malachea had said to her ten days ago seemed to have made her utterly indifferent to the queen one way or another.

"Are you sure your arm is ready?" Califia said, examining the polemarkos' limb for bruising but finding nothing but tattoos.

"I'll manage," she replied tersely, taking up a ready position as the queen did the same.

Califia thrust the head of her sagaris against Malachea's shield a few times, jabbing it like a spear. Malachea endured these annoyances at first, then suddenly smacked the left side of Califia's shield hard with the flat of her axe. The queen stepped to the right, then swung her shield hard against Malachea's axe-arm while hooking the woman's shield with her own sagaris' beard and yanking it hard to her right. Malachea swung her right arm around, trying to bring her axe in front of her but the queen planted her left foot against the woman's padded torso and thrust-kicked her to the ground.

Califia felt a surge of pride well within her as the polemarkos rolled over her shield and scrambled to her feet. Her movements felt natural, almost instinctual. There was no time to decide between actions; her body responded to the circumstance. Malachea approached again, tapping her shield menacingly as she charged forward.

Califia was expecting a heavy blow from the polemarkos' wooden axe but instead the woman charged directly into her with her shield, pushing against her as the queen braced her legs and held her ground.

"I'm sure you thought *that* was terribly clever," Malachea said as the women pushed against one another.

"You're the one who wanted to see my progress," Califia said, trying to work the beard of her axe over the rim of Malachea's shield. "How am I doing so far?"

Suddenly the queen felt her shield tilt upward from the bottom and she stumbled as Malachea suddenly stopped pushing and stepped back. She shoved her shield toward the polemarkos' face as she fell, hearing the thud of the woman's wooden sagaris behind her as she rolled out of danger.

"Confidence can be useful," Malachea gloated, "in *moderation.*"

It was Califia's turn to charge in this time, swinging her wooden sagaris overhead and locking its beard onto the rim of Malachea's shield. Malachea latched her wooden sagaris onto the queen's own shield so they ended up pulling together, their weapons and shields locked up in close quarters.

"You really won't be satisfied until you turn everyone against me," said Califia, her anger beginning to boil over now that her blood was up.

"Are you talking about Deanna?" Malachea asked, trying to free her sagaris from Califia's shield. "She wasn't doing her job."

"She wasn't doing it the way *you* wanted," Califia said, pulling with her shield to keep hold of her opponent's axe as she tried to free her own. "If I wanted you to train me, I would have asked you."

Malachea pulled hard with her shield, then suddenly pushed back against the queen, allowing both women to free their weapons. They exchanged a few blows, but all struck shield and neither could find an advantage.

"Your success in this duel is a matter of national pride," Malachea said. "You should have asked me to train you, but I had every right to make sure you were preparing properly."

"If your aim was to crush poor Deanna's spirits," Califia said, shoving with her shield and striking with her axe a few times, "then you succeeded."

"Deanna's spirits are not as important as securing your victory tomorrow."

They grunted and strained as each landed blow after blow but still neither could gain the upper hand. They locked shields and axes once more, Califia's muscles burning with strain from the continued effort.

"She was doing fine without you!" The queen hissed, pulling and pushing but not daring to break the hold yet.

"If you were being honest with yourself, you would know that wasn't true," Malachea said, grunting as she attempted unsuccessfully to free her axe. "She was going easy on you because *she is in love with you.*"

Califia broke the hold by shoving Malachea back just as she unhooked her axe from the rim of the infuriating woman's shield. As she took several steps back, she realized Malachea's axe now lay in the dirt between them.

The polemarkos backed up, sheltered behind her shield for a moment, then drew a wooden short sword from her belt and advanced upon her foe. Califia hooked the grounded axe with her own and tossed it to the side, then prepared to meet Malachea's charge.

They exchanged another flurry of blows, each blocking and parrying without either one making legitimate contact. Califia's heart pounded in her ears but she did not let up, nor did she fall for any of Malachea's obvious feints or tricks. Both women were breathing hard, however, and soon they were once more pushing shields against each other.

"Getting tired, old woman?" Califia said, feeling heartened that she was able to go blow-for-blow against the famously warlike polemarkos.

"Closer to bored," Malachea said, taking a swing with her short sword at Califia's helm. The queen ducked and easily avoided the hit.

"You probably always thought you could beat me in a fight like this," the queen said, loosening the fingers of her weapon hand until her fingers gripped just below the axehead. "How does it feel to be wrong?"

"You don't need me to answer that question for *you*."

Malachea swiped at her helm once more. The queen pulled the sagaris toward the blade and moved her shield up so that Malachea's blade was trapped between the underside of the axe's beard and the rim of her hoplon. Califia pulled hard down on the sagaris and shoved both weapon and shield to her left, forcing the weapon from her opponent's hand. Malachea yelped as the sword was pulled from her grasp but she quickly recomposed herself, stepping back and holding her shield with both hands. Califia did not give her time to recover, however, and once more they resumed their shoving match.

"I don't understand your need to constantly undermine me," Califia said, her blood coursing hot through her body.

"Think whatever you want about me," Malachea said, gritting her teeth as Califia hooked the top of her shield. "Everything I do is for the good of our people."

Just when the queen thought the sparring match was surely about to end, Malachea suddenly squatted low, holding her shield above her as the queen lost her balance and rolled over it. Califia scrambled to her feet, expecting Malachea to be already charging her, only to find the polemarkos appeared to be running away. She stopped, felt around in the sand for a few moments, then grabbed the wooden sagaris she had dropped before. She held it in the air like a trophy. Cheers erupted from all around her and Califia realized they had begun to attract a crowd. The spectators stayed far off, but they encircled the sparring fighters and cheered them on with words of encouragement.

The queen's skin burned with surprise and embarrassment. They had just seen Malachea rearm herself by playing an obvious trick on Califia. No matter what else happened, the queen was convinced she absolutely *had* to win this fight.

Califia banged her shield with her wooden axe. They charged at one another, pushing and swinging and hooking and countering until they once more settled into a stalemate shoving contest. The queen could feel her limbs begin to ache with weariness and her energy begin to wane from the burst she had received at the fight's beginning. *I need to find some way to undermine* her *for a change.*

"Everything you do is for the good of our people?" Califia said as she and Malachea grunted and pushed against one another. "If you had your way, Yakov would be dead and we might be at war against the Osmans!"

Even from under the shadow of her thick-padded sparring helm, Califia could see Malachea's eyes glance to the side as she tried to think of a retort. The queen bashed the woman's shield a few times with her sagaris, forcing her attention on the fight as she thought of something else to unnerve her.

"What about lobbying to become polemarkos behind my back? What did that serve besides your own ambition?"

More heavy blows from the queen, more exhausted defense from Malachea. Her breathing was heavy and her skin glistened with sweat. Califia's limbs burned with a renewed fervor at the sight of her opponent's fatigue.

"I know you don't approve of the lightning campaign I used to win the election," Califia said, her blood boiling, "but at least I never would have murdered my own *sister.*"

While the polemarkos was still stunned from the accusation, Califia rolled her wooden sagaris along the edge of her enemy's shield, let it drop after it reached the side, then hooked Malachea's ankle with the underside of her axe. She pushed forward and her opponent fell backward, flailing and dropping her weapon. Before the polemarkos could regroup, Califia stood up, placing her foot upon her fallen enemy's chest and resting the edge of her wooden axe to the side of her neck.

The crowd erupted in a roar far louder than the queen would have expected. They began chanting her name and trilling with an excitement that permeated the air like lightning. The queen raised her axe and somehow the shouting grew louder. She stepped off of Malachea and strutted around the sparring ring, letting the praise of her people wash away any insecurities she had been harboring about her martial prowess.

She looked to where Malachea had fallen, but the woman was already gone. She continued smiling for the crowd as their adulation gradually died down, but her stomach felt like a clenched fist.

Basilea was occupied that night, smoothing over some misunderstanding with their Osman neighbors which Califia would otherwise be handling but for the urgency of her training. The queen ate alone and while she spotted Deanna in the distance a few times, she did not see Malachea.

Dionysia was holding court once again, regaling her captains with some story involving a cougar and a bear which the queen did not doubt was spun from whole cloth. Still, where was the woman's mother? Where could the polemarkos possibly be during evening mealtime?

Califia made a plan. She would apologize, ask for Malachea's forgiveness. She lost her head in the heat of battle, everyone knows that happens sometimes. As she walked back to her tent, the queen occupied her mind with the speech she would give. When it was finished and polished and perfect, it would absolve her of having any suspicions about the polemarkos' unfortunate sister.

She saw the familiar flaps of her own tent and then suddenly they disappeared. No, not disappeared — something was obscuring them from view. In the dim haze of twilight, she realized too late that it was a person who now stood half a spear's length in front of her. A woman. An Amazon.

"Please don't scream," Malachea said. Her braids in the dim light of early evening looked like the snakes they were meant to represent. She was holding something small in her hand, but Califia could not see whether it was a weapon of some kind.

"Polemarkos!" Califia hissed, in a similar whisper with which the woman had greeted her. "You startled me."

"Why did you say that I murdered my sister today?"

Califia took a deep breath and prepared to lie her ass off.

"I'm sorry for what I said," she began, suddenly realizing she was rehearsing her half-baked speech with the elements out of order. "Everyone loses their head in the heat of battle sometimes, don't they?"

The large, imposing woman stepped forward so that if Califia bent one of her arms up at the elbow, her fingers would brush against the woman.

"Please don't lie to me," she said. Now that she was closer, Califia looked into her eyes and saw no trace of the hostility or aggression which she had expected. Malachea's eyes were red from weeping, her brows forming a perfect arch of worry and sadness. Califia felt compelled to speak on the matter in broad terms.

"Basilea believes that your sister and the captains with her did not fall victims to a random rockslide," the queen said, feeling a wave of relief as she finally admitted this suspicion. "She believes it was murder."

"And that mine was the hand that arranged her death," Malachea completed the thought. A fresh tear rolled down the polemarkos' cheek. She sniffled and sighed. Her breath formed a rolling cloud in the cool night air.

"Please don't be angry with Basilea," the queen said, growing increasingly uncomfortable with the unspoken tension that now filled the air. "And again, I am very sorry for—"

"No," Malachea said, holding up her hand. "You need not apologize for speaking the truth."

Califia just nodded at first, thinking that Malachea meant the truth that Basilea was suspicious. But the polemarkos' countenance was not merely sad. It was guilty.

"What truth have I spoken?" The queen asked, moving her hand subtly to the hilt of the triumvir dagger. Malachea brought her hand up and as Califia's fingers closed around her weapon's hilt, she saw that the item the woman held was not a small weapon, but a ceramic remembrance totem in the shape of a white feather.

"Basilea is correct," Malachea said, looking down at the clay feather with something approaching reverence. "I murdered my sister."

15

Her griffinsteel armor had been shined to a mirror finish. Califia stared at her own reflection, idly thinking about coronation day. It seemed impossibly long ago. For most of her life, she had never been completely comfortable wearing armor but now it felt comfortable, almost natural. Strapping on armor was almost like wearing a second skin.

After a fortnight of training, her muscles possessed a taut awareness, a constant readiness for action. There were still some things she was not ready for. Malachea's confession from the previous night haunted her and she had no idea what to do about it.

She actually killed her sister.

The full account was, of course, much more complicated but the fact remained that Malachea, the polemarkos of the Amazon army was guilty of *sorocide.*

"Finish quickly!" Basilea said, poking her head into the tent. "The people are ready!"

Are they?

She took a deep breath, feeling a slight resistance from the griffinsteel breastplate. She glanced down at her armguards, skirt slats, and greaves, pleased at how the alloy flashed golden even in the dim morning light of the tent. She stepped outside.

Raucous cheering filled the air. She raised her sagaris and the wave of sound somehow boomed louder, as if everyone in the islands of California were screaming her praises at the top of their lungs. She breathed it in as the Gorgon honor guard, composed of warriors chosen by Malachea, took up their positions around her. The queen recognized Deanna among them, her octopus tentacle beard tattoo visible just behind her cheek guards, but she did not return the queen's gaze.

They marched along the road that led to the Golden Gate, where challengers went to regain their lost honor. She had seen a few men die before that gate, and had seen just as many succeed in killing their foes or wounding them badly enough for them to yield. Her people walked on either side of her, following in a massive procession which the queen hoped would not look too much like an impending assault. At a point approximately halfway between the gate and the camp, most of her massive entourage stopped as Malachea raised her sagaris. The polemarkos stepped closer to the queen, passing between the Gorgon bodyguards who made way for her without missing a step.

"Don't forget to breathe," Malachea said. She tapped her own breastplate. "It's not too constricting, is it?"

"I puffed up like a frog before I tightened the straps," Califia replied, giving the thorax a good shaking to demonstrate that it was tight enough to stay on, but limber enough to allow for movement.

"Stay on his flank as much as possible. The helmets these people wear restrict their periphery."

"I *know*," Califia said, feeling instinctively defensive.

"We've discussed this a thousand times."

"Of course. Sorry," Malachea said, giving her head a shake. She took in a breath and let it out quickly as if centering herself.

"By the Triumvirs," Califia said, smiling and nearly giggling at the revelation she had just received. "You're more anxious about this than I am."

"Of course I am!" Malachea sounded as though she thought this would be obvious. "If you lose today, you get to be remembered as the queen who died heroically restoring Amazonian honor. I'll be remembered as the incompetent polemarkos who let it happen."

Califia turned away quickly; the longer she gazed at the polemarkos, the more her mind tried to ponder what ought to be done. This was no time to get lost in thoughts of the future. *First, win the duel. Then the matter of Malachea can be decided.*

Their party reached the Golden Gate, a name clearly inspired by poetic flourish rather than any physical reality. If there ever was any gold on this gate, it had been stripped away long ago, leaving behind only thick splintering wood held together by brass fittings.

The queen stepped forward and Yakov, who had been following with his own entourage of Osman guards, likewise approached the gate and nodded at the queen.

"I, queen of California," she paused for a moment to allow Yakov to translate her message, shouting it into a conical amplifier, "hereby challenge the honor of those who currently occupy Constantinopolis to a bout of single combat. Let any who think themselves brave enough come face me or else we shall know you as cowards."

When Yakov finished interpreting her words, she turned to him.

"What is the name of that language again?"

"Frankish, fair queen."

She nodded as if she understood, but was once again puzzled by these people. When she told Yakov she would challenge the squatters herself using Greek, he balked and told her that the champion almost certainly would not speak Greek. She had known that, just like their own alliance, the Christian faction was made up of many different peoples with many different languages and customs but she was curious why there were not more Greek speakers among them. Perhaps the language "Frankish" was derived from Greek but she didn't understand a single syllable that Yakov had shouted on her behalf.

"I have some news," Basilea said when Malachea had walked some distance away to speak with some of Yakov's men. "I think I might find the proof we've been looking for."

It took Califia a brief but flummoxed moment to realize she was referring to the investigation into Malachea's role in her sister's death. While the polemarkos had not sworn the queen to secrecy, she had not told anyone else about the confession, nor the actions of Kassandra.

"Malachea has served admirably as polemarkos," Califia said, nervously trying to change the subject. "Perhaps it would be better if we dropped the matter."

"Dropped the—" Basilea sputtered. "I'm sure you feel warm and friendly with her since she started helping you prepare for this fight, but you cannot trust her. Besides, we cannot turn away from justice merely because it's inconvenient."

Califia wanted to protest further but she could see from Basilea's rigid bottom lip that it would be fruitless at the moment. She decided to try a different tactic.

"What proof have you obtained?"

Basilea's stern expression softened into one of relief.

"Three of the Gorgons whom she was supposedly with on the day her sister went to Persephone's embrace confessed to me that they did not see her at all that day."

"You spoke with them about this directly?" Califia's neck stiffened with goosebumps.

"I've been drinking with them," Basilea explained. "I helped them construct a still and every few days we visit it together."

"What if one of them told Malachea?"

"I doubt our conversations are interesting enough to report to the polemarkos," Basilea said. "I'm being careful. I do know how to extract such information subtly."

"You need to stop, at least for now," Califia said sternly. "It's too big a risk to investigate any further while we are in this dangerous place. Wait until we return to our native shores before you pursue this matter any further."

Basilea looked at the queen as though she was about to launch into yet another passionate lecture, but instead she turned her gaze to the massive gate before them.

"No matter," the old woman said, as if the whole thing was an idle pastime. "We'll be on our way home soon enough."

"That reminds me," Califia said, slipping the triumvir dagger from her belt and being careful to hold it only by the scabbard. "I would like you to care for this during the fight."

"I am honored," Basilea said, taking the weapon and sliding its scabbard into her sash. "The polemarkos will probably be displeased you did not entrust it to her care."

"Actually, it was Malachea's idea to entrust it with you," Califia smiled a little at Basilea's surprise. "The griffins were bonded to you until recently, so she thought it would be best for them to be under your care if this all goes poorly."

"Don't even consider the possibility," Basilea objected. "You will fight and win, just as you did against their last champion, and we will return home with our obligations to these people satisfied and the national honor fully intact."

"Let's hope Nika agrees."

As the words left the queen's lips, a horn blast resounded over the mid-morning sky from the city walls. The large gates rumbled as they slowly opened, and a long pike jutted out through the space that appeared between the doors. Then there were two, then four, and soon after twenty pikemen marched out of the ever-widening gates, weapons at the ready. They wore conical helmets with flanged rims and burnished steel cuirasses that seemed to swallow the sunshine rather than reflect it. Their loins were covered by plates and their legs as well, which gave their marching a distinctive clanking sound. Lighter armored men followed, and Califia saw that they wielded loaded crossbows which they held across their torsos. Their eyes searched the horizon ahead of them, ever watchful for targets and threats.

Behind the crossbowmen strutted a single, heavily-armored man with a triangular shield strapped to his left arm carrying a large feathered helmet and a long-bladed sword which he rested across his plated shoulders. His jaw was angular and sharp while his cheeks were high and his eyebrows narrow and stern. His eyes locked onto her immediately and he permitted his mouth a curling little smirk.

She expected a sharper gut-wrenching sense of revulsion but she felt only further curiosity about these enemies. She decided that the man was attractive, as far as men *could* be attractive. His brown hair had an auburn shimmer and his lips were just full enough that in the right light he could almost be confused for a woman.

As her opponent drew closer, she noticed the many scratches and small impact dents in his armor. She had hoped that the enemy would send a young inexperienced fighter, underestimating her because she was a woman. Everything about this man — his confident swagger, the scarring on his armor, his practical tied-back hair — led Califia to believe that he was a dangerous combination of young, ambitious, and experienced.

"I do not like the look of him," Basilea said, almost mirroring the queen's thoughts.

"I'll give his head to someone else, then," Califia said, smirking in a manner which she imagined resembled that of the cocky young man she was about to face. As she and Basilea arrived with the honor guard and Yakov, the soldiers from Constantinopolis parted in the center to allow their champion to pass through. He drummed his fingers against his helm a few times and it sounded like a galloping horse.

He opened his mouth and spoke rapidly. Califia thought his language sounded very interesting but she didn't understand a single word of it.

"His name is Sir Guy de Saint Laurent and he is here to accept your challenge and fight for the honor of his King, his people, and his God," Yakov translated, smiling as he interpreted the man's pronouncement with a very sarcastic intonation. "I would not want to fight him if I were you, fair queen, but I suppose that's why I didn't become a warrior."

Califia nodded respectfully at her opponent, who set his helm on the ground and pulled a padded covering over his head, tucking its ends into his plate. She donned her own helm and pulled the chinstrap firm.

Focus.

Califia stepped forward and the others backed away so that she and Sir Guy had space to move about. She placed her hand in the boss of her shield and picked it up, lifting her sagaris likewise in a salute to her opponent. He smiled impishly and shoved his helm down over the padded covering on his head, lowering the faceplate so that all she saw of him were the whites of his eyes peering through narrow slits. He returned her salute, lifting his massive sword and then immediately pulled it behind his shield and appeared ready to begin. She did likewise, cocking her axe-arm back as she moved her hoplon to the fore.

As they circled one another. Sir Guy's movements were smooth and light, his posture aggressive but cautious, and his sword steady and threatening. Her pulse quickened as she felt the bloodrush of battle coursing through her muscles.

He shouted and lunged, raising his sword for an overhead slash. Califia raised her shield as the muscles in her right arm tensed instinctively to counter-swipe. He stomped his foot but then quickly sprinted backward and laughed as if it was all a big joke. She lowered her shield back to its ready position and her axe-arm unclenched. He did this several more times until she understood that he was studying her reaction, looking for weaknesses in her defense.

Good idea.

She likewise gave a battle cry and pretended she was about to strike him several times, noting his reaction time and trying to gauge his instincts. As she prepared to strike at his left elbow, suddenly he jabbed at her midsection twice, then let loose a big arcing swing at her head. She blocked the first two blows with her shield and ducked the swipe, unleashing a jab with her sagaris that dinged his chestplate and forced him to stumble back a few paces.

He lifted his faceplate and gave her an approving smirk with a little nod. Coming from Malachea, this would have been flattering, but she detected sarcasm in the gesture, a hint of being patronized. She swatted her sagaris against her shield as if impatient for the bout to continue. He lowered his faceplate and gave his own shield a couple quick smacks before charging toward her with frightening vigor.

She thrust out her sagaris to try and keep him at a distance but he swatted it aside with his shield and slashed down with his sword. She deflected with her shield and then rammed its rim into his faceplate, hoping to at least give it a dent. His helm rang but he continued his assault seemingly unfazed. He swatted at her shield with the flat of his sword, a blow which she first thought was a mistake. As she pushed her shield forward, hoping to shove him back, she saw his sword point appear over her aegis' rim, pivoting downward toward her right shoulder. He jabbed at her pauldron and she felt the point probing, searching for a space to slip through.

Califia bent her knees and hooked the beard of her axe behind his knee. She shoved. He stumbled over her axe and she raised her shield to strike him with its edge. He rolled out of reach and her aegis thudded against the dirt. This brought a cheer from her bodyguards and Yakov's, while the Crusader's supporters jeered at their champion and called out to him in their strange, nasal language.

He stood tall for a moment in a posture of defiance, then hit his left breast twice with his sword hand before once more barreling toward her. She thrust her sagaris for his left shoulder. The griffinsteel head bashed his chestplate but he pressed forward as though he hadn't noticed. His sword swung up for a big angled slash and she moved her shield to block. His feet shuffled quickly and suddenly his left hand was grabbing the shaft of her axe. He raised and swung his sword down once more, straight for her hand. She pulled the axe in vain as the blade came down and released her weapon just before his sword would have struck her wrist.

She sprinted backward, raising her shield and drawing her sword, expecting that at any moment he would continue his onslaught. Instead, he turned around and lifted the axe to show his comrades, who cheered uproariously at his new trophy. Califia's neck became hot with rage as the midday light glinted off the gold-tinged tip which she had sharpened herself earlier that morning. *Not sharp enough.* He ended his promenade by throwing the sagaris to the ground near the pikemen and taking up a ready stance once more.

Califia smoldered with anger as she circled her opponent, her sword ready and her muscles hot with a desire for revenge. She feinted toward his left, banging her sword against her shield as he moved to defend. She did this again but pretended to attack his right, then struck his left elbow with the flat of her sword. She dodged as he thrust his blade toward her, catching its edge against her shield as she directed it slightly upward. He realized too late what was happening and she saw his eyes grow wide through the narrow slits in his helm. She shoved her sword quickly so that her hand guard was just behind his and then jerked the weapon from his grasp with all her might. He grunted as he stumbled a few steps forward, then swiftly retreated.

She placed her shield gently on the ground and held his massive sword aloft, twisting her wrist back and forth so that it looked like a shimmering beacon as Basilea and Yakov cheered along with the bodyguards. She heard her opponent clear his throat loudly behind her and turned to see that he was waiting for her to rejoin the fight, a blunt flanged mace in his hand.

She approached cautiously, creeping closer with halting steps and peering from behind her shield. Sir Guy shoved at her with his shield and she stepped back just enough to keep her maneuverability. Her shield rung like a funeral bell as she deflected a strike. She managed to connect a glancing blow to his helm as she leapt back.

They continued this way for some time, exchanging a few close-range blows which mostly missed or which landed against well-armored body parts. Around their seventh scrum she felt a weariness in her left arm, a combination of fatigue and muscle cramp. As she backed away from the latest round of battering, she shook her left arm a few times, thinking that it must just be overtired from gripping her shield so tightly.

As the fight continued, she realized the relentless hammering of her opponent's mace was wearing her down. With every hit, her shield smashed into her forearm and sent spikes of pain throughout her arm and shoulder. She adjusted her grip on the boss handle, trying to keep her aegis flush against her arm like that of her opponent.

Amid a particularly harrowing series of blows, an animalistic panic blared at the fuzzy edge of her mind, a savage shriek of fearful defiance. *Why am I sensing the griffins?* As they broke away from one another, the knight

took a swipe at Califia's head that came uncomfortably
close and she felt another spike of terror pour into her
mind.

Sir Guy was striking faster but his blows were landing
with noticeably less force. *He's getting impatient.* She held
her ground beneath his hammering blows, her hand
getting numb from the repeated vibrations. As she was
unable to see his upper body, she turned her gaze toward
his lower section and noticed a gap between his leg plates
and the knee joints. When he finally paused, she assumed
from exhaustion, the queen thrust her sword toward the
gap, putting as much force behind it as possible.

She felt a gritty sort of sensation in her sword hand
and realized that she had struck a layer of chain mail her
opponent was apparently wearing beneath his plate. He
jerked his knee back and swung hard for her head. He
overcorrected and she swiped at his helm, nearly striking
it as he lurched back. He swung the mace again, swinging
too hard once more, and she ducked the blow but stayed
close.

For a tiny fraction of a heartbeat, she spotted a sliver
of puffy white between his breastplate and pauldron
where the plates had been pulled apart by his panicked
overcorrections. She plunged her sword into the man's
right shoulder, pulling it back immediately as he shrieked
in pain. She stepped back and glanced at the tip of her
weapon. It looked as though she had dipped it in
manzanita wine.

Her opponent wriggled his gauntleted left hand into
the gap where he had been wounded and withdrew metal
fingers covered in red. He gave her a curt nod, said
something in Frankish, and then charged toward her like
a griffin upon its prey. He swung quickly again, but these
strikes were forceful and soon Califia's shield arm was

aching once more. She struck back whenever she could, but only managed to slow him a little.

Once more she sensed the animal panic from the griffins and did her best to ignore it. *Any moment*, she thought, *his right arm will grow tired.* Then she would pounce. His wound must be filling his body with pain. He would make a mistake any moment and she could take control of this fight.

He continued his unrelenting assault, smacking her shield, her armor, her sword. She moved as quickly as she could but felt spikes of pain everywhere he struck. She leaped back out of range and he pursued. She dodged, ducked, and even rolled away as he shouted and swung. His compatriots on the wall were jeering him and Califia reckoned that his wounded pride was the source of his seemingly endless supply of vigor.

The griffins' fear flooded her mind like a ringing in her ear that suddenly spiked every time she was struck by the mace. Finally he stopped his swinging and stood ready for a moment, breathing so heavily that his armor was visibly shifting with each breath. Over his shoulder, she spotted a mysterious glowing red light. She cursed as she understood; Basilea was resting her hand on the hilt of the triumvir dagger. From the look on her advisor's face, she wasn't doing this intentionally. *I am still bonded to the flock.*

She waved her sword, desperately trying to wake Basilea from her apparent carelessness but to no avail. Sir Guy took notice of this gesture and interpreted it as an invitation to launch into a new series of strikes and blows. She countered as best she could, determined to find some way to damage her opponent, but to no avail. The few times she managed to wedge the tip of her sword into a gap in the plate, the chainmail beneath proved strong enough to resist being pierced.

They broke away from each other once more, Califia now breathing at least as heavily as her young opponent, whose weapon hand had developed a tremor. Basilea was to her right now, so the queen quickly turned and shouted, "The Dagger!"

The old woman looked down at her hand and gasped as she understood what had happened, then quickly released the weapon at her belt as if it had been replaced with a snake. Sir Guy tilted his head like a perplexed animal. Then he gave his mace a flourishing spin before once more swinging it at the queen.

She took to dodging this time, which was more difficult but much more satisfying as she heard his grunts of aggression quickly transform into shouts of frustration as he put more and more force behind his blows but struck only air. He was nearing the point where his exhaustion would make him vulnerable, she was sure of it. Finally he overswung hard enough that she saw once more a gap of a white padded undertunic in his exposed armpit and jabbed for it with her sword. This would not be a glancing blow, but a final thrust. As her blade neared its target, suddenly she felt something wrap around her wrist like a hungry octopus. Her blade stopped a hand's width from the vulnerable spot. Sir Guy had grabbed hold of her wrist with the hand of his shield arm.

Califia tried to pull away, lifted her shield to bash the offending limb but Sir Guy was quicker. He raised his mace and brought it down on her sword hand, forcing her to drop her weapon and cry out in pain as her gauntlet was dented and her fingers felt crushed. He swung his weapon upward and it struck the right side of her helm like a bolt of lightning. Colored dots swirled in and out of her vision and she realized she was lying face-down on the dirt with her shield and left arm pinned beneath her torso. She rolled to her right and immediately felt the crush of a steel knee upon her left arm, then the octopus crush of Sir Guy's grip on her right wrist as she tried to reach for her dirk - the last weapon on her belt.

She could not see his expression beneath his faceplate but imagined that it was proud and triumphant. He drew a dirk of his own and dangled the tip above her throat. She expected at any moment the blade would plunge into her neck and she would see her mother in the court of Persephone. Her heart beat wildly. Her limbs went numb with fear. She stopped wriggling and took a deep breath. This was the end; she had lost.

She felt a spike of terror and rage suddenly flood her mind from the griffins and glanced at Basilea to see that she was holding the hilt on purpose this time. The red gem glowed blindingly bright and the expression on the former queen's face was one of dark vengeance. She raised her eyebrows slightly, and Califia saw a fire in the old woman's eyes which frightened her.

On Basilea's left flank, Deanna stood ready, gripping the head of her sagaris where it sat in the sling on her hip. Her eyes also glinted with a desire for violence. Malachea held the head of her axe and wore a ready expression, glowering at the knight who had pinned the queen.

At first Califia believed they were offering to save her. Surely they saw that Sir Guy would dispatch her before they came close enough to prevent her execution? Then she realized her mistake. *Those are not expressions of salvation; they are the faces of vengeance.* Killing her would be Sir Guy's last act in this life, but what would come next? The crossbowmen near the gate would easily kill every member of her entourage in such an event.

Sir Guy said something — maybe a question? — and remained still as a statue for a moment. Califia glanced side to side, wishing Yakov wasn't standing in a blind spot.

"He asks if you wish to yield, fair queen," Yakov said. She could hear his feet shuffling as they always did when he was anxious, just as they had done that day when Malachea first brought him before her. She shared his anxiety, fearing what would happen to her friends and to the entire Amazon nation if she allowed them to act rashly.

"I yield," the queen said quickly, releasing the shield boss from her left hand.

Yakov relayed the message and Sir Guy stood up immediately, offering her a hand when she tried to rise. She considered swatting it away, spitting at it as though accepting help from an enemy was something her honor would not permit. Instead she took the gauntleted hand with her own and he lifted her swiftly from the ground. She unfastened the chinstrap and removed her helm, then presented it to him. He grabbed it and held it aloft for all of Constantinopolis to see.

The queen took the opportunity to look upon her friends for perhaps the final time. Malachea gaped like a trout, Deanna glared at the ground, and Basilea's bottom lip quivered as a tear rolled down her cheek.

Califia closed her eyes and felt her own cheeks begin to moisten with tears. She wiped them quickly away as Sir Guy exchanged a few words in his nasally language with Yakov. The great roar of cheers within the city sounded like a gigantic wave that was about to crash upon her head.

Part IV: Captivity

16

Sir Guy gently took her elbow and guided her through the massive open doors of the city gate. She gingerly probed her tender right hand, which her opponent had bashed with his mace, and was relieved that none of the bones seemed broken. She and her escort halted just inside as the gates continued their gradual crawl.

Even over the rumble of the closing gate, the thunder of the crowd was louder and more terrifying than a summer storm. The streets were packed with armored and commonly-dressed well-wishers alike, many of the latter group sitting atop the thatch-roofed buildings near the gate and shouting what she assumed was praise toward Sir Guy de Saint-Laurent. The knight started raising his right arm to wave at his admirers, but winced and opted to use his left instead. The queen remembered his wound and felt a short burst of pride.

While waving and smiling at his adulating crowd, Sir Guy's gaze fell upon her and he blinked as though he had forgotten about her. He made a summoning gesture to a short man wearing a rough-looking robe with a circular bald patch on the very top of his head. The newcomer came running and exchanged a few words with Sir Guy in their strange tongue. He looked upon Califia as if she were a wild animal.

"Are you wearing clothes underneath your armor?" he asked. At least, she believed that was what he asked; he spoke Greek with such a heavy accent that she could barely understand him. She nodded and he continued, "You must remove it at once. Prisoners are not permitted to wear armor."

Her heart sank like an anchor. *This is happening.* She began loosing the straps on the thorax and unbuckling the belt of her plated skirt. She unfastened the closure on her greaves and slipped off her armguards, placing all the pieces of armor in a pile in front of her. It looked like a memorial to a fallen warrior.

A young man nearby picked up the pile and fell in line behind the procession that formed with Califia and Sir Guy at its head. She was relieved that no one clapped any irons onto her or handled her in any way. She had the impression, however, that Sir Guy might grasp her arm if she lagged too far behind him.

She had resolved herself not to look upon the ground with shame as she reckoned they would expect. She forced her head to stay level and was soon glad she did; the interior of this city was even more impressive than its massive outer walls. They marched past an enormous palace with archways where the servants and residents stood and cheered. In the distance, she could see decorative columns stretching into the sky, many of which had statues of mounted warriors sitting atop them.

As they rounded a corner, she spotted several groups of men dressed in elaborately fancy coats and with impeccably neat hair and beards.

"Are those the kings of the Greeks?"

Her guide raised his eyebrow and pursed his lips. It seemed that he was trying to decide between whether Califia was mocking him or insulting him.

"Apart from a few no-account mercenaries, the only Greeks here are cooking our food, changing our bedsheets, and laundering our clothes," he spat his answer as if trying to emphasize his point. "The men you see before you are the King of the Franks, the King of the Muscovites, and some of their vassals."

She rolled her eyes. *More hierarchy to memorize.* The Californians used titles for the sake of public accountability. The people in this part of the world seemed to use titles to place themselves above it. Before this journey, she hadn't realized that tyranny could be so complicated.

They passed a large building topped by a magnificent dome and she gaped at it until they walked out of its sight. *Even tyranny is not without style.* She puzzled over what Yakov had told her of succession and politics and right-to-rule, and decided she was definitely missing a piece of this puzzle.

"If none of the kings are Greek," she said, hoping to avoid offending this litigious little man, "then how can they claim rightful rulership of this place?"

He gave her another searching look, then quickly glanced around as they turned another corner and passed a large square building whose exterior was decorated by beautiful mosaic artwork. He reached his hand inside the left part of his robe and scratched his shoulder.

"The last natural heir to this kingdom sold his inheritance and claim to the king of the Franks."

Califia didn't know what to think of this. *Inheritance can be purchased with money?* Sir Guy gave them a sharp look, still smiling and waving at his adoring crowd, and exchanged a few words with her conversation partner in their shared language. At first the man sounded defensive, but then their tones seemed to de-escalate, as if whatever conflict had just erupted was a matter of no great importance to either party.

"Sir Guy thinks you talk too much for a woman," he gestured to the knight, who was still playing the chivalrous hero. "He wanted to know what you were asking about and I told him 'the history of the city.' You need to be careful who you ask questions of, especially questions of who belongs on Constantinopolis' throne."

"I see," Califia said, pretending to understand. "Why is the king of — the Muscovites, was it? Why is he here?"

"He is married to the last emperor's daughter."

She shook her head once again at the silliness of leaving the important business of leadership in the hands of something as fickle as reproduction. Her mind wandered to the groups they had encountered in the countryside and wondered where they fit into this tapestry of rivals.

"We fought with Wallachians on the road to Gelibolu, do they also have a claim to this city?"

The man rolled his eyes in a way that made Califia feel foolish. She resolved that this would be her last question.

"The mountain savages are here to support the Russian savages, and only because they are tired from fighting one another. Their leader is here and you should pray you do not meet him. He is a foul pagan."

The way the man spat the word pagan gave her the impression that he would be most unhappy to learn that this label applied to Califia as well.

Suddenly she felt a flutter of panic as she remembered that in only a fortnight it would be Olympus Day. Who would wear the paper crown in her absence? Basilea, she supposed. Then again, perhaps Malachea would insist on wearing it as polemarkos. What other queenly honors did she plan to grab while Califia was indisposed?

Curse that woman.

She cursed herself as well for not telling Basilea about Malachea's confession. The polemarkos' explanation made sense, but was it true? Had she gone easy on the queen during their sparring just to give her a false sense of security?

Califia shook her head at these intrusive thoughts. Malachea appeared ready to tear Sir Guy's head from his neck with her bare hands when the queen herself was under his knife. There was no one to blame for this tragedy except herself. Califia was now a prisoner at the mercy of her enemies.

The procession halted before the steps of a tall, rectangular marble building with an arched wraparound portico on each of its four floors. A stone-faced man wearing a surcoat decorated with a two-headed eagle on a red field sauntered down the steps straight for Sir Guy and Califia suppressed a shudder at the cold, murderous glint in the newcomer's eye.

Sir Guy said something in Frankish. Another man came quickly down from the steps and whispered into the newcomer's ear. He responded to the man, who then jabbered at Sir Guy, who laughed and shook his head. Then he moved past the irritated man as if he were a mere annoyance.

The queen thought about asking her guide what that had all been about, but remembered his warning about asking too many questions. To her surprise, he volunteered an answer.

"Sir Vasily of Novgorod also wanted to fight you, but the honor fell to Sir Guy instead," he explained. She felt a little flattered until he continued, "Sir Vasily says that, from the look of you, such a fight would have been beneath his dignity."

The interior of the massive stone building was even more impressive than the arches, facades, and statues that adorned its exterior. As she followed her escort through the winding hallways and two narrow staircases, she gaped in awe of the mosaic art along the walls, the beautifully detailed marble statues in niches along their path, and the clever ways in which light filtered into the structure via slits in the walls and in parts of the ceiling. They snaked through three labyrinthine corridors before arriving at last at an old wooden door that looked like every other door they had passed— smooth-worn wood darkened with age.

"This is your chamber," her interpreter said, wiping his runny nose on the sleeve of his brown threadworn robe. "Servants should be here soon if you require anything. I suggest you make yourself ready should the king pay you a visit."

"Which king?" She asked. He turned to her with his mouth and nose twisted as though she were a skunk who had just sprayed all over the room. She realized why and held up a hand to interrupt his answer. "The king of the Franks, of course."

"*You* will address him as Your Most Christian Majesty," the man snapped, then turned back for a moment. "If that is too much to remember, you may call him Sire."

"And when might I expect a visit from His Most Christian Majesty?"

"Perhaps this evening," the man said, shrugging. "Perhaps tomorrow. I am but his majesty's servant, and not privy to the details of his schedule."

She nodded as if she understood. In her heart she felt as though any moment she might shake to pieces. As the door closed, she plopped herself on the bed. It was soft and decorated with fine, thin curtains that hung from a bar above. The large, puffy burgundy blanket atop the bed was embroidered with looping stems that displayed colorful flowers in a repeating pattern that she reckoned must have taken many days to create. She lifted it and found - to her very great shock - that the next several layers of bedsheets were bedecked with intricate embroidered patterns that were as fetching to her eye as they were exhausting for her to think about. She hated every moment of learning needlecraft in her youth—always wondering whether her fingers would cramp first or get stabbed. She didn't think even their most skillful seamstresses could produce a single sheet like this in less than four months without intensive teamwork.

Grimly she thought of the slaves she had encountered among the Osmans and their allies. Surely the Christians had people in similar circumstance who must purchase their survival with menial labor. She felt a wave of grief for the people she imagined had been coerced into crafting her bedding.

Her heart filled with dread as she found herself wondering whether Basilea would continue trying to find evidence of the polemarkos' alleged murder of her own sister. Her internal crisis was interrupted as two women in plain tan dresses and white open-backed bonnets burst in the room. One carried a bucket, the other an armload of towels.

"Oh!" said the first woman as they both came through the door. They bent their knees in a gesture which Califia had learned from Yakov was called a curtsy and she returned the gesture, which sent them tittering like children sharing a secret joke.

"See how civilized our pagan guest is - her curtsy is so refined!"

Califia blinked at the bare-faced rudeness of the comment and was about to respond in kind when she realized the two women didn't know that their guest spoke Greek. *Perhaps I can learn something by letting them talk awhile...*

"The Frankish king will be charmed by her tattoos, I'm sure," said the larger of the two women, who was putting towels onto a strange piece of furniture across the room. It looked like a desk but it was far too ornate to be practical. A large mirror was affixed which would allow a person sitting in front of it to stare into their own reflection. While it was beautiful, the queen was mystified by its existence.

"The priests are probably placing bets right now over which one will seduce her first."

It didn't seem right to hold her tongue any longer. These women would eventually be embarrassed to learn that she understood them. If she allowed this to go on too much longer, this embarrassment might transform into embittered humiliation.

"I speak Greek," she said, walking toward them in what she hoped was a friendly manner. Instead, they shrieked and ran toward the door, stopping just in front of it and lowering their eyes as they trembled in fear.

"Apologies, my lady!" The smaller one said, clasping the fingers of both hands together and holding them out in a begging sort of posture. "Please don't tell anyone - they'll have us beaten!"

"We are just poor widows who succumbed to the sin of gossip," the other said, likewise holding up her conjoined fist of interlocking fingers. "We mean you no harm, please."

"Be at peace, good women," the queen replied, stunned by the sudden change in their demeanor. "I will forgive both of you if you will but stay and talk with me a while."

They nodded and reluctantly came further into the room and sat upon the bed, following the queen's gesture. Both still looked equal parts guilty and suspicious, as if they worried she might still have them punished. Califia herself was quite surprised to learn that she *could* have them punished, but saved the questions about that subject for another time.

"First, I would like to know your names."

They exchanged a worried glance, then the larger one began.

"If it pleases your majesty, this one is called Sophia," she said, using especially formal language.

"Lydia," the other woman said, still breathing heavily.

"I am Califia, queen of the Amazons of California," she said, carefully choosing more casual words in hopes of putting them at ease. "And where are you from?"

"Venezia," said Sophia. Califia's face must have appeared blank because she quickly added, "It is many days west."

"This one is from Bologna, but my family is from Athenai," Lydia said, managing to squeeze a few more words out than before. "It is south of here but very beautiful."

"It is named for the goddess herself?" Califia said, her curiosity getting the better of her.

"Yes, I believe so," Lydia replied, raising an eyebrow. "You know of the goddess Athena?"

"She is one of the patrons of my people," Califia felt her heartbeat quicken. There was an old story of

Amazons who escaped the sinking of Atlantis but did not flee on Griffins. They founded a great city among the Greeks... could it have been this Athenai? She decided to investigate. "Had your people lived in Athenai for long?"

"My father said that the blood of Cleisthenes runs through our veins," Lydia began, "but he was prone to exaggeration and often told tall tales."

Califia set the matter aside for the moment.

"My people were from Constantinopolis," Sophia said, pursing her lips and wiping her hands upon the white apron that covered her skirt. "Mum said we were almost royalty until the Turks stole the city from us."

"I see," Califia studied the large woman's features for a moment, imagined her ears bedecked with jewels and her doughy features accented with make-up. There was something about her that definitely felt regal, although the queen wondered if that was just pride in her supposedly blue-blooded ancestry.

"You must understand, my lady," Lydia said, her eyes still wide with terror, "that any rancor we unleashed upon you was actually meant for the Turks. They took everything from our families— our homes, our liberty..." she glanced quickly at Sophia, "...even the virtue of our mothers."

Califia took a moment to understand the meaning of her words, then another moment to understand what it meant for Sophia. None of the Amazons knew even the first thing about their fathers, but at least their mothers had chosen to be impregnated. The hardness she saw in Sophia's eyes now made sense.

"Many years ago, my people were driven from their homes by invaders as well," she began, looking out the window as she recalled the all-too-familiar story. "One of their queens fled from her husband, a cruel and vicious king."

The women were enraptured and she could feel their anticipation. She decided to omit the part of the story where the queen of the Amazons fell in love with the queen of Sparta, something which, given its negative reception among the Osmans, seemed likely to offend some bizarre taboo here as well.

"For years they tried to take us by force but my ancestors defeated them in every battle. So they made it appear as though they departed, but had actually found a secret way into the capitol city. They took the city by surprise and my people had to flee."

"Sounds like something the Turks would do," Lydia muttered, glancing at Sophia. The larger woman lifted her eyebrows and nodded in agreement.

"As it happens," Califia stood and walked to the strange desk, watching the two women in the reflection behind her, "the people who stole my ancestors' land were Greeks."

They both blinked in surprise for a moment. She said nothing more, contenting herself to wait until they laid the fresh towels and soap bucket upon the ground and then left the chambers.

She spent the afternoon trying to find a familiar landmark in this labyrinthine place but she could not even see the ocean from her room despite the outside air's salty freshness. Beyond her window, the city hummed with what she assumed was its usual bustle of activities, something she may have found charming were this a friendly visit. A helpless frustration welled up inside of her at being so near to the sea but not being able to gaze upon its vastness nor hear its gentle whispers.

She waited for the king until the same servants whom

she had met earlier that day brought her an evening meal of roast chicken, boiled greens, and a fresh biscuit. The food tasted far better than she expected and her plate was emptied sooner than she intended. She laid on the bed and fell asleep before the servants returned to retrieve the empty plate.

The next morning she woke with a start. *Where am I?* Her mind settled after a few moments and she closed her eyes, wishing herself back to sleep. It had not been a dream, she really had lost the duel and was now in the clutches of her enemies. Her heart slowed from its initial panicked cadence, her muscles slowly released their tension, and she cleared her mind.

The panic made her think of the griffins and the panic she felt from them the day before. Califia wondered if she could still feel the creatures' emotions, so she sat cross-legged on the bed and closed her eyes, breathing slowly as she reached out through the mysterious connection with which she had previously been tethered to the beasts of Athena.

At the very edges of her mind, she felt them; they were mostly bored, some a little apprehensive. Was their anxiety tied to her imprisonment? She couldn't say. The beasts disliked their kennels, everyone knew this. Only now, as she gazed out the window at strange buildings and to the chorus of many strange languages, did Califia begin to understand why.

Someone knocked on the door and the griffins vanished from the edges of her mind.

"Apologies, radiant one," Sophia began, still speaking in elevated verbiage as she stuck her head through the door, "but would you be so kind as to break fast at your vanity instead of your bed this morning? We are under strict order to scrub this room until it shines!"

The large woman came in first and Lydia followed, soapy bucket in one hand and scrubbing rags in the other. Califia did as they wished and ate the salted meat, hard-crusted bread, and cheese from the plate they had brought, standing at the strange desk which she just realized they had named. *Vanity.* She wondered at this name for a moment, then giggled a little as she understood; women use desks like this to alter their appearance, using the mirror just as poor Narcissus gazed at himself in the clear waters of a spring. The whole thing seemed rather silly, but Califia decided that she probably didn't understand these people well enough to render a judgment.

"I hope your majesty slept well last night?" Lydia inquired as she began washing the floor.

"The bed was very comfortable, to be sure," Califia said, stacking her meat and cheese together as she was fond of doing back home. The taste was different than she was accustomed to, but it was similar enough to eat without complaint. "It is warmer here than I was expecting."

"Thick walls keep out the cold," Sophia said absently as she pushed a scrubbing rag up and down the wall next to the chamber door. "If you want something else for breakfast, we can probably get it. The cursed Turks might hold the land, but King Ivan rules the seas."

"We can even get you eggs if you really want some," Lydia added. Something about her tone led Califia to believe that acquiring eggs would be a difficulty.

"It's not necessary; this is quite good and more than fine for filling one's belly on a hungry morning."

The queen ate her last few bites of breakfast and then immediately grabbed a rag from the pile, dunked it into the sudsy bucket, then started scrubbing a part of the floor that Lydia had not cleaned yet. After a few moments, she jumped as she heard the two women shriek in horror.

They gave lengthy objections at the same time, and the queen understood very little of their protestations. Califia blinked at the mad flurry of words, then realized she had created a problem. Just as these people would never dream of a servant becoming their king, so they also could never dream of a monarch engaging in an activity as humble and base, in their minds, as the work left to servants.

"My mother," the queen said, hoping to assuage their fears, "would be most angry with me if I did not assist in cleaning my own chamber, especially considering the hospitality I have been shown by the two of you."

She saw conflict on their faces; royalty wasn't supposed to perform grunt work like this, but royalty was also allowed to do whatever it wanted. Also, neither seemed eager to displease Califia's late mother.

"Your humble servants only ask," Sophia said, grinning like a proud mom, "that you don't tell the Frankish King or anyone else about this."

"If my guess is correct, then telling them would only make them think less of me. Yes?"

Lydia and Sophia nodded, pursing their lips with concern. Califia wanted to roll her eyes at the sheer pomposity of these foreign leaders but she resisted the urge.

"I see no reason to inform the king or anyone outside of the three of us," the queen said, hoping that this was clear enough. The ladies nodded and returned to their work as though it had never happened, though Califia did catch them watching her with some amusement here and there. *What a novelty - a queen who scrubs floors!*

They finished just before mid-morning and thanked the queen for her help. Califia accepted their thanks and marveled once more that people would accept the leadership of someone who didn't help with simple tasks like cleaning.

She spent her time in prayer and meditation, still able to sense the griffins far off, but her connection was undoubtedly becoming weaker. She tried to send them her love, and hoped they found comfort in it. They gave no indication either way whether they received it or felt any comfort. She studied her linens, trying to trace the patterns of the embroidery and idly wondering what Ariana would make of this.

At midday, there was a rather sharp rap at her door. She expected one of the maids bringing food, but instead several men entered. They seemed to travel in pairs, one dressed in a flowing cloak and each with a companion dressed in plain sleeved tunics and breeches.

The first she recognized as the Frankish King, who stood just a little shorter than she and wore a blue felt cap upon his head. His face was young with piercing eyes and thin lips pressed together so firmly that his mouth appeared minuscule. The man who entered after wore a great black furred hat with the tips of its downy fur dyed white so it almost looked snow-kissed. The queen recognized him as the King of the Muscovites. His cloak looked like one of the tapestries which the teachers back home used to illustrate the histories of their people — a sharp contrast to the Frankish King's cloak, which was plain blue save for a set of three stylized golden lilies which adorned his left breast.

Several more entered after but it was clear to Califia that the King of the Franks and his dour-faced counterpart in the fuzzy hat were the most important men in the room. The other noblemen stood in a row behind them, each dressed finely with a plainclothes companion nearby. The Frankish King began speaking in a rapid-fire manner as if he was in a hurry to be done with this.

"His Most Christian Majesty welcomes you to his fine city," his plain-dressed companion said, "and would appreciate it if you would swear an oath that you will not attempt to escape his custody."

The man's Greek was so thick that Califia had trouble understanding him until he was finished and she could put what words she had grabbed into context. The other plain man whispered into the snow-capped man's ear and he likewise unleashed a stream of quick and articulate words in a language that sounded even stranger to her ears.

"His Radiance also urges you to pledge the oath that you will be bound by the Frankish King until such a time as your people afford the ransom demand."

Her head spun. It was jarring, going from the Osmans and Gurkani who would always talk around issues and needed a three-hour ceremony just to say good morning to these brusque and direct people. She wondered if they treated her thus because she was in their power or because she was a woman. *Probably both.*

"Your Most Christian Majesty," she offered a curtsy to the Frankish King and then the Muscovite King in turn, "and Your... Radiance, I am certain that my people will happily supply any ransom they can muster."

She did her best not to smirk at how she had sidestepped the question of swearing an oath. Yakov would be proud. Refusing to answer a question is not the same as lying, but her claim about her people meeting a ransom demand was absolutely a shameless falsehood.

She wasn't proud of this, but could not deny its necessity. *If they believe ransom is forthcoming, perhaps they will overlook the need to extract an oath.*

"Your Highness," the Frankish interpreter said firmly, "His Most Christian Majesty insists upon the oath. If you refuse it, then he shall have no choice but to move you to more... secure accommodations."

Something about the way he said *secure* conveyed that these accommodations would be much less pleasant than the lavish room she currently stayed in. From the firm look upon both kings' faces, she knew that this would be a difficult thing to writhe out of. She gazed upon the stern faces of the kings, certain that any such effort to convince them would be wasted. Still, it was her duty to try.

"I see that you bear an image of flowers upon your breast, Your Most Christian Majesty," Califia said, pointing to the three lilies that adorned the Frankish King's cloak. "Your people must be great appreciators of beauty."

After her message was relayed, the king nodded silently. The others in the room leaned close to their interpreters and Califia believed she saw King Ivan's lips twist with irritation.

"I have heard that the Franks are a noble people, that they especially protect the weak and vulnerable in God's name."

She hoped she was remembering correctly the details which Yakov had idly mentioned so long ago. She tried to stick to the kind of characteristics which she imagined *any* civilization would aspire to. The message was relayed, the king replied and the interpreter looked at her with an impatient expression.

"His Most Christian Majesty affirms that the Franks

carry the great banner of noble chivalry to every land which their feet bless," he said. "He is beginning to wonder, however, when you will get to the point."

Califia took a deep breath and did her best to appear sincere and vulnerable.

"While I understand His Most Christian Majesty's desire — his *need* — for me to take such an oath, I worry that extracting it from me under such an imminent threat will be seen as extortion — *or worse* — by other sovereigns and — worse! — his *chivalrous* people."

She felt her skin chill slightly and realized she was starting to sweat. She examined the face of the Muscovite sovereign and the other leaders in the room. Most were skeptical, but King Ivan's mouth curled into a wicked grin and she feared the worst. When her eyes alighted upon the Frankish King's countenance, however, she was pleased to see that he wore an amused smile. He spoke a few words to the interpreter, who turned to Califia and relayed the message.

"His Most Christian Majesty wants to know how much time you think would be appropriate to avoid accusations of extortion — *or worse?*"

Califia nearly laughed in relief but suppressed the urge. While she believed this particular argument would get farther than any others she might conceive, she did not truly believe it would work. She said the first thing that came to mind.

"A fortnight should be sufficient."

King Louis nodded at the interpretation and rubbed his chin thoughtfully with his forefinger and thumb. The nobles and sovereigns in the back of the room chatted amongst themselves and the interpreters appeared to be struggling with relaying various languages between them. Only King Ivan was silent, but he watched King Louis with an amused curiosity.

Finally the Frankish King turned his eyes upon her and spoke a short sentence in his nasally language. His interpreter pursed his lips and glared at Califia in a most serious fashion.

"His Most Christian Majesty has granted you five days to decide. At that time, you will either make the oath or be moved to less friendly environs."

As the mass of men filed out of the room, Califia tried to slow her racing heartbeat with steady breathing, but to no avail. When the door at last was swung closed, she released a sigh of relief which by now had become half a groan.

The elation of victory would later feel hollow, but in the moment it was better than life itself. She looked out of her window at the busy city sprawled before her, filled with people going about their various business and having almost no notion of her existence whatsoever. As she tried to see the city walls from her chamber, she realized she was too deep into the city to locate them. A feeling of dread crept into her heart, in spite of her victory of persuasion.

I am in prison, she thought. *Just like Amaltheia.* In her despair, however, she found a cause for hope. The Frankish King would not demand a promise against attempting escape unless escape was actually possible.

17

In other circumstances, the accommodations would have been quite enjoyable. The bed was perfectly soft and suitably firm. The vanity table, chairs, and stools displayed breathtakingly ornate craftsmanship. The room was neither too hot nor too cold. Still, she spent a fitful night tossing and turning on that comfortable bed, the chairs of the vanity felt stiff and confining, and her body alternated between sweltering heat and frigid cold.

A luxurious prison is still a prison.

A soft rapping at the door announced the maids, who briskly entered and went about their usual tasks after bowing politely to Califia. Sophia carried a plate of meat, cheese, and bread in her stout arms while Lydia hauled in two brooms under one arm and a basket wider than her hips under the other. The queen thanked them and ate swiftly. Sophia took the larger broom and Lydia the smaller, and they both proceeded to sweep at the far end of the room. They were about halfway finished when Califia stuffed the last piece of cheese into her mouth and picked up the basket.

"What should I do with this?" She asked, briefly

examining the item. Its reed construction and intricate woven design would have appeared very much at home on California— light but sturdy.

"That's for the sheets," Sophia said, her voice tinged with apprehension. "Honestly, your majesty, it isn't necessary for you to help with chores."

"It makes me feel more at home," Califia said, trying to ignore the pain in the truth of those words. Once more she found herself baffled by these people. Among the Amazons, those who served were held in high esteem. Both Muslims and Christians, as far as she could see, treated service as either a means of punishment or a lowly profession.

"Do a lot of laundry back home, do you?" Lydia said, with a wry smile.

"I do whatever is needed," the queen replied, stuffing the sheets into the basket.

"How do you manage without servants?" Sophia said. "Seems like you wouldn't have enough time to do queen stuff if you're constantly cleaning and preparing food."

Something about Sophia's tone gave Califia pause. *Does she think I am lying?*

"Our palace is staffed by volunteers," the queen replied. "They take care of most day-to-day needs, but they aren't forced to feed and clothe the queen."

Sophia raised an eyebrow and looked sidelong at the queen. Califia resisted the urge to become defensive.

"What would happen if some of those *volunteers* just decided they didn't feel like serving the queen?"

"That happens all the time," Califia replied. "Several palace volunteers resigned just before we embarked on this journey. There were no shortage of eager young women ready to take their place."

"Hmm," Sophia said, still sounding very skeptical. "It's

hard to imagine how such a society could function."

"Be easy, Soph," Lydia said, sweeping more dirt into the hallway. "Our ways probably seem just as strange to her."

Califia idly fiddled with the embroidered sheets in the basket, admiring their design but also wondering if extra threads made the linen stronger. She tugged it casually; it felt nearly impossible to tear.

"Something wrong with the bedding, your majesty?" Sophia asked, examining the stretch of cloth which the queen had been testing.

"I was only admiring it," Califia said, smiling broadly at the maid. "Do you serve King Louis or King Ivan?"

"We serve *you*, your majesty," Sophia said. Califia was about to clarify herself when the woman gave her a mischievous wink.

"We were living in Italy when the Frankish king made conquest there," Lydia said, scoffing and rolling her eyes at her companion. "I suppose we work for him, but it's not like he ever bothers talking with the likes of us."

"If the Turks and their allies abandoned the siege," Califia said, "then which of the two rulers would govern this city?"

Lydia and Sophia exchanged looks, and for a moment the queen worried that her question was somehow rude. Lydia checked the hallway, then nodded to Sophia, who looked at Califia with furrowed brow and pursed lips.

"King Louis had himself proclaimed the King of Constantinopolis a few weeks after they took the city," Sophia said. "He and King Ivan must have some kind of deal worked out for the future, but no one bothers telling us anything about that."

"At least old Louis promised to allow proper churches to be kept in place," Lydia said, nodding with approval.

"Last thing we need is the Pope and his lackeys throwing their weight around."

"The Pope," Califia said, trying to recall who that was. She remembered Yakov mentioning the man a few times, but the specifics escaped her.

"Just a Roman prince who thinks he's in charge of the church. Everyone says the kings worked out a deal," Sophia said gravely, "but we won't know whether it will hold until the Turks have been driven off."

"There could be war between the Franks and the Muscovites," Lydia said, pausing to shudder, "and us Greeks would get caught in the middle."

Footsteps echoed from the hallway and the maids went quickly and quietly back to their chores. Califia set the laundry basket by the door, which opened as she was pushing back the curtains.

In walked four ladies in sturdy gray dresses and matching gray caps. The leading woman stopped and gasped at Sophia and Lydia.

"What are you two still doing here?" She demanded, her voice as stern and unmoving as the stone walls. "Run along and tend to your duties elsewhere!"

The maids, color draining from their faces, cast their eyes downward and gave a quick curtsy before grabbing the brooms, as well as the basket full of sheets, and leaving the room in a hurry. The four new gray ladies exchanged amused glances and head shakes before presenting themselves to Califia with elegant and respectful curtsies.

"Your highness, if it pleases you, this one is called Konstantina," said the apparent leader of the group as she put her hand on her chest. Something about her annunciation led Califia to suspect that she was well-practiced in the kind of overly-polite language which the nobility here apparently expected. "I have the honor of serving as the royal seamstress to his most Christian Majesty, King Louis of the Franks."

"Did you embroider the bedsheets?" Califia asked, ready to shower compliments upon someone she greatly admired.

"Um… no, your highness." The woman stifled a laugh and shot a glare at one of her compatriots who let out a small snicker. "I do not know who made them but I am sure they are very fine, so I thank you for the compliment."

The queen tried not to appear disappointed.

"If it pleases your highness," Konstantina continued, "may we have permission to acquire your measurements?"

The queen's body tensed and she took a small step backward.

"Why do you need to… *measure* me?"

"All I am permitted to say, highness," Konstantina smiled the way an adult grins at a child, "is that this process is part of a gift."

Briefly the queen considered refusing, but did not see the point. This was odd, but it did not seem malicious.

"Fine," Califia said, stepping forward and standing tall. The women swarmed, placing long strips against her body and marking them with charcoal at various places. They moved her arms to the side and measured from her armpit, then put the arm down and measured from her shoulder. They even circled one of their strange bands around her waist and then her chest, marking each in turn.

"What is your favorite color?" Konstantina asked as the other ladies continued their measuring.

Califia thought for a moment before replying. "Blue."

"Ah! That will go very well against your skin tone, an excellent choice, your highness!" The royal seamstress took a few strips of fabric from one of the baskets and laid them against an exposed stretch of Califia's upper arm, making a noise of surprise as she pressed the fabric into the queen's firm bicep. "You are... very different from other queens and noble ladies that I have met."

"Oh?" Califia replied, holding back a giggle as one of the assistants dug her fingers a little too far into the queen's armpit.

"When word spread that there was a warrior queen challenging our champion, we scarcely believed it."

"Lydia and Sophia said much the same thing," Califia said, suddenly longing for the two unpretentious maids.

"Ugh, *those* two," Konstantina said, holding up one strip of light blue cloth against Califia's arm and then another darker shade. "Don't trouble yourself over them for another moment, your majesty. I'll see to it that the Chamberlain whips them raw and shoves them back into the kitchen for wasting a queen's time with their silly nonsense."

Califia's breath caught in her throat. Her thoughts immediately recalled the lashings she had witnessed aboard the Göke, the ribbons of blood that poured from the scarred backs of the limp sailors. For a moment she thought she could hear the humiliated howls and whimpers of the victims once more. She reflexively imagined Lydia and Sophia shrieking as rivers of blood streamed down their back and she locked eyes ferociously with Konstantina, who blinked with a start at Califia's countenance.

"No. You will not."

The assistants had finished their measuring and were now putting their tools away, but they froze at the queen's words, as did their mistress.

"I beg your pardon, majesty," Konstantina sputtered, scoffing and shaking her head a little. "This is but a... silly misunderstanding. Those maids in particular have a notorious reputation for sloth and ingratitude. Surely someone in your position understands the need for such correction."

Califia's fingers curled into fists.

"I am not dissatisfied with them in any way. This room is clean, I lack no comfort, and I delight in their company." She paused, remembering something Yakov said about royalty's tendency to favor subtlety. "If anything should happen to those two pleasant ladies, I would be most... *upset.*"

Konstantina's eyes grew wide and she glanced at her assistants, who quickly resumed their duties under her wrathful gaze. She turned back to Califia with a conciliatory smile.

"Humbly begging your pardon, highness, but this is a matter for the household and is surely beneath the concern of your royal person."

So much for subtlety.

"This royal person," Califia stepped forward, forcing Konstantina to retreat, "will concern herself with whatever pleases her."

"Of-of course, your majesty, I only meant—"

Califia stepped forward once more, forcing the woman back a few more steps.

"Should I not concern myself with those who feed me and keep the chamber tidy?"

The queen now abandoned taking one step at a time and started stalking forward, practically chasing Konstantina around the room at a slow but unrelenting pace.

"I didn't mean any disre—"

"You were right to call me a warrior queen, for that is what I am! And warriors do not leave discipline in the hands of useless boot-lickers, do they?"

One of the assistants yelped, leaping out of the way as the chase continued.

"My lady, please!"

Califia stopped and the royal seamstress paused as well, her chest heaving both from the exercise and the sheer panic which the queen could see in her wide eyes.

"If I am displeased with Lydia and Sophia, I'll beat them myself," the queen said. Konstantina didn't dare blink. Califia plucked a ruler from a bag as they passed by. "My will is absolute, and you will obey it or I will see to it *personally* that you are thrashed twice as hard as Lydia and Sophia."

Konstantina cried out and Califia advanced upon her, feeling something similar to the excitement of battle coursing through her veins.

"Mercy, your majesty!" The royal seamstress wept, clutching at her dress and bowing her head low. "Have mercy upon this one, your highness! I will leave those good women alone, just please do not hurt me!"

The assistants exchanged awkward glances and then stared at Califia as though she were Medusa herself, something horrible, frightening, and yet fascinating to behold. The queen turned her back to them. She hoped they would think she was disgusted by them, but in truth she felt strangely pleased to have caused them terror and this frightened her.

"As long as Lydia and Sophia are safe, you need not fear my wrath."

"Thank you - thank you! - your highness! You are the Savior's own compassion made flesh!"

As she heard the door close, she let the air out of her lungs and slumped her shoulders. Her head spun with the stress of her performance and she tried to release the tension she felt in her shoulders and back. Her legs felt like they were melting. She threw herself onto the bed before her strength failed completely.

Something about the wide-eyed terror she had inspired in the seamstress haunted her. It felt so good to lash out, to gain the upper hand over an opponent. Now she was filled with shame. She had acted like one of their sovereigns — petty, vindictive, and coercive. She was nearly in tears from her distress when someone rapped very loudly on her door.

A frowning old man entered dressed in flowing white robes with a short red cape adorning his shoulders and upper arms. His white hair looked strangely puffed and she realized he was wearing a small cap that covered a tiny portion of the top of his head. She was wondering what the practical purpose of such a head covering could possibly be when a second figure entered with the gangly walk and nervous air that often accompanied the middle teenage years. The robed man stood before her and, without waiting for his young partner to catch up, began speaking. His words sounded as though a drunk person was speaking the Frankish tongue. The boy sighed at the inconvenience and, when the long-winded gentleman finally paused, he began speaking Greek.

"Your majesty, this is Father Mignoletto and he has been instructed to provide you with religious education during your stay here. He hopes you will feel free to ask any question you like without fear of punishment."

Califia was struck speechless. She had not requested any kind of education, religious or otherwise, and it never occurred to her that anyone would be punished for asking questions. Something about the man's steely gaze and proud posture made her suspect that she ought to tread carefully, regardless of any promises against punishment.

"You are… his son?" she asked the translator, who chuckled a little too readily and earned a slap on the back of his head from Mignoletto. He hastily spoke a few words to the man in whatever language they shared and both smiled at the misunderstanding.

"*Father* is a title, not a literal descriptor in this case," the boy said smiling. "He's a priest, not my dad. I hope you don't think this handsome face looks anything like that sack of day-old dog shit?"

She nearly burst with laughter but, given how swiftly the old man had doled punishment to the boy, pretended she was only giggling politely at the misunderstanding. Father Mignoletto raised an eyebrow but the young man smiled amiably as if nothing could possibly be wrong. The priest uttered a *hmph* and continued speaking. The cadence of his words was so rapid, Califia worried that his interpreter would not be able to follow.

"He says not to worry about the confusion, that he is not offended. I'm Niko, by the way, nice to meet you. I can confirm that old splotchy-face here doesn't speak even a single syllable of Greek, so if you want to chat, I can always pretend that you're asking about some particular point of theology. Oh, and he says that he's here on behalf of King Louis."

"Thank you, Niko, your wit is greatly appreciated. I assume you are Greek?"

"Born Greek; raised in Italy."

She nearly asked if he knew Lydia and Sophia but, as she recalled the results of the last conversation about the two maids, decided against it. Idly she wondered about this Italy, how far away it was and how it apparently produced both impish young men like Niko and sour-faced codgers such as Father Mignoletto.

The priest gestured to the cluster of stools toward the far end of the room and the three each claimed their own wooden perch. Once more Mignoletto launched into a jarringly long chain of syllables, eventually pausing so that Niko could relay the message.

"First; how long have your people followed the teachings of Mo-ameth, and were they Christians or Pagans before that time?"

Califia briefly pondered which part of that question she should ask about first.

"I have never heard of this Mo-ameth - wait," the name sounded almost familiar, like one she had heard of when she was in the Osman camp. "Do you mean Mohammad?"

"Yes, Mohammad."

"I see. We do not follow the teachings of *Mo-ameth*," she replied, adding quickly, "although some of my people have begun learning more about them."

She could see the priest's eyes unfocusing as she spoke, no doubt imagining something more exciting far away. As Niko interpreted for him, however, his eyes grew wide with surprise, then narrowed with suspicion. He loosed another percussive flurry of sounds. Even through the language barrier, she sensed a deep distrust from him.

"It is strange, he thinks, that you fight alongside Muslims but are not Muslim yourself. He has never heard of such a thing except on rare occasions when people were coerced into serving the Sultan under threat of death," Niko waved his hand in circles as he explained, periodically gesturing to the priest when relevant. "I hope you understand he thinks you are lying."

"I understood that, yes," she sighed. "My people follow the way of our ancestors, worshiping Athena, Hera, and Aphrodite, as well as many other goddesses."

The priest interrupted Niko with questions several times as he translated the queen's words. When the lad finally finished, the priest clapped him on the back of his head and shouted at him aggressively, punctuating with words which Califia suspected were normally excluded from polite conversation.

"Now the paranoid old strip of boiled leather thinks that *I'm* lying. I told him everything exactly as you described, my lady."

"I see."

The queen gathered the right sleeve of her tunic and pulled it up over her shoulder so that the tattoo which lay atop her bicep could be seen. The artist who created it was renowned for her skill at realistic depictions and Califia was glad she opted for such an image rather than the simple oak leaf crown that she nearly chose instead.

"Hera," she said, pointing at the tattoo. The priest leaned forward to examine it more closely and after a little while nodded and retreated. He opened his mouth but she held up a hand to signal a pause and then gathered her left sleeve in a similar fashion, displaying her tattoo of Athena's head in profile, her warlike helm thick with plumes. "Athena."

Again he inspected, this time exchanging a few words with Niko which the queen hoped was an apology. From the boy's face, it probably wasn't. The old man shifted uncomfortably as she unlaced the top of her tunic and his eyes bulged nearly out of his skull as she lifted her left breast fully out of the garment so that he could see the full-figured tattoo of the goddess of love whose upraised arms stretched nearly to her collarbone and whose bare feet danced upon her nipple. "Aphrodite."

Father Mignoletto's face turned redder than a tomato and Niko's forehead erupted in sweat as he pulled his tunic lower as if trying to hide his hips. She put her breast back under the tunic and tied the laces.

"It would probably be for the best," Niko squeaked, clearly speaking his own mind and not Father Mignoletto's, "if you refrained from exposing any other... covered body parts in our presence, my lady."

She sighed, remembering the many times which Yakov reminded her that the Amazons should keep their breasts covered in public, even on hot days, to avoid offense. Both of these coalitions thought themselves superior to their neighbors, yet they swooned at the sight of a single areola.

Father Mignoletto cleared his throat and spoke once more, this time remarkably slower, as he glanced periodically at her chest.

"He says you are pagan, which is good. Pagans are much closer to the kingdom of heaven than the followers of Mo-ameth. He would like to leave you with a question to contemplate in your moments of peace."

"Alright."

The priest spoke once more, his eyes glancing toward her breasts less and less.

"Can a garment with a stain ever be made clean?"

Niko rolled his eyes at the question, but she couldn't imagine why. Some Amazons, considered the holiest among them, spent their lives in contemplation of the blessed triumvirs and other spiritual matters. She never had the patience to undertake such an ordeal long-term but she respected the effort. She did not understand why, but at that moment she recalled some words that Basilea had once spoken. *The most dangerous people in the world are those who are certain of the uncertain.*

"Thank you for your time Father," she said, careful to use the man's title, "and you as well, Niko. I shall think upon these things until I see you again."

"We'll return on the morrow, your highness," Niko said, explaining quickly to the priest what he had just said. The old man nodded and smiled. Califia was certain that it was not the smile of a friend.

Regardless of any duplicitous intentions of the jaundiced priest, Califia meditated upon his question that afternoon. She turned the question over in her mind and was still considering possibilities when there was a meek set of knocks at her door which she had come to recognize. She smiled as the maids walked in, bundles of sheets under Sophia's burly arms while Lydia carried the dinner plate.

Upon the plate was roast chicken along with ringlets of a white bitter-smelling vegetable along with some thin-sliced rounds of something red. She ate the chicken gladly, though it was rather dry and lacking in salt. The bitter rings she pushed aside. She took one crunchy bite of a red disk and then promptly decided she never needed to take a second.

"Do either of you know," she asked the maids as she pulled every last bit of meat from the thigh portion, "why the seamstresses took my measurements today?"

"They never tell us anything," Lydia said, shrugging. "They think themselves too important to bother with the likes of us."

"But surely," Califia reasoned, "even humble, hardworking maids such as yourselves must occasionally overhear things."

"This is just a rumor among servants, mind you,"

Lydia said, as Sophia struggled to compose herself, "but I heard from Lucinda, who cooked your dinner, that King Louis himself has ordered a special dress to be made just for you."

She looked down at her tunic, feeling suddenly conscientious about her appearance.

"Why would he do this?"

"There are only a few reasons why the king would try to win your favor," Sophia said.

"Win my favor," Califia repeated, trying to understand the secret meaning behind this incantation. "Does he want to have sex with me?"

The ladies paused as they stuffed the edges of her sheets beneath the mattress and exchanged a look, then burst into childlike giggles. Embarrassment warmed through Califia's cheeks and neck, and she resisted the urge to lash out in anger.

"Beg pardon, your majesty," Lydia said, wiping a tear from her eye. "We don't usually talk about such things quite so… *directly*."

"I thought the king was married?" Califia said. "The Osmans told me that Christians are only allowed one wife each."

Lydia's face twisted as if she were perplexed that she had to explain something which was extremely obvious. "Powerful men find a wife to make alliances and secure their inheritance, but that wife is not always sufficient to… satisfy their husband's *needs*."

"I beg you to speak plainly," Califia said, rubbing her temples impatiently. She considered examining the chicken thigh once more to see whether some small shred of meat was still hidden somewhere upon the bones.

"She's talking about sex," Sophia said, smiling impishly

at Lydia, whose face turned bright red. "Men are cursed with lust and when powerful men cannot contain that lust, they spawn illegitimate children who can cause a lot of trouble later on. Made a right mess of England some years ago, I understand."

Califia didn't dare ask what an *England* was, but still wanted to understand.

"So kings aren't allowed to have two wives, but they may have one wife and one... other woman they have sex with?"

"The church doesn't like it," Sophia said, "but as long as the king keeps their coffers full and doesn't go around promoting heresy, they don't seem to care too much. *Especially* in France."

"But the other woman—"

"She's called a mistress," Lydia explained.

"This *mistress*," Califia felt like her head was about to spin right off of her neck, "can still get pregnant, right? So there are still..." she forced the words out, "*illegitimate* children."

"Yes, but much fewer than the King might otherwise produce," Lydia said, speaking almost as if she approved of all of this. She shrugged as if she shared Califia's frustration but could offer no relief. "I can tell you this, my lady— I would never tolerate that kind of behavior from a husband of mine!"

"Oh, I don't know," Sophia said, much to the dismay of Califia and Lydia both. Seeing their consternation, she crossed herself as she explained, "My husband, God rest him, was always poking and grabbing at me like a child with a toy. It might have been nice to have a break from that once in a while. Let someone else get squeezed and tickled while I have a nap!"

Lydia laughed as if Sophia had just made a terrific joke

and Califia laughed along politely. It was unthinkable among the Amazons to purposefully make unwanted advances. Although their brightest scholars all agreed that the desire for sex should be treated like a hunger, they were likewise in accord that there were plenty of ways to satisfy that need without bothering someone who wasn't interested.

"Your majesty," Lydia said, after their laughter had died down, "I must confess something to you; I overheard you speaking with Father Mignoletto."

"Oh?" Califia was intrigued. "What did you hear?"

"Do you... that is, do your people really worship Athena?"

"I told you when I first arrived here that we do," the queen replied.

"I thought you were having a bit of fun with us," Sophia said, as Lydia nodded.

"We worship Hera who governs justly, Athena who fights cleverly, and Aphrodite who loves passionately," Califia said, a thrill sprinting up her spine that she remembered the words she had been taught as a child. "They are the triumvirs who help us in every aspect of our lives."

"And what of Zeus, Poseidon, or Ares?" Lydia asked, her voice ringing with unquenchable curiosity.

"The triumvirs and their allies overthrew the old order of the male gods," Califia said with the certainty of a zealot. "They still exist of course, gods can't be killed, but their power has been shattered and so now they can only deceive and mislead."

"We dare not ask more," Sophia said, pointedly. "We're good Christian women and we wouldn't want folks thinking we're secret pagans, would we?"

Lydia opened her mouth as if she was about to ask

another question but then closed it and looked down, nodding dourly as she finished adjusting the sheet they had just affixed to the bed. Califia recalled that the Osmans punished members of their own ranks who were insufficiently pious toward the official religion and sighed as she realized that the two factions were not very different in that regard.

"Not everyone on our isle worships the triumvirs," the queen added, feeling a sense of self-satisfaction as Lydia's eyes seemed to illuminate. "We have many women among our number who came over from the mainland and they worship as they please."

"Would you allow Christianity on your island?" Sophia asked, her voice deep and suspicious.

"Anyone may worship as they wish," she answered carefully, "but only women priests would be allowed."

Lydia and Sophia exchanged a perplexed look.

"There are no women priests in Christianity," Sophia said. "Why would the men be forbidden?"

"Don't you *have* men on your island?" Lydia said, eyebrows raised in confusion and perhaps some suspicion.

"The griffins keep them off. You yourselves must have seen or heard what they did to the men on your walls. They didn't do that because they dislike Christians, only because they dislike men. They are a divine gift and we treasure them."

Lydia smiled at the idea of a land without men but then quickly adopted a look of confusion. "But if there are no men, how do—"

"It's getting terribly late, don't you think, dear?" Sophia asked her companion. Lydia blinked quickly as if snapping out of a trance.

"Oh, yes. Yes, I do think it's getting late," she said,

yawning as though she was growing tired. "We must tend to our duties or we'll never get any sleep."

The ladies gathered their implements and took Califia's plate. Lydia took her leave and strolled quickly down the hall. Sophia lingered, looking up and down the hallway before turning back to the queen.

"The king may want to sleep with you, but he also may have another reason for giving you a dress," she said in hushed tones.

"Perhaps he believes this gift will help him extract the oath that he covets?"

"That's one possibility," Sophia said, twisting her lips as though she was considering unpleasant ideas. "Whatever his plan, you can be sure that he wants *something*."

Califia nodded as she considered possibilities herself. Sophia begged her leave and hurried after Lydia, whose footsteps were echoing from the stairwell down the hall. The queen thought of the Osman Sultan and how displeased he became at even the most polite refusal. She had a dark feeling in her gut that this was yet another area in which the Frankish monarch would prove identical to his sworn enemy.

18

Her new dress arrived with breakfast. Califia was impressed at first; the seamstresses had chosen a soft shade of blue which served as a canvas for intricate designs which shifted from free-flowing swirls to tight, precise geometric patterns. When she attempted to put the garment on, however, her love very quickly turned into hate.

Califia was still shifting the dress around when rapid, percussive knocks banged against her chamber door. She beckoned the visitors to enter as she made a few last-minute adjustments, fiddling with the way the cloth hugged her shoulders and trying to center the cursed thing. She spun around as she heard footsteps and smiled at Father Mignoletto and Niko. The priest smiled diplomatically while his interpreter smirked like a child with a secret.

"His shittiness says he likes your dress," Niko said, pronouncing the words in a formal-sounding cadence so as not to give his patron a clue to his actual verbiage.

"The maids brought it this morning," Califia said, remembering how the ladies had gawked at her tattooed form as she stripped out of her tunic and skirt to put on the fresh garment. "Am I wearing it correctly?"

"Well enough, I think," Niko winked impishly and she gave a curtsy as thanks.

Father Mignoletto began rapidly addressing her in his native language, which she remembered was called Italian. Niko rolled his eyes as he translated.

"He wants to know if you have an answer to the riddle he gave you yesterday," He frumped his lips as if he were already bored. "The question of stains and washing clothes, you know."

"I pondered that question for several hours and thought of many possible solutions," Califia explained, remembering the conclusion she had come to the night before. "Here is the first: Lay the garment in the sun until the stain is bleached away and then dye it once more."

Niko looked stunned at this answer, and after a brief awkward pause, he translated it for the priest, who raised an eyebrow and asked several questions.

"Though he won't admit it," Niko said, jerking his head subtly toward Father Mignoletto, "he doesn't actually know if your answer is correct or not. I can tell you, though, that it is not the answer he is *looking* for."

Califia was taken aback. The priest was looking for a specific answer? If he knew it, then why didn't he just answer it himself? She set her confusion aside for the moment.

"The stain could form the basis of a new design," she said, recalling the other options she had conceived. "The rest of the garment could be entirely transformed."

The way the interpreter twisted his lips told the queen that she was still very far from whatever answer the priest was waiting for. *Is this what passes for education among these people?* She swallowed her frustration as Niko and Father

Mignoletto appeared to debate the merits of her response.

"Your responses confuse him," Niko explained. "He doesn't actually know anything about clothing."

"Then why does he think he knows the answer to this question?"

"I will tell you what he wants to hear, if you like."

"Please," the queen said, irritated by this entire affair.

"He wants you to admit that it is impossible."

Califia looked at Father Mignoletto, who smiled warmly when he realized her eyes were upon him. Amazon philosophers also asked questions, but never for the sake of delivering flat truths as answers. *Questions are tools that can lead to the discovery of greater truths* was the central tenet of doctrine of nearly every religious and philosophical movement on California. She sighed and resigned herself to fate.

"Tell him that I said it's impossible, then," she said, sighing as the message was relayed.

"He says that you are correct," Niko said, beginning the translation before the priest had quite finished speaking. "For mankind, it is impossible to clean permanent stains from their garments. He says that such a task would be a miracle, and that there is only one being in the entire universe who is capable of such a miracle."

"Our people have a story about clothing," the queen said, "about a young woman who challenged Athena herself to a weaving contest. After it was over, she had woven much finer than the goddess. Athena rewarded her by appointing her as a handmaiden and now Arachnea weaves clothes for all the triumvir goddesses."

Father Mignoletto blinked impatiently throughout her story, then continued rehearsing what was obviously a prepared speech. Apparently the priest's objective was not to invite authentic conversation and well-reasoned debate, but to impress her with some grandiose theological truth after she had acknowledged the impossibility. Such tactics were generally viewed, among the Amazons, as the rhetorical equivalent of cheating.

"Because of something that happened long, long ago," Niko related, waving his hand in little circles for emphasis, "humanity itself, each and every one of us carries the stain of mistakes."

She squinted as he uttered the word *mistakes*. They had a similar word in Californian, but she felt like they used it differently than what the priest was trying to imply.

"Because of something that happened long ago," Califia repeated, hoping to comprehend the mystery of this strange teaching, "we carry the stain of tripping over our feet, or missing a target?"

Niko smirked as if she was making a terrific joke, but quickly adopted a serious countenance when it became clear she was asking in earnest. He uttered a few words to Father Mignoletto, whose face went blank for a moment, as if he couldn't conceive of a person who didn't understand the deeper meaning behind the word mistake. He and Niko puzzled over it together for a moment, leaving her free to glance out the window and see that the market just down the street from this building was starting to fill with people again, which meant that it was probably mid-morning. The city seemed, to her, like a vast and complex organism which she couldn't entirely comprehend. She wondered how she might avoid becoming its next meal.

"Apologies, your highness," Niko said, snapping her back into the moment. "We do not mean in the common way of making a mistake, but in the poetic sense, if you will? As in, King David was a wise ruler but his *mistake* was lust."

She nodded, believing she understood. Many believed that her pursuit of the office of queen was a mistake, that using the griffins to attack the walls had been a mistake, and that challenging a crusader to a duel in an effort to win back national honor was a mistake. Stuck in this richly-decorated prison cell, wondering whether she would ever see her people again, Califia was starting to agree with them.

"The original mistake was arrogance, and it is from this that the whole world has become tainted with the stain of mistakes." Niko translated as Father Mignoletto droned away. "The first humans which God created were named Adam and Eve. They were told they could eat of any tree in the garden except for one; the tree of knowledge about good and evil."

Califia held up a hand and the priest seemed irritated by the interruption but raised his eyebrows as he waited for her to ask.

"Which god are you talking about?"

"There is only one god, highness."

"And this god didn't want people to know the difference between good and evil?"

Niko translated her question this time, his cadence lazy and slurred compared to the confident punctuation of the priest.

"People who don't know the difference between good and evil are innocent and thus cannot be punished."

She blinked her eyes as she considered this line of thinking. Could anyone in this society commit a crime - even something serious like murder - and then claim they cannot discern good from evil when the talons of justice come hunting? Before she bothered to ask, it occurred to her that the priest had just indicated that all of humanity was stained from the mistake of eating the fruit that taught them the difference. In a world like that, no one could be innocent.

"So you believe in one god, who told his people not to eat from a tree and then punished them when they ate from it regardless?" The queen said, hoping she didn't sound disrespectful.

"That is more or less correct, yes," Niko said after consulting the priest. "But God also sent his son into this world to make a way for humanity to be forgiven for their mistakes."

"This god has a child?"

Niko nodded gravely as if this was a matter of utmost seriousness. She nodded as if she understood, assuming things would become clearer as the story went on.

"God's son is named Jesus and he lived a perfect life, free from mistakes."

"So people can be free of their mistakes if they live in the way that this Jesus did?"

"We can never be as free of our mistakes as Jesus was," Niko continued as Father Mignoletto prattled on. "But we can be forgiven our mistakes if we join with his church and humbly participate in the sacraments which he himself gave to us during his life."

She felt a yearning like nothing she had ever experienced. If the priest was right and all of humanity carried a stain of imperfection, then it made sense that god would provide a path to become cleansed of those mistakes. She thought of the previous year, of how many mistakes she had made during that time. The higher the office she attained, the more people suffered when she made errors. The collective weight of that suffering created an indelible burden on her heart. The thought of setting those mistakes adrift into an invisible sea was very appealing…

"Your highness?" Niko looked at her as if he was expecting an answer to a question.

"Apologies, I didn't hear what you said."

"I asked, well, Father Mignoletto asked if you would be willing to receive baptism and receive God's forgiveness for your mistakes?"

She longed to feel the weight of her mistakes lift from her shoulders. Deep within her mind, however, she felt alarmed. It was an instinct— a *feeling*, not a logical concept, but it was strong. Father Mignoletto leaned forward, licking his lips as he waited with eager anticipation for her reply. There was something conniving in his countenance, something coldly calculating about his greedy eyes.

"I have a few more questions," the queen replied, quickly trying to think of a few. She grabbed onto one open thread of a thought that had piqued a few moments ago but which she felt might be impolite to inquire. "How could your god justly condemn the first humans for eating from the forbidden tree when they were innocent at the time?"

"They committed a mistake, and did it on purpose. They disobeyed god." Niko said after some sputtering from Father Mignoletto.

"But how could they know that disobedience was wrong if they hadn't yet eaten from the very tree that provided them said knowledge?" Califia's body unclenched. She almost felt like she was back home, pondering imponderable questions with Arianna late into the night.

Father Mignoletto thought about this for several silent moments, his eyes wiggling back and forth as though some great internal debate was raging within him. Eventually he gave his hands a small wave as if dismissing some minor matter and spewed more strange words which Niko then transformed for the queen.

"He says he will ask one of the scholars, as they know more than he does about such things."

"There is a story among our people," Califia said, waiting for the translation. "May I share it with you?"

Father Mignoletto nodded, so she continued. "Poseidon trapped a beautiful young woman in the temple of Athena. He beat her, raped her, and left her for dead. When Athena discovered what Poseidon had done, she transformed the woman's hair into snakes and her legs into a great serpent's tail. Her face was so ugly that she turned men who looked upon her to stone. Why do you think Athena did this?"

The priest and Niko talked amongst one another for a moment and the queen noticed that Niko was leading their conversation more than usual. At last they seemed to come to an agreement and the young Greek man spoke.

"My mother told me this story when I was a boy. Athena punished the young woman for defiling the temple, cursing her to live out her days as a hideous monster until a brave hero killed her with Athena's help."

This interpretation filled Califia with a sudden onset of bubbling rage. Was *this* what the Greeks had taught their children after the Amazons left? It was no wonder they now followed after gods who so eagerly punished humans for breaking rules they couldn't possibly have understood.

"Athena was *protecting* the young woman," Califia said, forcing herself to remain calm and not take offense.

Niko and the priest consulted each other again, the

priest finally tossing his open hands toward his side as if he didn't think the current conversation was of any importance.

"Father Mignoletto would like to continue the lesson, if it pleases your majesty," Niko said. "You see, of those first humans who ate the fruit which God had forbidden, the one who was tricked by a serpent was the woman."

"Was it?" The queen felt herself rapidly losing patience.

"Indeed. Eve bears the responsibility for the first mistake, which is why women experience great pain during childbirth."

"I have a daughter back home," Califia said, practically speaking through her teeth. "Giving birth to her was painful, yes, but it was also beautiful."

"I'm sure she's lovely, your ma—"

"I don't know if I can believe in a god who blames women for creating all the troubles in the world," the queen continued, her mind unwilling to set any of this aside. "When Medusa locked eyes with a man, it turned him to stone, but do you know what happened when she locked eyes with a woman?"

Neither Niko nor the priest had an answer.

"When a woman looked into her eyes, their bodies underwent the same transition as Medusa herself and they became her fellow Gorgons. Athena created an army of them to overthrow Zeus, Poseidon, Hephaestus, Ares, and all the others. Do you know what happened to those Gorgons after the war was over?"

"If we have offended, your highness, I must apolo—"

"The goddesses combined their power and transformed the Gorgons into women, each giving them a gift of herself: the love of Aphrodite, the wisdom of Athena, and the grace of Hera. Thus were the Amazons born!"

"I think we are getting off the subject, your majesty," Niko said nervously.

"I am finished with my religious education for today. You are both dismissed."

"Please, highness, Father Mignoletto does not want to leave until you fully understand the consequences of refusing God's forgiveness."

"Then Father Mignoletto will leave disappointed," she declared, turning her back to them. She hoped it would be enough, but they were not leaving yet. After a sufficient amount of time had passed, she spun back around.

"King Louis will be most upset if you throw us out, majesty," Niko pleaded. She knew what to do.

"If you do not leave, I will rip this dress from my skin and shame you once more with my tits!" She shouted, grabbing at the top of her hemline so that the priest understood without needing the threat translated. Niko ran out of the room first, Father Mignoletto close upon his heels, leaving her in peace at last. She found little comfort in the silence and her attempts to meditate or pray were constantly interrupted by her newfound obsession with her own mistakes.

She felt haunted by every mistake she had made since becoming queen, and every potential mistake. Should she have executed Yakov straightaway without hesitation? Should she have acted sooner in lobbying to be named as polemarkos? Should she have stayed home and waited for Malachea to return reeking of failure?

This was not just a moment of overzealous self-examination; this was a siege of grief, an avalanche of guilt and shame for every time she had failed to live up to the ideals of Amaltheia. She was nearing the edge of despair when there were three loud, confident knocks at her chamber door. She sprang from her bed like a deer who spots the movement of a predator. As she trotted for the door, she felt a small wave of relief. A visitor would be a most welcome distraction from this relentless bombardment of guilt. She opened the door to see a man with raven-black hair wearing a stylishly embroidered vest-and-doublet and a curious smile.

"A thousand apologies, your majesty," he said, using the most formal possible Greek and bowing his head and shoulders while pressing his fist to his heart. "I am called Sir Alexios."

She curtsied in response, growing a little bit weary at the gesture because of the hundreds of times she had performed it recently.

"You are Greek?" She asked, surprised to meet a Greek who wasn't a servant or laborer.

"Born in Milan, but Greek nonetheless," he answered with a winning smile. Califia did not generally find herself physically attracted to men and while that was still true of Sir Alexios, there was something about him which made her believe that he might manage to be tolerable. "My family once owned this villa in which you are now staying."

"Truly?" The queen felt a twinge of suspicion that perhaps the young knight was having some fun at her expense, but nothing in his expression looked like anything other than earnest truth. "Well, it's lovely."

"May I come in?"

She paused as her gut instinctively tensed.

"What is your purpose here?"

He chuckled a little at her suspicion but shrugged and nodded as if he understood.

"I want to make sure King Louis is keeping the place

in good repair for me until I can press my claim." He held up his right hand. "Honest."

He looked harmless enough and she reminded herself that she had just prayed for a distraction only a few moments ago.

"Very well," she glided back into the room, feeling silly once more in the ridiculous dress they had forced upon her. No amount of servants promising her that she looked beautiful could convince her. This damnable thing constricted her breasts to the point of discomfort and was likewise so tight in the shoulders that she couldn't lift her arms above her head without shredding the back into pieces.

"Everything seems in order," Sir Alexios said, gazing around the room at the bed, the vanity, the sunlight that streamed in. He took a few steps to the open window and looked down into the courtyard below. For several moments the queen's hair stood on end and she felt her stomach twisting itself into knots with worry. Did this man suspect that she had been planning an escape? Was this really some overconfident Greek servant which King Louis had dressed up just to spy on her? "Such a lovely day today, don't you think?"

"The weather is especially nice," she agreed, grinning with as much friendliness as she could possibly muster and hoping he did not notice her sudden rush of nerves.

"It's a waste to spend it indoors," he said, shepherding a lock of black hair behind his ear after it strayed into his face. "Would you like to go for a turn about town with me?"

She blinked, shocked for a moment at the suggestion. She was under the very explicit impression that she wasn't allowed to leave the room, much less go on a leisurely stroll.

"I think I understand your hesitation," Sir Alexios said, illustrating his point with an outstretched index finger. "I assure you that I have permission from the King of the Franks himself to escort you around the city. Provided you don't leave my sight, of course."

She felt a sudden thrill at the thought of setting even a single foot outside this room, even more at the concept of going on a walk around town. Such a venture would also afford her the opportunity to mentally map this ridiculously labyrinthine place.

"I would like very much to *take a turn* about town with you, Sir Alexios," she curtsied for effect and smiled as he laughed at her clownishly formal performance.

He stepped into the hall and she followed, half expecting to be tackled at any moment. They passed by a few servants and a guard on their way to the outside door, all of whom nodded to Sir Alexios and didn't regard her at all.

Stepping outside was overwhelming. The skin of her face became taut at the sensation of fresh air. Her nose was bombarded with the aromas of cooked pork, fresh-baked bread, and a rich mixture of ground spices. The sky was brighter than she remembered and she squinted, stumbling backward in the doorway slightly as Sir Alexios passed by her. He glanced over his shoulder and immediately offered a hand. She took it, holding out her other arm for balance but the moment passed quickly as she stepped forward to join him in the vast outdoors. He proffered his elbow and she placed her hand upon his forearm.

Califia hoped he would lead them left through the nearby market, that she might eat some of the delicious-smelling food. Instead they went straight through a less-crowded avenue lined with large houses on either side. They were not quite as impressive as the solid stone villa where she had been staying but were constructed instead of lumber and brick.

"Who lives in these houses?" The queen asked, watching women on the upper stories beating their blankets which hung upon the balconies.

"Mostly Frankish tradesmen and their families," Sir Alexios said, waving amiably at one of the women who gawked at them from an upper story window. "I hope you'll forgive their stares, most of them probably think you're a Turk."

"Are all the Franks fair-skinned?" She said, suddenly overwhelmed by the sea of white faces that seemed to be glowering at her.

"As far as I know," he replied, sniffing indifferently. He turned to her and grinned playfully. "Why do you ask? Are your people looking for a new home?"

She was perplexed by this question and her face must have shown it because he laughed and held up a hand to gesture that he was only joking.

"So your family was driven out of Constantinopolis?"

"My granddad," Sir Alexios said, finally dropping his formal speech. "He died fighting alongside the last emperor, for all the good it did him."

"But his children escaped?"

"My dad was in Venezia at the time, safely stashed away from the horrors of the siege. Lucky thing for me."

"Indeed," Califia said. They were coming upon a large plaza lined with vendors selling decorative plates, cups, and other fine wares. In the center was a great pillar, taller than any of the surrounding buildings and atop that pillar was an ornately decorated golden cross.

"Used to be a statue of Constantine himself up there," Alexios said as they strolled toward one of the stalls. "He was the founder of this city."

"An emperor of the Romans," Califia said. When he looked at her with wide-eyed surprise, she elaborated. "The Osmans taught us much about the city's history."

Alexios picked up a plate from the stand and showed it to Califia. Upon it was painted a handsome young man with a crown that looked too big for his head. There were some letters below it, but she couldn't begin to guess what language they were written in. She surmised that he must be someone important so she took a guess.

"Is that Jesus?"

Like a clap of thunder from a mighty storm, so loud was the laughter that exploded from Sir Alexios' mouth. He wiped tears from his eyes and explained.

"He would fall in love with you if he heard you say it, your highness!" He snickered a few more times and then finally recovered himself. "Beg pardon, majesty; that's an image of King Louis."

"Ah." She gazed at the image on the plate and did her best to recall the appearance of the Frankish king. The eyebrows in the image were far bushier than their real-life counterparts and the chin depicted on the dish was far more prominent than the tiny neck bump which the king possessed. "Our artists often take liberties in their depictions as well. I do like the colors, though."

Sir Alexios laughed again, far less boisterous than the last time but still quite loud. The vendor himself harumphed at this and crossed his arms. His eyes were like little dots of ash beneath the hedgerows which he called eyebrows.

"I didn't paint them, I just sell them," he said, in a way that was so defensive that Califia suspected he was lying. "Are you going to buy them or not?"

"I meant no offense, sir, I— wait, you are Greek?"

"No, but I speak it well enough. Either buy something or move along!"

"Best of luck to you," Sir Alexios said, pulling Califia toward the next stand, this one also featuring various plates and cups but featuring a strangely different image.

"Now, who do you think this is?" The Greek knight held up a vase with the image of a man wearing a black coat with a large furry collar attached to a red cloak. Like the image of King Louis, he wore a crown, albeit a better-fitting one. She would recognize those sunken eyes, skeletal cheeks, and thin, frowning lips even without the clue that King Louis was depicted on the other plates.

"King Ivan of Moskva," she said, shivering a little as she remembered what a chill that man's presence inspired.

"Very good," he said, complementing her as though she were an animal whom he had just taught some terrifically amusing trick. "The likeness on these is much better, but I don't think I'd want to be found out in possession of a set like this in the city's Frankish quarter. Not in a few months."

She shuddered at the thought. No matter how much the Californians professed to love freedom and hate tyranny, their people had been forced to deal with tyrants of their own making on occasion and the results were blood-stained episodes of national shame. How would tyrants fight one another? She hoped she would never have to see firsthand.

"Do people really buy these?" Califia asked the shopkeep. He replied in a string of syllables which she couldn't fathom but believed was the same language that Father Mignoletto used. Sir Alexios replied rudely, or at least she guessed it was rude from his delivery and from the reaction of the shopkeep, which was to snort and ignore them until they left.

"People like the novelty, I suppose. I think the emperors of the past would sometimes reward people who displayed their images in public during festivals and the like, but I can't imagine Louis tossing coins to someone just for owning a plate. Ivan seems more likely to torture them just so he can enjoy their screams."

"I assume you serve King Louis?"

"I am sworn to him. Helped him press his rights in Milan and was rewarded with some land. Hoping I get some more by supporting him here."

"That is what you fight for then," Califia felt like she was beginning to understand these people. "Gifts of land?"

"Sometimes land, sometimes coin, it all depends," he waved his hand as if trying to shoo the subject away but she wasn't ready to let it go.

"Coin? You fight for little metal disks?"

"Sometimes, yes. Those little metal disks come in quite handy." He sounded somewhat perplexed at her response. "Don't your people use money?"

"We have nothing like that on California, save for perhaps some children's toys."

"Children's—" He scoffed. "How do you buy things? Hell, how do you sell things?"

"We devote our energies to meeting the community's needs." She could see from his face that he didn't believe her. "We do trade some items, but never anything that is needed."

"So no one sells any food?"

She was repulsed at the idea. "No."

"Who owns the land?"

"The people," she said, shrugging.

He shook his head.

"I see why Father Mignoletto was so flummoxed," he said. "Your nation sounds like no place I've ever seen or heard of."

"You talked with Mignoletto?" She felt her shoulders tense as her body raised its guard.

"That's the official reason for this constitutional," he said, winking. "King Louis came to me — he likes to keep the priests happy you see — and asked if I would secure a promise that you would not harm Father Mignoletto."

"Define harm."

He erupted once more in thunderous laughter.

"He told us that you threatened to strip naked if he didn't leave. I thought it was pretty funny."

"I won't do it again," she promised, blushing at the thought of everyone in the king's royal circle knowing about her outburst. "As long as he respects my wishes and leaves when I grow weary of his preaching, he is in no danger."

"Good enough for me," he shrugged. "So. Now that the unpleasant conversation is behind us, can I show you my absolute favorite plates of all?"

She nodded and smiled, doing her best to shrug the whole thing off. He guided her to another stand where the plates, cups, and vases depicted two figures standing hand in hand as they held crosses in their other hands. Though the depictions were not very good, she understood that these partners were meant to be King Louis and King Ivan working together to rule the city as equals to one another.

"Amazing, isn't it?" Sir Alexios stepped back and put his thumb and forefinger against his chin as though he were admiring a real piece of art.

"It's a lovely idea," she conceded, understanding

enough about these people to realize why Alexios found this so amusing.

"A fool's dream," he scoffed, offering his elbow once more. She put her hand upon it and he led her down a narrower street which merged with another large plaza that was filling rapidly with people.

"Why did the king make me a dress?" Califia asked as they strolled through the largely empty street. He turned to her, his eyebrows arched in an expression of genuine surprise.

"That's... erm... not for me to say, your majesty." He sputtered, his cheeks blushing bright and red as ripe manzanita fruit. "I'm sure he has only noble intentions."

"You have to say that," she said, rolling her eyes at the boringly safe response. "He's your king, after all."

"I suppose that is true," he laughed and offered her the same expression she had seen raccoons wear when they were caught stealing beans from a barrel. "Everything that I own is because of his majesty, so yes, it is difficult for me to express an unbiased opinion of the man."

"Try," she brought her left hand over and placed it intimately against his bicep, "for me."

She felt him tense slightly at her touch and hoped that she hadn't gone too far and once more offended these peoples' nonsensical sense of modesty. He sighed and relaxed a little, which gave her hope.

"King Louis tries to be a good man, which is more than one can reasonably expect from a king. That being said," he scratched at the back of his neck with his free right hand, "he doesn't always succeed. He set Italy to the torch just so he could rule over the embers. I helped him ignite the flames."

She shuddered as her mind conjured images of the

capital palace on California engulfed in flames, as all the capitol around it likewise burned.

"Does it seem likely that he might try and take me for his mistress?"

They walked in silence for eight whole footsteps, each moment only adding kindling to the flame of suspicion within Califia's heart.

"Nothing's impossible, I suppose," he shrugged. "That being said, I *don't* think he would. Some kings collect ladies' hearts like jewels in their crowns, but not Louis. It's well known that his single-minded pursuit in the bedchamber is producing a legitimate heir."

"He has no children?"

"Not a one," Sir Alexios scoffed and shrugged. "Not for lack of trying. Oh! I didn't mean that in a crude way! Only that he arranged to have his first marriage annulled when his wife failed to conceive."

"Annulled?"

"You need special permission from the church, which doesn't come cheap. You also need a good reason, like if your spouse is unfaithful or refuses to... erm... perform their duties," he said, his suggestive pronunciation leaving little doubt in Califia's mind what he meant.

"Is his wife here in the city?"

"Funny story that," he smirked. How this young man loved gossip! "The queen *was* here for many months after the initial conquest, but when word came that the Sultan was gathering a great army to besiege us, the king shipped her back to Paris."

"How awful for her."

"There is a rumor that he told her he'd be on one of the accompanying ships and that she didn't learn the truth until she landed safely on friendly shores," he winked, "but you didn't hear that from me."

She tried to catch a glimpse down a nearby alley, looking eagerly for landmarks but finding none. This venture was turning out less than useless; rather than helping her understand the layout of the city, she was only growing more confused about which streets led where. A company of guards passed by them, eying her menacingly. She sighed as she realized that was the third such group she had seen since they had been out. Running afoul of even one would be a disaster.

"I was wondering if you might indulge my curiosity about those winged beasts your people employ," Sir Alexios said. "One of them nearly took my head off a few weeks ago."

"The griffins?" Califia said. "It was nothing personal. They protect our island and have an instinct to kill any man who crosses their path."

"Young Niko told me that you don't allow men on your island. I thought he was spinning tales."

"It's true," the queen shrugged. "We have managed without men for thousands of years."

Sir Alexios stopped and looked at her intensely, "Yet, the creatures seemed to be under someone's control, at least at first."

"The queen controls them," she said, suddenly suspicious about his curiosity. "No one understands exactly how."

"Hm," he said curiously, clearly about to ask more questions.

"What is happening there?" She gestured to the plaza before them, now only thirty or so paces away, which she now saw was not only full to bursting with people, but that all of those people were facing the same direction. *Time to change the subject.*

"Not sure. This city thrives on spectacle."

As they finally moved past the wall on Califia's left which was blocking her view, she saw five people standing on a wide stage. No! They stood not on the stage, but upon stools on the stage and each appeared to be sprouting something thin and brown from the back of their heads that reached up to the rafters above them. Several men in puffy hats and fine robes were reading from unfurled scrolls, each speaking a different language. She caught only bits and pieces of the Greek.

"What is this?" She asked, suddenly filled with horrified certainty that something terrible was about to happen.

"A hanging," Alexios said, raising an eyebrow at the question. "What do you do with thieves in your homeland?"

"We do not have thieves," she replied, recoiling at the site of a man standing next to the five wearing a black mask over his face. "If someone takes more than they need, we put them to shame."

Her stomach clenched as she discerned a few expressions in the gathering crowd. While many were somber, she spotted a few faces smiling in delight while others even appeared to be jeering and shouting abuse at the condemned.

The black-masked man on the stage held up a hand and the crowd grew silent. A richly-dressed man standing toward the stage's front read something from an unrolled parchment - they were too far away for her to hear, but she guessed he spoke Frankish - and the crowd cheered as he rolled the scroll up and stepped to the side. The man in the black mask marched to the nearest person, a middle-aged man who was balanced precariously upon his stool with his toes. Reaching down, the black-masked man pulled the stool from under him and suddenly the poor, raggedly-dressed fellow was kicking his legs and jerking from one side to the other as if trying to free his hands which Califia assumed were bound behind him. He gasped and choked and the queen recoiled in horror. *These people are being murdered.*

"This isn't right," Sir Alexios said, shaking his head in disgust. "They should be doing this in the hippodrome, not in Theodora's plaza."

"Is no one going to help those people?" Califia couldn't believe that not even a single person was rising to assist these poor souls. The second stool was torn from underneath the next person's feet, a woman with an unspeakably dirty face and threadbare burlap for clothes.

"Anyone who helps will swing next to them," Sir Alexios said, incredulous that Califia still didn't understand.

"I can't be here," she said, backing away and bumping into someone she hadn't realized was behind her. She turned to see a sour-faced man in a fine tunic and doublet who glowered at her as if she had just spit in his soup. "Pardon me," she said, moving quickly past him only to see that more were packing in behind him. She moved past the next person and the next after that and then suddenly heard Sir Alexios' sharp voice some distance behind her.

"Your highness!" He shouted. She turned and saw his face just before the crowd began whooping and cheering as the last stool was yanked from its place and the final victim dangled, helpless and gagging.

Califia heard herself cry out at the sight and pushed her way past several more people before finding herself in an empty space of the plaza facing a narrow alley. She sprinted through out of pure desperation - no plan, no notion of where she was, no conscious thought outside her desperate need to get as far away as possible from the grim spectacle she had just witnessed. The alley opened into a wider street, so she turned left and continued fleeing, running past several street vendors carrying baked goods.

"Stop that woman!" She heard Sir Alexios' voice call out behind her. She turned quickly and saw him burst from the alley, pursuing at full speed. On her right there was another narrow alley between buildings. She slowed down to avoid knocking anyone over in the crowded street and started cutting toward the open alley. She heard the Greek knight's furious voice shout, "Stop her!"

Just as she reached the alley, a halberd suddenly jabbed across its entrance and its shaft knocked the wind from her chest as she ran straight into it. Everyone nearby screamed as Califia was suddenly surrounded by armored guards pointing the lethal end of their halberds at her. She breathed heavily as she considered her options, filled with terror and the unnatural strength that her flight had inspired.

"Stop!" Sir Alexios shouted as he caught up. The guards raised their weapons but appeared ready to use them at a moment's notice. He spoke something in Frankish and one of the guards replied. They had some kind of exchange that ended with the guard who was speaking shoving his index finger in the queen's direction and then likewise thrusting it toward Alexios, who held up his hands as if conceding some point in an argument. The guards fell back into formation and continued down the street on their patrol.

"Sorry," she muttered, feeling suddenly embarrassed by the whole affair. "I don't know why I did that."

"We all do stupid things when we are afraid," Sir Alexios said, scratching awkwardly at his neck. "Still, no reason to ruin an otherwise lovely walk. Come, I'll show you the Aya Sophia."

Califia knew she should agree. Her secret purpose in allowing Sir Alexios to take her into the city was to find a reasonable means of escape, and she certainly had not attained that yet. But continuing to walk the city could mean witnessing more unspeakable horrors. The thought made her feel nauseous. As eager as she had been to leave the confines of her chamber, she now found herself longing for the soft bed, the familiar furniture.

She sucked in a deep breath of outside air, savoring its various smells, flavors, and freshness. "I prefer to return to my chamber."

"But…" He began to object but the look on her face must have convinced him that it would be fruitless to argue. He sighed. "As you wish, your highness."

She took his elbow once more and they walked, largely in silence, back to her ornate and comfortable prison.

"Perhaps you would fancy another turn tomorrow," he said, as they ascended the steps to the front doors of the villa.

"I am not sure that is a good idea," she said, her courtesy returning as her heart calmed.

"There's still so much of the city that you haven't seen!" He exclaimed as the doors opened and they walked inside. "The Aya Sophia, the palaces, the hippodrome-"

Califia stopped and Sir Alexios halted as well. "Would you really take me to a place which you consider appropriate for public executions after today?"

"I… uh… I misspoke, your majesty."

She strolled quickly ahead of him and he jogged a little to catch up.

"It's more than that, though," he sputtered. "It's where

we used to elect emperors and have grand chariot races and public gatherings and—"

"Sir Alexios," she said, gently but with just enough command in her voice for him to listen. "I think I've seen all I need to of this city and will only be too happy when I lay my eyes upon it for a final time."

They arrived at her door at that moment. She quickly slipped inside and closed it behind her before he could follow her in. A plate of food was waiting for her on the vanity, the bed fitted with fresh, clean sheets. She sighed, realizing that she would not see Lydia and Sophia tonight.

Perhaps that's for the best, she thought. She ate with a heavy heart. As she shoved pieces of cold chicken into her mouth, the queen of California became steadily convinced of an incontrovertible truth: she absolutely had to find a way to escape from this city.

19

She spent much of that afternoon trying to reconstruct what she could remember of the city. The drawers of the vanity held a few useful items — some spools of leftover thread and three rusty thimbles — which she used to reconstruct what she could recall. Three times she tried to recreate her path using the faded thread, arranged the thimbles where she remembered spotting guard patrols, and each time felt certain that some detail was incorrect or at least unreliable.

Sleep offered no escape from her troubles. In her dreams she saw Malachea, Basilea, Arianna, and little Chloe standing on stools with nooses around their necks and each one was made to dangle from their ropes. As she watched her daughter struggle for breath, she realized that the fifth person on the gallows was herself. She felt the stool get quickly snatched and woke just before the rope went taut around her neck.

She woke early that morning with a clear mind in spite of her fitful sleep, as if all her troubled notions had been exorcised by the unsettling dreams. The guards arose that morning with a terribly effective quickness which she surmised was the result of good discipline and training. Every night since arriving here she had observed the patrols that passed under her window, striving in vain to discern a regular pattern. No single group ever followed the same route twice and the nearby streets seemed serpentine, narrow, and impossible to navigate at night without running afoul of at least one such patrol.

This problem had a solution; all problems did. She pondered her impending escape like a wolf gnawing the bones of its prey. She had not yet arrived at the marrow, but she was certain she had adequately chewed the outermost layers. The bedsheets could be tied together into a rope from which she could descend from the window. With the right timing, she might be able to pass for a lady taking an early morning stroll. Whether her Greek would hold up to the interrogations of the guards was questionable, but she wasn't certain which accent she should attempt to mimic.

The light raps which she had come to recognize as Lydia and Sophia struck her door and the two maids entered with their usual accessories; Lydia carried the food tray and Sophia held the linen basket and brooms. Diminutive Lydia set the tray down and took a broom, sweeping as Sophia began stripping the bed. After some courteous greetings, Califia picked up a broom and helped. No one objected.

"You've gone quiet this morning, your highness," Lydia said, fussing her broom into a corner several times to get some clump of dust to come free.

"My apologies, good ladies," Califia said. "I went walking the city with Sir Alexios."

"Oh, how nice that must have been!" Sophia said, yanking the bedsheets from where they were tucked in the underside of the mattress. "Did he take you to the hippodrome?"

She shuddered at the mention of that place, whatever it actually was. It took a moment for the shiver to pass.

"Just some of the nearby plazas," Califia said, hoping that she made it sound adequately boring so as to warrant no further worthwhile questions. "He said his family used to own this villa."

"Oh, *that* Sir Alexios! Alexios Papadoulos, Lydia!" Sophia exclaimed.

"High pedigree indeed," Lydia said, sounding very impressed for a moment before frowning slightly. "If King Louis keeps control of the city after the Turks have been driven off, this place will probably be his again."

Sophia sighed. Her voice was low and somber. "We'll still be laundering clothes and scrubbing walls whether the city belongs to the Franks or the Muscovites."

"Is every place like this one?" Califia asked. "For... servants I mean."

"A few are better," Sophia said, gathering Califia's sheets. "I have heard that many are worse."

Califia suppressed a shudder at the word *worse*.

"Did the seamstresses leave all this behind?" Lydia said, looking at the spools and thimbles which Califia had lain on the vanity's surface. "What a mess!"

"I found those in the drawer," Califia explained. Both servant women looked at her with raised eyebrows. "Sewing is a hobby of mine."

They stared at her for another moment and she worried that the lie was too obvious. Was her hatred of sewing written upon her face? The women shrugged and Lydia dutifully put the items back in the drawer.

"Do you think it would be possible," Califia said, "for me to borrow several spools of thread?"

"It might be," Lydia said, "but I think it would be

better if you requested it through Father Mignoletto or Sir Alexios. I don't know why, but the seamstresses don't like us."

Califia nodded and she began helping Sophia strip the bed.

"Do either of you have hobbies?" The queen asked, wanting to deflect attention from her sudden interest in embroidery.

"I enjoy weaving on occasion," Sophia replied. "My mom was a weaver and she taught me a lot about the craft."

"Cooking," said Lydia. "I know it sounds silly, but I love baking and frying and all of that."

"You really are too kind, your highness," Sophia said, hoisting the basket and striding toward the door. "We thank you for a lovely conversation."

"It is I who should thank you," Califia said, but already they were out the door and it closed behind them. She returned to the vanity and brought out the spools and thimbles, arranging them and rearranging them, gazing out of her window to try and spot landmarks she might use to navigate this labyrinthine city when the time came.

Sometime midmorning there was a knock at her door and she shoved the items back into their drawer before bidding the visitor to enter. From the sharp and confident rapping, she supposed it was a noble or someone important. As the newcomer cleared the doorway and came into view, she felt a tiny pinch of pride that she was correct; in walked King Louis of the Franks. He was closely followed by King Ivan of Moskva, and three other well-dressed aristocrats whom she vaguely recognized from her first day in the city.

The interpreters entered last and each shuffled to their patron. King Louis' translator was the same man who had accompanied him the first day he visited Califia.

"Your highness," the King bowed and Califia curtsied in return.

"Your most Christian Majesty," she replied, glad she could remember his official address.

"I see that you are making good use of my gift," he gestured toward her dress and she suppressed a shudder at the way his eyes seemed to consume her as they wandered her body.

The queen looked down at the dress she wore. The blue cloth shimmered in the morning light that streamed through the windows and when she moved the birds and flowers appeared almost animated.

"The dress is yours to keep," King Louis announced, pausing for the translation. "You wear it well."

"Thank you, Your Majesty," Califia said, stalling as her mind raced to think of a way to extend her delay. *Perhaps I can change the subject.* "Please tell Father Mignoletto that I am sorry for my outburst yesterday."

"That matter is already resolved," said King Louis, glancing at his well-dressed companions behind him. "Behind me are some of the rulers of the lands north of here. King Ivan you already know," he gestured to the Muscovite prince, who nodded grimly, "but the others have been at war with the Ottomans since before my people arrived. They would like to ask you some questions.

The questions began innocently enough. King Stephen of Moldavia, a bald man with a bristly mustache, asked about the food on California and the queen told him all about potatoes, bison, shrimp, tomatoes, and peppers. King Ivan inquired about Californian tattoos and the queen moved her dress to display hers, excluding Aphrodite this time, as she explained religious symbolism as well as the beard tattoos of the Gorgons.

King Vladislaus of the Majyars, a heavily bearded man with long hair, wanted to know why the ladies fought with battle axes, which he always considered a man's weapon. She explained that it was tradition, and tried her best not to think of how many of his people her own had felled in battle near Gelibolu. Lord Stefan of Zeta, a stern-looking man with a curly beard, asked about the history between the Amazons and the Osmans and the entire room was shocked when the queen informed them that the alliance was less than a year old.

The King of the Majyars asked about trade with the turks and the room was once more shocked to learn that no such trade had ever taken place.

"Forgive me, your highness," said Prince Radu of Wallachia, a fat man with curly hair, a bare chin, and a wavy mustache, "but why did your people join the war against us?"

"We were told we would be fighting the Greeks," Califia admitted, blushing with embarrassment. Thankfully each sovereign turned to their translator and spoke rapid-fire, so none of them noticed the queen blushing with shame. *It all seems so foolish.*

"What can you tell us," Prince Radu of Wallachia broke through the noise as he took up the conversation once more, "about the relationship between Sultan Bayezid and the Mamluk savages?"

The queen felt a bolt of suspicion at the question, as if the man asking was trying to trick her into giving something away. She thought of a suitable answer.

"The sultan appreciates their support," she said, slowly, "and they respect his leadership."

Prince Radu looked at her skeptically.

"What about the eastern savages, the Timurids?" he

said. "Perhaps they have not been happy with the way this war has been proceeding?"

Califia gave a similar response and even claimed that the two sultans saw one another as equals, which she was certain was a lie.

"How many of the troops belong to the Osman sultan?" King Louis asked, cutting off Prince Radu before he could continue his questioning.

"I really can't say," Califia replied, suddenly understanding what was happening. *They are trying to squeeze information out of me.* "I can tell you that we brought five hundred of our own warriors along with one hundred and fifty griffins."

Mentioning the griffins had the desired effect; the room erupted once more in chaos as each man chatted with his interpreter and Califia took a moment to calm herself. As the men finally began to quiet down, she decided it was time to bring this interrogation to an end.

"Oh!" She cried, sitting upon her bed and raising a hand to her forehead. "My apologies, your Majesties... all of these questions are making me feel faint!"

The men muttered and gazed regretfully at the floor for a moment.

"Our apologies, your Highness," King Louis said after exchanging some words with his fellow sovereigns via their interpreters. "I believe we have taken up enough of your time for today."

They all turned toward the door and Califia began to feel relief when suddenly the Frankish king turned toward her.

"I would beg your indulgence on one final matter," he said. "Have you given any more thought to swearing an oath against escape attempts?"

Her breath caught in her throat. She could not make

such a promise and then escape regardless. Even if she did not fear the retribution that would result from such duplicity — and after witnessing the fate of the thieves, she *did* fear that retribution — it would stain her honor to violate an oath. *I need more time.*

"Your Most Christian Majesty gave me five days. It has been only three."

"That was a demonstration of my generosity," the King replied. After the translation finished, he continued, "I had hoped you might reciprocate by not requiring the full length of time offered."

Califia's mind raced trying to conceive of an argument this man would find persuasive. She thought of Father Mignoletto, and the upsetting story which he had told her.

"It was not noble Adam who feasted upon the fruit of the forbidden tree, thus disregarding the Lord God's commands," she did her best to seem respectful and humble, "but Eve, in her haste and without consulting her husband, ate of the fruit and thus does the whole world continue to suffer."

The king pursed his lips after the translation finished but appeared impressed. He exchanged looks with his translator, who shrugged, and then gave a rapid-fire of words for the man to relay.

"The king says that your humility is a credit to you and your people. He is likewise impressed with your piety and hopes you will continue learning the Christian way of life."

Califia curtsied and King Louis smiled amiably.

"He certainly doesn't want undue haste to tarnish your conscience and prefers you give your oath of your own free will and not from fear."

He seems happy to make me afraid. The queen smiled

broadly through the thought, determined to remain a very picture of gratitude and humility.

"I encourage you, fair majesty," the interpreter continued, "to meditate upon the benefits of swearing the oath. You would have whatever food you desired, regular companionship with Greek speakers, even Sir Alexios."

Califia's mouth curled into a tiny smile at this. There was an idiom in California for what King Louis was doing by offering extra benefits. *He is trying to improve rotten meat by adding too much seasoning.*

"I will consider your wise words, Your Most Christian Majesty," she said, convinced by their expressions that she had succeeded in appearing charming and harmless. "Your people are fortunate indeed that you wear the crown."

"His Most Christian Majesty thanks you," the interpreter said said after the king had spoken. "If you require anything at all, please don't hesitate to ask."

The king and his fellow sovereigns turned and left the room, their interpreters following close at their heels. She spent the afternoon setting up thimbles, spools, and laying thread between them in a rough configuration which she *believed* matched the city's layout, working with her limited supplies as best she could. She leaned out of her window for a better look several times, trying to work out the destination of various winding streets and making a note of guard patrols where she could.

She had nearly finished with her model city's outer wall when she heard the gentle knocks on her door which usually heralded Sophia and Lydia. Califia was about to call out her permission for them to enter but, strangely, the door opened before she had a chance.

The queen tried to quickly open the top drawer so she

could sweep her city map supplies into it, but the drawer jammed and in her hurry to get rid of the evidence, she brushed it onto the floor. The spools, needles, thimbles, frames, and cloths sprayed across the stone floor as Califia yelped in surprise.

"Let us help with that, your majesty," Lydia said, setting Califia's dinner plate upon the vanity and stooping to gather her *sewing supplies*. Sophia carefully stepped wide of the carnage and set the sheets she carried upon the bed, then came to the floor to help.

"Sorry," the queen said sheepishly. "I don't know what came over me."

"My guess," Lydia said, picking up a spool wound with pinkish thread, "is that you didn't want us to notice the map you were making of the city."

Califia froze, her hand reaching to pinch a needle which had rolled into a small valley of mortar between stones. Lydia and Sophia continued gathering the sewing supplies as though nothing out of the ordinary had occurred.

"A map of the city?" Califia asked, laughing at the suggestion. "You two have quite the imagination!"

Without a word, but with smiling faces, Lydia and Sophia reassembled the map which Califia had been creating. Some of the spools were in different places, and the thimbles which represented city guard barracks were farther apart, but it was close enough to cause the queen to drop her pathetic denial.

"We thought it was strange that you were refusing to swear the oath," Sophia said, sharing a smirk with Lydia. "Now we know why: you are planning to escape."

The queen stood and backed away from the women, her mind flooding with terror and doubt. *What do they mean to do with me?*

"Please understand us, highness," Lydia said, looking anxious. "We have no wish to see you punished. We want to help you get back to your people!"

Califia's terror turned to confusion, then to wonder.

"You want... to *help* me?"

The ladies exchanged a look between them, as though deciding whether to say more.

"In the time that you have been here," Sophia began, "you have shown us greater kindness than any of our previous masters."

"It's true, your highness," Lydia said, her eyes welling with tears. "We know that it is because of you that we weren't punished at the behest of the seamstress. That alone makes you a saint in our eyes."

"Any kindness I have shown you," Califia began, "is but a reflection of the compassion which you have shown me. I would have surrendered to the despair of imprisonment if not for your companionship."

The three women stood quietly together for a brief moment. Califia believed that in the silence between them, an unbreakable bond was being forged. She believed that the two servant women could feel it as well. They were no longer master and servant— they were equals.

"The city is filled with rumors, my lady," Lydia said. "The Osman sultan is bringing a huge cannon just like the one that crushed the city walls fifty years ago!"

Califia thought about the cannons that her people had helped fetch near the beginning of their time in this land. Yakov had told her that those mighty guns looked like arquebuses compared to the great weapon with which the sultan's father had ruptured Constantinopolis so many years before.

"It will be worse than the last time," Sophia said,

nodding and pacing. "They knocked the walls down with their cannon and did whatever they liked to those trapped inside."

"My friends," Califia said, sensing anew the need for swift action, "I thank you profoundly for agreeing to help, but I'm afraid I haven't yet made much of a plan."

"Oh, your majesty!" Sophia said, beaming like a proud daughter. "I was about to beg you to accept the plan we already made!"

"It's all arranged for tomorrow afternoon, your highness," Lydia added. "The house where we are placed is near the wall facing the bay and I found a spot some months ago where if you shift the stones around just right, you can wriggle through to the water side."

"Oh," Califia tried to sound supportive but she was confused. "How will that help? I don't mean to be rude, but what about the Venetian ships?"

"They don't concern themselves with the wall," Sophia said confidently. "We ourselves have wriggled through on occasion to get some fresh air outside the city and enjoy the peaceful swaying of the sea."

"The darkness should conceal us from any prying eyes on the wall," Lydia said. "Most of the guards aren't concerned with the Golden Horn. They keep their eyes on the Turk army."

"Then the plan is to walk around the city under the cover of night," Califia said, "then make our way to the siege camp?"

"Something like that, yes," Lydia said, smiling widely. "We'll sneak you out of here after lunch tomorrow. The king was planning to leave you alone in the afternoon for the sake of your contemplation. We worked ahead in our chores so we won't be needed or missed. We'll throw a hooded cloak over you and lead you along the safest path to our home."

"My absence won't be noticed?" Califia asked.

"Not until the evening at least," Sophia said. "Lydia and I will come back to serve your dinner and keep up appearances. They probably won't even realize we are gone until we fail to report tomorrow morning. By then—"

"We'll be free," Califia said, nearly choking back a sob. *Free.*

"There's only one thing left to do really," Sophia said, stepping back and then putting her rearmost leg upon the ground. Lydia did likewise. "We are yours to command madame. We pledge to you our fealty."

Califia understood that this was an important moment for the two ladies and that it would be best if she didn't interrupt it. After more than a few moments passed by, however, she realized they were waiting for her response, so she quickly cobbled one together.

"I accept your... fealty..." she hated the way her mouth wrapped unnaturally around that word. "Please rise. If we succeed, you'll never need to bend the knee to anyone ever again."

20

Califia gasped as she woke, her heart racing like a fleeing jackrabbit. Every muscle in her body clenched with an urgent tightness. Her eyes adjusted to the darkness and as she was wondering what had awakened her, a set of explosions resounded somewhere in the distance.

What is happening?

Another cluster of explosions boomed, sending tremors through her room. She rolled out of bed and huddled up against its frame, instinctively trying to hide. Another set of booms thundered through the air and she covered her ears. Her eyes burned with fresh tears and her breathing became ragged from terror.

She realized it was cannon fire she was hearing, but it seemed to be coming from the east and north, not the walls to the west and south.

Are the Christian ships firing?

Califia's hands were shaking, her muscles tensing with terror. She crept back into her bed, pulled the covers up to her chin, and tried to stay calm until the guns went silent. Just when she started to doubt whether that moment would come at all, they stopped. A few more distant booms sounded, but it was clear that whatever had been happening was over now.

Her mind raced with possibilities. Was this part of a rescue attempt? Did the Sultan's fleet try to dislodge the naval defenders only to be driven off or killed? She stared at the seaside walls, wishing there was some way to see beyond them.

She tried to quiet her mind. It took some time, but eventually her breathing slowed and she fell asleep once more.

A knock at the door woke her up. Califia sat up and called for them to enter. Lydia placed the breakfast on the vanity and Sophia closed the door behind her. The queen rose from the bed and stretched, feeling a little embarrassed that she had slept so long.

"Everything has been prepared," Sophia said, plopping the laundry basket upon the bed as she began stripping the sheets. "When we bring your lunch this afternoon, I'll hide some plain clothes and a hooded cloak in the basket under the fresh sheets. You put them on, then we'll sneak you out."

"Just like that?"

Sophia cracked a wry smile as she pulled the sheet from beneath the mattress.

"The simpler the plan, the greater the chance of success."

Califia thought that Sophia's words had the ring of Athena's own wisdom to them.

"Not a moment too soon," Lydia said, sweeping the far corner. "That bombardment last night was surely a portent of another attempted assault."

"You needn't worry, m'lady," Sophia said. "They threw everything they had at the walls and they're still standing. We have some time."

The queen nodded and smiled. As she began to eat her breakfast, she was haunted by a new thought. This city was filled with people just like Lydia and Sophia — common folk who did not bear arms, but whom were driven to this place by circumstance. *Are the foremothers avenged by* their *deaths?* She gobbled up her fruit and bread, then picked up a broom to help.

"Be careful of your dress," Lydia said, her voice thick with admiration. "It would be a shame to get it dirty."

"Indeed," Califia made sure the skirt especially stayed clear of the broom, admiring the way the fabric made its swishy crushing sound when it bunched. Sadly, this beautiful garment would be left behind. She couldn't risk wearing it beneath whatever common dress Sophia would bring her. The noise alone invited curiosity.

"Thea is looking forward to meeting you," Lydia said quietly as they passed each other while sweeping. "My daughter."

"You told her about me?" The hairs at the base of her neck suddenly rose.

"I just told her that we were bringing a friend home tonight," Lydia said quickly, as if sensing the source of the queen's dread. "I didn't mention *who*."

"She didn't tell the child anything that might harm us," Sophia said, stuffing the last bedsheet into the laundry basket. "You have my word, highness."

Califia nodded and made peace with it. Everything was in the hands of the triumvirs now— all she could do was hope for the best.

The ladies stayed longer, as had become their custom, knowing that Father Mignoletto usually took another hour or so to arrive. They peppered the queen with questions.

"Will we be forced to join the army?" Sophia asked,

her eyebrow raised in suspicion.

"Everyone is trained for the militia in case of need," Califia said. "It's not difficult, but it is work. I went through it, as did my... friend, Arianna."

Her voice caught in her throat at the mention of her lover's name. Was it still appropriate to think of the wild artist as her lover? Their last moments together had felt distant and cold.

"And what if I wanted to spend my days carving little statues," Sophia said, her intonation giving away that she thought this was a ridiculous example. "Would I be beaten and forced to do some other job?"

"If work needed to be done where you live, then you would be asked to assist," Califia said. "You would not be threatened with violence, but my people think little of those who don't contribute to their community."

"We have *that* much in common," the large lady laughed. Lydia joined, shaking her head at some shared memory of which Califia had no part. These women were becoming very dear to her and she allowed herself a little excitement at the prospect of them joining her back home. *It all feels so close now...*

Suddenly the door swung open and young Niko, the Greek interpreter, stumbled inside. The maids yelped. Niko's chest was heaving and upon his brow glistened a thin sheen of sweat.

"Leave us," he panted at Lydia and Sophia, who carried the sheets away and took their brooms before Califia could even say good-bye. He closed the door as they left, nearly snagging Lydia's skirts in the process.

"What is the matter?" Califia put a hand on his shoulder.

"Your majesty," he backed away and bowed briskly, "King Louis is on his way right now, and he is in no mood to be refused!"

"But he gave me until tomorrow," Califia began.

Niko turned with a start as the door creaked, but the sound was caused by a gust of wind. He turned back to the queen. "I beg you, my lady, give him whatever he asks."

Califia felt fear icing its way into her heart.

"What has changed?"

"Did you not hear the roar of the cannons last night?"

"My maids told me that it was just useless bombardment upon the walls."

"A falsehood to comfort the people," Niko smoothed his doublet and seemed to have caught his breath. "Osman ships crept through the strait and fired upon the Genoese and Venetian ships unawares. Our allied fleet is utterly crushed!"

Califia's heart sank into her stomach. How could the Osman fleet have executed such a daring maneuver? Suddenly she knew the answer. *Admiral Kemal Reis was not marching toward his execution— he was getting his job back.*

In spite of everything, she smiled, glad that the man's death need no longer hang over her head.

Niko continued speaking through his panting. "There are rumors that King Louis offered to surrender the city to the Turks on condition that we be allowed safe passage home, but they refused."

Before Califia had time to ask Niko for details, the door burst open and King Louis himself walked in, followed closely by Prince Radu, Prince Stefan, and a host of armored bodyguards. Father Mignoletto stumbled in at the end of the group and promptly delivered a slap to the back of Niko's head. The translator winced and began a rapid, heated exchange with the priest until the king held up his hand and they fell silent.

"Your Most Christian Majesty," Califia curtsied quickly, trying to shake off the surprise of this visit. She curtsied again to the princes. "Your highnesses. You honor this one with your presence."

As Niko translated, the queen observed the Frankish king's face. His red-tinged eyes were supported by puffy eyelids, his pupils dull with exhaustion and worry. When the monarch spoke, his expression barely changed.

"His majesty regrets that he has no time for pleasantries today," Niko translated as the king replied. "The wicked Turks and their allies have forced him to… accelerate plans regarding your royal person."

Califia felt her left hand tremble. She rubbed it with her right hand as though easing a cramp. *Do not reveal your fear.*

The king babbled away but Niko twisted his face in confusion at the words. He asked some questions in the nasal, grunting language of the Franks and King Louis grew red in the face and began slapping the back of one hand in to the palm of the other as he shouted. When he finished, Niko nodded and looked at Califia sheepishly.

"His majesty demands that you call upon the winged beasts which killed so many of our brave warriors," Niko said, looking at the floor, "and command them to kill the Turks and their allies instead. If you manage to drive our enemies away, he will set you free."

Califia was too stunned to speak. She gazed at King Louis' face, searching for some sign that Niko had mistranslated or that this was some kind of joke. The pale king glared in return, his lips slowly curling into a sneer.

"He is wrong to—" She stopped herself and waved Niko off from translating. *I must not let emotion rule me.* She swallowed as she took a moment to compose herself.

"His Most Christian Majesty is clever and perceptive," she began. "Surely, however, such a maneuver would violate the principles of chivalry and the rules of warfare?"

She could see from the way Niko winced as he translated that she had made a misstep. The king glowered at Niko and Califia in turn. He unleashed a rapid-fire response which Niko struggled to keep up with.

"As a fellow sovereign," Niko flinched as though the king's words wounded him, "you should understand that the only dishonorable tactic in war is one which causes you to lose. Achieving victory, on the other hand, covers any dishonor committed in its pursuit."

"I disagree."

Father Mignoletto raised his hand as the king was about to speak. The king nodded, and the priest spoke with Niko for several moments, gesturing with his hands and glancing at Califia periodically.

"The good Father wants to assure you," Niko said, his eyes pleading, "that the Muslims are just as much your enemy as they are ours. They have done nothing to try and free you from this place - no ransom, no rescue. It appears that they are preparing even now to attempt another assault on this city without regard for your safety."

I'll bet Malachea is excited for that.

She felt a twinge of guilt at the thought, but then suddenly her mind was seized by a new terror.

"Does his majesty understand," she began, "that he is asking me to turn against my own people?"

"It is his understanding that the creatures do not attack women. Your people should be safe."

Prince Radu idly fiddled with his mustache and examined Califia with his piercing eyes. Prince Stefan muttered something to the man at his right, who then whispered something in his ear. She wondered where King Ivan was, but decided it was safer not to ask.

"They would never forgive me for such a betrayal," the queen said. "They would depose me as soon as possible and elect another queen."

After Niko relayed this message to the king, a brief discussion followed. Father Mignoletto was insisting on something, but the king seemed to be resisting his overtures. Finally they turned to Califia.

"You would be welcome to stay here under King Louis' protection," Niko said, gesturing to the king. "You would even be allowed to keep your religion and take a husband, if you wanted one."

"You would make me an exile," she glowered at King Louis, who looked back impassively. "The Osmans were right about you; your ambition is outweighed only by your arrogance."

The king did not appear especially insulted after the translation, but shrugged indifferently.

"I... softened your tone on that last remark, highness," Niko said, his eyes pleading with her to agree with this horrendous plan. "The king is resolute and will not be dissuaded by any argument or twist of scripture, and he certainly won't be swayed by *insults*."

"Even if I wanted to summon the griffins," Califia said, her anger bubbling to the surface, "I cannot do it without a special dagger which I do not currently possess."

"And if you had this dagger, would you use it to destroy the king's enemies?"

Califia considered what might happen if she agreed to

this. Would they set her free, trusting that she would keep such an oath? The thought made her dizzy with longing. The queen quickly shook the thought aside; she already knew what needed to be said.

"Among our people, it is the ruler's duty to take the people's burdens upon themselves. I could never agree to betray our allies just to spare myself discomfort."

"You would rather rot in a cold cell than accept the king's offer of friendship?"

The king's tone was aggressive, but Niko translated with great reluctance. Califia's heart was moved that the boy seemed to care for her.

"I have no use for his friendship, nor a need dire enough to sacrifice my people's honor for the sake of my own freedom."

The king listened coolly to the translation, his eyes examining Califia as though he was beholding some strange, unknown creature. Once Niko had finished, his eyes narrowed on the queen and he waved his hand dismissively.

"So be it," Niko interpreted, clenching his eyes shut as he spoke. "You will be escorted to your new chamber immediately."

The halberdier guards stepped forward, flanking the queen on every side and facing the door. The king and his party left, then the guards began marching. Califia wondered idly what would happen if she refused, but decided against the attempt. The possible humiliation of having her hands bound filled her with shame.

They took a winding path through the city but she couldn't bring herself to revise the map she had tried to construct in her mind. It was pointless; this place stretched in all directions like a squirming nightcrawler, twisting and counter-twisting in ways that made it unnavigable for anyone who didn't live here. As they rounded a corner into yet another broad plaza with a statue atop a pillar, she wondered if people born here didn't still get lost on occasion.

At last they arrived at a lone tower with a wide base that tapered as it climbed toward the heavens. She pondered briefly whether it had been built by the Romans, the Turks, or the Franks. Her guards took up position before and behind her as they went inside and began climbing the seemingly infinite stairs to her new accommodations. She counted for a while to keep her mind occupied, but around step number one hundred fifty-six she nearly fell over as the building swayed in the wind. She abandoned the counting in the interest of staying alert enough not to tumble down the winding staircase and break every bone in her body.

When she thought herself too exhausted go another step, they arrived. It was not the topmost cell in the tower — at least she assumed the continuing stairs led to more cells — but she could feel the altitude and it made her ill. She didn't like being this high on a griffin, much less in a wobbly building whose construction she did not trust.

They ushered her from the stairs to the landing, then into the cell. They slammed the wooden door behind them and she heard them clanking away back down the winding stairs until their steps were like waves crashing on a distant shore. Then she could hear them no longer and had only the whipping of the wind for company.

She rubbed her hands against her bare arms as she examined her new chambers. A dirty mattress lay in the far corner next to a wooden chamber pot with an ill-fitting cover. Crumpled near the mattress was a threadbare blanket which she quickly fetched to wrap around herself. Her shoulders warmed but the covering only reached her knees. Her calves shivered in protest.

There was a large window covered with bars on the far wall. She went closer, squinting through the faint light that trickled in from outdoors, and saw that beyond the bars lay an inaccessible balcony with sides so high that she would not be able to see beyond them even if the bars were not in place. She suspected that it had been constructed this way in order to torment the cell's resident. If so, it was working.

Her head filled with impossible questions. What hope did she have of escaping now? How would she even survive the night without a suitable blanket to keep her warm? What would become of her people now that she was stuck here?

Do not give in to despair. She had trained for the militia in a desert which was hotter than Zeus' farts during the day and colder than Hades' blood at night. She wondered then how she would survive. *I found a way then and I will find a way now.*

Califia leaned against the bars that blocked the balcony and closed her eyes, feeling exhausted. She woke with a start when a shallow bowl scraped against the gritty stone floor as it was shoved through the space beneath the door. She examined the grayish-green substance within; it dripped from her short-handled spoon and splashed back into the bowl in gooey chunks. The insufficiently-cooked grains crunched between her teeth. She was reminded of the time Karissa, her lover at the time, had tried to cook a dish with quinoa but hadn't waited for their curly tails to emerge before serving it. Califia had smiled and chewed through the wet, crunchy mess for the sake of their love. She did likewise now for the sake of survival.

Every morning, midday, and evening from that day

forward, a bowl was shoved under the door and she eagerly ate its contents as quickly as possible to shorten the unpleasant experience. She prayed and meditated every morning until Father Mignoletto and Niko showed up, panting and exhausted from their journey up the stairs. Califia politely listened as the priest lectured on the sacrament of communion, Judas' betrayal of Jesus, and, most confusing of all, the trinity.

She recalled an older school of devotees among the Amazons who believed that each of the goddesses was but an aspect of one all-powerful deity, neither male nor female. The proponents of that philosophy, however, did not label it an immutable truth, nor attempt to claim that those who disagreed had been deceived by Zeus or Ares. As to the other subjects, she found them needlessly complicated and confusing, and every attempt at questioning the issue eventually led Father Mignoletto to declare those questions themselves heretical. She wondered what the church did with heretics but her thoughts turned to the swinging bodies in the plaza and she decided against asking.

Her days were impossibly dull but she discovered little ways to pass the time. She found the correct angle by which she could lean her head against the balcony bars and see a vast swath of sky. When she caught fleeting glimpses of birds, she followed their path until they flew out of sight. Aside from a bored interpreter and a zealous blowhard, these animals were her only company. There was the gaoler as well, but all he ever did was slip disgusting food under the door, retrieve her dishes, and occasionally replace her chamberpot. Hardly actions that qualified as fellowship.

One day, she had already lost track of how long she had been here, a breeze blew in from the balcony and howled through the room, exiting beneath the door. At first it felt refreshing and she thanked the triumvirs for stirring up the usually stagnant air. As it persisted well into the afternoon, however, she took shelter beneath the threadbare blanket and shivered until the wind abated in the evening.

Her sleep became fitful, often due to the thunderous reports of cannon-fire that sounded in the distance. Sometimes she woke in a confused state and didn't understand her surroundings for several moments. It took a long time to calm herself from these malicious awakenings. When Niko and the priest arrived one morning, she felt utterly exhausted and spent.

"How long have I been here?" Califia asked Niko as Father Mignoletto was catching his breath.

"I'm not sure I am allowed to tell you," he said, as his red-faced companion wheezed and coughed.

Califia was too tired to be charming.

"Please."

Niko glanced once more toward the priest as though expecting the gasping, sputtering man to support him. Instead he looked Califia in the eye and sighed.

"Six days, your highness."

Six days. Had it really been so long? She thought it was, at most, the fourth day since she had been thrown into this miserable cell as punishment for refusing to use her people the way the Frankish King apparently used his.

Father Mignoletto started by lecturing on the actions of Jesus' followers after he apparently left to live in the sky with his father, who she remembered was also himself. He instructed his friends to spread the faith to every corner of the world. Califia was especially fascinated that he also endowed them with the authority to forgive mistakes, a power which, according to the priest, now rested with the Roman church alone.

It is no wonder these people define themselves by war and conquest; they serve a conquering, tyrannical god.

After they left, she scarfed her midday gruel, slid the used bowl under the door, and then fell into her usual habit of gazing out at the sky. What was taking Sultan Bayezid so long? Surely now that the straits and the golden horn were once more his, nothing could stop him from knocking down the Blachernae walls and saving her? Her mind darkened at the thought. Such an event would be liberation for her, but it would be slavery and slaughter for nearly every other resident.

She was shaken from her miserable trance by a rap at the door. She was about to shout that she had already returned the bowl but something about the knock was unfamiliar. The gaoler rapped with his whole forearm so that it shook the door. Father Mignoletto always barged in without bothering to announce himself. *Who could it be?*

"My lady?" called a familiar voice from behind the door, followed by another set of humble, demure knocks. Califia's heart fluttered as she recognized the voice.

"Come in!" She called out, far more eagerly that she intended. The latch slid back and the door opened, and there they were — Lydia and Sophia. They strode into the room and Sophia made sure to close the door behind them. Lydia began to curtsy but Califia sprinted forward and squeezed the maid in an enthusiastic hug. Sophia stood awkwardly for a moment until Califia waved her toward them and she joined the embrace. For a long, full moment, the three women just stood in the cell, subtle afternoon light streaming warmly in from the barred-off balcony.

"I thought I would never see you again," Califia wept,

tears soaking into Lydia's shoulder. "Either of you!"

Sophia also began to weep. "Please don't be angry with us."

"We came to help," Lydia said, pointing to the brooms they had brought and the basket, which was full of clean blankets.

"I was never angry with you," Califia said, releasing the women at last to look them in the eye. "How did you manage this?

"These are our things, highness," Sophia replied, gesturing to the basket and brooms. "We requested permission to bring them to you the day you were brought here."

"And the king agreed?"

"No," Lydia said, "not right away. We had to convince him."

"What did you do?" Califia was afraid of the answer but nonetheless asked the question.

"We didn't do anything by ourselves," Sophia said. "We told our fellow Greeks about you and word has spread. They've decided that you are one of us."

"It's been a little chaotic these last few days," Lydia said, grinning widely. "Between the work stoppages, mass demonstrations, and fighting with the city guard, the king very much regrets sending you to this tower."

Califia noticed that Sophia's left eye was somewhat puffy, as though it was healing from a bruise. Lydia's hand was wrapped in bandage which no doubt concealed some other injury.

"I am sorry to be the cause of pain for either of you," Califia clapped a hand on either woman's shoulder. "But, by Hera, it is so very good to see you both."

She could scarcely believe the news about the Greeks taking her side in this dispute. Hearing of their support for her made her feel strangely happy. She felt a small measure of shame at rooting for the descendants of those who killed Amaltheia. *Perhaps we have more in common with them than we realized.*

Lydia and Sophia unpacked the blankets and the queen wrapped one around herself like a cloak, her body filling with warmth at the garment's soft touch. Lydia leaned the infested straw mattress against the bars of the balcony door.

"This will help with the fleas," she said politely, taking a pillow from the basket and giving it a few fluffs. "Just take it down when the sun sets, probably before dinner."

"Of course," Califia said, remembering how she hung their own mattresses in the sunshine back home for that same purpose. "Thank you, truly."

"Your Highness," Sophia said, her eyes narrowing in a most serious way. "We have made another plan for getting you out of here, but it might take a few weeks."

"No!" The queen shouted, her voice echoing so much that all three ladies froze. "Sorry, no. I appreciate your devotion, and thank you for all your kindnesses but... the two of you already endured a lashing on my behalf. I will not risk your lives further for my sake."

The women both gazed upon her with solemn faces, their eyes wet with tears. They embraced her again, this time hugging her harder than she was able to squeeze them.

"My lady," Lydia said, wiping her eyes, "I would still like you to meet my daughter, Thea. Would it be alright if I brought her here tomorrow night, after supper perhaps?"

"It would be the honor of my life to meet the daughter of one of the best women I have ever known," Califia said earnestly.

The women eventually left and she was alone once more. In her prayers that night, she thanked Hera for giving her the strength to resist the temptation of Zeus. Whatever Malachea might think of her, whatever the Gorgons might whisper behind her back, Califia was not a queen who needlessly sacrificed the lives of those who served her.

The queen woke early the next morning, while the world was still dark. She felt almost too warm beneath her fresh, clean blankets but stayed snuggled within them nonetheless. She pulled them tighter around herself when she suddenly realized she wasn't sure when the Greek maids had brought them.

It was the day before, wasn't it? She remembered their tears, their kind faces, the warm embrace they shared— she was certain that had been the night before, which Niko had told her was the sixth day. Strangely, she felt as though she remembered another day in between the maids' visit. Had she been here 7 or 8 days? Had she been here even longer?

As she looked around at the cold stone walls and tried to recall her previous days, they became jumbled together. It was two days ago that Father Mignoletto had told her about the man who exiled his illegitimate son whom God then had to save. Or was that yesterday? Or two days before that?

She examined her dress, trying to recall the history of its decline. The first day she had ripped one of the shoulders when it snagged on a rough part of the wall. The second day she observed that the bottom hem was becoming threadbare. The fifth day had seen the lace on its upper portion begin to separate from the regular fabric. She poked her fingers through a hole in the upper part of the skirt near the outside of her right thigh. *How long has this been here?*

Her gruel that morning tasted no worse than usual, it was much easier to keep herself warm with the fresh clean blankets, and she itched much less in the morning thanks to Lydia's care of the mattress. She gazed at the sky, longing to feel the open wind against her face, to feel the sun warm her skin.

She found no peace that morning as she sat and thought. Escaping with the help of her maids was tempting because it was the only alternative to staying here, not because it seemed in any way feasible. And although the recent Greek unrest *might* mean a ready-made diversion, it seemed just as likely that security in the city would be much more active than usual.

The Greeks! How she wished that she had cut Yakov's head from his shoulders straight away and never heard him mention the name of their foremothers' great enemies! She should not be here— not in this cell, not in this city, and definitely not in this land. She had been robbed of her freedom, denied control over her life, and made utterly dependent upon the charity of two compassionate but equally powerless women. She threw the threadbare blanket against the wall and wept.

When he arrived later in the day, Father Mignoletto could see that she was upset but said nothing. Califia noticed that Niko muttered to him more than once and she surmised that the lad was encouraging the stone-faced priest to talk to her as if she were a fellow human and not a blank wall at which he could recite the finer points of theology. Niko may have also been trying to convince the old man to tell a different story.

That day, which she was certain was the seventh day of her imprisonment in the tower, Father Mignoletto told one of the worst stories she had ever heard. God commanded one of his prophets to sacrifice his own son. The tale made her seethe with anxious rage. After the prophet and his heir climbed to the top, he seized his son and tied him to an altar. Abraham raised a knife to murder his brood because the lord demanded it. At the last possible moment, a messenger from God appeared and stopped the dark ritual before blood could be spilled. He told the prophet that this was all a test from God and that Abraham had passed.

"What kind of God asks his believers to harm their own family?" Califia said, wearily.

"God would never let Abraham slay Isaac," Niko explained. "He was just testing Abraham's obedience."

She sighed, her bones aching from sitting on the hard floor.

"Athena would never ask me to kill my daughter," Califia said, bitterly, thinking of little Chloe thousands of stadia away. "And if she did, I would tell her to go *fuck* herself."

Niko made the sign of the cross over himself and then translated to Father Mignoletto, whose face became red as he opened his eyes wide. He jabbered away rapidly and Niko listened closely.

"He says that if you said something like that to our god," Niko replied, somewhat sheepishly, "then he might maim you or strike you dead."

Califia chortled to herself as she let her head fall back against the wall behind her. *Do these people truly understand nothing apart from violent coercion?*

"I would rather be dead," she clenched her teeth and spoke with a bitter edge, "than serve a god like yours."

Father Mignoletto started replying, wagging his index finger at her as he ranted.

"I will hear no more," Califia announced, interrupting

him and breaking his rhythm. "Please leave me in peace."

Niko translated and, she suspected, even argued a little on her behalf. The two men granted her wish, sliding the bolt into place before beginning their long descent down the spiraling stairs. She felt a stab of loneliness but determined that she preferred to be alone if the alternative was a sanctimonious windbag and his dancing monkey. It seemed a little cruel to characterize Niko thus, but it didn't matter. They would return tomorrow and tell her more dreadful tales of their tyrant god.

At lunch that day, there was a little cube of day-old bread sitting in her gruel, a heavenly treat compared to her usual fare. Idly she wondered if her friends had somehow influenced the quality of food she received as she munched on the bread and crunched her teeth against the nasty gruel.

She could not purge her mind of the story of the prophet and his son. Could young Isaac have ever trusted his father again, after nearly being killed? Could Abraham ever look his son — *either* of his sons — in the eye after such a betrayal? This god of the Greeks and their allies continued to disappoint her. They claimed that he was all-powerful and could strike people dead, but where was this god when the Amazons were being enslaved by the Greeks? She imagined that the priest would make the argument that the Greeks were god's punishment for worshiping idols. But didn't the Greeks worship this god when their great capitol was seized by Osman soldiers who raped, killed, and beat them in the streets, who displaced them and caused them to flee their homeland for the price of subservience to the other Europeans? Where was this god when they needed him?

Where are your *gods now?* She tried to stop the tears that this thought provoked, but they came too quickly. Soon she was drenched in the salty baptism of hopeless weeping and she lay on the floor feeling miserable, abandoned.

She woke to the sound of the dinner bowl scraping across the floor. How long had she been asleep? Had she missed Sophia and Lydia's visit? She assured herself that they had promised to come *after* supper. She took the straw mattress down from the balcony doorway, hoping that the late afternoon sky might light her cell a bit more. She frowned as she gazed upon the overcast sky, the clouds lumped together like badly mixed potato mash.

She leaned against the bars that denied access to the balcony, then turned her thoughts toward spiritual things. As she tried to let the goddesses guide her mind, her thoughts turned inexorably back toward her present dilemma. What could she do for her people, sitting in prison alone?

What did Amaltheia do?

The queen's heart thrashed in her chest like the roaring chorus of thunders that herald a fierce storm. Father Mignoletto was a long-winded sanctimonious hypocrite but he was right about one thing; every god respected sacrifice. She opened her eyes and looked down, examining the thick layer of dust that coated the stone floor. It wasn't enough to merely be *willing*. She needed to send a message.

Her fingers traced a simple shape in the dust of the floor before her. She crafted a simple image — a dagger about the length of her forearm, its tip pointed toward her.

Califia closed her eyes and chanted, speaking her intentions into the air and waiting for the goddesses to respond.

"Take my life and spare my people," she spoke over

and over again. She had spoken the words in earnest at her coronation, understanding in her head that leadership meant sacrifice. Now she understood with her heart as well, and with every recital of the phrase, her heart grew bolder and the stray thoughts in her mind fell away as she focused solely on the one thought she now entertained.

Take my life and spare my people.

She felt as though she had uttered the phrase hundreds, possibly thousands of times. She was halfway through speaking it yet again when something clanged in front of her. She looked down to where she had drawn the outline of the dagger to see a familiar silvery glint shining up at her through the dim evening light. A red gem on the handguard caught her eye and she realized - with horror and with joy - that she was looking at the triumvir dagger, that same weapon with which the first Califia had freed her people from the chains of slavery by giving her own life.

The queen reached out and touched it. The cool iron blade kissed her fingertips and she pulled her hand back with a start. How had the gods managed such a feat? It didn't matter. She had been given the means to set her people free so that they might return to California and live in peace.

She picked up the weapon carefully. It was heavier than she remembered, though she supposed that imprisonment had probably weakened her. She lifted the hilt, aiming the tip at her left breast and prepared to plunge the weapon into her own heart.

Part V: Liberation

21

Califia had faced death many times on this journey, but never quite this intimately. She thought of her daughter Chloe, of the taste of manzanita wine, of watching the sunset on the beach of Droseros.

When she accepted the office of Califia, she swore an oath to serve the Amazons' interests above her own, placing their desires, their needs, their futures foremost. *Even at the cost of my own life.* She had wanted to revive the peoples' memory of Amaltheia. What better way than by following in that queen's footsteps?

A voice in her mind continued its protest. How would the Amazons recover the dagger from this far-off cell? Would it create a succession crisis if the next Califia could no longer communicate with the griffins? What if her sacrifice caused Constantinopolis to sink, just as Amaltheia's death had predicated the sinking of Atlantis?

She bid the troublesome voice to be silent. Whatever came after was not her concern. She did not need to be guided up the mountain and tied to an altar, nor escorted through hostile crowds and nailed to a cross. The dagger's hilt began to feel warm in her hand and she knew the time had come.

"Persephone, receive my spirit," she said, lifting the dagger and angling the blade to pierce her heart.

"Don't!"

Califia jerked her head toward the sound of the voice, nearly dropping the dagger. Her heart pounded as she searched and, at first, saw no one else. Was she truly losing her mind, slipping away from sanity as she wasted away in this wretched cell? Her eyes spotted movement behind the bars of the balcony and she pointed the dagger in that direction as she rose. She squinted into the darkness beyond the bars.

"Who is there?"

The figure stepped closer to the bars and the queen's eyes focused on the black, tattooed face of a woman whom she had not seen in nearly a fortnight.

"Malachea?" The queen asked, still uncertain whether this was really happening or was the product of a dream.

"Califia," the woman replied, the warmth in her smile unmistakable. "It is good to see you, my queen."

"How did you—" she peered behind Malachea and saw her griffin Elena standing proudly on the balcony behind her. The queen realized her focus must have been deep indeed if she did not hear either the wings swiping the air nor the thump of the creature's feet against the stone. "You came for me?"

"I wanted to come sooner but..." The polemarkos trailed off and flinched.

"There was debate?"

"More than I would have hoped. The officers were mostly in favor of rescue. A particular faction of the gorgons, however, viciously opposed it and has been obstructing the effort for many days."

Malachea's face twisted strangely as she delivered the

news. Califia realized the polemarkos was in terrible pain, more than just the weariness that sometimes came with politics.

"Dionysia has done something terrible, hasn't she?"

Malachea nodded and looked at the floor. Califia wanted to inquire further, but the shame in the polemarkos' countenance led her to believe that it would be best to ask later.

"Whatever it is, you don't have to face it alone," Califia said. One of Malachea's hands was draped upon the bars and the queen rested her own hand upon it. The polemarkos' skin felt rough and warm and Califia's hands treasured the touch. Malachea smiled.

"If you are ready to depart, my queen, I will have Elena tear the bars from this cursed room and we will fly home."

"That sounds lovely," Califia felt suddenly invigorated at the thought of being free. "But we cannot leave just yet."

Malachea looked perplexed and as the queen was about to explain, a humble knock sounded at the door.

"Step back, please," Califia said, offering an apologetic look as she picked up the straw mattress. "I'll explain everything in a few moments."

The bolt rasped, the door creaked open and the two maids entered flanking a young girl whom Califia guessed was probably ten. They were all wearing simple dresses, but these were more colorful than their customary tan and brown. All three curtsied.

"Your highness," Lydia said, her voice cracking as tears began to fall upon her cheeks. "If it pleases you, I would like to present my daughter, Thea."

"It pleases me more than I can say," Califia said, smiling as her heart warmed with joy. "Lovely to meet you, Thea."

"Your majesty," Thea curtsied and the queen did likewise. "May I say that your dress is positively radiant?"

Califia gazed at the dress she still wore, the special dress that fit her perfectly and shimmered in the light. It was a shadow if its former self, a tattered garment which had become her only possession in the world. She smiled at young Thea, who appeared starstruck.

"I apologize for the interruption, your highness," Sophia said, stepping forward so that she was just a little in front of young Thea. "I insist that you allow us to tell you our plan for getting you - and us! - out of this city."

"Sophia, that really won't—"

"If you decide the plan is too risky, fine. But you must at least hear it, we insist. Forgive our impertinence."

"There has been no impertinen—"

"First, we will need to secure permission from the gaoler to launder that dress. He's close to saying yes already, it turns out he fancies women on the larger side."

Sophia winked and Califia was too delighted in the whole performance to interrupt.

"You change out of the dress and into a dress that is identical to the one that Lydia and I will be wearing. We need to take your measurements to make sure the dress we've cobbled together will be usable," she reached into her pocket and took out a long, notched stretch of ribbon but it slipped from her fingers. As she was gathering it, Lydia suddenly walked past the queen and took hold of the straw mattress propped against the balcony's bars.

"The night air will make it soggy, your majesty," she said, moving it aside before Califia could object. Having gathered the measuring ribbon, Sophia stood, went wide-eyed, and froze. Lydia looked to the balcony and uttered a sound halfway between a gasp and a yelp.

"Peace, do not shout! My friend unexpectedly arrived just before you did. Step forward, please, Malachea!"

She emerged from the shadows.

"Greetings to you all," Malachea said, smiling awkwardly.

Lydia's face went white and Sophia took a step back as if Malachea was a feral animal who might strike out at any moment without warning. Califia stepped between the Greek ladies and Malachea. She was about to continue calming the ladies when little Thea ducked under her arm and ran straight toward the polemarkos. Lydia whimpered meekly.

"Your hair is beautiful..." Thea said to the visitor, grabbing her own locks self-consciously.

"I like yours also, little one," Malachea replied, squatting so that she met the girl's eye line. "What is your name?"

"Thea," she answered, gasping as she peered at the polemarkos' face. "Do you have a beard?"

"It's a tattoo. Do you like it?"

The girl looked transfixed, staring at Malachea's face as if it the woman were a fine sculpture.

"I think it's amazing."

As Malachea and Thea continued idly chatting, Califia could feel the two women relax. Both looked to the queen and Lydia even offered a timid grin. She stepped past Sophia and stood next to her daughter.

"My name is Lydia," she said, curtsying. Malachea rose and Sophia joined them, introducing herself with a curtsy as well.

Califia gave them all a moment to get to know each other, then decided that she had waited long enough.

"Lydia, Sophia, Thea," she said. "If it is still in your

hearts to help me escape and to join with our people, the time has arrived."

Lydia stared somewhere past Califia as she pondered. Sophia cast her eyes from side to side as she appeared to deliberate.

"Is it true that we would have to leave this place and live on an island far away from here?" Thea asked, her voice tinged with concern.

"Yes it is," Califia said, "but you and your mother will be free to chart your own destinies from this day forward."

"She won't have to be a maid?"

"Absolutely not," the queen replied. She turned to Lydia and Sophia.

"Will you be there, Auntie Sophia?" She said, turning to the large woman and tugging on her dress.

"Well, child, I…" Sophia sputtered, clearly distressed at the whole situation. "That is, I would like to come, but I'm… I'm just not sure that I…"

"If I go, then you go," the child replied, clearly reciting some inside reference they shared.

"If you go," Sophia said, her voice growing stronger, "then I go."

"You don't seem terribly concerned whether *I* am going!" Lydia scolded, grabbing her daughter's shoulders from behind and pulling her into a tender embrace.

"Of course *you're* going," Thea said, as if the entire thing had been obvious. "You hate being a maid!"

"That will do, child," Lydia said, squeezing her daughter and sighing happily.

"I'll prep the harnesses," Malachea said, pulling a length of rope out of one of the saddlebags and looping it around the horn so that it hung down on either side.

"I don't suppose we can go back for anything," Sophia

said, sadly.

"What on God's earth could possibly be worth staying here even a moment longer than needed?" Lydia said, incredulous.

"I don't know…" Sophia shrugged and the queen noticed a tear streaming down her left cheek. "I used to have that locket my mother gave me, but that was stolen week before last."

"Sorry to hear it," Califia said as she heard Malachea grunting and the saddle shifting behind her. "Everything your mother gave you that was worthwhile, you already have with you."

Sophia looked a little confused but after a moment she appeared to understand the queen's meaning.

"She had stout arms like these, mum did," she proudly patted her biceps.

Califia nodded as Sophia wiped her cheeks.

"Saddle's ready," Malachea said.

The polemarkos gave clear, direct instructions for what needed to come next, how to quickly fasten the safety harnesses and how to keep hold once they were airborne.

"What if the beast attacks us?" Lydia asked, her voice rapidly filling with fear.

"The griffins only attack men," Malachea informed them.

"Makes sense," Sophia chuckled.

Those in the cell stepped back from the bars and followed Califia's example by covering their ears. The griffin walked to the bars and placed its foreclaws upon them, its talons wrapping around like snakes. At Malachea's command, it pushed the bars into the cell with a loud clang and dropped them unceremoniously on the floor.

"Let's go!" Malachea shouted. Califia glanced with

alarm at the chamber door, as she heard yelling and confused exclamations echoing up the staircase. "Move!"

The women did as the polemarkos had told them, affixing the large loop to their midsections and tightening the slip knot. Califia leapt onto the rearmost seat on the saddle and pulled the straps tight around herself. Malachea handed Thea to her. The girl fit right in her lap and didn't complain once when the queen affixed a safety strap to her as well.

"Everyone hang on!" Malachea bellowed as she strapped herself to the fore of the saddle. Elena flapped her great wings twice, then stretched them wide and leapt over the side, a maneuver which inspired panicked shrieks from poor Lydia and Sophia. The beast straightened itself and the queen could hear Malachea muttering calming words to them but couldn't hear them over the relentless howl of the wind. She heard Thea shout something unintelligible so she leaned closer to the girl's head.

"What did you say?" The queen asked as bolts from crossbows whizzed past them in the dark.

"I said, 'this my favorite day!'"

Mine as well, the queen thought as the wind whipped through her hair and chilled her scalp. The sensation was so refreshing she thought she might cry.

As missiles flew past them from below, Malachea pulled back on the reins to take them higher. The night was clear enough for her to get a view of the entire city from above, the glow of sconce torches and moonlight illuminating its many winding streets, monuments, and ruins.

A line of tall obelisks cast long shadows across a vast oval field surrounded by a stone wall whose topmost edge was missing so many stones that it now resembled a range of mountains. Somehow she knew that this was the hippodrome, the large public space that Sir Alexios had told her was used in part to host public executions. Several beautiful palaces lay in the structure's vicinity, as well as some domed buildings which Califia understood to be Christian churches. She had learned from Yakov that these buildings were converted into Mosques when Sultan Bayezid's father conquered the place and wondered if they had been temples to Athena or Aphrodite before that. She wrinkled her nose as she realized it was just as likely they had been dedicated to Zeus or Ares.

Even as high as they were now, well beyond the reach of their enemy's arrows and bolts, the city still looked massive. Califia had thought she had seen perhaps a little more than half of it on her walk with Sir Alexios, but it was as if she had mistaken a boulder for an entire mountain. *Trying to escape under my own power would have been futile.*

They followed one particularly wide avenue toward the double-walls in the distance. They passed a massive church sitting on a hill, what seemed like an endless ocean of houses, then a large open cistern with several churches and other large structures jutting out from the houses that surrounded it. Malachea directed her mount higher still as they approached the massive walls ahead.

Califia felt Lydia's hand clawing at her leg. The poor woman was wide-eyed and breathing fast as her face was starting to turn white. The queen recalled how the air grew less sufficient at greater heights, how even the bravest griffin rider did not dare to fly too high for fear of falling asleep among the clouds. She glanced at Sophia, who was likewise pale and blinking slowly. Images flashed in the queen's mind of the unfortunate maids slipping through their harnesses into the city below. Califia tapped Malachea's shoulder.

"We need to go lower!" She called.

"Too dangerous!" The polemarkos said. "There are musketeers on the wall!"

There was no time to explain.

"Lower!" Califia shouted, squeezing the woman's firm shoulder for emphasis. "Now!"

Malachea cursed and arced Elena downward, just a few degrees short of being a dive. The streets were empty save for a few beggars but even through the dim light of the stars and torches Califia could see armored men mobilizing upon the massive wall ahead.

"Everyone hang on!" Malachea shouted, veering her mount hard to the left as the Greek women shrieked in terror. An iron bolt whizzed somewhere overhead and Califia heard the sharp pops of musket-fire, but these were desperation shots which flew so wide that the queen did not hear the whistle of their bullets. They were soaring parallel to the wall now, its brickwork whizzing past in a blur of gray and black blobs.

"Mama!" Thea shouted, reaching out toward Lydia. Califia whipped her head toward the slender maid, who was spraying the houses below them in a sheen of vomit. Her hands still gripped the ropes and the hip harness held, so the queen breathed a sigh of relief. She turned toward Sophia, who was wiping her mouth as if she had also just loosed the contents of her stomach. For once, Califia was thankful for a meager evening meal.

"She's alright, little one," the queen soothed, patting Thea on the shoulder. Lydia turned toward her daughter and offered a weak smile, and Califia felt the child relax a little.

"Here we go!" Malachea shouted, veering her mount

toward the wall and pulling the reins back so that they tilted upward. They flew over the wall at the midpoint between two towers. The guards on duty in those towers streamed toward them as they vaulted over the structure. The few shots that sounded went wide, and the escapees quickly outranged the arquebuses and crossbows as they flew away from the cursed city.

Califia turned to look at the walls. The cannon fire she had heard so persistently during her time in the tower had done terrible work; she noticed many impact scars along the inner walls and a few places where the shorter outer walls had been reduced to piles of rubble. One of the towers near the northern end of the wall had collapsed, but the singular Blachernae walls appeared stable and strong in spite of the hammering she knew they had taken.

As the queen surveyed the walls of Constantinopolis, her eyes suddenly spotted a golden glint emerge from the holes of a nearby tower. She grabbed Malachea's shoulder.

"Cannon!" Califia yelled, hoping that her rescuer could hear her over the whipping of the wind.

"Everyone hold on tight!" The polemarkos yelled, inclining her head so that her right ear was turned toward the city behind them. The familiar boom of a cannon split the air and Malachea yanked her mount's reins to the right, turning them sharply in the air. An iron ball whistled behind them, striking a hill far below which exploded in a spray of grass and black soil.

"Thanks for the warning!" Malachea called over her shoulder, gently correcting their course as she cackled like a madwoman.

Califia's stomach unclenched. She gazed back at the shrinking walls once more, expecting at any moment to see the glint of another cannon barrel emerge. After a while she turned her attention to the camp before them, in which many torches and cookfires blazed. The place was so well lit that she could see the faces of the dirt-smudged soldiers who crowded around steaming pots. A wave of rich, spicy aromas wafted through the air and her gut gurgled jealously.

Califia knew that the siege camp was enormous but seeing it from above was overwhelming. Malachea had marshaled five hundred Amazons, by far the largest army they had fielded in centuries. Their meager militia was dwarfed by this dense collection of soldiers who outnumbered them by more than one hundred to one.

How will we find our people in this horde? Califia tensed as she thought of how hazardous it would be to land their mount among their allies. She had not dared try to use the triumvir dagger's magical properties yet and she certainly didn't think that trying to control an agitated beast was the best first step in reestablishing her bond with the creatures.

Malachea drew her sagaris from where it hung at her hip and raised it high above her head. From somewhere below, the queen heard raucous cheering and shrieking that caused her to grip little Thea tighter out of instinct. The girl giggled as though Califia had tickled her and she laughed along as though the whole thing had been a joke.

Far below them, among the many fires of their allies, the Amazons where cheering and shouting at their queen. Califia understood; the raised axe must have been a sign of success. She shuddered a little as she wondered about the sign of failure, though she supposed the ultimate sign would be the polemarkos never returning. That thought did not give her the guilty pleasure that she expected.

"Praise the blessed Virgin!" Sophia exclaimed as soon

as the griffin's talons touched solid ground in the middle of the Agora.

"I have a fondness for Artemis as well," Malachea said as she untied the knots that held the Greek women in place. "Though I think Athena deserves the bulk of the credit for seeing us safely from the city."

"Saints preserve us," Lydia said, laughing as she took a few stumbling steps after being unfastened. "We're at the mercy of Pagans now."

"Hooray for Pagans!" Thea cried as Califia handed her over to her mother.

Califia tried to unfasten her own safety strap but it was folded back inside the catch in a way that made it too bulky for her to easily manage. She cursed under her breath as she wore her fingers down to a nub working up a loop the size of a maize kernel.

"It does that sometimes," Malachea explained, turning around in the saddle and fiddling with the strap. "Clymena designed it that way as a safety measure. Better to err on the side of too secure, she said."

"That makes sense," Califia said as her legs started cramping with the expectation of freedom.

"Just hold still."

The polemarkos' fingers were deft in loosening the bulked material and soon had worked up a large loop. She grabbed the inner part of the strap and tugged it upward, brushing against Califia's upper thigh several times in the process. The queen's face felt suddenly hot as Malachea put her free hand upon her thigh for leverage in the process. *It has definitely been too long since I had sex.*

Amazons flooded the Agora and rushed toward Califia as Malachea finally defeated the safety strap. The first to reach the queen was Deanna, whose life she had saved and who had trained her for her duel. Califia gasped as the large, muscular woman compressed her ribs in an eager hug that lifted her off the ground.

"Apologies, my queen," Deanna said as she set Califia back on her feet. "It's just so good to see you again."

The queen smiled as she received hugs from several more women as horns, lyres, and drums sounded from the far end of the Agora. By her fifth hug, the impromptu band had started playing an upbeat, celebratory song which quickly inspired dancing and chanting among the Amazons. Califia joined in a dancing circle as they raised their arms and ululated along with the trilling in the song.

Women cut in and out during the dance and Califia felt drunk with the sheer volume of her people's joy. In her darkest moments alone in the dank tower cell, she had sometimes wondered if they would return home and abandon her to her fate. Not even the twinge of guilt she felt at having entertained such thoughts could even slightly quench the happiness she now felt.

Someone cut in on her left and she turned to see who it was. Basilea grinned warmly and she squeezed her hand. She gestured with her eyes toward a small, dense grove that lay just beyond the edge of the Agora behind them and the queen understood. She had celebrated long enough; the people deserved to continue but she needed to return to the important decisions which had no doubt multiplied in her absence. After a few more dance steps, she and Basilea discreetly departed and made their way into the grove.

While Califia was trying to think of something silly and clever to say, the old woman embraced her in a hug whose ferocity rivaled that of Deanna. The queen felt the air being squeezed from her lungs, and found herself returning an embrace that was just as enthusiastic. Basilea smelled of flowers and soil, and the queen hadn't realized how much she missed her.

"Praise Hera you've returned," Basilea began, pulling back from her embrace but keeping hold of Califia's shoulders. "Everything we've fought for was on the verge of being lost forever, but now that you're here you can set things right."

Califia had been feeling as though she were flying without the aid of a griffin, but now she felt as though she were plummeting to the ground. Malachea had indicated that some things had gone awry, but had not elaborated.

"Whatever has happened," Califia said, "we will face it together and find the solutions we need."

"I don't want to overwhelm you," Basilea said. "I can't even imagine what it must have been like, sitting in a prison cell for nearly a fortnight. We should engage with these problems one at a time."

"That sounds good," Califia said, feeling already as though she were thrashing underwater.

"It is my opinion that many of our difficulties can be solved by removing the current polemarkos. We must make public accusations against Malachea now, while you are strong and she is weak."

What Basilea was suggesting was, to the queen's mind, nothing short of a betrayal. Malachea had just rescued her; to choose this moment to dredge up the fate of Kassandra was an underhanded trick worthy of Zeus himself.

"That woman just saved my life," Califia said, shrugging Basilea's hands from her shoulders. "Are you really suggesting we seek justice for Kassandra now, when our people are unified in celebration?"

"Not all of our people are so unified," Basilea said cryptically. "In the time since your imprisonment, Malachea's leadership skills have been found wanting. Many blame her for your loss and subsequent detention. Some even whisper that she intentionally trained you poorly because she intended for you to lose."

"I wonder who started such rumors," Califia said accusingly. Basilea opened her mouth to protest, but the queen was not finished. "Whatever her faults, Malachea is no traitor. As to the death of her sister, that was a tragedy. I will not speak against her, however, nor will I authorize any such accusations from you."

"I have enough evidence now that I don't require your authorization!" Basilea huffed. "Malachea only saved you to recover her own reputation, you must see that. Even her daughter—"

"Any failure in leadership must surely rest upon your own shoulders as well," Califia spat, vexed beyond reason at the old woman's single-minded persecution of the polemarkos. "It was because of you that I was hearing griffins in my head when I needed to concentrate on fighting!"

"That was a mistake!" Basilea said, looking wounded by the accusation.

"It's easy to see how it might be misunderstood," Califia said. "Whatever our current circumstances, what happened with Kassandra is not what you think."

Basilea's eyes went wide at this. For a moment her mouth hung open and she seemed too shocked to speak.

"Did she confess the crime to you?"

"It was not a crime," Califia said. "Not in the broader sense."

Basilea looked at her as though she had just transformed into a bison.

"What justification could she possibly have for murdering her own sister?"

"Kassandra was plotting to *murder you!*"

Califia clapped her hands over her mouth. A long moment of silence passed between them as both women examined their surroundings to see if anyone was close enough to have overheard. It seemed that any Amazons in the area were celebrating in the Agora, dancing to the music, kissing one another, and singing songs of praise to the goddesses.

"This cannot be true," Basilea said. "She was my most trusted captain."

"She was not the only soldier who fought the Cochimi and came back changed," Califia said. "Many captains and a few strategoses clamored for an invasion against the mainlanders and the establishment of permanent colonies there. When you were elected as queen after my mother retired, they hoped you would lead them into a new era of conquest."

"I supported her nomination as strategos of the Gorgons to mollify her," Basilea's eyes looked into the distance as she recalled the circumstances of those dark times. Her shoulders slumped, and a tear began inching down her cheek. "Even then, I suspected that she would not be satisfied. She seemed to content herself with rigorously training the Gorgons, no doubt preparing to use them against me until…"

"Until Malachea intervened and saved your life."

Basilea squatted and then sat upon the ground. She put her face in her hands and sobbed. Califia couldn't help but feel pity for the poor woman whose personal history was now being rewritten by these revelations. Kassandra and Basilea had been close friends; that Kassandra would plot not only to overthrow the elected government but also to have her killed was more shocking than anything Califia had experienced.

"Whatever troubles have arisen since my captivity," Califia said, squatting and putting a hand on Basilea's shoulder, "we will face them together."

Basilea looked up, her face wet with tears, and nodded. Califia decided to leave her with her grief, for the moment. Her people were celebrating and she belonged with them.

As she returned to the Agora, satisfied that they had not been overheard, she spotted an Osman delegation of armed guards flanking Yakov, who was peering intently at the dancing Californians.

"Fair queen!" He exclaimed when he spotted her approach. "Hashem has preserved you and indeed rescued you from certain doom!"

He bowed politely. The guards who accompanied him nodded.

"In truth, it was Malachea who rescued me," Califia replied, offering a curtsy. "Though no doubt the sultan will say that it was God who ensured our success."

Yakov blinked in surprise and grinned like a child receiving a gift. Her suspicions about the similarities in Christian and Muslim theology had been correct. Both thought far too highly of their one god and his constant activity here on earth.

"The timing is most providential," Yakov said. He seemed positively unable to stop smiling. "In three days, the Sultan will crack this city open like a pistachio and your people's revenge will be at hand!"

Califia turned aside as she thought of the many people within the city who would be subjected to the deprivations of the Osmans, Gurkani, and Mamluk soldiers.

"Your majesty, are you ill?" Yakov asked. "The Frankish king promised to keep us apprised of your health, if he has been lying to us, I swear by—"

"I'm quite alright," Califia replied, smiling diplomatically. "It's a little overwhelming— the rescue, the celebration... This time last night I had given up hope of ever being free again."

"Understandable," Yakov said, gazing at the festivities with an expression of wonder. "His illustrious majesty Sultan Bayezid requests the pleasure of your company tomorrow before midday."

"The Sultan and I have much to discuss," the queen waved back at one of her well-wishers in a dancing circle. "How much... money... do you think might be required for passage back to California?"

"Passage back..." Yakov repeated the words to himself as if trying to make sure he understood them. "Once the city is taken, I'm sure his majesty will be only too happy to—"

"I have no intention of waiting until the city is taken," Califia said. "I mean to assemble my people tomorrow and convince them that we should leave for home as soon as possible."

"But your highness... you'll miss our moment of final triumph against the invaders. Would you really deprive your people of their vengeance?"

"That will be for my people to decide," Califia said. "I just want to understand our options."

"Surely you don't think the Sultan will allow the Blades of God to come with you?" Yakov said, tilting his head like a confused squirrel.

"Who?"

Yakov pursed his lips and squeezed his eyelids together the way he always did when he was about to give bad news. The queen prepared herself.

"They have not told you yet," he said, sweat starting to glisten on his brow. "Shortly after you were taken, many of your people expressed an interest in learning more about Islam. They renounced their native gods and the Sultan placed them under his protection."

"His protection..." Califia closed her eyes for a moment, feeling a familiar sense of dread at the way these people twisted words. "Can I assume this means they will not be allowed to leave without his permission?"

"There's more," Yakov said, wincing. "They are led by one of your former generals."

"Not..." Califia didn't want to say her name. "Not Traesta?"

"That doesn't sound right," Yakov said, tapping a finger against his bearded chin. "Something like Donatella or Denise or-"

Califia realized what name he was searching for. He looked at her expectantly and she hesitated, feeling that if she said the woman's name out loud, it would become real. Finally she forced herself.

"Dionysia."

Yakov nodded grimly and the queen felt as though the whole city of Constantinopolis, along with the whole world, had just landed on top of her.

22

Califia never imagined that the sight of Sultan Bayezid's tent would fill her with relief, but she could not deny the warmth that flooded her heart when she laid eyes upon the large brown tent. Square flaps along the upper portion had been pulled open, no doubt to cool the structure from the humid days of late spring. The entrance flaps had been tied open, which Califia took as a good sign.

The guards who flanked the open doorway nodded when she and her party stopped at the entrance and gestured for her to enter. Califia had kept the party small — Malachea, Basilea, Olympia, and Traesta. The Sultan was sitting upon silk cushions on a finely-weaved rug flanked by the Yenisherry commander Balyemez on his right and Alishir Nava'i on his left. They all held steaming ceramic cups and before them lay a silver serving tray with a pitcher that smelled of coffee along with several unused cups. Cushions were strewn upon the stretch of rug in front of the serving tray.

"Your majesty," Califia said, curtsying along with the rest of her party. Sultan Bayezid motioned for them to sit upon the empty cushions, an unprecedented event.

"We celebrate your triumphant return, fair queen," the Sultan said, raising his cup as the others did the same. The men took sips of their coffee as Califia took up the pitcher and filled cups for the Amazons. Sultan Bayezid smiled and waved for a young man clothed in bright white silk who came rushing over from his corner of the tent.

"It is not right for a sovereign to take work from servants," Bayezid said, wrinkling his nose at the pitcher.

Califia paused mid-pour as Malachea's cup was half-full. The servant stood above her, his eyes lowered but his hands outstretched to take the pitcher.

"Among our people," Califia said, gripping the pitcher tighter, "we consider service to be the chief function of a sovereign. One who does not serve is not worthy of the office."

"Your people have many strange ideas about sovereignty," said Balyemez as Califia continued pouring coffee. She raised an eyebrow at this seemingly rude comment, so he clarified. "General Dionysia has been regaling us with fascinating stories of your... *civilization*."

He pronounced the word snidely, his Greek dripping with condescension.

"From what she told us," Sultan Bayezid continued, waving the servant away as Califia poured the last cup, "it is a wonder that your streets are not clogged with idle, shiftless commoners. Surely you agree that such people must be forced to work?"

"Perhaps our people," Califia said, her face growing hot, "possess an industrious nature that yours simply lack. It could be that women are better at doing necessary work without coercion than men."

This comment inspired a burst of laughter from

Alishir, who nearly spilled his coffee. Sultan Bayezid twisted his mouth in annoyance as the man composed himself.

"In two days," Sultan Bayezid said, clearly eager to change the subject, "we shall destroy the walls that protect our enemies and retake the capital city which they have stolen. You will prepare your army for the assault."

Califia blinked at the sudden change of tone. Gone was the cordial, charming nobleman who had treated her with deference as an equal. Here at last she met the true Sultan: a man who saw her as a servant to be given orders. A servant with axes, spears, and swords, but a servant nonetheless. She glanced at Balyemez, who was sipping his coffee quite calmly, and wondered how much of this confrontation had been his idea. Did the Sultan understand that he himself was a servant of this man and the ambitions of the soldiers he commanded?

"Will we assemble near the Mamluks, as we did last time?" Califia asked, taking a long sip of coffee afterward.

"Our allies from Egypt were unable to honor their commitment," Sultan Bayezid replied. "Their most recent Sultan has *once again* been assassinated and so their army left to avenge him and probably put General Al-Khulani on the throne."

Alishir suddenly twisted his lips as he looked into his cup. He set it down but the pained expression remained on his face.

"You look troubled, Alishir," Califia said. "Are you feeling ill?"

"There have also been disturbances in our homeland," he said, glancing warily at Sultan Bayezid, who sipped his coffee as though he were uninterested. "We need to embark soon. We have agreed to stay a few more days, but once our troops ransack their fill from the great city, we will return to Persia to set things right."

"You mentioned rebels before," Califia remembered. "Perhaps your Sultan's absence has emboldened them?"

"That is what we fear," Alishir said, a look of deep concern passing across his face. He replaced it swiftly with a confident smile. "It is not the first time someone has tried to remove Sultan Bayqara from power. We will chastise them mightily upon our return!"

"Of that, we have no doubt," Sultan Bayezid said, setting down his empty cup. "Once the city is securely in our hands and the Wallachians and Majyars punished for their misdeeds, we shall send any soldiers you may require."

Alishir nodded affably at this, but something about the twisting of his lips looked to Califia like skepticism. Perhaps Alishir suspected that Sultan Bayezid might delay sending this military support indefinitely, leaving the Gurkani to fend for themselves.

"If you would indulge me," Sultan Bayezid said, turning his attention back toward Califia, "I would like to know the manner of accommodations you received from the infidels."

Califia suppressed a shudder as she remembered the dank cell, the flea-ridden mattress, the fogginess of her mind in isolation. She turned her attention toward the less unpleasant part of her captivity.

"I was held, for a time, in the room of a lovely villa," she said, smiling as she remembered the fresh sheets, the tailored dress, and meeting Lydia and Sophia. "I was fed freshly-prepared food and even walked about the city with an escort, once."

She felt the eyes of her compatriots turn toward her. She had not yet shared any details of her captivity with them.

"Tell me about the cell," Sultan Bayezid said, waving over a servant to refresh his cup of coffee.

She told him everything — how the Frankish king had tried to purchase her betrayal, how she shook with terror at the sounds of Admiral Kemal Reis obliterating the crusaders' navy in a daring night attack, how she feared she was going mad when they trapped her in a cold stone cell and fed her undercooked gruel twice a day. He listened with rapt attention as steam wafted from his cup and only when she finished did he dare to take a sip.

"I am glad you survived," Sultan Bayezid said, his eyes becoming vacant and distant. "There are many who did not."

A solemn pause filled the room as the Amazons and their allies sipped coffee. Califia enjoyed the thick, bitter drink for its richness and the way it made her body feel as though it were becoming more alive. She wondered who the Sultan had been thinking of when he referred to those who did not survive captivity.

"You mentioned Dionysia before," Califia said, setting her empty cup back on the silver tray. "I know that she and many others are interested in becoming Muslims, but I wanted your assurance that they are free to return to us if they choose."

The Sultan took a deep draught of his coffee. He gazed at her with an imperious expression, as though she had asked to borrow his jeweled turban.

"Their interest in converting to the one true faith places them under my protection," he said, placing a hand over his ceramic cup to illustrate. "They have also sworn solemn oaths to serve me; oaths which can only be dissolved at my pleasure."

Califia thought of several ways to protest this but felt Basilea's hand on her knee, indicating that further conversation in this regard was useless. She nodded as though she assented and gave the ladies in her party a concluding look. They set their cups on the tray.

"We must begin our preparations," Califia said, offering the Sultan a respectful nod. She and the other Amazons rose to depart.

"I expect no delays, fair queen," Sultan Bayezid said. "I also expect your monsters to participate, unclean and vicious though they are. Make sure that each is saddled and mounted for this battle and that your riders are prepared to suffer appropriate *consequences* if their mounts harm even a single hair on my soldiers' heads."

Califia paused at the threshold of the open flaps. She turned only slightly and spoke over her shoulder.

"I will see to it personally that everything is in place when this siege concludes in two days."

The sultan nodded, then held up his hand and made a motion in the air as though he were waving away a fly. Califia's skin burned at the gesture, and she left quickly to avoid the temptation of responding with a gesture of her own.

Once they had walked some distance from the sultan's tent, she heard a man's voice apologizing for His Majesty's brusqueness, attributing it to the sovereign's notorious indigestion. She whirled around to see that Yakov had joined them.

"I did not see you in the tent," Califia said, stopping her band in its tracks as they all turned on Yakov.

"His majesty ordered me to stand with the servants today," the emissary said, turning his eyes to the ground.

Califia felt suddenly ashamed. She had hardly looked at the servants' faces at all. *I'm becoming just like them.*

"Why did he do this?" Basilea asked, putting a hand on the poor man's elbow.

"I informed him last night that your people may leave soon and he flew into a rage. He thinks I've grown too close to you, fair queen. I thought he was going to have me beaten. Instead he had me stand with the servants to remind me that I, too, am *his* servant."

"It seems," Malachea observed, "that he thinks *we* are his servants as well."

"He is a good man," Yakov said, wiping away a tear. When he noticed the Amazons looking at him with incredulity, he chortled. "In the times before this jihad, he enjoyed telling jokes. He is actually very witty."

"He is not telling jokes anymore," Califia said, looking disdainfully at the man's cylindrical tent in the distance. "He seems to grow more tyrannical every time we visit."

"Fear brings out his cruelty," Yakov turned his head aside and seemed, for a moment, as if he was about to spit something distasteful out of his mouth. "He is afraid that he won't get his moment of triumph, that he won't be able to repeat the mighty conquest of his father who sacked Constantinopolis so many years ago."

Alishir's words came to Califia's mind. *He wears a face of anger, hoping we won't notice his fear.* It was not hard for the queen to imagine what the sultan currently feared most.

"The Mamluks left," Califia said, feeling as though she was beginning to understand the man. "If we leave as well, and also the Gurkani..."

Yakov gasped and his eyes went wider than Califia thought possible.

"Do not speak of such a disaster!" He exclaimed, looking around fearfully as though he feared they might be overheard. "If the Gurkani were gone it would mean... we wouldn't be able to take the city with Osman troops alone. We would have to accept the crusaders' surrender."

"Surrender?" Olympia said, sounding surprised. "Have they offered surrender?"

"I heard rumors of this when I was imprisoned," Califia said, suppressing another shudder at the memory. "The Frankish king was trying to bargain for a way to evacuate his people from the city. The Sultan refused."

"He will not betray the army," Yakov said, holding up his hands in a gesture of helplessness. "For them to have besieged this place for so long and be denied any plunder…"

"Gods forbid they are denied the pleasures of rape and pillage," Basilea said snidely, shaking her head.

Califia thought about everything Yakov had told them. He normally spoke in much more vague terms and had never before been this forthcoming. *He gets talkative when he's been hurt.*

"Yakov," she said, waiting for him to look up and meet her eyes, "is there any way the Sultan might relinquish his… *claim* upon the Amazons who followed Dionysia and now fight among his troops?"

"I overheard him speaking to the Agha," Yakov paused to wipe his eyes again, "who objected to their inclusion. He said he only intends to keep them under oath until the city is taken. He has no desire to keep them long-term."

"I see," Califia thought about this for a moment as Yakov composed himself.

The queen thought about what needed to be done. The others looked at her as if waiting to follow her lead, even master-of-plans Basilea. She could rightfully leave the Californians who had renounced their birthright to their fates in the Sultan's custody. No one would question that decision. But she did not believe the triumvirs had sprung her from a prison tower in a miraculous rescue by a woman who had been her most vocal opponent just so she could abandon fellow sisters who had perhaps made a rash decision.

"Olympia, Traesta," Califia said, looking at each of the strategoses as she spoke their names. "You should return to the camp and begin preparing your divisions for the coming assault."

The women nodded and went on their way. Califia was hoping Traesta would look back and wave or nod or do something to indicate she was glad the queen had returned, but the woman jogged on as if eager to do her duty somewhere else.

"Are we going to visit the Blades of God?" Basilea asked.

"We can pay them a visit if you like," Malachea said glumly, "but I doubt it will do any good."

"I want them to see me," Califia said, curling her fingers into tight fists and then releasing them. "Let them lay eyes upon their queen and tell her to her face that they would rather fight for a *man*."

"They are not far," Basilea said, pointing south of the Sultan's great tent.

"You should be armed," Malachea said, her fingers idly tracing the swirling inlay of the axe sheath on her hip.

"I have you to protect me," Califia said, hurrying in the direction Basilea indicated when she realized she was starting to blush. *Why am I flirting with Malachea?*

They made their way through some idling Osman soldiers who took time away from their dice, sword-sharpening, and bathing to gawk at the traveling Amazons. Califia considered what arguments she might make to move the hearts of her sisters who, in her mind, had put themselves in terrible jeopardy. She doubted she could convince them all, but perhaps a few might see reason and return to the fold.

Among the simple bivouacs of the Osman foot soldiers, there was one particularly large tent that had been erected from which raucous music and laughter could be heard. The flag that flew from its peak featured a white griffin holding a white sword in each of its forepaws against a yellow field. The tent's massive door flaps had been tied open just like the Sultan's, so Califia walked inside with Malachea and Basilea close on her heels.

The queen stopped almost immediately upon entering the tent as a man ran in front of her with a laughing Amazon slung over his shoulder while three of his compatriots chased him. Dionysia was holding court toward the back of the tent dressed in a fine embroidered maroon coat, loose-fitting sandy brown tunic, and billowing breeches which were tapered dramatically by knee-high leather boots.

"The queen!" shouted one of the Amazons. The tent seemed to choke with a sudden silence as the musicians stopped their playing and every conversation died immediately. The Amazons stared wide-eyed at Califia, frozen in place. Only one dared to move.

"Apparently the Greeks don't build prisons as well as they build walls," Dionysia said, marching toward the tent entrance with her chin in the air. "Did you come to join our little *omadha*, your majesty?"

Califia bristled. She had grown accustomed to members of both Muslim and Christian factions constantly calling her *highness* and *majesty*, but to hear the words come out of an Amazon's mouth was worse than any curse the young gorgon could have conceived.

"You call yourselves an omadha, but that's not accurate," Califia said, locking eyes with each errant

Amazon in turn. "Since you have sworn yourselves to fight for the Osman Sultan, you are not free to leave. No omadha in all our history has been so restrictive."

"You are trying to frighten us," Dionysia countered. "The sultan has promised us a portion of the riches he will take from this city. What could you possibly offer us in comparison?"

"I came with an invitation to return," the queen said, after letting the revulsion pass through her. "You are missed, all of you."

"Strange," Dionysia said, glowering pointedly at Malachea. "This is the first time since our departure that we have been blessed with any visit, royal or otherwise."

"I am not *royal*," Califia said, interjecting before Malachea. "I was legitimately elected by the majority of Amazons throughout our land and as soon as they tire of my leadership they may be rid of me."

"Your mother was a queen," Dionysia said. "You're the closest thing we've had to a dynasty in a thousand years."

"I serve the people," Califia said, as the other truant gorgons shuffled closer. "I do not *rule* them."

"That is because you are a coward."

Califia became suddenly aware that everyone in the tent had gathered around to hear the arguments and were waiting eagerly for her response. *I did not come here for a debate, but I've got one.*

"It is not cowardice to heed the will of the people. Would you follow a queen who crushes dissent, who rules through coercion and intimidation?"

"I would rather *be* the queen. Those who are strong should *rule*; those who are weak should *serve*."

"Weakness is no more permanent than strength," Califia scoffed. "Have you not read Nabatea's *Treatise on the Illusion of Permanence*? The strong should protect the weak not in order to rule over them, but because they will themselves one day need such protection!"

A hush settled over the Amazons at the invocation of Nabatea's name. Arguably the most influential of Californian philosophers, her words often commanded respect among both the learned and illiterate. Dionysia even hesitated for a moment, biting her lip as she conceived a retort.

"Nabatea spoke in theory about a world she did not understand," Dionysia declared, looking into the faces of her nearby followers. "Before Admiral Kemal brought us thousands of stadia across the oceans to fight on this foreign shore, we needed only concern ourselves with our islands and a few groups of mainlanders. Now that we have perceived the great vastness of this world, we must change our ways."

"Why?"

The left corner of Dionysia's mouth curled up very slightly but the queen saw it and she felt the unmistakable dread that she had fallen into a trap.

"Because the world knows about us, too," Dionysia said, smiling as though her point was obvious. "How much time will pass, do you think, before the Frankish armies seek revenge, or the Muscovites or the Wallachians? Perhaps they will come upon us in a great alliance, the way that their enemies have now assailed them?"

"That is why we need you — all of you — to rejoin us," Califia said, looking into the eyes of the truant Amazons who stood solemnly around them. "We are like griffin feathers: weak individually but strong together!"

"Scripture is the last refuge of the fool," Dionysia said, shaking her head. "I am reacting to changing circumstances, so it is I, not you, who embody Nabatea's teachings about the permanence of impermanence."

Califia gritted her teeth and prepared to make the argument she had been trying to avoid.

"My mother nearly destroyed our society by pursuing a pointless and cruel war. I thought that *our* cause was justified," the queen paused, looking into the faces around them and hoping some were truly listening, "but I was wrong. Coming here was a mistake, but I cannot change the past. Rejoin your sisters, your mothers, your daughters. Make us whole again and we can work out whatever differences have emerged since my imprisonment."

Dionysia's nostrils flared and her brow furrowed.

"I understand your disappointment in *your* mother," she said, glowering darkly, "for I have recently been disappointed with my own."

She looked pointedly at Malachea. For a moment Califia worried that the polemarkos was going to interject but instead the woman's eyes welled with tears and she winced as though her daughter had stabbed her in the gut. The queen was perplexed for a moment but quickly understood Dionysia's deeper meaning. *Malachea told her the truth about Kassandra's death.*

"Whatever has transpired between you," the queen said, "I am sure it can be overcome. But no problem is solved by absence."

"Then join with us," Dionysia said. "Swear yourselves to me and thus, to the Sultan. He respects us, he treats us well, and all he asks in return is that we shed blood on his behalf, which I remind you is the very reason we came to this place."

Califia sighed softly. *This woman is twice as bull-headed as her mother and this is going nowhere.* It was time to end this conversation and hope that her words would find purchase in the minds of those who had listened.

"If you trust the sultan, you must do whatever your conscience dictates," Califia said, looking beyond their leader and once more into the eyes of the Blades of God. "But if you have any doubts about his character, especially whether he will really treat a group of women with the same deference and equal standing which he would extend to men, then return to us quickly. The time to depart will be upon us soon and I don't want to leave *any* sisters behind."

As Califia turned to leave, her entourage following at her heels, Dionysia called after her.

"Any who choose to stay are your sisters *no longer*. The world has changed and we are merely changing with it!"

23

The world has changed.

The queen was still haunted by those words the next morning. She recognized the fallacy — the world had *not* changed, it was only their understanding that had been altered — but the deeper meaning lingered. The vast ocean had long served as a natural bulwark against theoretical threats from the west but now real threats had emerged regardless. The Osmans had found them. How long before the other factions sent expeditionary forces? How long before invasion, war, emergency powers, and personal ambition swallowed up any remaining vestiges of freedom?

These things rolled through the queen's mind as she joined Malachea and Yakov the next morning on Thrace's northern shore. Califia never expected to lay eyes upon a ship larger than the Göke, Admiral Kemal's flagship, but there it floated in the waters known as the golden horn. Like a whale that had somehow managed to float, the lumbering boat inched forward as its three rows of oars pushed against the waters of the Golden Horn. Its four masts held sails large enough to cover the

Sultan's tent and other ships in the bay were moving quickly out of its path.

"Has the Sultan brought reinforcements?" Malachea asked, gawking at the ship as it approached the sandy shallows of the north shore.

"You could call it that," Yakov said, his voice filled with a strange awe. "The sultan understands that the *way* a victory is achieved is often just as important as the victory itself."

The queen raised her eyebrow at this, but was distracted by an intriguing thought. *If that boat is full of fresh soldiers, perhaps the Sultan might release us from our obligation to partake in the coming slaughter.*

A large group of men unloading supply ships along the northern shore sent up a cheer when the ship anchored neared the shallows. The Osman and Gurkani soldiers who happened to be idling about in the area joined in the whooping and trilling, clearly ecstatic at whatever was onboard the hulking craft. The queen's heart fluttered with hope.

The anchored boat rotated so that its rearmost section — the *aft*, Califia recalled — faced the shore. The queen gasped as the aft wall seemed to detach from the rest of the vessel, steadily lowering from the top as if it were falling open. It continued its descent until the back of the ship hung open like a gaping mouth of a foul monster.

Califia spotted the chains that held the aft wall and realized something big lay inside its massive hull. Along the floor, a flat pontooned section was easing its way straight out. Its sides were flecked with indentations which, along with the clanking sound, led her to surmise that some kind of internal gear system was pushing the flat segment forward.

There was a loud bang as the segment reached its limit

and another segment began rolling out from inside the recess of the first. The gears turned slowly but steadily as the platform extended closer to the beach. This segment of the platform was also recessed and when it was fully extended another internal section likewise began rolling out.

Something now jutted from the open hole at the ship's aft. It was a large, cylindrical object that was wrapped in a thick layer of straw. As the platform continued extending and unrolling, more of the object came into view but Califia still could not discern what it could possibly be.

"Behold: *reinforcements*," Yakov said, coyly. "Soon all of the Sultan's enemies shall tremble at the thought of this mighty weapon."

"I hope the sailors did not anchor too far from the shore," Malachea remarked, "or this mighty weapon is about to rest on the bottom of the sea."

Yakov shuddered and suddenly became very serious. "The Sultan would have them skinned alive for such an offense. They know there is no room for mistakes."

"Sufficient motivation, no doubt," Califia said. She decided not to investigate whether Yakov was exaggerating.

He continued instructing Malachea about the Sultan's expectations for the coming battle while Califia hoped that some of the women who had followed Dionysia in serving Sultan Bayezid would respond to the pleas of their sisters. The correspondences should all be delivered by now, earnest letters of affection and camaraderie which Basilea thought might sway the hearts of those who had grown uncertain about their new allegiance.

Malachea had *not* written a letter. When the basket came round to her earlier that morning, she had passed it along without so much as a sorrowful glance. Whatever was happening between mother and daughter was certainly none of the queen's concern, but nonetheless she felt pangs in her heart at the thought of their estrangement.

The expanding platform upon which the massive, straw-wrapped cannon sat performed its final extension, comfortably settling upon the sand as the cannon came rolling forward and stopped with a massive clang that was almost as loud as a cannon firing.

The queen's breath caught in her throat. The assault was supposed to begin the following day but if the cannon was here now, did that mean the plan would move forward sooner than expected?

"Yakov," Califia said, interrupting him, "how long will it take to prepare this cannon?"

"It will be ready by tonight," he said, "but the Sultan has promised great festivities this evening to celebrate the coming destruction of our enemies. Your highness - what troubles you? Are you feeling ill?"

Califia turned away and took a moment to gather herself. It was a relief that they still had another day. The frustration of these last few days suddenly bubbled up inside of her. She turned back to Yakov, who stepped back when he saw the fiery look in her eyes.

"You speak to us as friends but your liege treats us as enemies," Califia said, pointing a finger at him accusingly. "He smiles to our faces and then threatens the lives of our sisters whom he holds as hostages."

"He will not hurt them!" Yakov sputtered, flustered at these sudden accusations. "Many serve the Sultan who are not Osmans - many who are not even Turks! To harm a foreign legion would threaten the loyalty of the many Arabs, Georgians, and even Greeks who fight for him!"

"You've been wrong before," Malachea said, circling the man from behind. He whimpered. "His probing questions about the queen's imprisonment felt like a veiled threat regarding the fates of our wayward sisters."

"That was not why he asked about—" Yakov stopped himself and shook his head. "He has his own reasons for wondering about imprisonment. I cannot say more."

"If you expect us to trust you," Califia warned, wagging a finger in his face, "then you'll need to convince us that he wasn't threatening the Blades of God with imprisonment."

Yakov sighed and looked pained. Califia felt a little guilty— Yakov had generally behaved as a friend in the past— but she pushed her compassion for the man aside.

"When Sultan Bayezid's reign began," Yakov said, "the Grand Vizier - that's like our Basilea - tried to set the sultan's younger brother upon the throne in his place. The rebellion failed, obviously, but Chem escaped. He was captured by Christians in Italy, and the Sultan paid them generously to keep his brother in prison. Five years ago, he died there. Thoughts of imprisonment have haunted His Majesty since that time."

"I can see why," Malachea said, gaping at the tale.

The workers on the shore lashed ropes to various knobs and rings along the big gun's hull. Nearby was a long line of iron carriages which had been hooked together and at least three dozen grooms coaxed horses into a massive harness apparatus.

"Speaking of my imprisonment," Califia said, suddenly curious. "Did the sultan or anyone else in the alliance ever make a plan to rescue me, or offer to pay the ransom?"

"Ah," Yakov said nervously. "Much of our attention was focused on supporting Admiral Kemal's efforts at taking the Golden Horn," he gestured to the body of water north of the city, "and as for paying the ransom, I'm afraid a large portion of the official treasury had already been dedicated to a... different cause."

The queen puzzled what this different cause could be, then suddenly remembered the peculiar absence of one crusader the morning after Admiral Kemal's triumph.

"You... bribed King Ivan?"

Yakov looked at her with wide eyes, then burst into a good-natured chuckle. "No, fair queen. King Ivan's grandson had only a few supporters until the sultan sent him several chests filled with gold coins. In the absence of their monarch, some of the more ambitious nobles have decided they prefer the young Dmitri to sit upon the throne."

Califia's mind spun with the usual confusion she felt at the notion of hereditary monarchy. Certainly it was possible that an ambitious Amazon might try and hold an election in her absence and seize the throne for themselves, but it didn't seem likely. And if they did, another election could just as easily be arranged upon their return. If power was concentrated on her bloodline, would the Arkozhas try and crown young Chloe in her absence? She shuddered at the thought.

"Couldn't the sultan have used a collective volley from his other cannons, rather than one big gun?" Malachea asked. "I don't understand these weapons very well, but that seems like it would work."

"Our engineers have confirmed that you are correct," Yakov said, shrugging. "He could have ordered this many days ago but he is trying to follow in the footsteps of his father, who used a single large cannon to demolish the wall."

Trying to follow in the footsteps of his father. The words struck Califia like an arrow in her chest and for a moment she felt a twinge of sympathy for Sultan Bayezid. She knew what it was like to live in her parent's shadow.

Califia gazed at the row of cannons arrayed against the Blachernae wall and observed an enormous dugout trench in the center. Clearly this was meant to be the home of the massive cannon that was now being loaded onto the metal carriages by placing logs along the floors that allowed the cumbersome thing to be rolled on board. *This will be over tomorrow,* she thought, looking toward the great walls of Constantinopolis. *Our foremothers will be avenged.*

The thought made her stomach turn. Avenging the foremothers was a concept with such visceral appeal that it could not be ignored politically, but now that the hour of their vengeance was at hand, who would suffer the wrath to come? The Greeks who caused the destruction of Atlantis were moldering at the bottom of the Mediterranean. The people inside Constantinopolis — who had never harmed the Amazons except in self defense and who even supported her while she had been imprisoned there — were about to be subjected to wholesale slaughter, abuse, and enslavement.

The queen left Yakov and Malachea to discuss the tactical arrangement for the upcoming assault and wandered through the trees back to the Amazon camp. At the edge of the agora, amid a throng of women laughing and chatting, was Arianna.

Califia's heart fluttered with joy as she strode toward the young woman. Her eyes burned with tears to come as Arianna locked eyes with her, said something to her group, then jogged to the queen. Califia grabbed the sides of Arianna's head gently, tenderly, and laid a passionate kiss upon her lips.

Arianna grunted, pushing the queen gently but firmly away. Her cheeks were bright red and her eyes wide with shock.

"It's good to see you too," Arianna said, looking upon the queen as though she was a two-headed lizard.

"Sorry, I… sorry…" Califia blurted, her cheeks burning with embarrassment as Arianna gave her a pitying half smile. "How have you been?"

"Much has happened since you went away," Arianna glanced back at her group of ladies, who were listening to a story from one of the shorter Amazons. The sides of her head were shaved and the patch of black hair that remained was short and bushy. Her lightly tattooed arms gesticulated wildly as she wove an exciting tale for her rapt audience. Below her lips there was a thin-lined rainbow which stretched down her chin, over her throat, and disappeared beneath her chestplate. The queen wasn't sure why, but the young woman looked familiar.

"You know Natolee," Arianna said, gesturing to the speaker as the women in the group laughed at whatever punchline she had just delivered. "She and I are… involved now."

Califia felt the blood drain from her fingertips and suddenly realized her breathing had stopped. She and Arianna had severed their relationship before the duel, but she had hoped the fortnight they had spent apart would reignite their flame. Now she saw that the rift between them could not be repaired. She may as well place a remembrance totem on its corpse and light the pyre.

"I don't believe we have met," Califia said, flustered.

"This doesn't feel like the right time for jokes," Arianna replied, lifting an eyebrow and staring hard at the queen. Califia smiled as though she *were* joking, but really she just wanted the awkward moment to end. *How would I know Natolee?*

"I've been looking for you," the queen said, regretting the words instantly. She had wanted to open with something casual and friendly, not clingy and desperate.

"You have?" Arianna said, raising her eyebrow in an expression of genuine confusion. "Surely the queen would have resources to locate one soldier out of five hundred?"

"I mean... I have been looking for you around camp. Seeking you out personally would have been..."

Desperate.

"Intrusive," Arianna said, finishing the sentence with a half-smile. An awkward silence passed between them. "Well, you've found me. What did you want to say?"

Come back to me.

"Only that I'm... sorry... for the way we left things," Califia managed, doing her best to keep back the flood of emotions. "I should have listened to you, and I shouldn't have belittled your opinion."

Arianna set her bag on the ground. "Watching you get taken into that place..."

She shuddered.

"It was even worse than I imagined it would be." Califia told her.

"Something you have in common with Amaltheia," Arianna said, sardonically. Her voice dropped to a whisper. "Is it true that the city will fall tomorrow?"

"Whether it does or not," Califia said, "we will be leaving very soon."

"I'm not sure how I will endure another half a year aboard those floating prisons."

Califia's stomach clenched at the thought. Six months

of half-assed holiday celebrations, gradually losing the war against crushing boredom, and hoping the griffin kennels held up. Not to mention avoiding Arianna and her new lover.

"I'm sure you'll find something to occupy your time," Califia said, glancing at Natolee and then back to Arianna. The young woman's face winced as though she had been slapped and the queen realized she sounded much bitchier than she intended.

"I really tried to make it work with you," Arianna said, her bottom lip quivering as a tear trickled down her cheek. "Honor and glory held more interest for you than I ever did."

"I didn't mean—"

"Do you have any idea what it is like being joined with a woman who the rest of the island wants to *fuck*? The insecurity that brings?"

"Arianna, I never—"

"Stay away from me and Natolee," she said, her voice rising enough by now for bystanders to take notice. "Whatever pleasure you get from crushing my hopes and dreams, you will have to find it somewhere else!"

The agora fell silent and the queen wished she could somehow vanish. Instead she cast her eyes downward until Arianna rejoined her cohort, who whispered loudly as Califia walked out of the public square by the shortest route possible.

As she walked through the thin forest south of the agora, she saw Malachea standing with Basilea, both of them waving their arms to summon her. From their left, she saw Olympia and Traesta approaching together and realized she was being summoned to a War Council meeting.

"Any responses from those who defected?" Califia

asked, despairing of the hope that they all might return to the fold.

"A few have found their way back," Olympia said with a wry smile. "The Turks disapprove of women having sex with one another."

"The Franks and their allies seemed to have the same attitude," Califia said, shaking her head. "One wonders if they're allowed to enjoy themselves at all."

"Regardless," Basilea said, "there are still nearly fifty who have stayed with Dionysia and it seems unlikely that they'll return."

"We should set the matter aside for now," Traesta said, "and discuss our plans for the coming battle. Is it true that the Osmans will breach the wall tomorrow?"

"Unless Hera herself transforms that cannon into a flock of birds," Califia said, "then I don't see how the walls can survive a blast from a gun that size."

"So this is really the end?" Traesta sounded almost hopeful.

"The Sultan has promised us safe passage home," Malachea said, "once the battle is over. It occurred to me, however, that he did not specify *when* we should go home."

"He insists that we stay, yet he also seems eager to be rid of us," Califia said, glad that Malachea had broached the subject. "I believe as soon as the siege has ended, he will be glad to see us board the ships."

"We can spare a few more days, surely," Malachea said, sounding incredulous at Califia's suggestion. "We wouldn't want to leave until we had exhausted every avenue regarding our departed sisters."

They all looked at Malachea with sorrowful faces.

"After they have drenched themselves in enemy blood and treasure," Olympia said gently, "they'll never want to leave. And worse, those who still fight for us might envy their fortunes and defect."

"I am not willing to give my daughter up for dead!" Malachea said, glowering at Olympia.

"No one is suggesting that you do!" Califia stepped between them and locked eyes with Malachea. "Dionysia and her fellows made a choice when they left our army for the Sultan's service. If you are so eager to convince her to return to us, you should have written her a letter."

"I know my child," the polemarkos said. "Written words mean little to her."

Malachea's expression softened and she heaved as she exhaled, as though someone had punched her in the gut. Tears began to fall from her eyes and the other members of the council were quick to embrace her. Califia pressed against the polemarkos, sharing in the devastation she must feel. The queen thought about Chloe, how painful it would be to leave her behind on a foreign shore thousands of stadia away.

After a few sad moments, Malachea recovered herself and gently pushed the others away. She pursed her lips and sighed.

"Have you spoken with your soldiers?" She asked the two strategoses, who nodded.

"Mine will not object to a swift departure," Traesta said. "They long to set their feet upon our home shores."

"Mine as well," Olympia said.

"The Gorgons have no objection either," the polemarkos declared. "I spoke only of my own reservations."

"Your reasons are personal," Basilea said, "but you shouldn't give up. There is a great feast planned for tonight — try to speak with her again. If she turns you away, you can take comfort in knowing you did all that you could."

"Small comfort," Malachea grunted, "but comfort nonetheless. Thank you."

Basilea nodded.

"We are in agreement, then?" Malachea continued. "We shall tell our troops to prepare themselves for the assault tomorrow and for a swift departure once the battle has ended."

The council affirmed unanimously and then adjourned, each attending to a different corner of the camp to spread the word. *This will all be over tomorrow, and then we can go home.*

The Amazon camp was soon abuzz with activity as word of the war council's decision was passed along. Stations were quickly erected for the maintenance and preparation of arms and armor, and lines formed around the various wheelstones, oiling benches, and leathering tables. In the time it had taken Califia to fetch her sagaris, there were already several queues at the sharpening wheels so she took her place on the shortest one she could find.

The women around her were chatting about everything from their choice of wardrobe to which omadhas they wanted to join or create when they returned home. The two women behind her were holding one another close as they kissed and snuggled. The queen's heart felt like a stone.

The feast began on the Osman side of the camp but soon their servants and slaves brought huge platters of food into the Californian quarter. Musicians followed, playing a variety of squawking horns and twangy stringed instruments. Many of the musical groups were tailed by a company of beautiful women who danced by rolling their abdomens as they clanged tiny cymbals in their hands in time with the music.

"I still say that this is a mistake," Basilea said, eying a nearby plate of spiced cubes of meat wrapped in green leaves. She grabbed a few of them from the serving platter and the slave paused only long enough to allow the transaction. "Gods, but I love this food!"

Califia took a bite from a pita stuffed to bursting with savory meat, tilting her head back so that the juices wouldn't drip down her chin. She watched as Malachea approached the Osmans with whom the rogue Amazons had taken refuge. Dionysia was dancing nearby. The queen smiled as she saw Malachea talk briefly with one of the outlying soldiers and he slowly demonstrated the dance steps so that she could follow.

"I wish her the best," Basilea said, clearly gazing at the same scene from a distance. "I think those sisters are lost to us, but perhaps Hera might act through Malachea and repair the breach."

"I rather hope that it is Aphrodite who acts," Califia said, smiling as she saw Dionysia notice her mother on the dance space. The young gorgon quickly turned her head away but even from this distance, the queen believed she spotted the faintest signs of consternation and uncertainty. *Please let this work.*

A great cheer suddenly erupted far to their left; Califia turned and saw that the cannon had finally been installed into its dugout. Engineers near the back of the cannon were still making adjustments to the barrel's angle, but the gargantuan task of getting the massive thing in place was over.

"Is that the great and terrible weapon which shall end this dreadful war?" Basilea said sardonically.

Califia imagined the walls collapsing, the defenders making a doomed last stand, the Osmans and their allies casually murdering women like Lydia and young girls like Thea as they ransacked their homes and tore down their places of worship.

And yet, she thought gloomily, *the Franks and the Muscovites did the same to the Osman people when they seized the city.*

"It may end the siege, perhaps even the war," Califia said. "But the next one won't be far behind. Plunder, slavery, oppression and coercion is all these people seem to understand, whether Frankish, Osman, Muscovite, or Gurkani."

The queen sighed and her heart became heavy. Bigger guns, bigger armies, higher stakes, dire consequences... Ares truly thrived in this land, even if they did not worship him by name. *They praise him with their deeds.*

Malachea and Dionysia at last looked at one another and left the dance floor, talking with animated gestures. Malachea's face looked determined but also loving, welcoming. Dionysia looked uncertain and conflicted. She crossed her arms against her chest and gazed at her own feet.

The queen's mind suddenly flooded with voices of concern, each worried about her emotional state. She took her hand from the pommel of the Triumvir Dagger where it had been resting, laughing a little at how easy it was to forget about the weapon.

"I'm going to visit the griffins," Califia said to Basilea, who nodded absently.

The walk to the kennels felt longer than usual, the land between those cages and the camp now sparse with so many Amazons attending the party. Eight gorgons guarded the griffins, and two handlers were distributing food to the beasts. Even without touching the triumvir dagger, Califia could feel their excitement as they spotted her approach.

She visited Ektra first, reaching through the bars of the kennel to stroke her shoulder. Ektra purred softly and closed her eyes as the queen probed her fingers through the feathers and gently scratched between her shoulder blades. The creature across from Ektra snorted, as though demanding equal attention from Califia. The queen obliged and as she stroked the beast she realized it was Elena, Malachea's griffin. She stayed with it a few moments longer, massaging and scratching, knowing she could never possibly repay it for its role in saving her life. She set her hand on the pommel of the dagger and concentrated on the great catbird before her.

Thank you.

Of course.

We're going home soon.

That's good.

I am sorry for bringing you here.

The great catbird looked at her askance.

I don't understand.

It doesn't matter. After tomorrow, we all go home.

What is wrong?

Califia carefully considered her response. She could feel the presence of other griffins listening in on their conversation, waiting with baited breath for her reply.

We never should have come here.

A flurry of emotions flooded her mind through the dagger's connection. Many agreed with her, but some were angry and others demanded further explanation. She took her hand from the dagger but still felt their objections, their demands, through the faint connection that lingered.

"Are you giving the griffins a vote?"

Califia recognized Malachea's voice and did not need

to turn around. She gave Elena a final shoulder scratch.

"Perhaps we *should*," Califia said. "I am certain they won't like what happens tomorrow."

"None of us *like* it," Malachea said. "What choice do we have?"

Califia shrugged.

"Dionysia, did she—"

"No."

The word felt like an anchor, sinking the conversation for a moment. Even in the relative darkness at this remote end of the camp, Califia could see the polemarkos' eyes welling with tears.

"Does she still insist that we are hypocrites?" Califia asked.

Malachea leaned against a nearby tree. "She claims that this was always a mission of conquest, and that we have merely lost the stomach for it."

Califia sighed. The brash young Gorgon lieutenant was right. Reluctant as she was at the beginning of this war, the queen herself had gladly slaughtered the enemy to enhance their standing among their allies and reassert her own control over the Californian army. *It had been so much easier before I realized our enemies were just people like us.*

Califia felt a tear trickle down her own cheek. The words of Queen Helena, who led the Amazons to California so long ago, echoed through her mind. *Do not visit upon others the evils which have been visited upon you.* Califia felt like she was spitting in the foremothers' faces before stabbing them in the gut.

"I should get ready for tomorrow," Malachea said, pushing away from the tree she had been leaning against.

"Wait," Califia said. Malachea had begun to turn away, but paused. The queen did not see a way out of their present predicament, so she spoke from her heart. "We did not come all this way to participate in wanton slaughter and shame the foremothers."

The polemarkos gave her a pain-filled expression and even in the darkness, Califia could see the exhaustion written on her face.

"We either fight or abstain," Malachea shrugged. "Either way, we lose."

Califia's mind raced with stubborn determination and, to her surprise, she began to conceive of alternatives. Many were bad, but she discarded them as quick as she would have disposed of rotten eggs. Her mind narrowed on the workable concepts, the few actual possibilities amid idealistic scenarios.

"What if there was a third option?" the queen said, the plan still forming in her mind like a crude lump of clay. "What if we could maintain the integrity of our principles and proved to Dionysia and her followers that the Triumvirs did not send us here to make slaughter and conquest?"

Malachea clenched her eyes shut for several moments, as though deciding whether to take Califia seriously. The queen would have prayed, if she had thought of it. At last the polemarkos opened her eyes. She gazed at Califia for a long time and the queen felt like she was being measured, weighed, and judged. Malachea gave a little smile and Califia knew the infernal woman would at least hear her out.

"What do you have in mind?"

They talked together late into the night. A few times, they nearly fell into their old pattern of locking horns but both women kept their heads and pressed forward, discarding bad ideas and developing those few that might work. Malachea provided a practical edge to Califia's idealism, and by the end of the night, they had their plan.

Califia did not know whether the Blades of God would be convinced, but she was certain that the foremothers would approve.

24

The early morning air was frigid but its chill refreshed Califia as she strapped on her thorax, skirt, greaves, and armguards. The inviting scent of chai wafted from somewhere close, and she saw that many Amazons were gathered around a large pot with their thick ceramic cups in hand. She searched through her luggage and found her own, then waited in line.

"I couldn't find you last night," Basilea said. Califia turned and saw the woman's puffy eyes, chaotically random locks of hair, and disheveled tunic. "I had an idea you might like."

"Tell me," the queen said, moving forward in line as another pair of Amazons were served.

"It is not enough for us to simply stand by as the people in this city are subjected to horrors beyond our worst nightmares," she said, in a voice full of bold conviction. Califia saw the spark of the woman's old self, the indomitable queen who inspired the nation to lay down its arms.

"I agree, of course," Califia said, taking another step toward the steaming pot of chai. "What do you think ought to be done?"

She held her breath in anticipation of the old woman's response.

Could it be that Basilea has conceived of the same idea that we worked out last night?

"We must send a clear message that we will not be party to butchery," Basilea declared, drawing a few intrigued eyes from the Amazons in line around them. Califia's own heart raced with excitement. "When the cannon begins to fire we will, all of us, turn our backs."

The intrigued bystanders went immediately back to their conversations and Califia's chest nearly collapsed, the air rushed out of her so quickly. Basilea appeared undaunted, as though she had not noticed the reactions of anyone around her, including the queen.

"Turn our backs?" Califia repeated, as though making sure she had heard correctly. "You think that will send the appropriate message?"

"It will signal to Sultan Bayezid that we want no part in any of this, that we object most strongly. And who knows? Perhaps some of the others will join us in this protest."

Finally it was Califia's turn and as the hot chai was being ladled into her cup, she took a few moments to think of a suitable response which did not also alienate her adviser. Her heart was in the right place.

"As bold as that would be," Califia said, pausing to blow on her steaming beverage, "the polemarkos and I formulated a... *similar* show of protest last night."

"Malachea wishes to protest the killing of innocents?" Basilea sounded a little indignant and, in the queen's opinion, she was not keeping her voice low enough considering the many fellow Amazons who were flocking to the chai pots. Califia walked a few steps away from the crowd and looked her adviser in the eye.

"She is not the woman you thought she was," Califia said firmly. "You need to let go of your prejudice against her."

"She undermines me— and you!— nearly every chance she gets!" Basilea hissed, looking to the crowd of women near the pot as though remembering to be discreet. "I understand I owe her my life and our people's liberty, but this entire adventure was her doing and we ought to ensure she is held accountable for it!"

"There will be a time for accountability," Califia said, pushing away the images of their home that tried to flood her mind. "Today is not that time. Today, I need you to trust me."

Basilea looked at Califia as though this was obvious. Then she raised an eyebrow. "Why? What exactly is this *plan* the two of you concocted?"

"Do you trust me?"

"That is not the—"

"Do. You. Trust. Me?"

Basilea sighed and looked as though Califia had just slapped her across the face.

"You know that I do."

Califia grasped her shoulders and looked her in the eye. "Then follow my lead."

The queen's chief adviser opened her mouth as if to object, but nodded instead. She muttered something about the need to clean herself up and prepare, when a chorus of horns suddenly sounded in a unified blast from the Osman camp. Apparently it was time for them to ready themselves as well.

Malachea found her shortly after Basilea left to prepare. The armor of the polemarkos shined in spite of the overcast sky. Califia pictured Malachea staying awake late into the night, polishing her armor as she pondered the plan they had made. Whether she was kept awake by excitement or doubt remained to be seen.

"I informed the strategoses privately this morning," Malachea said when she approached the queen. "I noted their objections and addressed their concerns. They are willing to accept the consequences."

Califia let her breath escape. She had thought that they would go to the strategoses together but for once she was glad of the polemarkos' direct intervention. Califia was not naive enough to think that their actions would have no consequences, nor was she fool enough to believe that every Amazon would survive. This would cost them.

The queen was gripped by a sudden dread.

"What if the captains and lieutenants refuse to follow?" She said, picturing a bloody mutiny of sisters killing sisters.

"It is too late to ask such questions," Malachea replied. As though she noticed Califia's continued unease, she continued. "If we - you and I - act together then I believe our people will know what to do. Half might follow you, half might follow me, but all of them will follow *us*."

Califia's heart was strangely warmed by these words and Malachea clapped a hand on her shoulder. She gave the queen a single vigorous nod and then walked toward the kennels, affixing her griffin-skull helm on the way.

Before another hour had passed, every Amazon was dressing for battle, their griffinsteel suits glistening as the midmorning sun finally peeked over the clouds.

Per the orders of the polemarkos, the Amazons deployed in porcupine formation - the winged cavalry in the center surrounded first by a layer of archers and then spear-wielding heavy infantry protecting the perimeter. It was a defensive formation, and Califia overheard some of the captains expressing dismay that they weren't arranged in a more aggressive manner.

She set her hand on the hilt of the Triumvir Dagger, feeling the griffins through the connection. They had noticed the increased activity and knew that something big was about to happen. They paced in their kennels, loosed the odd shriek, and tapped the bars with their beaks.

The queen could relate.

It was nearly midday when Califia spotted Yakov rushing up the hill where the Californian army had assembled. The foot soldiers allowed him through, and he exchanged pleasantries with many of them on his way.

"Most illustrious queen," Yakov greeted her, bowing respectfully. "My Sultan wishes you good fortune on this glorious day when we finally liberate this bright city."

"Send him my thanks," Califia said, smirking as she added, "and tell him I am not offended by whatever you're here to apologize for."

Yakov laughed far too enthusiastically at the barb. "As witty as you are beautiful! I assured his majesty that the griffins will be under control today, but he insisted I hear this from you."

Califia sighed. *He wants to indemnify himself so that he can blame me for any battlefield accidents.*

"We only brought them out at his request," Califia said. "If you recall, his majesty was quite insistent that we use them."

"Of course," Yakov said, waving his hand at the absurdity. "I am sorry for how he has treated you and your people. I am only doing as I was asked."

The queen felt a twinge of sympathy for the Jewish emissary, the man whose presence on California had directly led to their involvement in this jihad. It had occurred to the queen the night before that the Sultan might have the unfortunate emissary killed after she executed her plan, but that was beyond her control. *I have already saved his life once.*

"Tell his majesty," Califia said, "that I personally accept all responsibility for the actions of our beasts, and the consequences thereof."

He smiled and bowed his head.

"I thank you for your time, fair queen," he said, "and I hope you understand… that is, I never meant to…"

"I understand," Califia said, feeling a little sad that when this was all over, she would never see this man again. "Keep yourself safe today, Yakov. Not even the cleverest generals can truly predict the outcome of a battle."

"Thank you, fair queen. I must beg my leave of you; the Sultan will want me close at hand to help record the day's proceedings."

There will be much to record, Califia thought grimly as Yakov made his way out of their formation and rejoined his entourage of guards who had stayed far away from the griffins. He strode down the hill and through the broad spaces between the assembled Amazons.

From her vantage on the hilltop, Califia could see nearly the entirety of the vast army assembled below. Arrayed like a phalanx were rows upon rows of cannons at the left-most end, the rearmost raised upon earthen platforms so that they could safely fire over those in front. In their center was a large carved-out space where the newly-arrived gun had been placed. The queen thought wryly of how the weapons looked like a gathering of bronze penises with one particularly gigantic member plopped in their midst.

Malachea was using a scope that one of the sailors had gifted her to monitor the cannoneers' progress. "They are nearly finished filling it with powder."

Califia took a deep breath, then slowly exhaled. The hour was upon them. She gripped the hilt of the Triumvir Dagger and closed her eyes, feeling the excitement of the griffins as they detected her presence among them. They settled quickly as she quieted them and told them to be ready.

"It is time," she said to Malachea, who nodded and held up her fist. Behind her, a series of signals would be passed along via the captains and lieutenants, but she did not need to look for confirmation.

The air was thick with battle fury and bloodlust. The Osman soldiers were singing in some areas, chanting in others, while those waiting on the walls of Constantinopolis were readying their own cannons which were being splashed with water by white-robed priests. Califia idly wondered if Father Mignoletto was among them.

"Are you ready, beloved?" She said as she tilted her head to look her mount in its eye. She was startled, for a moment, by her own reflection in Ektra's wide black pupil. The queen's lower eyelids sagged slightly and the creases on her forehead and brows had deepened.

Ektra tilted her great head. The queen put her hand upon the creature's shoulder and stroked her feathers, then embraced her. The griffin purred. Califia patted her mount's shoulder twice and shouted *Hyah!* Ektra pushed hard off the ground, flapping its great wings furiously as they quickly ascended.

Califia's heart leapt in her chest. A strange euphoria absorbed her worries; the anxiety over the plan, over Arianna, over this entire expedition melted from her as she soared through the air like a hawk seeking prey. She spotted her quarry below— soon it would be in her talons. As long as the rest of the pack joined her.

As Ektra turned and dove back toward the earth, the others took flight and followed the queen, soaring over the frightened Osmans below. They passed the Sultan's pavilion— he was standing, red-faced, shaking his fist and shouting words that she could not hear. Yakov quaked nearby, blanching with terror.

Ektra landed near the newly-arrived cannon, frightening the loaders away with a shriek as her feathers flared aggressively. Eight other griffins landed around the great monstrosity and still the queen was uncertain that it would be enough. Ektra leapt to the top of the cannon in a single bound and grasped some of its bands with her talons. The other eight riders did the same and together the mounts flapped their wings hard in unison. At first it seemed fruitless but then the queen heard the groan of metal and felt the cannon rise slightly. The other griffins flapped in furious unison, encouraged by this progress. They lifted the great cylinder off the ground about waist-high. Califia gripped the Triumvir Dagger and gave the order.

Ektra and the other griffins flew gradually northward, inching closer and closer to the Golden Horn. The ships near the shore were steering away, clearing a path. She reckoned that the sailors were trying to avoid having their ships destroyed by the falling cannon. As they neared the water, several other griffins sailed quickly past them, smaller cannons gleaming in their talons falling quickly into the sea. Great dunking splashes heralded them into Poseidon's dark domain.

Suddenly there was a series of twangs from the deck of one ship and iron bolts whistled through the space around them. The queen looked back and forth to the other mounts and riders, and all were unharmed. The crossbowmen on the ship who had tried to down them were reloading their weapons but it was too late. The Amazon cavalry had already crossed the shoreline and were nearing the dark part of the water, where the cannon could rest safely.

"Now!" Califia shouted as they crossed over the dark waters. The griffins released the great weapon and it splashed down with a massive blast of water that sprayed the nearby barques and schooners. The waves generated by the impact were like the swells of a great storm. The ship which was attempting to attack them began rocking and bobbing in the cannon's wake. Their bolts flew harmlessly beneath Califia and her compatriots.

The Osman alliance camp was in chaos now, filled with panicked running and shouting. Califia dropped two more of the smaller cannons into the bay as Malachea led her special team of griffin riders to harass any groups of soldiers from among their former allies who were attempting to assemble an assault upon the beleaguered Amazons who now formed a massive circular phalanx upon the hilltop. Upon returning after dropping the second small cannon into the sea, she saw that there were no more weapons like it left along the Osman alliance's lines. She turned her eyes to the tops of the walls where the Franks and their allies were cheering the Amazons' apparent defection.

"With me!" Califia called to those griffin riders nearby, gathering about eight of them into formation behind her. They soared toward the walls, where the Christian soldiers quickly abandoned post and sought shelter in the towers and covered hallways. They landed upon the Blachernae walls and made straight for the cannons.

Once more they all grasped the cannons around them, then carried them to a watery grave. As she turned and led the cavalry from the sea back toward the mainland, a massive ship barred their path, its cannons aimed toward them. She recognized the ship in an instant — the black hull and the red oars — it was the Göke, Admiral Kemal's ship.

The admiral stood atop the upper deck and peered at her through his looking glass. As Califia's mind scrambled to think of what to do, Admiral Kemal shouted something unintelligible which his officers repeated. The muskets aimed at the Amazon cavalry were shouldered and the cannons withdrawn as their windows shut. The Admiral drew his sword and held it aloft in a kind of salute. Califia drew her sagaris and raised it above her head in a similar gesture as she banked to the side of the great boat with her cavalry close behind.

Thank you, Admiral.

They returned and seized more cannons from the crusaders' walls. Bolts, arrows, and even the occasional spear flew past her more than once, but the defenders were shooting through tiny slits in the stonework. Some of her followers were wounded, but a large number of arrows either bounced off of their armor or stuck only just into the plates without piercing flesh.

After clearing all but three of the cannon on the Blachernae walls, they flew around the perimeter of the city, grabbing and disposing of guns as they went. There were hardly any defenders on the other walls but Califia could hear the terrified screams of the residents. This kind of combat was not honorable, it was not glorious or regal or in any way particularly challenging. Nevertheless it had its own kind of satisfaction and the splash of each cannon made her feel like Athena herself.

They nearly had all of the cannon removed, but left three guns on the Blachernae walls so that the Christians would not be completely defenseless. The Amazon cavalry flew toward the hilltop where their foot soldiers were defending themselves on all sides. The Osman forces pressed against the circular phalanx but quickly retreated to avoid the swooping, shrieking griffins who struck from above.

Califia had told Malachea to avoid casualties of their former allies but this situation was about to demand a violent, bloody response. Califia called to Malachea as soon as she was within earshot.

"It's time to go home!" She shouted, swooping over a cluster of spearmen and disrupting their attempt to charge one side of the phalanx.

Malachea held up her fist and gave several hand signals to her lieutenants. As the griffins landed, they shrieked at enemy soldiers as three members of the phalanx broke off from their line and grasped the rope-holds on the saddle. The four of them lifted into the air as quickly as possible, dodging arrows, bolts, and jabs from pikes and halberds as they ascended.

Califia broke away as the rescue effort began, scanning the vast army for Dionysia and the wayward sisters who had followed her into the jaws of Ares. As her eyes fell upon a large number wearing the lizard-scale lamellar armor of the Gurkani, she realized she must be searching in the wrong direction. She turned Ektra around and went across a different swathe of the army, her eyes searching for some clue in the sea of armor and weapons. Something flashed in the corner of her eye, a sudden burst of color among the gray iron mass.

There were dozens, perhaps hundreds of banners designating the many segments of the Osman and

Gurkani army but only one was currently waving side to side. It was a yellow standard bearing a white griffin holding two swords, the symbol of the Blades of Heaven. She turned Ektra toward the flag. The griffin landed hard after a few swift flaps drove the nearby Osman soldiers back. Califia jumped off as Ektra turned and hissed at the terrified soldiers around her. Those around the banner, whose hands had been waving it, were the very gorgons she had been searching for.

"My queen," one said, nearly in tears. "You came for us."

There were at least twenty gorgons awaiting rescue; Califia could not take them all herself. She grasped the hilt of the Triumvir Dagger, found several griffins who hadn't yet been loaded up with extra riders and summoned them straight away.

"I am taking those who wish to leave!" Califia shouted at the nearby soldiers who all had their weapons drawn but didn't dare advance. Ektra snarled, her eyes continually moving about as if eager to fight anyone foolish enough to try their luck. She hoped some of those soldiers spoke Greek, but when she saw some whispering to their neighbors who in turn whispered to others, she assumed her message was being passed along. "Back up, or you will be hurt."

As the message spread, the soldiers withdrew, none daring to sheathe their weapons nor take their eyes from the monster who threatened to bite their faces off at any moment. Wanting to give room behind her for the incoming griffins, Califia slowly stepped forward and Ektra followed her lead, pushing the terrified warriors farther away from those she was rescuing.

The first of the griffins arrived and four Gorgons quickly jumped on each one and fastened their safety ropes. This continued, Ektra still snarling, until finally Califia saw that there were none standing in the space any longer. It was time to go. She backed up a little, Ektra following once more, in order to give herself a wider area from which to launch.

"Califia!"

The queen turned to see that it was Dionysia calling her. The gorgon leader sprinted toward Califia's mount, as though she were afraid that the Osmans might grab her along the way. The queen jumped from the saddle and ran toward the troublesome gorgon as well, thanking Aphrodite for the young woman's change of heart. When she was but three strides away, Dionysia held her sagaris aloft and cocked her arm back for a swing.

Califia shoved her forearms toward the axehead, her vambraces ringing as they were struck. She stumbled backward a few steps but kept her feet. Pain coursed through her left arm. She drew her own sagaris just in time to receive Dionysia's next strike, their hafts pressing against each other as Dionysia tried to shove her blade into Califia's neck.

"Do you feel it, my queen?" Dionysia said as their axeheads locked together and they each pulled the other close. "*This* is our true legacy — the triumph of strength over weakness!"

Keeping hold of her axe with her left hand, Califia brought her right arm back and punched Dionysia directly in the face. The blow dazed the young woman and the queen unhooked her sagaris rather than disarming the errant gorgon.

"I offered you my hand, and you tried to cut it off," Califia said. The Osman troops still did not interfere, and she hoped that they saw this as a private matter between herself and this infernal young warrior.

"I will do far more than cut off your hand," her opponent snarled, twin streams of blood trickling from her nostrils.

Dionysia dropped her sagaris into the dirt and brought her left hand above her head in triumph. Wrapped in those fingers was a dagger about a forearm's length with a glowing red gem adorning the place where its blade joined with its hilt. Califia looked down at her belt in disbelief. Dionysia had swiped the Triumvir Dagger.

"Should I order your griffin to devour your head in a single bite, or eat you slowly, feet first?"

A wicked grin spread across Dionysia's face. The red stone glowed and Califia turned to see Ektra advancing upon her, hissing and spreading her wings.

Please, no.

As the queen backed away, she reached out to her mount with her mind, hoping the residual connection might be enough to sway the beast. Two more griffins landed on Ektra's flank and began stalking steadily toward Califia, glowering at the Amazon queen.

Listen, please!

Califia felt their presence in her mind, along with the insecurities, confusion, and contradictions the great beasts now wrestled with. She turned back to Dionysia, who was sweating profusely. The red gem on the dagger was dim, blinking randomly rather than holding its usual solid glow, just as it had during Califia's disastrous assault.

The three griffins were nearly upon Califia now, but she felt her fear suddenly melt away in favor of a very different emotion— indignant rage. The beasts walked past her, growling and hissing at Dionysia. The young Gorgon pointed the dagger at them as though hoping she might win against three griffins armed with nothing but an antique short blade.

"It's over, Dionysia," Califia said, hearing other griffins land behind her and riders dismount. "Drop the dagger and I will order the griffins to stand down. Otherwise they will eat you."

Dionysia spun, her wild eyes searching for a way to escape. As one of the beasts snapped, she yelped and tossed the dagger at Califia's feet.

Those who had dismounted from the griffins now surrounded the queen, shields and axes raised. Califia picked up Dionysia's axe where it lay on the ground nearby and shook the dust from its blade. A red-plumed lieutenant picked the dagger up and handed it to the queen. She took the dagger proffered by the lieutenant and sheathed it.

The young gorgon leader hung her head and fell to her knees. Califia tossed her lost sagaris into the dirt in front of her. Dionysia lifted her head and for a moment they locked eyes.

"You are still welcome to join us," the queen said. She was certain her words were spoken in vain but felt duty-bound to speak them nonetheless.

Dionysia picked up her axe and stood. Keeping her eyes locked with Califia, she threw the weapon aside, discarding it as though it were nothing to her but a piece of rubbish. She turned her back to the queen and shuffled toward the Osmans. Califia sighed and walked back to Ektra, whose head continued to dart randomly as she eyed the surrounding Osman soldiers. The small ember of hope that Dionysia might come with her now transformed into heartache. *At least I can tell Malachea I tried.*

"My queen," said the lieutenant who had fetched the Triumvir Dagger from Dionysia. She handed Ektra's reins to the queen and smiled. Califia recognized this young woman, but couldn't remember her name.

"Would you like to ride with me?" Califia asked, determined to bring her name to mind.

"I am honored," she said, smiling so broadly that the queen could see her teeth in spite of her helm.

A few of the surrounding griffins leapt into the sky, each carrying four Amazons apart from the rider. Three warriors shoved their weapons and shields into Ektra's saddle bags and Califia raced to fasten the pouches and help her new passengers into their harnesses. Ektra turned to the right and shrieked, intimidating the Osman pikemen who had been approaching while the queen busied herself with preparations. She jammed her foot into the stirrup and swung her other leg over the beast, checking the harnesses one last time.

Suddenly the lieutenant, whose name she had still failed to remember, gasped as an arm adorned with griffinsteel armor wrapped around her throat from behind. Califia drew her axe, but could not strike without hitting the officer.

"A parting gift, my queen," Dionysia said, grinning from behind the lieutenant, who was hindered by the harness. "Call it a remembrance totem."

The lieutenant shrieked in pain. Califia could not see what Dionysia had done. Ektra turned toward the sound and, feeling Califia's terror, she whipped her tufted tail and wrapped it around the gorgon's throat. Dionysia gagged and choked as Ektra dragged her backward and then, in a swift motion, flung her spinning away from them.

The queen pulled the reins upward and the beast was aloft with a few massive flaps, shrieking her battle cry as the surrounding crowd closed in where they had just been standing. Califia looked into the lieutenant's eyes, which appeared to be draining of their life.

"My queen, are you alright?" She asked, half-shouting over the din of battle.

"I am unhurt, lieutenant," Califia said, cringing that she had to use the officer's title instead of her name. Suddenly the woman's head lolled back a little and as the queen saw the thin rainbow stripes that began below her bottom lip, Califia recognized her. *Natolee. Arianna's new partner.*

"She stabbed me," Natolee said, reaching behind her as if grasping for the blade.

"Don't disturb the wound!" Califia shouted, putting a hand on her shoulder as she tried to steer Ektra one-handed. "I will get you help as soon as we land. You will be okay!"

"I trust you," she said, resting her head upon Ektra's shoulder and gripping her harness until her knuckles were shock white.

The queen felt tears traveling a well-worn path down her cheeks as she flew toward the hillock where the Amazons had been defending themselves in the confusion. There were enough griffins already upon the hill to transport the Amazons who still remained, but they were having difficulty getting into the harnesses while defending themselves from Osman incursion. Every time they would get close, the surrounding army would make a racket and feign a charge and the evacuees would be forced to get their weapons out to defend themselves.

Califia put her hand to the hilt of the Triumvir Dagger and seven nearby griffins followed her command, creating a perimeter around the evacuees to allow them to escape. Ektra joined them, and Califia raised her sagaris threateningly every time any of their former allies seemed too aggressive. The final Amazons were loaded onto their mounts and their defenders launched as well, dodging bullets and iron bolts as they launched into the air and darkened the sky with their many wings.

As their great flock traveled eastward, Califia wondered whether the second part of this plan would really work. Getting the Amazons out while refusing to visit upon others the evils which they had suffered had succeeded. The Gurkani would soon depart, and the Osmans would stand alone. She was certain, as certain as she could be, that Sultan Bayezid would be forced to accept the Crusaders' surrender in exchange for his promise of safe passage to their home lands. Whatever happened was in the Triumvirs' hands now.

They crossed the Bosporus Strait and flew over several large cities before they reached a high plain which was empty enough to accommodate a safe mass landing. Califia tried to engage Natolee in conversation as they flew, but the only replies she received were moans and flops of the head. When they landed, she called for a medikos and told the young woman to hold still while they undid her straps. Natolee's hands appeared to have become tangled in the upper portion of the harness but as the queen unwrapped them, she realized the woman had done this on purpose.

They carefully lowered her onto her side, her body limp and heavy. It was too late. Somewhere between the Bosporus and the stretch of Osman land they had covered before arriving on this plateau, Natolee had breathed her last. Jutting from the right side of her lower back was a crude knife with a handle of rotting wood. Dionysia had shifted the woman's chainmail aside and murdered her with the same weapon that she had won

from the poor Majyar on their journey from Gelibolu to
Constantinopolis.

25

The blade barely spanned the length of Califia's hand. The queen ran her fingers along the corroded wood of its hilt which had been worn smooth in some places, remained pitted in others. She wouldn't normally have thought of this implement, which had clearly been used as an everyday tool, as a deadly weapon. It had taken a life, nonetheless.

Natolee was not the only fallen warrior laid to rest on the plateau where the Amazons had landed. Many had been struck by iron bolts or other projectiles, some succumbed to wounds from swords or spears. One poor dead woman was caked in blood; her helm and skull viciously cratered by something blunt and heavy. Medics saved who they could but as the sky began to transform from blue to pink, the count rose to twenty-nine.

Califia gathered kindling and timber from a large patch of inter-connected shrubs on the eastern end of the plateau, overhearing snippets of conversations from scattered groups. Some were displeased that they had no opportunity to avenge the foremothers, others approved of Califia's course of action. All sounded relieved that they were finally going home.

The bodies were gathered and placed on the makeshift pyres. Someone discovered a clay deposit near the northern edge of the plateau. Those who knew the departed as close friends - about a hundred or so - gathered the clay and shaped their remembrances as the sky grew dark. Califia joined Basilea and Malachea, who appeared to be deep in discussion.

"Someone should say something," Basilea said.

Califia's shoulder pinched with a sudden twinge and she massaged it with the heel of her thumb. "The army needs to hear from their queen."

"I could address them," Malachea said, taking a swig from her water horn. "I am the polemarkos, after all."

Basilea gave Califia a hopeful look, but the queen shook her head.

"This failure is mine," Califia said, looking upon the stiff, cold face of Natolee. "I will take responsibility."

Califia walked some distance from the bodies as their friends returned to place clay remembrances upon them. What words could she summon for this occasion? The usual platitudes and encouragements all sounded hollow in her mind. It seemed like sacrilege to invoke the triumvirs, and she wished she could cast some spell to hide herself from the goddesses. Footsteps thumped behind her; Malachea approached, pressing her fingers into a small bit of clay in her hands.

"This was not a failure."

"Tell it to the dead."

"We saved the lives of every person in that city and countless lives of Osman and Gurkani warriors who would have died in the assault. Saving lives is *not* failure."

Califia squatted, then plopped herself fully on the ground. She sat in the dirt and wept. Malachea worked her index fingernail around the remembrance she was crafting.

"What have we gained by this excursion?" Califia sighed, wiping her tears. "How are we better now than we were before?"

"We know more about the world, more about the neighbors we didn't know we had."

"I would rather have preserved the lives of those lost."

"As would we all," Malachea held up her remembrance and, after eyeballing it, seemed satisfied. "But we cannot go backward."

"What are you making?" Califia asked.

"On the journey to Constantinopolis," Malachea said wistfully, "I saw the strangest fish. It surfaced, swam on its side for a few moments, then dove back into the deep."

The polemarkos handed her the remembrance - a fish that was round and flat like a coin with spiky fins at its rear. Califia smiled at its goofy appearance, which reminded her of a child's toy. She handed back the totem.

"Who is it for?" The queen asked.

Malachea paused.

"Dionysia."

Califia's thoughts drifted once more to her own daughter Chloe, and to the many mothers and sisters on California who awaited those who would never return. She thought suddenly of Kassandra, the polemarkos' late elder sister.

"Did she *know*?"

The queen felt unable to speak her entire thought out loud, even though she was certain they were alone. Malachea stopped her sculpting and locked eyes with her.

"Yes," she said quietly as a tear grazed her left cheek.

"She suspected it for a long time. When you were imprisoned, she told me to declare myself the new Califia. She guessed at the... circumstances around Kass's death and my reaction gave me away."

"Gods," Califia said under her breath.

"She cursed me for a fool when I told her my motives," Malachea's voice became shaky. "She told me she wished that *I* had been killed instead, and Aunt Kassandra put upon the throne."

The polemarkos wept and Califia sat silently for a few moments, her chest now feeling heavy with the crushing weight of guilt.

"I should have found a way to prevent all of this," the queen said. "I failed to protect Dionysia from herself just as I failed to protect every one of our fallen."

Malachea wiped her tears. "My oldest daughter chose her own path. Besides, don't you remember the popular fury that whipped up when we learned that Yakov's sultan was fighting the Greeks? Who knows what she may have attempted if you had somehow prevented our departure?"

Califia shuddered at the thought. Whether through a violent coup or through a lightning election campaign, she was certain that her time as queen would have ended if she had obstructed this voyage.

"My apologies," Califia said. "Dionysia was not a child."

"Few will forget how she attacked you without warning," Malachea said. "Many watched from above, horrified at her conduct. The dishonor burns my heart even now."

"It is not yours," Califia said, standing and putting a hand on the polemarkos' shoulder. "You are wise to let her go."

Malachea nodded, then turned away and continued sculpting.

As night fell, the Amazon army converged around the unlit pyres and laid their remembrance totems upon the fallen. Califia stood in the center of the circle and spoke loudly so that all might hear her.

"We gather here to remember the great heroes among us who paid the ultimate price and prevented the wholesale slaughter, rape, and degradation of those within the walls of Constantinopolis. Our foremothers struggled against their neighbors— not to dominate, enslave, or eliminate them, but to encourage them to turn away from coercion and tyranny. We honor the legacy of those foremothers tonight."

Few expressions changed, as far as she could see in the torchlight, though a few nodded their heads in agreement. For some awkward moments, silence reigned. Then a voice suddenly lifted in song.

"Return to me the love I lost
　"Fill my whole heart with peace and kindness.
　"When comes the day I stand alone
　"I will by no means ever falter."

More voices joined as Califia recognized the initial singer. It was a familiar voice; it belonged to Arianna. Califia joined in, her heart moved by her former partner.

"There is a spring high in the mountains
　"It fills my soul with Hera's tears."
　"She wept for all our present troubles
　"And she's weeping with us still."

"Return to me the love I lost,

"Fill my whole heart with peace and kindness.
"When comes the day I stand alone,
"I will by no means ever falter."

Most of the Californians walked toward their tents as the torch-wielding attendants lit the pyres. The flames seemed to lick the heavens and the stars above were blocked out by the billowing column of smoke. The scouts had reported that the plateau and the area around it was largely abandoned save for a few small villages. The queen wondered whether the flame or smoke could be seen from Constantinopolis.

Califia strode to her tent, holding her chin high so she would appear dignified to her people. Alone at last in her small tent, she sat on the ground and wept. The tears sprang from grief, but also relief and a longing to once more lay eyes upon her home.

****

It was the third day since their flight from Constantinopolis and still they captured no glimpse of the Great Western Sea. The irony that this body of water now lay to their east was not lost on Califia. The air they traveled through was wet and heavy like the summers along the southern coast.

Califia peered at the distant horizon but still saw only trees. There was much excitement the day before when the land was broken by large bodies of water but since then the land below them varied from sand to grassland to forest and still they flew onward, stopping periodically and sleeping only as much as needed. Through the connection of the Triumvir Dagger, the queen felt the griffins' confidence that they were going the right way.

Malachea's map seemed to confirm their path and the queen had no reason to distrust either source but she still felt a gnawing anxiety that would not be fully extinguished until she set her feet on the shore of her country.

The rich forested hillsides below looked beautiful, like the tops of large green clouds. She worried she might never see the end of them when suddenly on the horizon she spotted the barest sliver of dark blue. The queen suppressed her excitement, wondering whether this was merely a wide river or another gulf inlet. As the distant blue became wider and broader, she allowed herself the luxury of temporary relief.

She turned to her left, peering over Lydia's head to spot Malachea, who was pointing at the horizon and smiling. Califia smiled back, then held out her flat hand, palm down, and pushed it toward the ground several times, a signal that meant "Land soon?"

The polemarkos responded by thrusting her fist in the air once. Yes.

The trees below gradually thinned into a broad meadow with several streams running through. The queen gripped the hilt of the Triumvir Dagger and signaled to the griffins that they would be landing soon. She led the way by gently pulling Ektra's bridle back so that the creature angled slightly toward the ground and they began descending.

Ektra's landings had been especially soft since Califia took the Greek women aboard her saddle. The queen had rewarded this with a few extra helpings of smoked pork which she pulled from a saddlebag. She patted Ektra's nose and hugged the great beast's head in gratitude.

"Is this Africa?" Sophia said, stretching her legs which

had no doubt grown stiff from hours in the harness.

"I think it is Hindistan," Califia said, hoping that Malachea's map and the griffins' instincts were correct.

Sophia wore a blank expression and turned to Lydia.

"India, I think," she said, helping her daughter out of the rope harness.

"Ah yes," Sophia said. She turned back to Califia with a strange smile on her face. "This place is nice."

Califia blinked. Sophia had spoken the words in the Californian language, not her native Greek. She giggled at the queen's expression, then bowed with a flourish as Lydia and Thea clapped politely.

"Not a bad start," Califia said, nodding and scratching behind Ektra's ears.

"Once we get to your kingdom," Lydia said, pushing her hands against her back and tilting her head and chest skyward as she grunted, "I think I'll be done with traveling for some time."

Califia smiled at this, happy that these blessed women had decided to join the Amazons. Little Thea had already run off, chasing some nearby frogs and giggling as they hopped away.

Several griffins launched straight into the air after they had been released from their saddles and soared over the ocean, busying themselves with catching fish. She scanned the nearby faces, but Arianna was not among them. The two hadn't spoken since Natolee's funeral two days ago and the queen wanted to break the silence.

While searching through the crowd, she spotted Basilea, who was gathering fallen wood from a nearby glen. The old woman likewise spotted the queen and summoned her with a jerk of her neck.

"I wish you had told me what you intended," Basilea said, gathering twigs and dried brush along with Califia, "but I understand why you didn't."

The queen paused. She could sense the old woman's pain and she regretted her own contribution to it.

"Why do you think I didn't tell you?"

Basilea sighed.

"At first, I assumed it was because you didn't trust me to keep it secret," she said, snapping a large branch off a nearby tree which had been previously broken and was only hanging on by a few splinters. "I later realized you thought I would try to talk you out of it."

The queen winced and Basilea nodded at the expression.

"It was never my intention to—"

"Please," Basilea held up a hand. "You do not owe me an apology. Especially because you were right. I *would* have tried to convince you not to execute such a plan, and I would have been wrong."

"You must understand, Basilea," Califia bundled all of her branches under her left arm and put her right hand on her adviser's shoulder, "I never meant to make you feel... inadequate."

"And yet, I do. Close your mouth, I do not need your words of comfort. I know myself well enough by now to understand when I have reached the end of a journey. I've grown cautious in my old age — too cautious. When we return home, I will set things in order and retire as Basilea."

Califia wanted to object, to grab the old woman by the shoulders and tell her that she needed her to stay, but she knew it would be wrong. The former queen, the woman who had led their society away from the pointless war of the Califia before her, deserved to retire on her own terms and in her own time.

"I only hope," Basilea said, "that I helped contribute

to this great triumph."

Califia nearly choked on her own breath.

"Do you really think the people will see this as a victory?"

Basilea grinned as though she thought Califia was joking. "You stuck your fingers in the eyes of both the Osman Sultan and the Frankish King! Everyone's talking about the incident as a show-of-force, a warning to anyone who might try to oppress our people."

Califia's breath paused for a moment.

"*That* is what they think I was doing?" She nearly dropped her bundle of twigs. "Intimidating the other powers to discourage them from invading us?"

She shot Basilea an accusatory glare.

"The rumor was well-established by the time it reached my ears," her adviser said. She sounded just exhausted enough for the queen to believe her. "I will admit I have done nothing to stop its spread."

Califia stooped to grasp at a cluster of kindling twigs, but they were tangled in a mossy growth. In her frustration, she dropped the rest of her load as she jerked the twigs free.

"Whatever your intentions," Basilea said, shifting her load onto her left hip, "keep them to yourself. This solves every problem we had with your candidacy and reign. The *Gorgons* are raving about you, Califia! Any doubts about your military prowess have vanished like those cannons we dropped into the sea!"

Califia wanted to object but by the time she gathered her bundle of firewood back into her arms, Basilea had already skipped away to add her load to a great pile that was developing. The queen sighed, suddenly aware that many nearby Amazons were smiling toward her as they busied themselves with making camp.

She thought of the palace, of her mornings breaking fast on its great porch. How nice it would be to eat her food in peace without a thousand angry messages. She could finally put her plans into motion, arrange the building of great statues and the renovation of older temples, revive the academies, and support trade with the mainlanders.

An army of musicians would be drafted to make new songs and even create new instruments, while thousands of artists across the land could apply their skills toward reinvigorating national aesthetics. She thought suddenly of Arianna. How wide would her former lover smile when the queen asked her to take charge of renovations of the temple of Hera?

After depositing her meager stack of firewood onto the larger communal pile, the queen flitted about camp superficially helping with various tasks and hoping to catch a glimpse of Arianna so that she might give her the good news. As she set down a basket of fresh-caught fish which she had hauled from the shore, she turned around intending to continue her search but instead she collided with something and fell back. Initially she thought it was a wall or tree or other immovable obstacle but as she looked up, the frame of Malachea came into focus.

"Apologies, my queen," the polemarkos said, proffering a hand to Califia.

"I am unharmed," the queen answered, glancing behind Malachea but still not spotting Arianna.

"If you have a moment?" the polemarkos said.

Califia dusted herself off and felt a twinge of suspicion at Malachea's tone, which sounded almost somber. The energy that pulsed through the camp was optimistic and hopeful; the polemarkos seemed to have something weighing heavily upon her mind.

The queen followed Malachea to a large, fat stump where the map which Admiral Kemal had given to them so long ago was laid flat with its corners anchored by stones. Califia took in a sharp breath as she looked upon the world, her eyes following the gentle curve of southern Africa, the tooth-like protrusion of Arabia, and the sweeping slope of the peninsula labeled Hindistan.

"I believe we are here," Malachea thrust her finger onto the eastern edge of Hindistan. "There is a decent amount of landmass between us and home, but there is also a massive stretch of ocean."

"We could try and shelter on some of these islands," the queen suggested, tapping her finger against some small clusters that lay in the heart of the Great Western Sea.

"Locating those islands will prove tricky. While some of our more ingenuitive sisters have created their own versions of the navigation tools employed by Admiral Kemal, I doubt any of them would be able to use them with his skill."

Califia traced her hand along the several land masses that lay to their east, stopping at the furthest edge of a small cluster of islands.

"How far is California from these little islands?"

"Therein lies another problem," Malachea said, gesturing to the vast, empty space east of where Califia's fingers rested. "We aren't exactly certain."

Califia removed her hand and rested it, quite without thinking, on the hilt of the Triumvir Dagger. As she worried over the problem, she suddenly felt a response from the griffins, as if she had asked them a question.

We will get you home. Trust us.

She relayed the message to Malachea, who shrugged but nodded.

"If the griffins aren't worried, then neither am I," she said, removing the stones from the map's corners and rolling it back into a cylinder. Califia blushed as she caught herself admiring the cord-like sinews and rippling muscles in the polemarkos' arms as they curved the edge of the flat parchment and rolled the document slowly and carefully.

"I… uh…" Califia said, snapping out of her trance.

"My queen?"

"I was thinking of something…" Califia wanted to punch herself. Daydreaming about the polemarkos' arms had pushed some stray thought from her mind. She wrenched it back just before Malachea was about to reply.

"We should fly in a loose, spread-out formation," the queen explained, "on the day we embark from the islets in the east. Increase our chances of finding the small islands between there and home."

Malachea looked impressed. Califia's heart gave a flutter at the approval. "I'll see that it is done."

Califia nodded, certain that she had made a fool of herself. "Thank you for bringing this problem to my attention."

Malachea locked eyes with her for a moment, but the queen turned away as though she had urgent business on whatever side of the camp was furthest away from the Gorgon leader.

After a few dozen paces, her cheeks cooled and she felt comfortable sparing a laugh at herself. She must be weary indeed for her heart to start nurturing a crush for Malachea, of all women. She attributed their recent lack of arguments to mutual exhaustion, nothing more.

She turned back to make sure that Malachea had also gone about her business. Instead she saw the polemarkos still standing where she had left her, staring in her direction as she walked away. Malachea turned quickly after the queen spotted her, and Califia felt her cheeks become embarrassingly warm once again.

The next morning, she emerged from her tent to see that she had slept longer than most. The camp was abuzz with Amazons packing their tents and saddling their griffins. At the far end of camp, the strategoses and a few captains crouched around a map as Malachea pointed and gestured.

She collapsed her tent and was busy stuffing it and its skeleton into its pack when she spotted Arianna sitting on a rock overlooking the sea with her back to the camp. Her bright, colorful bracelets gave her away.

"Is that you, Califia?" Arianna said as Califia approached.

"I am sorry for your loss, Arianna," Califia said, her heart sinking into her stomach with the weight of grief. "This war has cost us too much."

"Yes," Arianna agreed, clutching her hands together atop her chest. Califia realized she was holding something in one of the hands and caressing it with her fingers. "Natolee was far braver than I am."

"I wish I had known her better," the queen added ruefully, sitting next to her former partner and dangling her feet from the cliff. "I owe her my life."

"She died for nothing" Arianna said, bitter tears drenching her cheeks.

Califia tried to catch a glimpse of the totem that Arianna was cradling. "Her sacrifice saved thousands of lives."

"Why was *she* the one who was sacrificed?" Arianna spat, glaring darkly at Califia.

"We cannot know the will of the triumvirs," Califia

replied, feeling an icy chill begin to creep down her back. "We must trust that all th—"

"Trust? *Trust?*" Arianna shouted the words as though they were swears. "I was not asking for theology, o wise queen — I was asking why *she* was sacrificed *and not you.*"

The words stabbed Califia in the heart. Arianna stood and walked toward the camp. The queen scrambled quickly to her feet and sprinted to catch up. Arianna turned, her face red with fury.

"The queen is supposed to sacrifice herself for her people, not the other way around!" She shouted, opening her palm to reveal the totem she had made the night before. It was an exact replica of the Triumvir Dagger, a hundred times smaller than the real knife which hung from Califia's belt. Arianna had even managed to include the red gem at the intersection of the blade and the handguard. She closed her hand around the totem and marched toward the queen.

"When you said that you didn't know Natolee," she continued, "I thought you were joking but you were serious, weren't you?"

The queen nodded solemnly. Arianna stepped in close, whispering the answer to this riddle.

"She drove your chariot at the coronation."

The queen closed her eyes and a tear ran down her cheek. She remembered the young chariot driver who gawked at the capital. The light tattoos on her arms, the rainbow markings on her chin and throat... all of it came back and the queen was suddenly overwhelmed. She stammered, struggling to find sufficient words.

"Nothing you can say will possibly help," Arianna said, in a voice that was eerily calm and cold. She balled up her fist around the tiny dagger totem. "To me, it is as if *you* died in the mud near Constantinopolis right next to

Natolee."

She cocked her arm back and flung the remembrance into the sea. Califia watched it disappear beneath the waves with barely a plop. Arianna sprinted away. The queen tried to convince herself that the despair that now sank her heart was the result of her former lover's harsh words and nothing more.

The truth was that Arianna had cut her more deeply than she may have intended. Basilea had encouraged her to continue as queen when she was ready to step down, but now she was given fresh reasons for self-doubt. Could she really accomplish an agenda of peace, culture, and prosperity with so much blood on her hands— not just the blood of her wartime enemies, but of her fellow Amazons? Perhaps her initial instincts had been correct.

The Amazons left behind a pile of some of the coins leftover from the massive collection which the Osmans gave them in exchange for their alliance. They had been distributed to the army, but they had no use for them other than as mementos. She hoped that the people who lived in this place would find some use for these and accept them as thanks for allowing the Amazons to use their land. She spotted some of the locals peering from between the trees in the denser parts of the surrounding woods, gawking at the griffins and their riders. She waved and they scattered.

Califia tried to remember the shapes on Malachea's map as she examined the coastlines far below them. For a long time they soared over the open ocean, a terrifying portent of their eventual voyage across the vast expanse of the Great Western Sea which lay still ahead. They landed at the western edge of another island, this one more densely populated by people whose skin was only a few shades lighter than the Amazons'. They retreated at the sight of the griffin flock and kept their distance from the shore where the Californians struck camp.

Basilea and a contingent of devotees of Hera - skilled in communication and diplomacy - trekked about a thousand paces from where the Californians were encamped and drew an image in the dirt showing the griffins sleeping under the moon and then taking off when the sun rose. Next to it they left a pile of clothes, spare cookpots, and some griffinsteel daggers. After Basilea relayed the events to Califia, she went to check on the evening's meals while the griffins happily dove for fish in the ocean nearby.

Califia sighed. Was this how the foremothers had traveled to California so many years ago — heartbroken and lost? Nights of fitful sleep and fear of what the morning might bring?

The next day they flew only until midday, when they finally came to the far eastern edge of a small island chain. One of the islands was unoccupied and it was there that the Amazons encamped, leaving another offering before they left the next day.

The queen dreaded this terrible final stretch, even with the precautions they had taken. They embarked just before first light, the griffins spreading into a broad, loose formation and the passengers all given orders to look for islands. The rider in the saddle would busy themselves with keeping their neighbors within sight so that none would go astray. After consulting the map the previous day, Malachea recommended a slight northeasterly course toward the northwestern coast of California, which jutted out farther than the southern stretch.

The day wore on and Califia forced herself to only eat as much of her remaining salted meat as needed to quell her hunger. She tended to snack when she was stressed, but this was no time to waste resources.

The sky began to take on hues of purple and pink which would have been enjoyable in most circumstances. They continued to fly over vast, dark water and still there was no land in sight. Could the griffins continue in the dark? She was about to grasp the hilt of her dagger to ask them when a hornblast sounded from somewhere far to her right. She was on the leftmost wing of their wide formation so she wheeled Ektra toward the sound after she made sure that the neighboring riders on her left had heard the call as well.

As she drew nearer to where the griffins converged, she spotted a small chain of several islands. They were mountainous, covered in trees, and ringed by white sand beaches. She breathed a sigh of relief as the cavalry landed. It wasn't home, but it would suffice.

The air was warm and the sky was quickly becoming pitch black as Califia dismounted and helped the Greek women out of their rope slings. High on the mountainside she saw small flickering lights of cookfires or torches. Like everywhere else, the natives kept their distance and, just as they had done everywhere else, the Californians laid out offerings of gratitude for allowing them to use their space.

Early in the morning, before the sky would become light enough to allow for flying, Califia suddenly woke and heard a noise outside of her tent. *A local beast? A native warrior trying to prove their bravery?* Her heart quickened and her eyes sharpened in the dim light of her tent. She grabbed her sagaris by the haft near its wide blade and spiked tip, readying herself for action.

She sprang out of the tent with her weapon before her. Her assailant jumped back.

"Peace, my queen!" the polemarkos hissed as she took another backward step.

Califia lowered her weapon.

"What are you doing here?" She asked, her words slurred slightly with the lingering effects of exhausted sleep.

"I wanted to talk with you," Malachea explained, eyeing the battle axe still in the queen's hand.

Califia tossed the sagaris gently back into her tent. They walked along the beach far from the tents and even farther from where they had spotted the islanders' lights the day before.

"My term as polemarkos expires upon our return" Malachea said, with a sigh. "I wish it had been more nobly spent."

"I feel the same way about my tenure as queen," Califia said, her heart heavy. "I am thinking seriously about stepping down upon our return."

Malachea scoffed. "You're more well-loved than ever — after a month of veteran's stories up and down the isle, you'll be more popular than your mother. Even *I* don't want to see you step down."

"Not *anymore*?" Califia said, melting Malachea's annoyed glare with her smile.

"I admit that I misjudged you. I am sorry if I was bothersome, but I believed I was protecting the interests of the nation."

Califia's cheeks became red-hot and she turned upon Malachea with a fury which had been simmering but was now boiling over.

"Were you protecting the nation when you brought Yakov for me to decapitate?"

Malachea looked befuddled, as though she was only hearing about this issue for the first time. Then she winced as though the queen had stabbed her.

"I... I can see how that may have appeared... malicious, but please, let me explain."

Califia nodded as Malachea composed herself.

"When you were first elected," the polemarkos explained, "a faction began to form within the Gorgons, led by Dionysia. They believed you were weak, and that your election might embolden our foes."

The queen felt the impulse to interject, but resisted.

"I had already criticized your lightning election, and they thought I agreed with them. I overheard them talking one night about how they would accompany me to the capital, slaughter you and your supporters, and place me on the throne in your stead. They never involved me directly but believed I would acquiesce once the blood had been shed."

Califia pictured Malachea sitting on a blood-stained throne with the bodies of Basilea, Arianna, and herself decorating the dais. The queen shivered as the polemarkos continued.

"I led them through Droseros that morning, claiming that jaguars had been harassing a local bison herd. I planned to walk them through every rough ravine and overgrown footpath in the region to ensure that they would be too exhausted to execute their plan when we arrived. We found Yakov and I thought the triumvirs had provided a sacrifice. *If the Gorgons see the queen execute a trespasser,* I thought, *they will no longer question her willingness to protect our home.* I honestly never expected you to refuse."

Califia's head spun at Malachea's logic. *She thought she was helping.*

"What about your campaign for polemarkos?" The queen felt certain that this question would elicit a guilty reply.

"I did that to save your life. Dionysia convinced her group that you had placed us all in jeopardy by sparing the trespasser and inviting his people to the island. They swore upon Athena that if you became the polemarkos, they would murder you even if it cost them their own lives."

Califia's skin felt suddenly clammy and she swallowed in spite of a dry throat. How many times had Malachea saved her life in the last year? She looked the polemarkos in the eye.

"I really thought you hated me," Califia said, her head still spinning at the revelations.

"Don't get too puffed up!" Malachea said, smiling as they continued walking. "Opposing you for polemarkos is my right as an Amazon and I'm of the opinion that serving as Califia and polemarkos at the same time is far too much power to entrust in a single person."

Califia felt the impulse to defend herself, but instead let the matter go.

"You're probably right," she said, gazing upon the wine-red sea as dawn's rosy fingers stretched over the horizon.

"Any opposition I had for you was never personal," Malachea said, touching the queen's elbow. "I've constantly defended your decisions and advocated on your behalf to the other gorgons and even, on occasion, to Olympia and Traesta."

The queen felt a stab of shock that Traesta, whom she considered a close friend, would criticize her behind her back. *It seems Malachea is not the only person I've misjudged.* She was grieved by the thought, especially thinking of all the times she had plotted with Basilea to try and find proof that would incriminate the polemarkos.

"I have been terribly unfair to you," Califia said, stopping as Malachea halted.

"It's understandable. You couldn't have known the truth of what was happening."

Califia wrapped her arms around Malachea's waist and embraced her. The polemarkos squeezed tight and they held each other for several moments as the waves lapped against the nearby shore.

"I'm sorry," the queen said, resting her head upon Malachea's shoulder. "I've assumed the worst of you and now I find all of my assumptions mistaken."

"I learned something when you were taken prisoner," Malachea said, speaking softly, almost tenderly. "I was terrified that something awful would happen to you. At first I thought I worried purely because you are the queen… but I realized that I would not feel the same way if the Califia were anyone other than *you*."

Califia released from the embrace and dropped her arms to her side. Malachea did the same. A tear trickled down the polemarkos' cheek and Califia gasped as she saw her pained expression. It was as though even the memory of her feelings when Califia was captured caused her to experience an intense dread all over again.

The queen embraced Malachea once more. The polemarkos' body was warm and inviting; the queen's mind wandered as she felt the taut squeeze of a woman she once considered an enemy. The queen brought her head away from the polemarkos' shoulder and the other woman did likewise. They locked eyes, each seeing in the other exactly what they didn't realize they had been looking for. They closed their eyes and kissed deeply, neither pulling away until the passion of the moment was exhausted.

The queen glanced at the camp up the beach and saw

that their people were already rousing themselves for another long day of flying and searching. A few curious heads had been turned in their direction, but they swiftly turned away once they realized she had spotted them spying on what was clearly a private moment.

"We should help with the preparations," Califia said. Malachea nodded and they walked toward the camp, hand in hand, breaking at last when they arrived at Malachea's tent. After a brief flurry of packing and harnessing, the griffins launched into the air for what the queen hoped would be the last time.

During the early hours of the journey that morning, the only thing in sight was the sea. The riders had adopted a loose formation, though not quite as spread out as they had been the day before. As midday approached, fear began to take hold of Califia. The vast blue expanse seemed infinite, and what had before seemed an object of shimmering beauty now seemed like a large tomb waiting to swallow her army into its depths.

She felt dizzy as she looked down upon the deep sea. Was Ektra drifting closer to the water's surface? Was the creature's strength about to fail and doom the queen to a watery grave?

What would become of her people in the event of her passing? They would need to hold an election, and quickly. Perhaps Malachea would put her name in the running and even win. They would mourn the late Califia, of course, and probably remember her fondly as a mighty warrior queen who dared to defy the powerful and feared no one — man, woman, or beast.

The queen clutched at the reins as Ektra's body suddenly lurched forward. Her passengers yelped with the motion and Califia felt as though a great wind was suddenly at her back, carrying them homeward with greater speed than they were otherwise capable. The windblown locks of her neighbors told her that she was not imagining things. Surely some agent of Hestia was ferrying them back to California, summoning them home.

While she appreciated the increased speed, many hours still passed without any land in sight. The sun was starting to sink behind them. Soon it would be too dark to see anything. How long would the griffins last with no place to land and no food available to eat? How long would they continue flying in the dark without any visible target ahead?

Just as her heart was about to fall fully into despair, a horn blew from somewhere near the front of their formation. Several more horns followed in agreement. The Greek ladies in their slings exchanged excited glances but Califia kept her eyes locked on the horizon, refusing to look anywhere else until she caught sight of what lay ahead.

Slowly, steadily, the distant flickering lights of torches came into view. This was not home, but it was good enough; the torches were used by fisherwomen luring squid into nets by night. They kept close to the bay, which meant that the shore itself, the shore of California, could not be far behind.

They stayed aloft in the swift upper wind as long as they could, then descended quickly. As they grew closer she spotted Nika's Harbor, the twin gates of the peninsula, and even the astonished faces of the fisherwomen as the griffin flock soared over their heads.

"Is that it?" asked Sophia, who finally seemed to be relaxing in her harness. "Is that California?"

"Yes it is," Califia said, enjoying the little thrill she felt at the Greek ladies' stunned gasps.

"Our new home," Lydia said wistfully, wiping a tear from her eye and then quickly grabbing the harness once more. "Even in the dark it's beautiful."

As the griffin flock neared a vast plain to make their landing, Califia felt strangely alienated, as though she were laying eyes on Nika's Harbor for the first time. It seemed larger than she remembered, like a gaping mouth swallowing the entire sea. The village beyond, however, looked smaller than she recalled. She felt as though she had arrived in yet another foreign land. As Ektra slowed and then set her talons upon the ground, Califia felt uncertain whether she should think of herself as a refugee or an invader. Their home had changed since they had embarked on their quest. If they were honest with themselves, those who landed on the plain near Nika's Harbor that night would admit that they had changed as well.

We are home, the queen thought, watching her people kiss the sand, kiss each other, and kiss their griffins. *For good or for ill, we have returned.*

THE END

Acknowledgements

The first person I must acknowledge is my amazing wife. Her support and encouragement were especially vital to this novel and I honestly would not be able to do this without her. Second, I need to thank my parents, who also listen with rapt attention whenever I have a story idea to share. The encouragement of my family is vital life-blood to my creativity.

I also would like to thank the listeners of my podcast, A History of Japan, for their patient forbearance when I have needed to take extra time away from creating the pod in order to work more deeply on this book. My supporters on patreon obviously get an extra measure of thanks here for continuing their generous support during these times.

My daughters especially I must acknowledge, for while they have heard a lot from me about this book, neither of them are of an age where I would be comfortable with them reading it. Nevertheless, they have helped me in times when I have been stuck, and for that I thank them deeply and wish them a good journey when they do become old enough to understand this book's more mature content.

Lastly, I have to thank everyone who has patiently listened to me describe this story for the last three years which it has taken me to craft it. This includes uncles, several cousins, many close friends, and the occasional unfortunate acquaintance at social functions who have dared to ask me what I've been working on after I informed them that I am a novelist.